LEGION OF THE QUEEN
After the Fall Universe, Book Two

D.M. SIMMONS

COPYRIGHT © 2022 BY D.M. SIMMONS

All Rights Reserved. No part of this book may be reproduced or used in any manner without the written permission of the copyright owner except for the use of quotations in a review. For requests, contact the author at www.dmsreadwrite.com.

This is a work of fiction. Names, characters, places, and incidences are either the products of the author's imagination or used fictitiously. Any resemblance to actual persons, living or dead, events, or locales, is entirely coincidental.

ASIN: B0BC6W8CCV
ISBN: 9798358797772

Published by Foggy Day Publishing

Cover Design by RFK Designs

AUTHOR'S NOTE

Legion of the Queen is a dark paranormal romance told in dual POV. It contains enemies to lovers, forbidden love, stuck together, soulmates, found family, and alpha hero tropes.

It is the second book in the first duet of the After the Fall series. It should be read after the first book, Fealty of the Fallen. It is intended for mature audiences and contains adult language, sexual scenes, and situations that may trigger some readers. Read at your own risk.

BLURB

You come for him, she's coming for you.
You come for her, he's coming for you.
You come for their family, the legion comes...and they always protect their queen.

PLAYLIST

#1 Crush by Garbage
Exile by Enya
Angel by Aerosmith
Fire In A Nameless Town by Angels & Airwaves
Heartbreak Beat by The Psychedelic Furs
Lips Like Sugar by Echo & the Bunnymen
London Calling by The Clash
Rampage by GRAVEDGR
Play With Fire by Sam Tinnesz
Gangster by Labrinth
Losing My Mind by Angels & Airwaves
Fell On Black Days by Soundgarden
Ceremony by New Order
Parasomnia by Angels & Airwaves
Thousand Miles by Tove Lo
Birds by Imagine Dragons
Not Gonna Die by Skillet
Hysteria by Def Leppard
Legends Never Die by Against The Current

1
DIABLO

I stare vacantly out the window, drinking in the turbulent sky. Gray clouds billow against a deep purple backdrop, as rain pours down onto the streets below. I may as well be looking into my heart because the world looks as I feel–dark, cold, and miserable.

Drawing a heavy breath, I turn my attention from the raging storm to where Dante lies quietly in bed. He looks like he is sleeping–chest rising and falling slowly, his chiseled jaw at ease–only he's not. What he is, exactly, I don't know. No one does.

Since the battle in Eden, his condition is the same as when we arrived in London six months ago. He healed from the wound that ripped open his chest, but never regained consciousness. With each day that passes, my anger grows hotter, and despair, greater; both burrowing inside me, bone deep.

The only thing that keeps me from succumbing to either, is training with the legion

The army of fallen angels once loyal to Luke, is now my own, and they share my anger and need for revenge. Working out with them has made me stronger and I have promised them the day will come when we make Luke pay for his lies.

But when I am alone, and the quiet surrounds me, I give in to the emotions that gnaw at me and allow their release. Last night, when I broke the mirror in the gym, it was vengeance that pumped through my veins. Cold and powerful, anxious for its time. But today, as I stare at Dante, desperate for him to wake up, it is a profound feeling of hopelessness that sits on my chest. I miss him so much it hurts, and I need him to come back to me.

Willing away the unbearable heaviness, I make my way over to the bed and sit down, reaching for his hand. The tattoo he had inked of my name stares back at me, as the quote I had etched for him on the back of my neck, pricks in memory of the day we got them–*Thus, from my lips, by thine, my sin is purged.*

The foundation of this existence had been rooted in the sins of the past, but when Dante and I found our way to one another, it felt like I could finally let go of the guilt and regret I had carried, for five thousand years. He was convinced our forever was right around the corner and I was, too. If only I'd known then, how our world would be turned upside down, I'd fought harder.

The sound of gunfire echoes in my ears and I close my eyes, watching the moment he was shot, playing like a movie in my mind. I see blood on my hands and fear in his eyes, as he drops to his knees in Luke's throne room. Even now I feel the whip of time– as if I'd traveled back to the night of the Fall, my spirit desperate to save him, all over again.

"Come on, Dante," I shake off the memory and pull his hand to my cheek. "Wake up." But like every plea before, it goes without a response.

I may not have been strong enough back in Eden to stop what happened, but I was now. Dante *was* my forever, and I was fighting for us. I wouldn't give up. I never would. But some days are harder than others, especially when he should be awake.

The wound in Dante's chest healed months ago and he is

in perfect health. His vitals are strong and his body warm. But the longer he remains this way, the greater my fear grows that it will become permanent, and the idea paralyzes me. I couldn't imagine this existence without him because the simple fact was, he was my reason for being.

Long before we were confined to these mortal forms and Heaven was our home, it was my wings that beat for him and not my heart. I'd never known anything other than my ethereal purpose, but the moment I saw his spirit, I was drawn to it. He fascinated me–his essence beguiling–and my desire for him could not be denied. But then came The Fall, and we were bound, trapping us in an irrevocable contract of pain and heartache.

For five thousand years Dante was obligated to pursue my loyalty–returning to Eden at the beginning of each century, with the goal of doing whatever he could to secure it. And it had been a particular kind of cruelty to be chased by the one I wanted and could never have, while at the same time being kept from seeing him, except for ten days every one hundred years. But torment was Luke's specialty, and he cared not about my heart, but the thrill of the game between those who swore their allegiance to him, and those who wished to remain free.

Yet, no matter how angry I'd been at Dante over the centuries for all he'd done in his pursuit of my fealty, my existence didn't make sense without him.

I'd do it all over again to save him. Fall a thousand times, because he would always be worth my sacrifice. I just wish I knew what he needed now, because I would give anything to see his cobalt eyes staring back at me. If only he would give me a sign. But nothing–not my voice, nor my touch, not even his favorite music–wakes him.

A knock at the door cuts into my thoughts, and I turn to find Vinny standing in the doorway. "Hey," he smiles, gold-brown eyes shifting from Dante to me. "Any change?"

"No," I sigh and place Dante's hand back down on the bed. "He's the same."

"Well," Vinny crosses the room, coming up to the other side. "It's been a long existence. My brother needs his rest."

His mouth tugs up at the corner and I know the casualness of his response is meant to reassure me. But I also know, no matter how hard he tries to hide it, he too, is concerned by Dante's condition.

Vinny and Dante are like brothers. Best friends since before The Fall, it's always been the two of them. Between them exists a bond that is unbreakable, and I know the last few months have taken as much a toll on Vinny, as it has me.

"Trust me," Vinny crosses his massive arms. "Dante's been through worse. If anyone can beat this, he can."

While my deal with Luke saw that my existence was confined to Eden with the rest of the Fallen who refused to swear their loyalty, Vinny and Dante were rewarded for theirs. As such, the world had been their proverbial oyster for thousands of years.

The two have seen the rise and fall of empires and toppled a few on their own. Yet, no matter the time, no matter the story, one thing was clear–there had never been a problem that Dante couldn't work his way out of and come out on top.

I know that's why Vinny shares stories of their time together. So that I understand everything Dante has been through and see what is happening now as simply another chapter in his infinite story. But it was time for this chapter to end, so we could start a new one. One that began with payback and ended with a peaceful forever.

"Well, it's time for him to wake up," I turn my attention back to Dante. "Luke has to pay for what he's done to me, Dante, and all the legion."

Luke may have plotted against us for centuries, using the way I felt about Dante to get what he wanted, but he never counted on Dante's feelings for me, being as strong in return. When Dante promised he would do whatever it took for us to be together, he meant it, and I carried that same commitment for us now.

The angel who was afraid of her own heart, had changed since leaving Eden. I was no longer afraid of Luke. He'd done his worst to me twice, and both times, I remained standing. I was strong, and committed, and would be his undoing, if it were the last damn thing I ever did.

"Well," Vinny says with a hint of mystery. "I have some news in that department."

I turn to him and arch a curious brow; the idea of burning Luke's kingdom to the ground, giving my need for revenge a small taste of satisfaction.

"It's surprising, but then again, not really," Vinny says cryptically. "I have one more thing to look into, but if it checks out, tomorrow we will finally know where Luke has been all this time."

"Good." To know we may finally have an answer after all this time, stirs something I haven't felt in a while–hope.

"Dante's going to wake up," Vinny says when I grow quiet. "And when he does, he's not going to let Luke get away with any of this. He would burn the world for you. You know that, right?"

I did know that–Dante had said those very words to me the first night we spent together here–and a part of me burned with the anticipation of wanting to see him reduce Luke's empire to ash. But the other part just wanted him back. One night together where it was just us, before setting that kingdom ablaze.

"Well," I turn back to Dante. "He can't do that if he's in this bed now, can he?"

"If he hasn't made it back yet, there's a reason. Trust in him."

I push up from the bed and blow out a frustrated breath. "I do trust him. More than anything. But that's exactly what worries me. What if he needs us and we don't know?"

Vinny looks at me in understanding. How many times had we asked those very questions of one another? "We just have to remember he's strong," he says calmly. "And trust that will come back to you, to us, when he can."

"You're right," I straighten my shoulders. Vinny didn't beat around the bush. He told you what you needed to hear, even if it wasn't necessarily what you wanted. And right now, I needed to hear that.

He holds a hand to his ear and grins. "Come again?"

I shake my head, trying to stop my own smile from tugging at my lips, but failing. "Stop."

"Never," his smile widens. "While my brother has been getting his beauty sleep, I've been seriously lacking in the 'Vinny-you're-right department.' So," he motions for me to repeat myself, "say it again, please?"

I shake my head and manage a soft laugh, which admittedly, feels good. "You're right, Vinny."

"Atta girl," he claps. "I knew you could do it."

"Does Lila know you're this impossible?" With the levity of the moment, the weight I'd been carrying lifts from my shoulders, and for the first time in days, it feels like I can breathe.

"Are you kidding," he smirks. "She's hot for it."

Just as Dante and Vinny were best friends, so too, were me and Lila. Bound to Vinny since the Fall, the two had been smitten with one another for centuries. Lila was fun and full of spunk and impossible not to adore, so it was no surprise the pixie-sized redhead stole the heart of the strongest among the Fallen.

Before everything happened in Eden, she'd sworn her fealty and was planning to leave it behind for a forever with Vinny. Thankfully, we broke the contract and I never had to know what it would feel like to be without her because the idea alone, had been too painful to consider.

Without Lila and Vinny, I might have self-destructed months ago. But the two had been there for me since we arrived and never left my side. They'd moved into Dante's penthouse, instead of into Vinny's place a few blocks away, and I'd grown so used to having them around, that not seeing either of them every day felt weird.

"How about you join Lila and I for dinner?" Vinny suggests. "She's taken over the kitchen and is planning a feast."

"How did she manage that?" I shake my head. The kitchen was particularly fussy about who was in their domain, and everyone followed Wills' order to stay out of their way. No one dared defy him or Lillian.

The two had been with Dante for hundreds of years and were attendants–eternals who gave up their lives to serve daemons, not their souls, as Luke required of those who served him. They ran Dante's house, as well as his personal affairs, and I'd come to care for, and trust them, as Dante did.

"Oh, you know Lila," Vinny grins. "She has a way of getting what she wants."

"Oh, I do indeed." Knowing the tenacity of my best friend, I could only imagine what she'd said or done to get them to oblige.

"If I'm being honest, losing never felt so good," he winks, and I can't help but feel a pang of envy. Dante and I were supposed to be together right now like Vinny and Lila. Instead, I was holding vigil at his bedside, feeling sad, angry, and desperate.

Suddenly, I didn't feel like eating. The only thing I wanted was to curl up next to Dante and hope when I opened my eyes, he would be awake

"You know what Vin," I chew the inside of my cheek. "Tell Lila thank you, but I'll raincheck."

"Oh, come on," he exhales. "You know she won't take no for an answer. And I don't know about you, but I'd rather not have her mad at me."

Vinny was fierce and strong and would go to Hell for any of the four of us–which he did the day he helped save me from Luke. But Lila could bring him to his knees in a way only the one who owns your heart can.

"Please," he nearly begs. "If not for her, for me? Dante would kick my ass if he knew I let you wither away."

I look at Dante, willing him awake for the millionth time. "Well, he'll just have to wake up and kick your ass then, because I'm not leaving."

Vinny looks at me, clearly concerned. "You need a break, Diablo."

I know I needed a break. The walls of Dante's suite were beginning to feel like they were closing in on me. But lately when I'm with him, something about leaving makes me anxious. Like, if I do, he'll wake, and I won't be there.

"Fine," I sigh. "Tell her I'll be down in a bit."

"Great," Vinny smiles with relief and his shoulders visibly ease. "I owe you."

"We both know that's not true." Vinny may appear all brawn, but his loyalty was the biggest thing about him. Memory of him carrying Dante out of Luke's will forever be seared in my mind. I know there wasn't anything he wouldn't do for his best friend, and I also know that loyalty extended to me.

"He's going to wake up," Vinny says for a second time. "He knows you're here, waiting to spend forever with him. And if there is one thing I know, it's that he would walk through fire to get back to you."

I once likened Dante and I to a cosmic joke. It was the only way to describe our fate. But even though our time together over the millennia had been limited, just knowing he was part of my existence was enough.

It wasn't until he was gone however, that I realized just how vital to me he truly was. Every day without his smile, his voice, that confident countenance that once drove crazy, but now crave, feels like an eternity. How could we have gotten what we wanted only to fail in the final stretch?

"Alright," Vinny dips his shoulder towards the door. "I'll see you downstairs in a bit?"

"Yep," I force a smile. "Just let me know when it's ready."

"You got it." He looks from me to Dante again, then turns and leaves, closing the door softly behind him.

Once he's gone, I queue up the playlist Dante created on my cell phone and connect it to the sound dock on his nightstand. It's full of his favorite music and a few new discoveries of my own.

I curl up next to him and place my hand on his chest. "Where are you?" I wonder, hoping wherever it is, he can feel me watching over him, just as I did in the beginning.

2
DANTE

From the dark I hear it, faint, but distinct–an unusual cadence of guitar and drums. It is a familiar melody that stirs something deep within me. An ache, or a longing…an overwhelming feeling that something is missing.

I reach out to pull it closer, but it fades, and a new sensation takes hold as a heady aroma fills my lungs, rousing my nerves and making my skin tingle. I'm bathed in light and for a moment the gentle stillness and sweet decadence are a soothing salve to my burning spirit.

Then the dark returns, and my peace vanishes; every muscle tightening as red eyes bore into me. Rage from the depths of my spirit sends heat ripping through me as I remember what's gone. Diablo–my angel. He's taken her and I need to get her back. If I don't, she'll be gone forever, and it will be the end of me.

Luke, the one I swore my loyalty to, will pay for this, and everything else he's done. I will take his kingdom and burn it to the ground because Diablo is mine. She has always been mine.

The thought of my beautiful angel starts to sooth my rage, but then I see him in the distance, holding her close. There is fear in her eyes and agony in her scream, as he twists her arm and whispers vile desires in her ear.

I know her concern is for me. It's why she fell…why she gave up what she was and her very purpose. But she needs to know I would do anything to keep her safe. Even if it meant stepping in front of a bullet.

The sound of a gunshot ricochets in my mind and I'm prepared to do exactly that. Only, it isn't meant for her. It's meant for me. And when it strikes my chest, I'm pushed back by a force that steals the air from my lungs and sends pain shooting through me.

The moment it hits me, I feel the burn, and with every beat of my heart, it carries through my body, circulating faster and faster until my blood is boiling.

She watches me, frantic; pupils swallowing the green of her eyes, as blood seeps through my fingers, covering the tattoo of her name on my hand.

I don't want her to worry, but I can't move. Can't speak. Can't reassure her that I'm okay. And when darkness pulls me under and she disappears, the realization I failed, suffocates me.

It plays over and over, an endless loop of memory, anger, and failure, until finally it stops, and light, bright and unyielding, reaches out and grabs hold of me. My eyes scream open, and I reach for my chest, gasping for air.

I draw in a deep breath and then another, as my heart races and every nerve ending comes to life. Then I turn to find her asleep next to me–one hand tucked under her head, the other on the bed next to me–and everything stills. Diablo–my home, my peace. Her exquisite spirit fell for mine and I will forever be in fate's debt.

I ease back down on the bed and turn to face her, gently placing my hand on hers. She is breathtaking, and as warmth passes from her hand to mine, I know it was she who pulled me from the dark. The magnificent being that saved me once, did so again. Her light, brighter than all others, always.

I can tell from the bed we're not in Eden, but London,

which means Vinny did what I asked. He got Diablo away from Luke and to safety. Only, as my eyes drag across the room, it looks different than it did when we left. Papers stacked on my writing desk and a teacup on the nightstand are markers of time. How much, however, I don't know.

The sound of a gunshot again echoes in my mind and when I feel the bullet pierce my chest, I look down. My shirt is clean, and my body feels no pain. In fact, I don't feel anything at all. How long has it been? Clearly long enough for me to heal.

Diablo stirs and moves her hand to my chest, as her eyes flit under their lids. "Dante," she says softly, my name barely a whisper, and my anxious heart thuds against my ribs, in response to her voice.

I lean over and kiss her forehead, the smell of sugar and peonies, filling my lungs as I try to soothe her. But when her hand flinches and breathing picks up, I realize something is haunting her sleep.

"Shhh," I soothe, "it's just a dream."

It takes a second, but slowly, her eyes open, and when they find mine, she reaches out and touches my face. "Dante?" she asks, hesitantly.

I smile and grip her hand. "Hi angel."

"Is it really you?" her voice falters. "If it's not...if this is a dream..."

"It's not," I trail my thumb along the apple of her cheek and down to her lips. Gone is the bruise and cut inflicted by Luke's hand.

She closes her eyes and takes a deep breath. As if she is preparing for me to disappear the moment that she opens them. But when she does and sees me lying next to her, she gasps, then pulls her hand from mine and throws her arms around me.

"I don't believe it," she says breathlessly as her lips ghost my cheek. "It's really you."

The feel of her in my arms chips away at the ache I've felt since waking and I pull her closer and kiss the side of her head. "Guess I've been out for a few days, huh?"

She tenses for a moment, and when she pulls back, she answers my question with her own. "What do you remember?"

Memories of our time together plays in my mind. From the day we were bound to our first kiss to the promise left unspoken the night Luke took her from me. "All of it. Which is why I need to—"

"You don't need to do anything," she cuts me off, a beautiful smile lighting up her face. "All you need to do is rest."

"No," I shake my head, the question of how long I'd been asleep suddenly the furthest thing from my mind. "I need to tell you something. I should have told you that night, but I wanted to wait until you could say it, too. But it kills me to think I might never have had the chance to tell you. That you may never have known…"

"Dante," she insists when my words trail off "It's okay. You don't have to say anything right now."

"I do," I cup her delicate face in my hands. "You have to know how much I love you, Diablo. That it is you, and only you, who owns my heart. I am yours forever, irrevocably."

Her eyes fill with tears, and one breaks free, and rolls down her cheek. "I love you, too. Across time, and this existence, as well as the one before. It has always been you and only ever will be you."

I know how long she has waited to confess the truth of her

heart. Heaven punished her for loving me, and she has carried that weight, all these millennia.

As if freed from the ties that have bound her for thousands of years, Diablo falls into me, and when our lips meet, my heart skips a beat. I taste the salt of her tears and the sweetness of her love, and when a moan curls from her mouth to mine, my body comes alive.

"Vinny said you'd wake up," she pulls me down on top of her. "That you'd walk through fire for me."

I stare into her eyes, thankful to be here with her, and free from that endless loop of pain and darkness. "I would do anything for you."

She runs her fingers through my hair, staring at me intently. "Where have you been…all this time?"

I know she has questions. My angel is curious and will want to know everything. And I have questions too, like what happened after I lost consciousness, and how long I have been out. But I don't want to think about anything right now but us.

"I'll tell you everything." I run my thumb along her lower lip. "But right now, I don't want to talk."

She flashes me a bright smile and trails a finger down my cheek, her touch drawing fire along my jaw, and down my neck. "Shouldn't you rest?"

"No fucking way." I crash my mouth down onto hers and we kiss hungrily, while undressing one another with anxious hands.

Once we are free of our clothes, my hands travel slowly over her body, remembering every inch of her skin, and she does the same, moving her hands up my chest and down my back. It feels like I've been starved, and the way she is touching me, like she has been, too.

I savor every touch, every kiss, every whisper of devotion, and when I finally ease into her, and feel her tight and wet and warm around me, my scalp tingles and warmth floods me with her breathless approval.

We alternate between slow and fast, hard, and soft; every kiss, every touch reconnecting us on a cellular level. And when she comes undone and cries out my name with her climax, I too let go, and clamp my mouth down on hers, riding out the high together as our tongues dance.

As we lie together afterward, I can't stop from thinking about our last morning in London–before we returned to Eden, and everything started to unravel.

"Do you remember what I said to you the last time we were here?" I ask, while running my hand through her hair.

"Mm-hmm," she looks up from my chest where she is quietly tracing the ink on my chest. "You said that you would fight for me. For us."

"And I meant it, with all that I am." I look down and find her eyes on mine. "I will destroy Luke for what he did to you. But I need to know how long it's been?"

She pushes up and pulls the sheet around her and I can see that despite the question's simplicity, it troubles her.

"I need to know, angel," I sit up and lean my back against the headboard. "I need to know what he stole from us this time, so I can make him pay for that, and all the other pain he's caused you."

She starts to say something, then shakes her head and looks down.

"Please," I reach for her chin and tip her head up gently.

She's quiet for a moment, but when she finally looks up and I see the pain in her eyes, it levels me. Already I hate the answer. "Six months," she says quietly. "For six months, three days, and seven hours my world has been without you in it."

I freeze, her response both disturbing and angering me. It was longer than expected and yet, explained the darkness in her eyes and hunger of our touch. Every cell in our body could feel the absence of one another.

"I lost you," her voice falters. "After five thousand years I finally had you, and then you were gone in the blink of an eye. And for months, the only thing I have been able to think about is the unbearable possibility of an existence without you."

"Listen to me," I scoot closer and reach for her hand. I don't have to imagine what the last six months has been like for her because I can see it staring back at me.

I want to kill Luke for taking more from us, but it's not about my anger right now. It's about Diablo. She'd already hurt enough in this existence, and I didn't want her to hurt anymore.

"You never have to worry about an existence without me because no matter what happens, I will always come back to you, angel." Tears again fill her eyes, and one breaks free. "You are my tether to forever," I brush it aside. "Do you hear me?"

She nods and I pull her into my arms and kiss her fully and completely. It's a promise of what we are, and always will be.

We were forever, and nothing, not a bullet, nor time, not even Luke, could tear us apart. But Luke...I would. Piece by piece, until he was no more.

3
DIABLO

I breathe him as our tongues dance, a heady mix of orange and spice filling my lungs, stirring memories of us across the millennia. I may be Dante's tether to forever, but he too, was mine.

Long before we fell, he captivated me, and over time, no matter how hard he pushed for my fealty, no matter how great my anger was over his efforts to win my loyalty, I was drawn to him like a moth to a flame. His strength and confidence, wit, and poise–everything about him fascinated me. But I had been so blinded by his power, that I didn't see my own.

When Luke first bound Dante and I, it nearly broke me. Being confined to an eternal existence with the one I gave up my wings for, made me feel things I'd never felt before. Jealousy, pain, anger, and regret all became a part of me, giving way to thoughts and actions that had a mind of their own.

But our endless cycle of push-pull also created a strength in me I didn't know I possessed, until I was forced to face the possibility of an existence without Dante.

Love changes you. And when you have to fight for it, over and over, that fire that burns forges you into something new. Like the blade of a knife, you become impenetrable, and at the same time, capable of cutting deep.

It was this strength that carried me through these past six months. It was there for me when I wanted to give up, reminding me that anything worth having, was worth fighting for. That *we* were worth fighting for. And it was there in me now, fueling my desire and igniting my possession. Dante is mine, and I'll be damned if anything ever tries to take him away from me again.

That was the reason for my tears. The surge in relief that he was back and knowing soon, my thirst for revenge would be satisfied. Together, Dante and I would make Luke pay for what he'd done and that craving for payback was just as delicious and just as satisfying as the hot lips working their way down my neck.

I pull back, and drink in the cobalt eyes of the one I love, seeing the same fire that I see in my own eyes when I look in the mirror. Need, want, anger...we were two halves of the same whole.

I fell for the angel he had been and loved irrevocably the daemon he was. Both parts of his spirit spoke to me. It had taken me thousands of years to realize that it didn't matter if he was dark or light, I loved him, totally.

Dante was passionate, and loyal, and carried the pain of abandonment, just like all the Fallen. But you had to look past the brooding, and anger, and the need for control, to see it. You had to move past who he wanted you to see, to find who he truly was. And that being was beautiful. That being was magnificent. That being was so undeniably hot.

While my sexual awakening had only recently begun, I'd had enough of Dante to know six months without his touch and kiss was way too long. Seeing him lying naked beside me fills my mind with the most carnal thoughts and I want to drown in his body and own it, just as he did mine, the night he first staked his claim on me.

I push him onto his back and straddle his legs, tracing the

ridges of his abs with the pad of my finger. He meets my touch with his own, running his hands up the top of my thighs.

"Angel," he whispers as I bend down and kiss his chest.

"Mm-hmm," I murmur, drawing circles with my tongue.

"What...happened after Sam shot me? How did you get out?"

I shift on his lap, brushing against his growing erection. "I thought you remembered everything?"

A low moan rumbles his chest, and he thrusts his hips up, and rubs against me. "I remember being shot," he punches out, "and telling Vinny to get you out, but fuck ..." he watches me raptly as I push up from his chest, my naked body on full display. "I can't think when you're riding me like that."

I wiggle my bottom and feel his now hard erection digging into the back of my thigh. "That's the point,"

I don't want to talk about what happened in Eden. I need him to fill me and fuck me and bring me to climax over and over until the burn of anger and ache from missing him dissolves, like the last six months never happened.

My mouth waters with the anticipation of how it feels when he commands my body under his will. and I'll gladly let him do whatever he wants to sate his need. But first, it's my turn. I've waited long enough.

I crawl down his body and take him into my mouth, flicking the tip with my tongue, then working my way down his shaft. I go slowly, taking him inch by inch, until I can bob all the way up and down easily.

He grabs my head with both hands guiding my rhythm as I lick up, and suck down, and when I graze the purple vein on his cock with my teeth, his body jolts and he blows out a ragged breath.

With the rhythm we set, it's not long before I taste the salty tang of pre-cum on my tongue, and knowing he's primed and ready to go, I place my hands on the sides of his legs and push up, hovering over him so my breasts brush against his body.

He looks at me, pupils blown, as I lace my fingers through his and hold our joined hands over his head and slide my slick folds up and down his erection.

"Fuck," he blows out as I lower down onto him, and once he's seated in me fully, press my hands to his chest and straighten, rocking my hips slowly.

I savor the feel of him filling me up as he runs his hands up my body and plays with my breasts. Then I pick up the pace, and he sits up, gripping the back of my neck with one hand, while putting the other on my lower back, and pulling me down onto him.

We're kissing and fucking like rabbits, hips grinding, skin slapping, and when I push him back down on the bed and brace my hand on his shoulder, he lays his head back and closes his eyes, panting my name in ecstasy.

Earlier, we were two lovers reconnecting, solidifying the covenant of the words we'd waited so long to say–every kiss, every touch, fueled by the euphoria of being back in each other's arms. But this…this is primal. A hunger that begs to be fed. Six months of desire left unfulfilled, creating a strong, pent-up need for release.

He feels good. Scratch that. He feels fucking amazing, as the force and friction of our joined bodies spreads fire through me and fuels my building climax.

"Take it," he whispers. "Take all of me, angel."

I drop my head back, relishing the way we feel, and he sits up and cups one breast with his hand, and moves his other between us, rubbing my clit feverishly.

"Don't stop," I bit my lip, feeling the pressure building.

He rubs harder, and with every circle of his thumb, my climax builds. I want to fall off the edge and fill my body with warmth and release.

I thought I would never feel this again. This connection. This high of us. And the idea I could have lost him for good, fills me with blind fury.

He stares at me, drunk with love and devotion, and as I slow my pace, then detonates, letting out a guttural moan as his climax shoots into me. I follow, my body clenching, and pulsing around him, and once I've come down, I collapse on his chest, breathless.

We lay quiet for a while, his hand running up and down my back as I rest mine on his chest, then he kisses the side of my head and whispers in my ear. "I need you to tell me what happened in Eden. How did you escape?"

"Why does it matter?" I ask softly, not wanting to go back to that day.

"Because it feels like you're not telling me something and I have to know. I need to know if he hurt you or…" his voice trails off, words hanging in the space between us.

Dante was right. I wasn't telling him everything. But how could I? How could I tell him the very thing I gave up once to save him, had been the very thing that helped me save him again?

I remain silent for what feels like forever, and then I answer the question I'd been avoiding. "We were able to escape because of me."

I lay my head flat on his chest and close my eyes–the memory of the moment my wings returned, slamming into me. The sound of flesh ripping, and bones breaking, was a cacophony of agony I would never forget; the combination of pain and elation seared forever into my mortal body.

"My wings," I draw in a pensive breath. Dante's body stiffens and his hand freezes on my back. "They...returned."

I wait for the barrage of questions I know will come, but Dante is strangely silent. When I look up, I see why. He is neither confused or in awe, but expressionless.

"But...that's not possible," he manages to say finally.

Dante was right. Even though I did not fall with those who rebelled, my punishment had been the same. Heaven stripped me of my ethereality and confined my spirit to its mortal form. The return of my wings should not have been possible. Yet, they had come back. When I asked begged to save Dante for a second time, it complied.

I look down, remembering how they felt extending behind me, strong and powerful, and when I saw their color-red, the color of love-I knew my spirit and heart had fused.

"Angel," Dante presses a finger under my chin and tilts my head up. "Tell me what happened." The confusion is gone from his face, and in its place, concern.

"You were dying." I place my hand on his cheek. "I could feel your spirit slipping away and I was desperate. So, I begged Heaven to save you and they did. That's how we got away. They gave me back my wings and you should have seen them," my chest warms with the recollection. "They were so beautiful, and stronger than before, and they were red, not gold."

Dante runs a hand along the scars on the inside of my shoulder blades. "But I can't feel them. Where are they?"

"They're not there anymore," I look down.

He sits up. "What do you mean?"

I do the same and pull the sheet to me. "Once we made it past Luke's guards—"

"Wait," he holds up a hand. "There shouldn't have been any guards. Vinny and I eliminated them."

"I know you did." The moment Dante rushed into the throne room to save me, flashes in my mind. He looked like he'd battled an army to get to me. His shirt slashed, and a cut on his temple, dripped with blood.

But then another flashes. We're making our way down a darkened corridor, trying to escape-Vinny carries Dante, Lila's on my side, and the legion behind us-and evidence of just how hard Dante fought to get to me, is all around.

Dozens of Luke's army are lifeless on the ground. Some shot, others beat to shreds. The carnage is great but there's no time to take it all in. The thundering steps of more guards approaching shakes the stone walls of the hall, and I know none of us are going to make it out unless I do something.

"My wings," I pause, trying to find the words to describe how powerful they were. "I had to get us out. I had to save you. It was the only way."

Dante's eyes widened. "What did you do?"

"They were as strong as a thousand angels. With one clap, I'd shattered the windows in Luke's great hall and cracked his throne in two, sending him running. But the army," I shake my head, "all it took was one clap, and they were gone."

He arches a brow. "They ran, too?"

"No," I swallow. "They were gone…vaporized. Reduced to dust."

"No," he closes his eyes.

My head snaps back. "What do you mean, no?"

"I didn't want you to have that on your spirit."

"Have, what?" I shake my head, confused.

"Taking a life."

"They were soulless," I let out a tense laugh. "Luke took

their lives. I freed them."

Dante looks at me, in silent contemplation.

"Hey," I tug on his hand when he remains quiet. "I love you. I fell for you once, and I will fall for you always. There is nothing I wouldn't do for you."

He runs a hand through his hair and blows out a worried breath. "Heaven did not give them willingly. They will want something in return."

"I don't care," I reply stubbornly. "You can't think that way," he turns his body towards mine. "You are important. Not just to me, but the legion. You are their leader now. You must care about what anyone may want from you, especially Heaven."

"And you?" My lip hitches up.

"What about me?"

"Where does what you want from me fall?"

His blue eyes turn dark and wicked. "At the top."

"Well," a grin pulls at my lips. "You're in luck because that's where I placed it. And...." I take a deep breath, "I didn't really feel like fighting you on the matter."

Dante shakes his head and smiles. "My angel is full of fire now, is that it?"

"Yes," I say with confidence. "Are you okay with that?"

"Oh, I'm okay with it," he wraps an arm around my waist and pulls me close. "In fact, I love it. But just so we're clear, you are at the top of my list, forever."

He leans in to kiss me and I fall into his arms, enveloped by his warmth. "And you will always be at the top of mine."

"Promise me we take Luke down together," I say as he tucks my head under his chin.

"I promise," he kisses the top of it. "We take Luke down, together."

We fall asleep that way, arms wrapped around one another, and when my dreams come, they are no longer of longing, but vengeance. Sweet revenge I'll finally exact, with Dante by my side.

4
DANTE

The sound of Diablo's breathing soothes my anxious energy. I could stay here like this forever, with her head on my chest, surrounded by warmth–but no matter how much we want moments to last, something always gets in the way. This time, it's the need for revenge and the desire to protect what's mine.

I once promised Diablo I would burn Heaven and Earth for her, and I wasn't lying. I would do anything to keep her safe and make her happy. But the only way I can ensure both, is to end Luke once and for all. *Me.* Not her. And not the legion.

Sure, her newfound strength and confidence are a major turn on, and I am eternally grateful she saved me not once, but twice. But the truth is, I love her too damn much to let her near Luke ever again. I still haven't forgotten what he had planned for her. His words haunt me, burrowing into my very marrow, driving my wrath.

An heir. Luke wanted Diablo to have his child. The very thought makes me red with rage. After reliving those last minutes in Eden over and over for what I now know is six months, the memory of him putting his hands on her, is forever seared into my brain.

I slip out from under her slowly, careful not to wake her, and once I am out of bed, make my way over to the window. Pressing my arm overhead against the glass, I look out across the skyline, trying to process everything.

Six months, I clench my fist and blow out an angry breath.

Six fucking months since Luke put a bullet in me and tried to take Diablo. Time may have passed, but the terror I felt that morning when I woke up and saw that she wasn't there is still fresh, my anger, still raw.

Turning away from the window, I make my way over to the writing desk in the corner and find JJ's sketchbook buried under a mound of papers. I reach for it and flip through the pages until I get to the picture he sketched of Diablo after the Fall. It guts me, just as it did when I first saw it–the way she lay over me protectively then, the same as she did earlier.

The irony was, I should be the one protecting her, and I failed. I wanted to throw the book across the room and take her away from this world of pain and loss and surround her with nothing but love and light. But I can't do that if Luke is still breathing.

The sound of the door opening catches my attention. Remembering I am naked, I drop the sketchbook back down on the desk, and rush over to the bed to slip on the sweats I ripped off earlier.

"Dante!" Vinny calls from the doorway, looking at me with a surprised smile on his face.

I hold a finger up to my lips and point to Diablo sleeping in the bed. He nods and backs out of the doorway as I hurry out of the room.

"Why the hell are you coming in without knocking?" I whisper as we step into the hall and close the door softly behind me. "I was naked, and she could have been."

"Hey," he holds his hands up. "We have an agreement. If it's not locked, it's safe to come in. She made the rule, not me. You know, for care and what not."

"Oh," I say flatly. The fact I had been bed-ridden for months and likely needed round the clock attention, hadn't dawned on me until now.

"Granted," he smiles, "she made it a point to take care of you most of the time."

I look through the crack in the door, wondering what the last six months must have been like for her. But the thought cuts short by Vinny's fist hitting my arm.

I swing my head around and rub my bicep. "Hey man."

He arches a brow. "Did that hurt?"

"No," I look down at my arm. I had not lost any muscle tone. Come to think of it, I was still in great shape; my body perfectly preserved. "Surprised me, that's all."

"Good," he laughs, then pulls me into a hug and pats my back. "It's really good to see you brother."

"You too," I do the same.

"How long have you been awake?" he asks when we pull apart.

"A couple of hours."

"Does she know?"

My lip tugs up at the corner, and Vinny knows me well enough to know what that means. "Right," he smirks and shakes his head. "Making up for lost time has already begun."

For thousands of years, Vinny had given me shit for my insatiable appetite and my reputation preceded me. But the moment Diablo and I finally found our way to one another, that was it. My desire for her transcended everything. She was it for me, forever. Just as Lila was for Vinny.

"How's Lila?" I ask. The pint-size firecracker that had stolen my best friend's heart earned my eternal gratitude when she went to Hell with us to save my angel.

"She's good, man," Vinny smiles. "She's been here with me every day."

Of course, she had. Lila, like Vinny, was loyal, and there

was no place she would rather be than with her best friend in her time of need.

Diablo and Lila were a lot like Vinny and me. Lila was like my sister, and there was no doubt in my mind in the months I was asleep, Vinny had watched over Diablo like a protective brother. The four of us were family, and no one fucks with family.

"I'm glad she was here. I'm glad you both were. I mean…six months?" I shake my head and close my eyes, still trying to process how long I'd been out.

"So, she told you," Vinny eyes me carefully.

"She did. And I'll tell you Vin, the pain in her eyes when she did, leveled me. What the fuck happened? How could I possibly lose that much time from one stardust bullet?"

"What do you remember?" Vinny crosses his arms and eyes me carefully, as he waits for my response.

"Every…fucking…thing." I try to shake the memory of Sam pointing the gun at me and the feel of blood seeping through my fingers. "But I want to know why that resulted in me losing months!" Vinny holds up his hand to keep my voice down. "When we tested stardust we lost hours," I whisper heatedly. "I could see a day, or two, but months? How is that possible, Vin."

"We tested the rounds Luke gave Sam and found they contained a lethal amount of stardust. You're lucky you woke up this decade, brother."

"Son of a bitch," I clench my fist. "How did he get a hold of that much stardust?"

"He created it. It was a synthetic that was so damn close to the original, the markers that differentiated it barely showed up on the tests."

"Well shit," I look away in disbelief. "He really wanted me

dead."

"He knew he couldn't kill you, but wanted you down as long as possible, that's for sure," Vinny nods.

When Luke wanted something, he would stop at nothing until he got it. The truth behind the contract that bound the Fallen, was proof of just how far he was willing to go. But Vinny heard what Luke said in Eden. He didn't just want me incapacitated. He wanted me out of the picture.

"I want to know everything," I curl my hand into a fist. "Every breath, every move, every shit he has taken since that day."

"Tomorrow," Vinny grips my shoulder. "We will fill you in on everything, I promise. But tonight," he looks at the door, "you need to be with her."

There was nothing I wanted more, than to hide away with Diablo for the next decade, free from the liar's contract that had kept us apart for five millennia. But Luke had to pay. He could not be allowed to exist after all he'd done. Especially with an arsenal of weapons that could render any of us lifeless for who knew how long.

"Do we know what else he has stockpiled?" I ask. "Anything similar or worse to what I was shot with?"

"We studied what we could get our hands on," Vinny nods and removes his hand. "It's the one thing that traitorous asshole Sam did right."

Anger pricks my skin. I didn't know Sam well. He'd been on Eden as long as Diablo and was barely noticeable during Luke's rebellion in Heaven. But I knew Viper, the daemon he was bound to, and she was strong and trustworthy. His betrayal had to have cut her deep.

"Where is he?" I ask, tersely.

"He is doing reconnaissance for me, while looking for his

daughter."

My brows shoot up, surprised by Vinny's response. "You trust him?"

Vinny had been livid with Sam after he shot me. In fact, at one point before I lost consciousness, I thought he was going to break Sam's neck with his bare hands.

"Trust is a funny thing, brother. As you know, the best way to find out if you can trust somebody is to trust them. Besides, Viper is on him like white on rice. She knows what to do if he steps out of line. That said, you'll have your day with him," Vinny grins. "You can trust me on that."

The legion was family. And when family disagreed, we settled those arguments the way we had been since The Fall. With a little sweat, and a little bloodshed. I couldn't wait to beat the shit out of Sam and see what he had to say for himself.

"And Diablo?" I rub my chin. "Has she talked to him?"

"No," Vinny shakes his head. I turn and peer through the crack in the door, remembering the frantic look in her eyes when the bullet struck me. "Probably for the best. Pain still too raw."

"That's some of it," Vinny laughs. I turn back around, confused by the lightness of his response. "I won't lie, she was a wreck at first. But your angel…she's stronger than I anticipated."

I know Diablo is strong. She has a heart of fire and determination and has carried more weight than any of us these past five millennia. Yet, the look in Vinny's eyes tells me it's more than just strength he's referring to.

"What aren't you telling me?" I ask, curious.

"Well, let's just say she asked us to keep Sam from her for his safety, not hers."

His answer surprised me. Then again, not entirely. I felt her strength and fire earlier–when she commanded me and took what she wanted and needed. It was hot as hell, and I was curious to see how that fire and determination shaped her.

Still, I knew no matter what she went through the past six months, the reason she was here and safe at all, was because of Vinny. When I felt myself slipping away and asked him to get her to safety, I knew he would, no matter what. He would do anything I asked, just as I would for him.

"Thank you," I look at him, full of gratitude. "For getting Diablo out of Eden and keeping her safe."

"Brother," Vinny puts his hand on my shoulder. "We've been through some shit, and I would do anything you ask. But you must know, she is the reason we got out."

"Her wings," I take a deep breath and nod. "She told me."

"It was the most incredible thing I'd ever seen," he says excitedly. "It's like they were on fire. And their strength. Shit," he lets out a low whistle. "They were stronger than mine or yours ever were. I mean dozens of Luke's minions, reduced to ash in a second," he snaps. "And now the legion worships her. Of course, it doesn't hurt she's been training and can kick ass, too. But man, it's wild."

I knew when the legion rescinded their loyalty to Luke and swore it to Diablo, they would protect her at all costs. A couple hundred fallen angels who'd been lied to for five thousand years, was a force no one would want to face. Still, the idea of her as our leader filled me with both pride and possession.

"She's been training?" I ask, trying to ignore the idea of the legion watching my angel in adoration.

"When she's not in the gym, she's here with you. And

man," Vinny laughs. "I've never seen so many tough ass daemons willing to move mountains for one being."

"Well, she is their leader now, so they better watch her back. But they also better fucking remember who she belongs to."

"Trust me," Vinny grins. "They remember. None of us have ever seen someone as fiercely devoted to another as she is to you. She is hell bent on finding Luke and destroying him. She reminds me of you in every way, man. There is not a doubt in my mind it's not a matter of when Luke will pay for what he's done. But when it's time, you'll pour the gas and she'll strike the match."

I look back to the room. My need to be with Diablo visceral, pulling at me with centrifugal force.

"Dante," Vinny asks while I look at my angel sleeping peacefully. "Do you remember anything from when you were out? Could you hear us, or did you know where you were?"

I turn back around, wanting to explain to him where I've been. But I'm not sure I can because the truth is, I don't really know. And he's right…the only thing I need to do right now is go back to bed and be with Diablo. Just, hold her close, and know that she is safe.

I run a hand up and down my face and blow out a tired breath. "You're right. Let's talk about everything tomorrow."

"Alright man," he grins. "You go love on that angel of yours. But know this–we will get revenge for what happened to you. I promise."

No matter what the millennia have brought, we've weathered it together. But saying thank you for keeping the most important thing in the world to me safe, just doesn't seem to suffice.

"Vin…I owe you. I don't know what I would have done if

I'd lost her."

"Brother," he grips my shoulder. "You, me, Diablo, and Lila…we're family. I would fight for any of us. Know that. Now, and always."

I feel the same. Diablo was my heart, but Lila was Vinny's, and he was my brother. No one had bled for me more, and that bond was forever. "And it will be the four of us who take that son of a bitch down."

"Hell, yeah it will," he smiles. "By the way, guess it's time to start knocking before entering, yeah?"

"That would be smart," I give him a shit-eating grin. "You don't need to see my naked ass."

"Trust me, I've seen enough of it to last this existence," he laughs heartily.

We both laugh and then he sticks his fist out. "It's good to have you back brother."

"Thanks man." I bump mine against it, then watch as he turns, and makes his way down the hall.

Once he's out of sight, I head back inside and crawl into bed next to Diablo. Luke will die for what he's done, but not tonight. Tonight, I'm going to curl up next to my heart, and fall asleep with my arms around her, knowing she's safe by my side.

5
DIABLO

I wake up and find Dante standing next to the bed looking down at me with a cup of coffee in his hand and a grin on his face. "Good morning, angel."

I can't help but smile back while pulling the pillow close, snuggling into its softness. "What time is it?"

"Nearly noon," he winks. "I let you sleep in. We had kind of a late night."

Heat fans my face as I sit up, holding the duvet close, and reach for his cup. He shakes his head with a bemused expression as I lift it to my lips and take a sip.

It's the roast Dante likes, prepared just how he takes it, and there's only one person besides me who knows the secret ingredient. "So, you've already been down to talk to Wills, I see."

"I have," he shoves a hand in the pocket of his slacks. "And Lillian. She's anxious to get housekeeping in here to straighten up. I told her they should probably change the sheets, too."

"You didn't," my cheeks grow warmer.

"I did," he laughs softly. "This room could use some tidying. Not to mention, we worked up quite a sweat last night."

I look around at the papers scattered on the desk, sweater on the chair by the window, and stack of books on the nightstand. It was more lived in compared to Dante's minimalist style, that's for sure. And he wasn't lying, we did work up a sweat.

"So, come on," he waves for me to get out of bed. "We've got a little payback to plan, while this room gets a thorough cleaning."

As Dante stands there looking down at me, I'm reminded of how magnetic his presence is and how raw his sex appeal.

"Looks like you'll be heading down to the office as well?" I ask, swallowing down my hunger.

He's wearing black button-up shirt and gray slacks, both tailored to perfection to compliment his chiseled frame. While his face is smooth from a close shave, and hair combed back on top, and short on the sides. Every inch of him is delicious, down to the ink peeking out from under his rolled-up sleeves, and he takes my breath away.

"Later, yes," he nods. "There's a lot of stuff to catch up on."

Dante's corporation, Primordial Holdings, was a global juggernaut with offices all over the world. Between Vinny and Wills, it had been in good hands the last few months. He was no doubt anxious however, to check in on things. It was the foundation to the empire he'd built, and he was proud of it, rightfully so.

"Before I do that, though, I want to get briefed on everything I've missed," he adds, taking his cup back and taking a sip.

Today was no doubt going to be busy, and I didn't want to share him with everyone just yet.

I lower my eyes and pretend to pout, the way I'd seen Lila do a thousand times to get her way with Vinny. "Well, there goes my idea of spending the day in bed."

"Angel," he leans over and runs a thumb along my lower lip. I plan to spend forever in bed with you, just as soon as we finish what Luke started."

The flicker in his eyes and smoke in his voice stirs heat in my core. I wrap my hand around the back of his neck and squeeze. "Promise?"

"One of many I never plan to break." He kisses me and hums in pleasure as he sucks my lower lip between his teeth. "Damn, the taste of coffee on your lips is still my favorite."

If he can stand there tempting me with how good he looks and that kiss, who said I couldn't do the same. I push the covers off me and get out of bed, knowing full-well I'm naked, and press my hands to his chest, and look up from under lowered lashes.

"What are you doing?" He clears his throat and draws in a shallow breath, as I press my body against his.

"Nothing," I shrug innocently as I finger the buttons of his shirt and tip my head up for a kiss. "Just saying good morning, properly."

He sets the cup down slowly on the nightstand, nearly missing it altogether, then wraps an arm around my waist and draws me into a kiss. "You're killing me, you know that?"

"Am I?" I ghost his lips with mine. "Well, Shakespeare did warn us about the joy in little deaths, did he not?"

Dante scoops me up and kisses me again, this time deeper and hungrier, as I unbutton his shirt and he lowers us down to the bed.

His breath hitches as my fingers brush against his skin. "We're not leaving this room yet, are we?"

I bite my lip and look at him wantonly, while running my leg down the back of his thigh. "Up to you."

"Fuck it," he bends down and trails kisses down my neck, as I press against him.

After freeing the last button of his shirt, I push it off and run my hands over his shoulders and down his back. His mouth is hot, his touch, hungry. But when he pulls up and looks at me, blue eyes burning with intensity, I know he doesn't want to leave this bed any more than I do.

He traces the outline of my lips with his finger, and when my tongue darts out to graze it, he crashes his mouth down onto mine, and slides one hand between my legs.

"Is this what you want?" he asks, while rubbing his fore and middle finger up and down the sides of my entrance.

His touch is teasing, and I moan with need, as I tip my hips up and grab a fistful of his hair. "Yes," I sigh.

He presses down on my clit with his thumb and continues rubbing up and down, sending fire shooting through me. "Like that?"

"Shit, yes," I press the back of my head into the pillow and widen my legs, wanting him to take more of me.

He looks down and licks his lips as I grind against his hand. "Fuck, now I won't be able to think about anything else all day, except you writhing under me."

"We could change that." My breathing is airy, my body charged. "I could be on top and then you wouldn't be able to think about anything else but me riding you."

He laughs and the rumble of his chest vibrates against mine. "You like being in control, don't you?"

"Yes," I admit, surges of heat ripping through me as he continues to thrum me expertly. Last night when he gave his body to me to do with it as I pleased, I won't deny…I liked the way it felt.

I'd never craved control. But as he lay back and let me take what I needed I realized… power was an aphrodisiac. Commanding the one you loved, stirred a delicious, wicked pleasure, and submission was a line I *definitely* wanted to cross more.

He eases up on my clit and runs his thumb down my slick entrance, then dips two fingers inside me, making my hips buck. He moans with approval as I rock against his hand harder and grip his arm.

His breathing picks up and watching him watch me only heightens my arousal. Too long I'd been without his touch, and I can't get enough. "Fuck angel, I'm going to come just watching you."

"Let me help you with that." Reaching for the zipper of his pants, I pull it down slowly, the click of teeth pulling apart, then wrap my hand around his girth, and start stroking him.

He pumps his fingers in and out of me harder, as I stroke him faster, and soon we're both breathing so hard we're panting. "I'm close," I say through a pinched breath.

In a matter of seconds, he's replaced his fingers with his cock and the moment I feel him in me, we both let go and moan in sweet release.

When we're both fully spent, he falls onto the bed next to me and we both laugh, dizzy with pleasure and relief. "Guess you'll have to put something else on," I look over at his rumpled shirt on the bed.

"Guess so," he puts a hand on his chest and blows out a spent breath. "And fix my hair."

I laugh again and when it grows quiet, I turn my head towards him. "What?" I ask, chest tightening with the way he's looking at me.

"What was all that about?"

"Nothing," I shrug innocently. "I wanted you."

"Angel," he grins. "If we do that every time I want you, we're going to be fucking all over this house."

I push up on my elbow and bite my lip. "Promise?"

He brushes my hair over one shoulder and leans over, pressing his lips to it. "Always."

I bury my face in his chest and take a deep breath. "I missed you. That's what that was about."

"Missed you more." He looks at me, eyes full of love, and a piece of my spirit that was still finding its way out of sadness, fuses back in with the rest of me. "Now get ready. We need to get downstairs."

Once done, I make my way into the room and find Dante sitting casually at the writing desk, with his cell phone in hand. When I enter, he looks up, and sets his phone down. "Damn, you look good in my color."

"Your color?" I look down and realize he is right. From my boots to my leggings to the oversized sweater, everything I have on is his color of choice…black. Come to think of it, of all the clothes Lillian stocked in the closet of the beautiful suite Dante built for me down the hall, everything I'd worn the last few months was black.

He gets up from the chair and crosses the room, coming over to where I stand. "Yes," he smiles down at me. "My color."

"Does that do it for you?" I look up playfully. Even though my body is satisfied, my hunger for him is unending.

"My color on my angel, what's not to love? But if you must know," he leans in and whispers, "everything you do, does it for me."

Heat pools in my stomach and I press my thighs together to stop the need I feel growing in me again. "We are never going to make it downstairs if this continues."

"You're right," he kisses me gently on the lips and then straightens, reaching for my hand. "Save it for later. The buildup will be the best kind of foreplay."

Heat surges between our palms and I savor the feel of us together again as we make our way out of the suite and down the stairs.

Everything feels...different. More alive. The world had changed in the blink of an eye. Even the clouds were gone, in their place, an azure summer sky.

When we hit the foyer, I tug on his hand and pull him back as he tries to head down the hall that leads to his study.

He looks down at my hand and back up. "You said you saw Wills and Lillian earlier?"

"Yeah," he smiles.

"Did you see anyone else?"

"Vin stopped by last night while you were sleeping, but that's it. Why?" he asks curiously.

"Come on," I pull him down the hall that leads to the kitchen and stop outside one of the spare rooms on this floor. "I have a surprise for you."

"Angel," he shoots me a devilish smile. "You can't go five minutes without—"

A door next to us pulls open and when Dante sees who's standing on the other side, he stops cold. For a moment he looks too stunned to speak. But when the old man throws his arms around him and claps his back, words start tumbling out.

"JJ?" he asks in disbelief.

The old man laughs and pulls back, and I can tell by the look on Dante's face, he's stunned. "What... I mean how is this possible?"

"Well," JJ looks at Dante for a moment then me. "I guess you can say your angel is now mine, too."

Dante turns to me, eyes wide. "What?"

"He's an attendant," I say matter of fact.

"You're a what?" he turns back to JJ.

"That's right," JJ nods and smiles wide. "Your angel saved me."

"Is that even possible?" Dante asks, shaking his head with disbelief.

"Well, it appears since I too, was bound by Luke's contract, I was able to free myself from Eden, the same way the legion was able to–by swearing my allegiance to Diablo."

"I don't believe it," Dante looks from JJ to me again. "You did this?"

"Well, I had some help," I look at JJ and smile. "Vinny told me what to say and well…it worked."

"Of course," Dante looks at me in wonder. "The legion is bound to you and so too, are our abilities."

"I look good, right?" JJ straightens his shirt and steps back. Gone was the pallid color of his skin, and gray in his hair.

"You look a thousand years younger," Dante agrees, and the two laugh. "But why are you down here? There are plenty of rooms upstairs that are bigger."

"Don't bother," I shake my head. "I tried to get him to move up there, but he hates the stairs. Prefers to be next to the kitchen."

"And you feel…okay?" Dante asks, the shock starting to wear off and giving way to joy.

"I feel like a million bucks, old friend. Honestly, between your angel and Lillian, I am being well looked after."

Dante looks at me, eyebrows raised. "Oh yeah?"

"Later," I mouth as JJ beams at Dante. I couldn't wait to tell him about the crush I suspected JJ had on her.

"Well, this is your home as long as you want," Dante assesses the room. "I can get you whatever you need, just let me know. Or, if you want, I can get you set up with your own place and a shop if you'd like. Just say the word, and it's yours."

"In time," JJ dismisses the idea. "Right now, I'm just enjoying this. Freedom…and you two." He puts one hand gently on my shoulder and the other on Dante's. "You're together, after five thousand years. The angel that fell, and her angel. It's like a dream."

I look up at Dante who reaches for my hand and pulls it to his lips. "It sure is," he agrees, kissing it. "I want to catch up with you," he turns back to JJ. "But I have to get caught up on everything right now."

"Of course," JJ motions for us to go. "Do your thing. I'll be here when you have time to catch up."

Dante reaches for JJ and pulls him into another hug. "I'm glad you're here, old friend."

"Me too," JJ pats his back.

After promising to come back later, Dante and I say goodbye and make our way back down the hall. Just before we reach the study, he pulls me into a smaller room and closes the door.

"What are you—" I start to ask but he cuts my question short with a searing kiss. It's hot, and charged, and full of emotion as his arm snakes around my waist and flushes his chest against mine.

When he finally pulls back, I'm breathless. "You're remarkable, you know that?"

My heart pounds as the air between us crackles. "I don't know about that," I lick my lips.

"No," he shakes his head. "You are. You saved me, you saved JJ and the legion. We're all free from Luke's lies because of you."

"JJ is important to you…well us, really…and I wanted to

make sure he was protected. I wanted to make sure they were all protected. You would have done the same."

He cups my face and stares into my eyes. "I don't know how I got so lucky, but I plan to spend my existence honoring that luck. Whatever you want, it's yours."

"I think I can live with that." My chest practically bursts with happiness as he folds me into his arms and kisses me again.

We steal a few more minutes alone and then I run my hand across his chest to straighten his shirt, as he swipes a thumb over my lips. "Ready?" I ask.

He grabs my hand and squeezes it. "More than you know."

The time had come to fill Dante in on everything that happened while he was sleeping.

6
DANTE

The moment Diablo and I enter the study, I'm hit with the memory of us. It feels like we were just here; shadows of our first dance, first kiss, linger. Then I remember, it's been months, and even though those moments are still so fresh I can still feel them, the reality of that loss hits me.

I tighten my grip on her hand as Vinny and Lila greet us. "About time," he sticks his fist out and I press my free one to it. "Although, if it were me, you wouldn't have seen me for a month, maybe more." He looks at Lila and winks and she swats his arm.

"Don't worry," Diablo flashes me a dazzling smile. "The door will be locked every night for the next decade."

Lila laughs and makes her way over to us, throwing her arms around me. "Good to see you, Dante."

"Hey sis." I let go of Diablo's hand and return Lila's hug. "Thank you for taking care of our girl."

"Anytime." She holds on for a moment longer then squeezes my shoulders and steps back. "Now, can we finally get this payback show on the road?"

"Hell yeah," Vinny throws an arm around her. "I mean, I was beginning to wonder if it would be this century or the next."

We all laugh, but as it dies down, I know we're each thinking about the same thing–the last time the four of us were together.

Lila is, unsurprisingly, the first to speak. "Can you believe it? We're all here, finally."

"It's pretty incredible," I agree. We'd all been waiting for this very moment. But now that it was here, we were planning for war, instead of celebrating. "Didn't think it would look quite like this, though."

"That's for damn sure," Vinny tucks Lila closer to his side. "I expected more booze, and less drama. But man, look at us, we're still standing."

"We are," Diablo takes a breath and looks at each of us. "So, why don't we get to work so we can get to drinking."

The determination in her response makes me smile. Diablo's innocence and naivety had always charmed me, but this new, take no shit confidence, electrified me.

"Agree," I wink, then head over to my desk, and press both hands down onto the wood. "Let's get started."

Lila steps away from Vinny's side and he follows, coming to a stop on the other side. "Let's begin with Primordial," he reaches for a stack of folders in the corner and slides them towards him, and hands me the one on top. "In a nutshell, performance is strong, and everything is running as normal. The team thinks you've been on a global scouting trip, and we've used previous video conferences to stitch together monthly updates for the execs. But you should visit them today. It will be good for them to see you in person."

"Already planning to," I read the first few pages and see everything is on track, just as Vinny said.

Between him and Wills, I knew Primordial had been in good hands. I'd set up a contingency plan decades ago, to ensure things would continue as normal, in the event I was incapacitated. Turns out, the plan was effective.

"That's good," Vinny nods as I close the folder and set it down. "Figured you were planning to. Next, let's talk about the building."

He hands me another folder and I open it, flipping through pages of diagrams and product details. "I've completely overhauled the security system," he says proudly. "Added new layers of encryption, remote firewalls, and server routing. And the pièce de résistance…titanium doors have been added at every external entry point, including the garage. They require retinal scanning, and anyone who tries to enter without will trigger their closing. In the case that happens, only you, me, and Wills have clearance to open them again."

"Anyone complain about the new protocols?" I look up.

"Nope," he shakes his head. "Staff have already given their consent and had their scans done. They were totally on board. Makes them feel more secure, too, given the kind of financial information we handle. Nothing, and I mean nothing, is getting through."

"This is really excellent," I nod, impressed. "You've outdone yourself, Vin."

"Oh, but wait brother, there's more, he says gleefully. "We all have new cell phones, as well. They are on the network of the carrier we purchased last year in Jakarta. Customers were notified of their accounts being moved to a new carrier given our plans to shut it down, so we are the only ones on the network–the four of us, the legion, and attendants. Every phone has a tracker, remote monitoring, security…all that."

I pull my phone out of my pocket and look at it. I didn't even know it was different. "Man, you're a wizard."

"Ha," he smirks. "I wish. Now, just a few more things about the building. We activated the elevator bank in the back of the building for floors thirty-four through fifty. Each apartment has been key carded, and every member of the legion given a key. And the gym on fifty is also done and fully functional. The legion trains there in the afternoons, and they know the rules-no visitors, and no leaving for their own places, until this is over. Although, I think more than a few will stick around. The apartments are sweet."

"I can't believe half of the building is apartments for the legion," Diablo looks up at me admiringly.

"We had the space," I shrug. "It made sense."

"Well, there's sense, and then there's generosity," she smiles softly. "I think creating safe houses for every member of the legion falls into the latter."

"Funny you should mention safe houses," Vinny smirks and hands me another folder.

Diablo looks at the folder and then up at Vinny. "Is that the news you were waiting for?"

"Open it and see," he says mysteriously.

I close the folder with the building updates and set it down on the desk, then reach for the one in Vinny's outstretched hand.

"For six month's it's been quiet," he presses his thumb and forefinger on each hand down onto the desk and leans in "Not a move, not a sound from either he or his army. And now, we know why."

I grip the folder tight; the whites of my knuckles showing under the strain. *Luke*.

"Open it," Diablo demands. I can hear the anger and anxiousness in her voice. It matches that surging through my body and down my arm, to my fingertips which burn with their hold of the folder.

I look over at Diablo. Her eyes are wide as she stares down intently at the folder, and Lila, too, has come over to get a closer look.

I turn my attention back to the folder and open it, finding a stack of photos inside. They are of Luke, each a different point in time, dating back a hundred years.

Billionaires and royalty, politicians, and crime lords, he has walked among them all, and I'd known this. We all had. It's how wrought the devastation he had. Through power. But it's the last picture that catches me by surprise. He's in a red robe of the purest silk, and he's standing in the middle of a place more over the top in its display of pomp and circumstance, than any other.

I pull it from the stack and hold it angrily, as the folder and all the other photos fall onto the desk. "He's a fucking Cardinal?" I look up at Vinny, my anger racing.

"Cardinal Lucius Raphael Giancarlo," Vinny's nods, jaw tight. "It seems, the depth in which he is in bed with the church, is far deeper than any of us realized. He's been at The Vatican the whole time."

"So, he didn't just make a deal with them to hide the contract?" Lila grips Vinny's arm.

"Nope," he shakes his head. "And we've learned something very interesting about Cardinal Lucius."

"What is it?" I slam the photo down on the desk, the source of the church's knowledge of Heaven and the Fallen–including Luke's own notoriety–now making sense. "I'll give you one guess to tell me what Cardinal Lucius is in charge of at The Vatican," Vinny challenges. "Actually, I'll give you two."

Luke was a Cardinal. That was as close to the top of the piety food chain as you could get. I think about it and then look at Diablo who stares back at me, just as stumped by the question as I.

"Well, what is it, Vin?" Lila taps her foot impatiently.

50

We all wait for Vinny to answer, but instead, he hands me another folder. "Man, you're like a fucking magician," I grab it.

"With the cutest assistant," he blows Lila a kiss. "But don't expect me to pull a rabbit out of my ass."

"I think you mean hat," Diablo corrects.

"Ass…hat…same thing," he laughs.

"Pretty sure they're not," Lila rolls her eyes, while at the same time, shooting Vinny a naughty smile.

"Well, what's in that folder, I may as well have pulled out of a unicorn's ass, because that my friend, is the Holy Grail, literally." I shake my head and look up. "The church's digital vault. The one that had the contract…Luke's in charge of it."

Diablo pulls my arm down and looks down at the list in the folder. "What?"

"Where did you get this?" I flip through the pages. There had to be well over a thousand items listed.

"David," he says matter of fact.

"David?" I ask and look up.

The relic hunter we'd enlisted to help translate the contract that bound the Fallen, had been instrumental in helping us discover the extent of Luke's lies. He was connected and resourceful, not to mention more knowledgeable than most mortals about ancient civilizations and antiquities. Vinny was smart to seek his help.

I flip through the pages, taking in the myriad of items on the list. "What did you tell him we needed it for?"

One of the reasons we'd worked with David so much over the years, was his discretion. We could tell him very little, and he'd still do the job, no questions asked–just as long as the items he found for us didn't wind up on the black market. Since nothing ever did, our working relationship had always been in good standing.

Vinny levels his eyes on me and draws in a deep breath. "The truth," he says simply.

Diablo's hand falls from my arm and I look up at Vinny, not sure I heard him correctly. "Come again, brother?"

"It was the only way we could get what's in that folder," he nods down at the desk, then reaches for the last folder in the stack. "And this one."

"What do you mean?" I ask, not liking both what he said, or how he said it.

"This," he hands me the last folder, "is everything we know about the bullet that shot you. Its composition, its effects…everything that could be known, and ever will be known about stardust."

I reach for the folder and open it quickly. It's filled with pages of lab results, diagnostics, and composition charts. "Did David do all this?"

"No," Vinny replies. "James did."

"Who the fuck is James?" I shake my head and reach the last page. It's a history of vitals, dating back months. "And whose vitals are these?"

"Yours," Vinny crosses his arms. "And he's a doctor. David's partner."

There is only one way this kind of information could have been compiled. It required access. Access one could only have been granted if they knew the truth about what we were.

"Vin," I close my eyes. "Tell me you didn't…"

"Before you say anything," he holds up a hand, and I know then, that I don't have to bother finishing my thought. He's already answered my question.

"Damn it!" I blow out my breath, forcibly. "Attendants! You made them both, attendants?" It was the only way one could know the truth of our existence, aside from being soulless.

Diablo places her hand on my arm, and warm rushes to my elbow. "Dante, let him explain."

I turn to her, voice tight. "You knew about this?"

Both her voice and eyes soften. "It was the only way." It's the first time since last night that her strength has dipped, and it tugs at my chest. "You weren't waking, and we didn't know what else to do."

"But we agreed," I swing my head back in Vinny's direction, her despondency making my chest hurt. "No more attendants."

"I know," Vinny kicks his feet shoulder width apart as if preparing to battle. "But it had to be done."

"What, the fuck Vinny!" I push up from the desk and turn to the window.

"Hey!" Lila shouts. Everyone turns to look at her, including me. "He was losing his best friend, and Diablo, her reason for existence. You can't be mad at him for doing what needed to be done. He did it. Man up and get over it."

I snap my head back and let out a surprised laugh. "What did you say to me?"

"I said," she places a hand on her hip, "man the fuck up, brother."

I shake my head and laugh again in disbelief. "Man, being with him has given you balls, Lila. Steel ones at that."

"You bet your ass," she lifts her chin. "So, listen when I say it a second time. Get…over…it. His decision saved your life. End of story. We have other things to focus on."

I look at Diablo, who shifts her eyes to her best friend and nods in agreement, then looks back at me. "She's right. We did what we did to save you, and we would do it again in a heartbeat."

I turn my attention to Vinny. "It was a mortal injury, man. You were dying. If there was any other way, I would have done it. But there wasn't. So, I broke a promise. Sue me. I've got a good lawyer."

Diablo presses her forehead to my shoulder, and I bury my face in her hair, breathing her in. If Vinny hadn't done what he did, I wouldn't be here with her…with any of them.

I stroke her cheek and take a deep breath. "Okay," I say finally.

"I think you mean, thank you," he shoots me a look of triumph, then strides over to the wet bar and pours a couple of drinks. "Look," he continues as he comes back over and hands me a glass. "I know attendants can be pains in the asses at first. But they're adapting well."

"That's why you didn't want him to make more attendants?" Lila rolls her eyes. "Because they're a little work?"

"A little work," I lift my glass and take a drink. It rolls down my throat and warms me. "Try rabid dogs on steroids."

"You talk about them like they're baby vampires or something," she scoffs. "What's the big deal?"

"Well, that's something the movies got right." I take another sip and feel myself relaxing a bit, not realizing how tense the last few minutes had made me. "They're messy. Do things they're not supposed to and risk exposure. When that happens…"

She looks from me to Vinny. "When that happens, what?"

"They get handled," he says pointedly.

"Handled?" her brows shoot up. "As in…"

"Removed…disposed of," Vinny downs his drink, waits for me to do the same, then grabs my glass and makes his way to the bar to pour another.

"What about JJ?" Diablo looks up at me, clearly surprised. "Will he be, okay, or will he need to be…disposed of?"

I had the same thought when I first saw him, and admittedly, had concerns. I still didn't know how it was possible he could be an attendant since he'd already given up his soul. But if he'd been here for six months and hadn't had any problems so far, he was probably going to be okay.

"He'll be fine, angel." The reassurance is for me, as much as it is her. But I needed to talk more with Vinny. I still had questions about JJ's transition.

"Whatever our baby attendants throw our way we'll manage," Vinny comes back over and hands me a fresh drink. "We'll manage. We like a little mayhem, remember?"

"You do recall some of the shit we've had to cover up thanks to careless attendants, right?" I look down into my glass and swirl the amber liquid. "There's mayhem, and then there's messy.

"Yeah," he knocks back his drink. "But they will also have the best teachers around. Wills and Lillian are pros."

"It's not their job to teach the new attendants, decorum," I counter.

"I know," Vinny nods in understanding. "Just saying, they can guide them."

I draw in a deep breath, let it fill my lungs, then exhale slowly. "I just don't want enthusiasm over their newfound immortality to get in the way of what needs to be done."

"Trust me," Vinny knocks back his drink then sets his glass down on the desk. "They've been laser focused so far. But you can see for yourself. They'll be here in a few."

"Oh yeah?" I finish my drink and put it down next to his. "You were that sure I was going to be cool with it, were you?"

"Well," he shoots Diablo a knowing look and grins. "I had a secret weapon in my corner."

I snake my arm around her waist and pull her close, kissing the top of her head. "You mean, my secret weapon."

"I think you mean, our leader," Lila corrects both of us. Diablo blushes and damn, if I don't want to kiss those cheeks and take whatever order she wants to give me.

Vinny reaches for the folder with the pictures of Luke and sets it down on the desk, pressing his finger down on it. "This is our focus. This asshole right here."

We're looking at one another in silent agreement when there's a knock at the door. Vinny looks up as Wills enters the study first. "Well come on in, gentlemen. We've been expecting you."

7
DANTE

After reviewing the ground rules with David and James, including a few new ones I added for good measure, I'm a bit more at ease. They appear to be taking their new existence in stride–as much as a mortal could after becoming immortal and learning there really were angels and daemons–and admittedly, could be of use.

I'd always liked David and long suspected he didn't believe the explanation Vinny and I gave him of being billionaire playboys, so it was a bit of a relief to no longer have to maintain the ruse. But James I did not know and wasn't sure how I felt about him knowing what we were or our world.

"So, tell me David," I reach for the folder with the list of items in the church's digital vault. "Why is Luke interested in these?"

"Well," he adjusts his glasses and taps on the tablet in his hand. "It's what I consider an artifactual history of mankind."

"But the contract that bound the Fallen was in there, and that's not relevant to mankind," Diablo counters.

"No," he agrees. "Not technically. But there are millions who believe in The Fall and its role in the creation of good, evil, and ultimately, faith."

Diablo chews the corner of her lip, considering his response.

"What I am more interested in, is the importance of some artifacts over the others." David sets the tablet down on the desk and turns it towards the four of us. "See this," he taps on the lower right side of the image and zooms in, "it's only on a handful of images."

"What is it?" Vinny asks tersely as I lean over to get a better look.

"It's a sigil," David explains. "Well, three of them, interconnected. The Moon, Sun, and Stars."

"Do you know why it is on some images, and not others?" Lila asks, appearing just as confused by the marking as the rest of us.

"No," he exhales. "And my contact at The Vatican doesn't either. It doesn't correspond to any meta data in the vault's database, nor does it appear on the original artifacts. Only the image."

"What contact?" I straighten and cross my arms.

"The one who gave me this list." I'm about to interject with a lecture about who we can and can't trust but David puts his hand up as if he knows exactly what I'm about to say. "I wouldn't be in this line of work if I didn't know how to work a contact for information without tipping my hand. I haven't said a word and I won't. Plus, this contact is a friend and I trust them."

His answer satisfies me. He's never given me any reason not to trust him, and I'm not going to start now. "So, any guess as to why it's on the images?"

"I was hoping you could tell me," David removes his glasses. "But you look just as perplexed as I am."

"May as well be chicken scratch," Vinny quips.

"Same," I nod. "I haven't seen it before."

Diablo reaches for the list and scans the pages of items in the vault. "Is there any relation between the images with that marking?"

"Not really," David shakes his head. "They're from different civilizations and time periods. No rhyme or reason that I can see. I've created an album and put all the images with the sigil in it," he taps the tablet. "I thought seeing them together could trigger a thought."

"Here's one," Vinny smirks. "Luke's a sneaky bastard and he's playing games."

I lift my chin in agreement. "I second that."

"Well, there has to be a reason some images have it, and others don't," Diablo muses. "We're just not seeing it yet."

My angel was smart. If anyone could figure this out, it was her.

"Perhaps when all the images are available, the answer will be more obvious," David rationalizes.

"They're not all in?" Lila taps a finger against her cheek.

"Not yet," David shoves a hand in his pocket. "The items on the list with an asterisk are still waiting to be scanned. They could have this sigil or not. We won't know until it's complete."

"When will that be?" Vinny asks.

"My contact says it will be the end of summer.

"End of summer?" I blow out a frustrated breath and clench my fist. "We don't have that kind of time. Luke needs to pay for what he did, *now*."

"What do you mean?" David looks at Dante, confused. "That's only a few weeks away."

"Weeks?" I shake my head, then remember…it's July. Not January. The end of summer is nearing.

Diablo sets the list down and wraps an arm around my waist. "When, specifically, will everything be scanned in?" she asks David. "Is there a deadline?"

"Two weeks from tomorrow," David confirms.

"According to my contact, there is a big gala planned where they will showcase the vault and have the real artifacts alongside the renderings. Sounds to me like a bragging rights event for the company that did all the renderings.

"So, in two weeks, the digital vault will be complete, and all the images that have a sigil in the album you created," Diablo repeats.

"More or less," David nods.

"More or less?" I arch a brow. "What's the less."

"Well," he clears his throat. "Knowing who, well, what Luke is, makes his oversight of the vault…alarming. Whatever he wants, it can't be good."

"No," Diablo agrees. "Nothing about his partnership with the church is good. And?"

"And, well," David clears his throat, "I was wondering if there is anything I should know."

"Such as?" Lila cocks her head. "Are there any dates that hold a particular significance, or any sort of passage of time anniversary coming up?"

"You want to know if Luke plans to end the world in two weeks?" Vinny lets out a hearty laugh.

"Maybe," David says with seriousness. "Or anniversaries and events that may occur to honor them? Like, the anniversary of the Fall."

"No," Vinny says with a smile. "That already passed, and it was one hell of a party."

David considers Vinny's response and asks another question. "Could it have to do with what happens to his domain? The vault could be part of his plan to take it back."

I bristle at the question. I hadn't had a chance to talk with Diablo about the ramifications of the legion swearing their loyalty to her, and now certainly wasn't the time. But the day would come when I would, and when it did, I would be the one to tell her, and not in front of an audience.

I look at Vinny and can see he's thinking the same thing. "He is who he is," I say as casually as I am able. "Luke's purpose does not change."

"And Hell?" David takes a deep breath and holds it.

"It's...complicated. But, if it will help you sleep better at night, Luke doesn't have the power to end the world. And even if he did, why would he? With the flock of mankind at his disposal, he has an endless pool of sheep to manipulate."

David lets out an audible sigh of relief. I can tell he still has questions, but for now I want to move on from this subject before Diablo starts asking her own questions.

I stretch my neck, twisting my head slowly from one side to the other. "Will you let us know once all the images are uploaded?"

"Of course," he nods with assurance "You have my word."

"Alright," Vinny rubs his hands together. "So, we wait until the vault is complete." He looks from Lila to Diablo and then me. "Agree?"

Waiting wasn't exactly what I had in mind, but I'd talk to Vinny about that later. Seeing I neither agree nor disagree, he claps his hands together. "Alright, next up."

James pushes up from where he's been sitting patiently in an armchair next to the fireplace and makes his way over to the desk. He'd been so quiet, I almost forgot he was here.

I didn't know what to make of him, yet. He seemed smart and was obviously credible given his degrees, but I was reserving my judgment for now.

David collects his tablet and leather briefcase, then drops back from the desk and takes a seat on the couch, while James takes his spot on the other side of the desk.

"Let's begin with the stardust," he hands me a folder. "The tests you and Vinny ran previously on the element were primitive," he begins. "Injecting a dose of a foreign substance into one another and observing what happens is neither scientific, nor reliable."

"Well obviously," Vinny shrugs. "One, we were being cautious based on what we knew about it. And two, there isn't much in existence."

Vinny was right. Stardust was composed of the same ethereal makeup we once were. When what we were, meets what we are, it can be toxic. Where it touched us, it purged our immortality in that spot, and made injury possible. Thankfully, it was quite rare and new discoveries of it, few and far between.

Regardless, we may not be scientists, but neither Vinny nor I were stupid. Our approach was what it had been for a reason, and I didn't appreciate James' tone.

"So, tell us, *doc*," I look him dead in the eye. "What findings did you come up with…scientifically?"

Appearing unfazed by the challenge in my tone and stare, James opens the folder in my hand and points down at the first page. "You were shot with a bullet that was laced with a very high concentration of stardust that was both the actual element, and a lab created synthetic that was a close enough match, it took dozens of tests to identify."

Looking down at the sheet of lab work, I can see he's right. The markers were near identical. "That's why I lost six months?" I look up. "Because Luke made a version of stardust that was more potent that the real deal?"

"Yes," James says evenly. "That is exactly why."

I hold my hand over my jaw, studying the lab work closer.

"Vinny and I injected it into our bloodstream and the impact was nowhere close to what happened to me in Eden. How is that possible?"

"An injection is a very precise method of distribution," James explains. "I understand the amount you tested was very little. Spilled salt if you will. Think of the bullet that shot you as an oil spill in the ocean. Combined with the velocity in which it entered your chest and the rate in which the human body pumps blood..."

"And the damage was done the moment it struck," I finished his thought.

James hands me another folder and I set the one in my hand down and reach for it. This one is filled with hospital records, including details on the wound from the gunshot, the surgery performed to remove the bullet, and my recovery.

"Once we removed the bullet your vitals started to improve almost immediately," he says as I skim page after page of notes. "But the healing process was slower than what I understand it normally is for your kind."

I look up and give him an unnerving smile. "Don't you mean, our kind? You too, are now immortal."

"Right," he clears his throat. It was the first sign of discomfort he has shown.

Good. I turn my attention back to the folder. This clown needs to learn his place, fast.

As I scan the pages, I realize Diablo and Vinny weren't being dramatic. I *was* dying. Luke had not only meant to incapacitate but kill me.

"And the stardust," my jaw tics not, realizing until this very moment, just how far he was willing to go to take what belonged to me.

"To a human, it would have been a mortal injury," James

says with authoritative candor. "But for you, the stardust had to run its course. It did not change all your DNA. You still had enough immortality in your blood to keep your body alive while it healed and purged the stardust from your system."

I close the folder. "And now?"

"A small amount is still traceable, which means there are small portions of your DNA that are mortal. With Diablo's blood we have—"

I hold up my hand. "What blood?"

"Thanks to Diablo, and Vinny and Lila, I was able to collect samples and create a solid baseline of the immortal genetic makeup."

"You took her blood?" I throw down the folder with force.

"Well, yes," he looks over at Vinny, confused.

"Hey," I snap my fingers, and his eyes whip back to me. "Diablo is off limits. No one touches her. Is that understood?"

"It wasn't—"

"Is that understood!" I shout.

"Dante," Diablo puts her hand on my arm. "It's okay."

I look down at her hand and back up. "No," I grit my teeth. "It's not. No one touches you but me."

She lets go of my arm and snaps her head back. "Is that so?"

"Yes," I stare back at her. "It is."

"Well," she crosses her arms, eyes flashing. "It's my body, and if I want to give it to science so they can get some answers that will help you and me, then that's my decision. Not yours."

I lean in and whisper, low enough so only she can hear. "The only one you will give your body to is me. And it won't be for science, that I can assure you."

Her cheeks flush, and for a moment her fierce nature gives

way to the shy one. "We needed answers, Dante. I needed answers."

"The blood we've collected has helped immensely," James explains. I keep my eyes on her for another minute before turning my attention back to him. "In fact, Diablo," he smiles, trying to diffuse the tension. "I have an update I think you may be interested in."

The pink in her cheeks starts to fade, but I know she can feel the heat between us. The air is charged, and if no one were here, something else would be laying across this desk, and it wouldn't be folders.

She rolls her shoulders and turns to James, drawing in a deep breath. "I'm listening."

"Something appeared on your latest scans."

Just as my anger starts to fade, red flashes behind my eyes. X-rays? They've not only drawn her blood but looked at her body? I fall asleep for six months and everyone starts putting their hands on my angel, is that it? Um no. Fuck, no.

I want to hit something. Better yet, someone. Sensing this, Vinny comes over to me and puts a hand on my shoulder and grips it with force. It's the only thing holding me back from reaching across the desk and grabbing the spiny-necked mother fucker across from me by the throat. Attendant or not, I don't know him and could dispose of him and not feel an ounce of guilt.

"I believe it boils down to internal conflict," James explains to Diablo, not realizing how close he just came to taking his last breath. "Based on your recollection of what happened before they appeared in Eden, and your activity level and emotional state before each of your scans the last few months, it is my belief your wings are dormant, and possibly triggered by adrenaline."

"Adrenaline?" she repeats.

"Before each scan we do a routine intake: mood, activities, sleep patterns. Before some scans, you were anxious. Other times you were tired. Sometimes you were on your way to the gym, and other times coming back from a workout. The scans taken after your workouts show consistently a faint outline along the shoulder blade, whereas the others do not."

"Why is that?" she asks. I, too, want to hear his answer. I've been curious about her wings ever since she told me they returned in Eden.

"When adrenaline is high, the human body releases an excessive amount of epinephrine. What they call the feel-good hormone. When it's low, the body does not."

"So, to get my wings to return, I need to become an adrenaline junkie?" she asks wryly.

My chest twinges with her response. Shy or bold, I was drawn to every side of her, and couldn't wait until we were alone again so I could kiss that sexy, sassy mouth.

"I'm working up some recommendations," James continues. "And when I stop by tomorrow, we can discuss in more detail. For now, just know we're making progress."

"I bet you fucking are," I mutter. Hearing me, Vinny squeezes my shoulder again. Shit, I forget how strong he is. I take a deep breath and he eases his grip.

"Well," David comes over to the desk, standing next to James. "That was a lot for one day."

"You can say that again," Lila agrees.

"We don't want to overwhelm you on your first day back Dante, so we're going to go," he looks to the door.

"You're right. It was a lot," I acknowledge and stick out my hand. "But thank you."

David reaches for my hand and gives it a shake. "When all

this is over, I have a lot of questions."

"Oh," I nod knowingly. "I'm sure you do. Word of advice, though? Give it time. You have lots of it now."

"I suppose you're right," he lets go of my hand. "Time is on my side from now on, isn't it?"

"In everything but where Luke is concerned," I correct. "When it comes to him, time is of the essence."

"Right," David reaches for his leather briefcase. "Duly noted."

While David says goodbye to Vinny and Lila, Diablo nudges my shoulder. "What?" I whisper. She nods to James as he gathers his stuff and I know what she wants.

I knew David. I liked him. But his partner…I didn't know him just yet. James had clearly saved me, and I suppose, I had to be thankful for that. But the jury was out…for now.

"James," I stick out my hand. "Thank you for what you did."

"You mean saving your life?" he deadpans. "Don't mention it. All in a day's work."

"Well," I look at the stack of folders on the desk realizing just how much work had gone into saving me, tracking down Luke, protecting my company and the one I loved. "Something tells me it was a little more than that and well," I stick out my hand, "thank you."

He takes my hand and gives it a simple, yet firm shake. "I suppose, I should be the one thanking you. David is honored by your gift. And while I may have been hesitant at first, what makes him happy, makes me happy."

I watch as he sneaks a glance at David and can see the same warmth and affection in that look, as there is in those Diablo, and I share.

Maybe, James wasn't so bad. He was willing to do

anything for the one he loved, so in that regard, we were the same. It was a place to start.

We say goodbye and once they're gone, Vinny turns to me. "So," he takes a breath. "What do you think?"

What did I think? Honestly, it was a lot to process. David was great, the jury was out on James, and everything about Diablo's wings and stardust was a lot to process. No to mention, everything I learned about the vault and Luke and the church.

I open my mouth to answer but a question I hadn't asked yet, comes to mind. "What about Eden?"

"What about it?" Vinny asks.

"Has anyone been there?"

"No," he shakes his head. "Not since the day we left."

"What about your place?" I turn to Diablo. "Your books, and library?"

She chews her cheek, pensive. "It doesn't matter. What does matter is right here."

My anger from earlier flares. How much else would Diablo have to lose because of me? "We'll get it, angel."

"No," she puts her hand on my cheek. "I don't ever want to go back. We look forward…to the future, together."

I lean into her touch. She is the calm to my burn. "We are going to make him pay. I swear."

She shoots me a bright smile, filled with warmth and confidence. "I know we are. Now, don't you need to go to Primordial and make an appearance?"

"Yes," Vinny points at me. "He does. In fact, why don't you go with him, Diablo?"

"No," she shakes her head. "That's—"

"A great idea," I reach for her hand.

"It's your first day back. Don't you need to focus?"

"You help me focus," I hold it tight. "Besides, I'm anxious to show you off."

"You mean, you're anxious to show the company off."

"Right," I spin her around, and pull her against my chest. "That."

"Well, if you two don't need me for anything," she laughs, craning her head away from me as I try to kiss it.

"No," Lila watches us with a smile. "We'll see you in the gym later."

"You two have fun," Vinny nods towards the door. "We'll see you later."

I hold my hand out. "Alright. After you, angel."

I clap Vinny's shoulder on the way out and know he and Lila are watching us with smiles on their faces, because I feel my own tugging at my lips.

What I'd just been through…no one should have made it. Mortal or immortal. But I did, and it reminds me that fate has other things in store for me and the beautiful angel beside me. I can feel it.

8
DIABLO

When we finally make it back to the penthouse, it's time to meet up with the legion for training. We're in the closet getting changed for the gym as I think back to our visit to Primordial.

"Everyone was so nice and obviously, thrilled to see you. But I can't believe no one has figured out all the men in those portraits are you."

I kick off my boots and wriggle out of my jeans. It's hard not to see Dante in the paintings that hang from the walls, illustrating the company's founding and history.

Dante makes his way over to a set of drawers and pulls it open. "No one ever said mankind was sharp," he laughs drolly.

"Still, there's such a thing as bearing a resemblance, and then there's, mirror image. I don't know," I shake my head. "I guess I didn't think—"

"People were so gullible?" he quips.

"Well, when you put it that way." I laugh and reach for the hem of my shirt and yank it over my head. "I just thought–"

The feel of his lips on mine surprises me and I drop my shirt as he pulls me into his arms.

"Mmm," he moans while his tongue dances with mine.

I could kiss him all day, every day. His lips are perfect; the power in which his mouth commands mine, total. Too long I've been without his kiss, and I want to spend forever in his arms.

I tilt my head as his lips trail down my neck, and wrap one arm around his back, and grab a fistful of hair with the other.

"Remember when I said people see what they want to see?" He runs a finger along my collarbone, which sends my heart racing. My skin tingles and I nod, biting my lip. "When people look at those portraits, they see powerful men that created a dynasty, and the entitled billionaire that inherited it. They don't see the eternal being that built the very empire that feeds them.

"That's not what you are," I brush his cheek with my thumb.

"Because *you* know me," his eyes burn into mine. "So well, in fact, I bet you know what I'm thinking at this very moment."

He leans in to kiss me again, but I slip out of his hold. "I do," I smile cheekily. "Which is why we're getting dressed."

"Why?" He rubs his jaw, eyes roving over my body. "I'm dying to peel those panties from your body and taste you."

Heat pools in my stomach and my thighs tingle at the thought of his mouth on me. As much as I want to keep Dante to myself, the legion needs to see him.

I swallow down the idea of going at it in the closet and open the drawer for my workout clothes and remove a pair of shorts and matching cropped top.

"If we start, then we won't stop. And not that I'd mind that, obviously," I shoot him a wicked grin. "But it's important that the legion sees that you're okay."

"You're right," Dante turns his attention to the drawer that's open in front of him and blows out a frustrated breath. "I don't like it–not the fact you're right, but not being able to have you at this very moment. They do need to see me, and I, them."

I step into the shorts and pull them up, then slip out of my bra and slide the workout top down over my head. "Don't worry. Tonight, I'm all yours."

"Correction," he slips out of his button-up and slacks, then pulls out his own workout shorts and shirt. "You're always mine."

While he's hunched over to slip into his shorts, I stare at the wing tattoo on his back. Among all the ink Dante has, it's the most stunning. Instead of feathers, the plumes are flames, and when he moves, the muscles in his back ripple, making it appear as if they're flickering like they're on fire."

I push down the urge to ignore my own advice and jump into his arms and grab my workout shoes and make my way over to the bench in the middle of the closet.

"Do you think James is right?" I sit down and put on my shoes.

Dante comes over and sits down next to me, doing the same. "About?"

"My wings. Do you think they're still there and getting them to come back is a matter of adrenaline?"

"Honestly?" he turns to me. "At this point, anything is possible."

My eyes scan his and when they fall to his mouth, I get an idea. "How about we test the theory?"

He presses his thigh against mine; heat blooming where our skin touches. "What do you have in mind?"

I climb onto his lap, and run my hands up his chest, and clasp them together behind the back of his neck. If there was anything that got my adrenaline going, it was him. And when I think back to last night, the surge of excitement and anticipation for when it will happen again is overwhelming.

"How about a game of restraint? A little, delayed gratification if you will. Today, while working out, we do not touch each other."

His lips curve up at the suggestion. "And if one of us caves?"

"Then they lose and are at the mercy of the other."

He grips my hips and slides me back and forth, so I feel his growing erection. "Meaning?"

"Meaning, whatever they want, the other has to oblige."

He rolls his lower lip between his teeth, eyes flashing. "Anything?"

I run my thumb along his chin, wanting so badly for him to be the one that loses so he can be at my mercy. "Absolutely anything."

"Starting when?" he asks, pulling me so close his breath fans my face.

I weigh the options: hot, fast sex now, to relieve my craving for him that's building by the second, or slow, languorous sex later, to make up for waiting.

"How about now?" I propose.

He looks at me in disbelief. "Now?"

The harder his erection gets, the greater the ache to feel him inside me grows. At the same time, I feel a slight tingle in my back. While it's too early to know if I'm onto something, it's worth a try, no matter how torturous. Besides, we'll be training. He can't very well have his way with me in front of the whole legion.

"Right now." I ghost his lips with mine. "It will be so worth it."

"Fuccckkk," he moans, watching me raptly, as I climb off his lap. "You never used to be this cruel."

"It's not cruel," I wink. "It's determined."

"No," he reaches out and pulls me right back down onto his lap. "You're bolder, and it's hot, and shit, I don't care if I lose. You can do anything you want to me."

I shoot him a devious grin, excited more than he knows by that very idea. "Come on," I place my hand on his chest. "I'm serious. I want to see if he has a point about adrenaline."

"And giving me blue balls is the way to do it?" He stares at me, the heat in his eyes turning the ache between my legs into a pulsing throb. "Like I said angel, cruel."

I trace the outline of his jaw with my finger, licking my lips with intent. "Please?"

He sighs and picks me up off his lap, sets my feet on the floor, then spins me around and spanks my butt.

"You're on. But don't think I've forgotten your little, 'I'll do what I want with my body' comment from earlier."

"I haven't," I look over my shoulder. "I said it, so you would remember."

"Well," he stands up and shakes one leg and then the other. "Two can play this game. Just remember that."

"Oh yeah?" I cross my arms.

"Yeah," he winks.

"Well, game on," I stick my hand out.

He places his hand in mine and surprisingly, gives it a shake, and nothing more. "You go on and head downstairs. I'll catch up in a few."

I stop at the door, hand on the frame. "Are you sure?"

"Yeah," he insists. "One," he looks down at the bulge in his shorts, "I need to cool off. And two, I want to stop by and see JJ for a minute."

"Okay," I turn on my heel. "But don't be long."

"I won't," he calls after me.

***

It's a good thirty minutes before Dante finally makes it to the gym, but when he does, silence falls over the legion. He stands there, looking around with a proud grin on his face.

One by one, the legion makes their way over to give him a fist bump or clap on the back, and by the time every member has paid their respects, the energy in the air is palpable.

"So," he steps onto the sparring mat in the center of the gym. "I hear you've all been training hard to impress our new leader."

A chorus of whoops and whistles breaks out, and I can't help but blush when he looks at me and winks.

"Well," he swings a confident jaw back in the legion's direction. "Who thinks they've got what it takes to fight me?"

Vinny, who's standing next to me with Lila, laughs. "Here we go."

"Come on man," Caro shouts from where he stands at the perimeter of the mat. "You've been out for six months. That would be like beating on some poor fool's grandma."

I look at the legion member with the shaved head and skull tattoo at the crown. He's always been respectful to me, but in Dante's presence, his bravado has shifted.

At the same time, the smirk he wears, tells me this is how it is between all of them. It's not about respect. It's about strength.

"Is that so?" Dante pulls his hand into a fist, popping one knuckle after the other with his thumb. "Then how about you take my old ass for a walk?"

"You're kidding me, right?" Hayden, another member, with wavy brown hair that swoops down over his forehead, calls from the back of the group gathered around the mat.

"You just got back, man."

One of the smaller members of the legion, he's nicer, less intimidating, and told me on a few occasions that fighting isn't really his thing.

"No," Dante says, deadpan. "I'm not."

"I take it you're not volunteering?" Vinny goads Hayden.

"Naw man," he holds up both hands and takes a step back. "I'll leave it to one of these other assholes."

Dante's mouth lifts at the corner and he nods at Hayden, then eyes the rest of the group. "Well, if no one volunteers, I'm going to choose."

"Alright," Gabe pushes through the crowd and steps onto the mat. "I'll fight. But if I win, you're buying drinks."

Bigger than Caro, and with an appetite that is very much pro fighting unlike Hayden, he accepts Dante's challenge, with his shoulders back and his head high.

"Shit," Dante shakes his head and laughs. "Then you better have your money ready, because the only one buying is you."

Dante peels off his shirt and tosses it to the mat. Seeing him among the rest of the legion, I'm reminded of his size and presence.

Vinny may have trained him, but Dante is the one that carved his body to precision. And what he's doing now, is reminding everyone that while Vinny may be the strongest, he's the most dangerous, no matter how many months have passed.

Gabe steps onto the mat and meets Dante in the center, and the two press their fists together then step back. Dante holds his hands up in a ready position, as Gabe jumps up and down, trying to rouse his energy, and for a moment it feels like they are never going to start. Then Dante sweeps Gabe's leg and he falls to the mat.

The legion laughs as Gabe pushes up, eyes narrowing, then lunges at Dante, and the fight is on. He lands a punch to Dante's waist with a sickening smack and follows it up with an undercut. Dante is ready for it and weaves, then comes back with a punch high to Gabe's ribs. I know it hurts because Gabe grabs his side and winces but continues with his attack.

I chew on the inside of my cheek, watching the two make their way around the mat, ducking, and hitting, blocking, and weaving. I can't take my eyes off Dante. He's like a wild stallion–unbridled and exquisitely fierce, with stamina that's off the charts–and all I can think is he's hot, and he's mine.

"Whatcha thinkin'," Lila singsongs in my ear as Vinny makes his way over to the mat. I turn to her and the flush in my cheeks tells her *exactly* what I'm thinking. "Thought so," she gives me a cheeky smile.

I don't try to feign ignorance or innocence. "He's been gone for six months, Lila. Tell me you wouldn't want to be with Vinny every second if he had been gone and was suddenly back."

"Hey, you don't have to explain to me," she pats my back and laughs. "You know I would."

We both turn our attention back to the fight. Dante has just punched Gabe so hard he's pushed off the mat.

"You know what he's doing, don't you," she says. I look at her and shake my head. "He's telling them all to back off."

"Why would he need to do that? He's clearly as sharp and strong as he was."

"No," she looks at me and grins. "Not back off him. Back off *you*. He wants them to know you may be their leader, but you're his, period."

I turn back to the mat and see Gabe has tapped out, and

another member jumped in. Dante fights him for a couple of minutes, then he too, taps out. With each member he beats, the fire in his eyes grows brighter.

When no more members step onto the mat, and Dante stops, and draws in a deep breath, those he fought approach and stick out their fist, and he bumps it.

Vinny throws his arm around Dante's shoulder and the two walk off the mat, heads together. But before they disappear into the throng of the legion, Dante turns and looks at me, shooting me a grin that tells me Lila was right. I may be their leader, but Dante is the alpha, and no one fucks with what belongs to him.

***

An hour later, I'm taking a break by the water station when Dante comes up behind me and blows on the bare skin of my shoulder. "I'm going to win," he says huskily.

I spin around, and my mouth falls open. Every muscle on his body is corded and dripping with sweat. Whatever Vinny had Dante doing, has given him more of a workout than battling half a dozen legion members had. Heat rolls off his body in waves; his muscles practically vibrating.

I can now run for miles, and box with the best of them. But when Dante looks at me the way he is now, it sends my heart racing in a way nothing else does.

Remembering our little wager, I curl my hands into fists to stop from touching him. "Didn't you do that earlier?"

His lips pull into a shit-eating grin. "You bet your ass I did."

"In case you need reassurance, they know who you are and what you're capable of. Not to mention, they know you're the one to thank for all this," I wave my hand to indicate the space around us. "They still worship you, nothing's changed."

"Angel," he leans in closer, a bead of sweat dropping onto my chest. "The only worship I care about is that which I plan to do between your legs. But they needed a reminder that I am the *only* one who kneels at your sweet altar."

My nipples pebble under my workout top and my heart thumps wildly. "Is that what that little display was all about?"

"Absolutely," his eyes flash. "Vinny was right. I saw it the moment I walked in. They adore you. I just want to make sure they know the boundaries."

"Are you jealous?" I ask, curious, and yet, strangely aroused by his possession of me.

"No," he grins. "I just don't like others, including the legion, looking at what belongs to me."

"Well good," I take a step towards him, careful not to touch, but wanting him to feel the heat coming from my own body. The intensity of not touching is electrifying and fills me with anxious energy. "Just remember, you are the only one that kneels at my altar, and I damn well better be the only one to kneel at yours."

"You bet your sweet ass," he growls and a bolt of heat shoots down my spine.

If it's adrenaline I'm feeling, I want to stoke that fire. "Well," I step back, changing gears at an impressive speed. "Time to get back to it."

As I turn to leave, he stops me. "Hey angel?"

I turn and look at him over my shoulder. "Yeah?"

"Time out." He grabs my wrist and spins me around, cupping the back of my neck with one hand, while gripping my waist possessively with the other and kissing me. It's full of heat and power and sends my heart pounding against my ribs. "You are my always, and forever," he whispers in my ear. "There will never be another. Don't ever forget it."

My breath hitches and my heart soars. "You can't just call a timeout," I pull back and find his eyes on mine and full of fire.

"The fuck I can't," he kisses me again, then runs his thumb over my mouth when done. "Now, what kind of regimen does Vinny have you on?"

"He's…not training me," I stammer, trying to shake the kiss from my mind.

"Who is?" His smile starts to fade.

I nod over his shoulder at the legion member headed towards us, and his jaw clenches, ready to exchange words with whomever it is that dares to train me. But when he sees who it is, he turns back to me, and looks at me not in anger, but surprise.

9
DANTE

Viper strides up to Diablo and me, giving her a high-five, while lifting her chin in acknowledgement of me. I can see the two are clearly at ease with one another. There's both comfort and camaraderie in their stance.

"So, this isn't a joke?" I look from Diablo to Viper. "You're training her?"

"Don't sound so surprised," she crosses her arms. "When the Big Guy has his hands full with his pint-sized play toy, I work with our leader. Vin thought she could use some one-on-one time with another big gun."

Viper wasn't joking. One of the toughest members of the legion, she was as strong as she was clever. In the War with Heaven, she was our Master of Arms, and since the Fall, been one hell of a fighter and rebel rouser.

"So, you train her," I repeat, still trying to wrap my mind around the fact.

"Yup," Viper smiles proudly. "And it's an honor."

Viper was the first to swear her loyalty to Diablo in Eden. Even though Sam, her undecided, had been the one to shoot me, I trusted her. If there was anyone besides Vinny I both wanted and was comfortable training my angel, it was her.

"I couldn't do half the stuff I can do now, if it weren't for her," Diablo looks at Viper with gratitude.

I'm curious what training Viper uses with Diablo, considering how aggressive she can be, and her preference for weapons. There was a reason she had the name she did. She was deadly when needed. "What do you have her doing?"

"We do a little bit of everything," Viper rubs her hands together. "We mix it up. Martial arts, ancient combat, some knife play. Vinny wasn't comfortable pushing her on that one, for obvious reasons," she shoots me a knowing look, then shrugs. "But I am."

"Is that so?" I look at my angel.

To be honest, I was still in shock that Diablo was able to keep up with Viper. Then again, her body and stamina were noticeably stronger last night. She kept up with me easily. Come to think of it, at one point, I almost had to chase to keep up with her.

"I don't mind knives as much as I thought," Diablo says with a hint of glee. "They can be fun."

"She's damn good with them, too," Viper laughs.

Diablo turns and sticks her hand up at Lila who's just called her from where she and Vinny are sparring on the mat. "I'll be back in a few. You two play nice," she turns to me and shoots me a playful smile.

"Oh, you don't have to worry about me," Viper winks. "Dante knows I can take him."

"Right," she runs a hand down her long ponytail, then tosses it over her shoulder. "Okay, I'll see you in a bit, V."

If any of the stardust lingering in my system doesn't kill me, my angel's newfound ferocity or those workout shorts, will. Both send my pulse into overdrive to the point it feels like it's going to beat right out of my chest.

"Earth to Dante," Viper snaps her fingers in front of my face.

"What?" I swing my head around.

"Man," she shakes her head. "Never thought I'd see the day you lose focus."

"And I never knew you were a fan of nicknames, *V*." I emphasize the letter just enough to annoy her.

"Diablo can call me whatever she wants. You, however, cannot."

"Oh, I see how it is?" I cross my arms and try to process the past few minutes. "So, you two are friends, really?"

"Sure are," Viper mirrors my stance. "She's not what I thought she'd be."

"And that is?"

"Beautiful…soft."

Diablo was beautiful and soft, as well as smart and feisty and hot as fuck.

"She's tough as nails," Viper continues. "You should be proud."

I glance over at Diablo who is now sparring with Lila against Vinny. She comes at him with a front hook that I must admit, looks damn good.

"I am her biggest fan. Although," I turn back to Viper, "I'm surprised you two, click."

"Well," Viper considers the comment. "You know what they say about oil and water. It mixes well sometimes."

"They never say that Viper," I roll my eyes.

"Well, I did, and we do. She asked me to train her, and I was happy to. She is our leader, after all, and her wish is my command."

When I first saw Viper walking towards us, I thought I might have to ask her to go easy on my angel. But glancing back at the mat, and seeing Diablo do a kick, punch combo, I realize I don't have to. She's learned more than a thing or two the past six months.

"How is she, really Viper? And don't sugar coat it for me. I want the truth."

The fact Viper and Vinny had trained Diablo, the strongest among the legion, and that Diablo had kept up, was a bit of a mind-bender. I believed when Vinny said she was strong, but was curious if Viper's compliment was real, or for my benefit. Her training was unconventional and could be ruthless.

"Dante, I'm serious," Viper says with complete candor. "She's a natural. Under that delicate appearance is a fighter. Her stamina is strong, and she bounces back from a hit well. Not to mention, she has a punch that packs surprisingly a lot of power."

I clench my jaw at the thought of someone hitting Diablo. I better never see it, or the ass-handing I dealt earlier, would be nothing.

"She's strong, and hard not to like," Viper continues. "I mean, look at us. The legion is under one roof. When was the last time that happened?"

She's right. We hadn't been together, really together, for a long time. Sure, we partied and raised hell, and of course there was our time in Eden every century, but training and living together…it had been more than a few millennia since that happened.

It didn't matter where time had taken us, however. If any one of the legion needed something, we were there, no questions asked. To see them not only here, but committed and united was incredible. Luke's bullshit contract may have been what drove us all these millennia, but I knew the unity I saw now was because of Diablo. They wanted vengeance for her, the one who saved them.

"I've never seen the legion as dedicated to anything as they are now," Viper says as if reading my mind. "She leads, Dante. Really leads. And she doesn't play favorites."

"Pretty sure she has one," I smirk.

"You know what I mean."

"Well," I take a deep breath. "As long as they remember who she belongs to."

"I think you reminded everyone of that earlier," Viper laughs.

She's right. When I entered the gym and saw the way some of the members were flocked around Diablo–standing so close to her it made my skin itch–I needed everyone to know she was off-limits.

"But you can't stop the others from admiring her," Viper cuts into my thoughts. "She's the closest thing to what we were–kind and hopeful, but also fire and fury. They can't help but be drawn to her. She's special."

I've always known Diablo was special. The first night we were together, when I confessed my darkest pain and worst truth, she listened, without judgment, looking at me only with love and understanding. It didn't surprise me to hear the others could see how unique she was. I just didn't want to lose any part of her to the others.

"Some advice?" Viper looks over at me. "You have to let go of the idea that she can't defend herself. She can. If someone tried to make a move on her, she'd drop them easily."

I grind my teeth together, molars gnashing with the force. "Is that right?"

"Yeah," she turns to me. "And it's a good thing. It means she's not vulnerable."

Whether Diablo could take care of herself wasn't my concern. She'd created her own business and existed for thousands of years without my help. If anyone could take care of themselves, it was her. And the fact that she could, only made me love her more. The issue was me.

After thousands of years, she was finally where she belonged, and she was everything to me. I didn't want anyone near her. I wanted her to myself. To make up for all the time she wasn't mine.

"I know how strong she is," I look at the mat again and notice Diablo has stopped sparring with Vinny and Lila, and now talking with a few legion members. They all appear comfortable around her. Too comfortable. "It's not her I worry about."

Viper follows my gaze. "If you saw her wings that day, and the way she watched over you the past few months, you'd know what we all do. Everything she does is for you, and only you."

My chest tightens as I stare at my angel. As if connected by an invisible thread she looks over and meets my eyes and smiles.

"I mean, I get it," Viper shrugs. "You've got the goods."

"I'm flattered," I reply flatly.

"Don't get too excited," she grins. "You're not my type."

"Oh," I shoot her my own right back. "I'm aware."

"You know," Viper laughs. "Luke was right to run because he doesn't know what's coming. Between the two of you, he doesn't stand a chance."

"No," I agree, determined to make him pay for all the pain he's caused Diablo. "He doesn't."

We both look back at the legion and grow quiet again. "How is Sam?" I ask. The fucker may have shot me, but Viper had been good to my angel, and it was only right I ask about hers.

"He's okay," she looks down. "Feels like shit. Knows he owes you, big time."

Sam didn't owe me. He flat out should be kissing my ass,

thanking me for not ending him the moment I woke up. "I hear he's looking for his daughter?"

"He is," Viper nods and looks up. "Luke didn't release her before he disappeared, so Sam is searching everywhere trying to find her. He's not having much luck, though."

"Viper," I start, but she holds a hand up, knowing what I'm about to say.

"I know he needs to pay for what he did. And I won't stand in the way. But…"

"You don't want him to get hurt," I finished the thought.

"You know what it feels like to be bound," she shakes her head. "The legion is my family. But so is Sam."

I understood. I did. Every daemon was connected to their undecided. Whether love, like Vinny and I found, or like the need to protect them was embedded in our very existence.

"Did you know about his daughter?" I ask, curious.

I know the soulless brought mortals to Eden for recruitment, but never heard of any engaging with the undecided. It wasn't allowed, and that rule had kept my jealousy at bay in the decades I was away from Diablo.

"I did," she says slowly. "Luke was the one who found out. He keeps tabs on all the mortals that come to Eden and leave. Most don't, so those that do, he's only that much more determined to bait. He told me that he let Sam know he had a daughter and asked me to look out for her."

Of course, it was obvious Luke never wanted Viper to look out for the child for Sam. He wanted to keep tabs on her so he could use her when the time came.

"Do you know Luke tried to get me to use her to secure Sam's fealty?" My brows raise and she continues. "Right before we arrived in Eden this last time. I said I wouldn't, but it didn't matter. By the time I arrived Sam said the words before I could even say hello. Luke must have worked whatever angle he had before we got there."

Viper exhales, and I can see she is torn in two: her loyalty to the legion and that to Sam. "Just, give me some time and I will get him back here to answer for what he did, okay?"

I nod but say nothing. That's all this existence seemed to revolve around–time.

"Alright," she hits me on the arm, trying to ease the weight that had settled over us. "I'm going to get to it. It's good to have you back, man. I mean it. And by the way, don't mess this up," she nods in Diablo's direction. "I'll have to kick your ass if you do."

"Are you kidding?" I shake my head. "I would never."

She flashes me a peace sign and makes her way over to Diablo. I'm at ease watching the two. I know Diablo is safe around Viper and that she would step in front of anything, or anyone, trying to do my angel harm. But when Caro picks her up and spins her around, that ease fades and anger floods me.

My hands ball into fists and I lurch forward but Lila steps into my path. "Out of my way," I seethe.

She puts one hand on my chest and wags a finger in front of my face with the other. "No can do, big brother."

"Lila," I bare my teeth. "I mean it, move."

"Nope," she drops her hand, and stands her ground. "If I do that, you're going to lay Caro out. Then Vinny will be forced to intervene, and Diablo will be mad and well, we can't have any of that, can we."

I look over at Diablo and see Caro's put her down and she's taken a step back. From where I'm standing, it looks like my angel put him in his place, and he listened.

"See?" Lila crosses her arms, triumphant. "Aren't you glad I stopped you from making an ass out of yourself?"

I uncurl my fists and take a deep breath. "He's lucky."

"What you're supposed to say is, thank you Lila."

She smiles at me sweetly and I shake my head. "You and Vinny are two peas in a pod, you know that?"

"I know," she waves her hand at me. "The words, please?"

"Fine," I blow out. "Thank you, Lila."

"Now see," she looks over at where Viper and Diablo have just left the group and made their way into a smaller room for one-on-one training. "No need for any more fights."

I take another calming breath and look down. "Sorry, just…getting used to everyone wanting to be around her."

"Dante," she laughs. "Everyone has always wanted to be around her. She makes them feel safe and at ease."

"I don't want to share her," I admit, and the confession surprises me.

"Share her?" she laughs. "Dante, she's only ever had eyes for you, and everyone knows it. So, you can put the BDE away."

"BDE?" I laugh.

"Um, yeah."

"Man," I shake my head. "You're such a brat."

"Don't I know it."

Lila is a royal pain, but most sisters are, and that's what she is to me. I'd beat the shit out of anyone who tried to hurt her.

"You know, I meant what I said earlier. Thank you for being there for her. You and Diablo share the same bond Vinny and I do, and I'm glad she has you."

"Well, you know I adore her," Lila smiles. "And that's what family does. We watch out for one another and have their backs, no matter what."

"And apparently teach one another how to throw a mean right hook," I look at her, impressed. "I saw you two earlier and Diablo's punch has improved since she clocked that server in Eden."

"It has," Lila agrees. "She's trained hard the last six months. Diablo is tough."

"That's what Viper tells me."

"You know," Lila looks down, kicking the floor with the toe of her shoe. "She really missed you."

"I know," my throat tightens. The raw honesty of her words hit me more than I expected.

"It was hard to see her in so much pain," she looks up. "It changed her. Not for the worse. She's still kind, as always. But she's not as naïve and willing to fight for all of us."

I knew Diablo had changed, but it didn't change how I felt about her one bit. If anything, I loved her even more, if that was possible.

Lila draws in a deep breath and looks at me. "So, can you do me a favor?"

"What's that?" I hoped she wasn't getting ready to read me the riot act like she did back in Eden. I think I'd more than proven that I would never hurt Diablo.

"I need you to make Luke pay for what he did to my best friend. Can you do that for me?"

I throw my arm around her shoulder and pull her to my side the way a protective brother would. "Trust me, sis. He is going to reap what he sowed."

10
DIABLO

We've just wrapped up for the day when the feel of Dante's lips on my neck makes my heart skip a beat.

"Mmm, angel, even your sweat is sweet."

My cheeks bloom with heat as his hair tickles my ear. "Admitting defeat?"

"Hell, no," he wraps an arm around my waist. We're in the back of the gym in a small alcove across from the showers and no one can see us.

I angle my head, relishing the feel of his mouth on my skin. "Well, we're still in the gym, and I do believe that means you have caved my friend."

"Workout time is over." He moves his hand down between my legs and moans in my ear. "And I see our little game has made you as hot as it has me."

"That's sweat," I arch into him.

"Is that right," he rubs his palm up and down my crotch; the seam of my workout shorts, creating a delicious friction.

He's right. Our little game of delayed gratification has made me hot. All afternoon I've tried my hardest not to give in. But the sweat glistening on his muscles and the wicked look he gave me every time our eyes met, made it nearly impossible.

"How about another workout?" he suggests, licking, then nipping my skin.

I draw in a pinched breath, relishing the feel of teeth and tongue. "Here?"

"Sure," he slides his other hand under the bottom of my workout top and brushes his fingers against the bare skin of my breast. "Live a little. I dare you."

A tingle forms in my shoulders and rolls down my back. It's a new sensation. "Dante," I close my eyes and reach up and grab his neck.

"Mm-hmm," he hums.

"How about we extend the game a bit?"

"No fucking way. I'm ready to strip you naked, right here, right now."

"But I think it's working." My words come out in airy breaths as he turns me around and pulls my body against his.

"Oh," he runs his hands up and down my back. "I'd say it's more than working."

I press my hands to his chest and look up. "I meant my wings."

"Really?" his brows shoot up.

"Mm-hmm," I look up. "I feel something in my back."

"Yeah," he leans in and goes for my neck again. "My hands."

"No," I press my nails into his skin and push him back again. "It's more than that."

"If you were trying to get me to stop doing that, trust me, feeling your nails dig into my skin only makes me hotter for you."

"I'm serious," I look up, his blue eyes heavy and full of desire.

"Angel," he lets out a pained sigh. "I need to have you, or I'm going to explode."

"Please?" I plead for the second time in hours. "I'll make it worth your while."

"Yeah?" He looks at me, curious. "How?"

"Let's say, if they haven't appeared by midnight, then you are free to do with me as you please."

"Midnight?" He drops his head back in frustration. "Tonight?"

"Midnight," I confirm. "Win or lose."

He lifts his head slowly and looks at me. "I win, no matter what?"

"Yes," I offer a suggestive smile. "You just, keep your hands to yourself until then. Do you think you can do it?"

"And you're not going to extend it longer once it hits twelve o'clock?"

"Um, no," I laugh. "I'm not a glutton for punishment."

The heat between us builds and he glances at the door to the showers. "When does this new round start?"

I step back from his hold and wiggle out of my workout shorts. "Now."

Now?" He watches me raptly as I reach for my top.

"Yes," I pull it over my head, then bend over, pick up my shorts, and carry both with me to the showers, naked.

I don't have to look to know he's right behind me. I can feel the heat emanating from his body as he closes, then locks the door behind us.

I take my time showering, lathering up, paying special attention to all the places that burn for his touch, then washing off. His pupils are blown as he watches me, and when it's his turn to, he pays me back with his own visual torture.

I'm parched by my thirst for him, watching as soap suds roll slowly down his chest, then his ass, and from his calves to the drain. I'm seconds away from calling the game off but the fire in my back and tingle in my nerve endings encourages me to stay the course, no matter how turned on I am.

Once we're done showering, we reach for two towels and

wrap them around us, then unlock the door to leave, carrying our workout clothes with us. The gym has emptied so we're alone as we make our way across the cavernous space.

We've just pushed through the glass doors to head back upstairs when we bump into Vinny and Lila. The two exchange a look and shake their heads at us, grinning from ear to ear.

"What," I ring the water from my wet hair. "You don't shower after a workout?"

"Of course," Vinny winks at Lila and her cheeks turn pink. I think it's the first time I've ever seen her blush.

"So," she clears her throat, changing the subject. "Vinny and I were talking, and well, we think we should celebrate."

Dante runs a hand through his wet hair. "Oh yeah?"

"Yeah," Vinny throws an arm around Lila's shoulders. "After the day, well, year we've had so far, we're due. What do you say?"

"Sounds good," Dante adjusts his towel. "What are you thinking?"

"A little booze, a little dancing. Maybe even, some good old-fashioned debauchery," Vinny grins.

I look up at Dante, waiting for his response. It will certainly be interesting to go out dancing given our little game of look but no touch.

He looks at me and I know he's thinking the same thing. "Will it be safe?" he turns back to Vinny.

"We've got eyes on all of London," Vinny says with confidence. "If Luke shits, we'll know."

"Come on," Lila begs while pressing her hands together. "We've been waiting for this. We should be out, living it up."

"Yeah," Vinny sticks up his hand and she slaps hers to it. "Listen to my pocket full of kryptonite."

"You're sure it will be safe?" Dante asks again.

"Brother, I wouldn't suggest it if I didn't think it would be. And my firecracker has a point. This is the first time in five thousand years we're all together, free from Eden and all its bullshit. This is huge, man."

"They're right," I look up at Dante, wanting to ease the hesitation I hear in his voice. "We should go out, all of us together. Even if Luke is watching, who cares. He needs to know he didn't break us. That he didn't break you."

"Is that what you want?" Dante runs the back of his hand against my cheek.

"It is," I nod. "I want to be out with you, with all of us."

"Alright," he drops his hand and turns to Vinny. "But one of our places. Not some posh spot where the drinks are weak and the people, even worse. I don't want any hedge fund fucks ruining my night."

"Already on it," Vinny pulls out his cell phone. After a couple of taps, he shoves it back into his pocket and claps. "Okay, we're set. We'll meet everyone at *Riders* at eight. How about the four of us meet up downstairs at seven?"

"It's a plan," I smile excitedly.

I link my arm through Lila's as we make our way to the elevator, as Dante drops a couple steps behind to walk with Vinny.

"You're sure about this?" I hear him ask.

"Brother," Vinny says coolly. "I would not have agreed if I thought for a minute, it wouldn't be safe."

"No one but us tonight," Dante presses. "I meant what I said. I don't feel like beating the shit out of some asshole in five-hundred-dollar loafers, for looking at something he shouldn't be."

"I hear you, brother," Vinny laughs. "I don't want to kick

any ass tonight, either. I need a break. It's been a long couple of months."

"You do," Dante claps him on the back. "I just hope none of those assholes from the financial district show up. You know how they like to rough it down by the docks now and then."

"Sure," Vinny laughs. "Maybe once upon a time, but not anymore."

"What do you mean?" Dante slows his steps. "Something change while I was out?"

"No," Vinny pulls Dante back in step with him. "The last few minutes. I just bought *Riders*. Now I own all the docks in Tilbury. *Riders* was the last holdout, but just made the owner a deal he couldn't refuse. He's closing it down for us as we speak."

"Man, Lila," I shake my head, listening to the two behind us. "We lucked out."

She looks back at the two and smiles. "Don't I know it."

I lean in and speak low enough so only she can hear. "Did you ever think we'd be here?"

"Where," she asks just as quietly. "Away from Eden?"

"No," I shake my head. "In relationships, with those two."

"D," she shakes her head and laughs, pressing the up button as we reach the elevator. "We've always been in a relationship with them. Literally, the longest one the world has ever seen."

I can't help but laugh. She's right. Being bound for five thousand years is one for the history books.

The doors open and we step inside with Dante and Vinny on our heels.

Once the elevator reaches the penthouse, Dante scoops me up and strides out of the elevator. "Come on angel, time to get dressed."

"See you in a bit," I wave over my shoulder as he marches through the foyer and up the stairs.

When we reach the suite, he pushes through the doors, and deposits me onto the bed. "What are you doing?" I watch as he drops his towel, then crawls towards me.

"I agreed to your little game," he unwraps my towel and drinks in my body. "But that doesn't mean I have to play fair. You sure as hell didn't in the shower."

I draw in a shaky breath, feeling the kinetic energy between us as he lowers his body down to mine, stopping just shy of touching. My nerves tingle with anticipation as I drink in his perfection. Hypnotic eyes, full lips, body like a god. Maybe I was wrong. Maybe torture wasn't the way to encourage adrenaline.

"Dante," I whisper.

His nose ghosts the outline of my jaw, as my heart starts pounding and goosebumps prick my skin. "Don't give in, angel."

"Why?" I swallow. I don't know if it's my need for him or my wings, but every inch of me is on fire.

"Because I want to see them," he pulls back and watches me intently. "I want to see those wings that everyone else has seen but me."

I know he is fighting every muscle in his body for control right now, because I am, too. I'm about to give in, but a notification on his cell phone stops me.

He pushes up and reaches for it on the nightstand as I take a deep breath to relieve the heat and tension of the moment. As I do, a notification on my own phone chimes.

I roll over and grab it and see that Vinny has started a text thread about tonight, and responses are starting to come in at a rapid pace.

"I guess it's time to get ready," I put my phone down and get up from the bed.

Dante watches me like a hawk as I cross the room and make my way to the closet. He's sprawled out on the bed, with a hand behind his head and shit-eating grin on his face. It takes everything in me not to climb on top of him.

By the time I'm done putting the finishing touches on my outfit I'm more than anxious to blow off some steam and pent-up frustration.

Dante whistles as I walk into the room. He's sitting in the wingback chair by the window, arm draped over the side, drink in hand.

"Where did you get that?" he straightens.

The dress I have on is different from anything I used to wear, but at the same time, fits me perfectly. It's a black halter style, with a gold chain that wraps around the neck, and cuts into a deep v in the front and drapes low in the back. The skirt skims the top of my thighs, and with the sky-high heels I have on, my legs look endless.

"Lillian bought it for me," I twirl around, and the skirt fans out, revealing a hint of the lace G-string I'm wearing. "Do you like it?"

He sets his drink down and pushes up from the chair. "I think it's time to take away her access to my charge accounts."

"You don't like it," I frown and look down.

"No," he crosses the room and stops inches from me. "It's hot as hell. I won't be able to take my eyes off you."

My frown turns into a smile, as I realize the dress has had the exact effect I wanted. By the time midnight hits, I want Dante to be so hot for me he can't stand it.

"Well, you're looking pretty good yourself," I look him up

and down.

Dante's wearing close-fitting black slacks, a white button-down shirt with the sleeves rolled up and top two buttons open, and a handful of leather bands on one wrist, and steel watch on the other.

"Nowhere close to you," he winks.

I reach for the small gold clutch that I paired with my outfit as his compliment fills my cheeks with warmth. "If you must know, Lillian bought this for me and told me to save it for a special occasion. And I did. This very one."

"She's been good to you, hasn't she?" He shoves a hand in his pocket.

"More than good," I nod. "I don't think I would have made it through everything without her."

He looks at me and I know he's waiting for me to say more. And I want to. But those first days after Eden were filled with so much sadness and uncertainty, I wasn't sure how to describe what felt like the darkest days in all my existence.

"When we first arrived, I looked like hell because that's exactly where I was. In those clothes Luke made me put on, covered in your blood." I close my eyes to steady myself, and when I open them again, find Dante looking at me pensively. "I couldn't move or speak. I was frozen, and at the same time, my body felt as if someone had broken it. It was Lillian who drew me a bath and cleaned me up and fed me, and she who cared for the wounds on my back from my wings."

"I had...no idea," he reaches for my hand.

"No touching, remember," I smile softly.

"Momentary truce," he pulls me into his chest, and I close my eyes and take a breath and fill my lungs with his familiar scent of orange and spice.

"She was like my angel," I finger a button on his shirt. "Every time she went out, she came back with something for me. Books, or lotions…even sweets from her favorite cake shop." I look up and find his soft eyes on mine. "Little things to make me feel better. It may not sound like much to you, but she made me feel safe and loved when my entire world had gone dark, and well," I draw in a deep breath, "this dress was the last thing she bought for me, and I am wearing it to do exactly as she suggested. To celebrate the most special occasion I can think of…your return to me, to us."

He places a strong hand on my cheek, and I lean into it. "Remind me to give her a raise."

"A big one," I smile. "And Wills. The two of them…you have no idea how thankful I am for all they did for me."

He tips my chin up and I see so much love staring back at me, it takes my breath away. "No one will ever love you the way I do, angel. But I am glad you had them, and Vinny and Lila, to take care of you, because I couldn't."

We stand that way for a moment, arms locked around one another, nothing in the world but us. Then he kisses me softly and reaches for my hand and laces his fingers through mine. "Are you ready to celebrate?"

"I'm ready," I hold his hand tight as he pulls me towards the door.

"Okay," he gives it a squeeze. "Truce over. Four hours until midnight."

"Game on." I squeeze his hand back, then let it go. The next four hours were going to be torture.

11
DANTE

Vinny lifts a shot and knocks it back. "You know something brother, seeing all of us together like this makes my dick hard and my palms twitch."

"It's quite a sight," I agree with a laugh.

"Times have changed," he slams the glass down on the table. "And you know, I don't mind one bit."

Vinny's right. Normally, on a night like tonight, we'd have left by now and taken our antics to the streets and started a little chaos. But now that the Fallen are no longer divided, the legion seems less interested in destruction and more into debauchery. And it feels right.

The drinks are flowing and the laughs unending. There are even hookups happening on the dance floor and in dark corners.

Daemons no longer have to pursue the fealty of their undecided using whatever method they need to, because all loyalty was secured before everything happened in Eden. Those who wanted to party, could party. Those who wanted to fuck could fuck. And those who wanted to explore all the world had to offer, could do so. They were finally free, and at the same time, part of something bigger.

For the first time since the Fall, we are all together, united against a common enemy, and it's all because of the radiant being I haven't been able to take my eyes off all night.

Diablo is mesmerizing. The way her hips sway when she dances and the sound of her laughter when it carries across the room, stirs warmth in my chest and ignites desire in my core. She may be our leader, but she is my reason for existing, and there is nothing I wouldn't do for her.

I tap my finger against the wood tabletop of the booth and look at my watch. Twenty minutes until midnight. Shit, could the minutes go by any slower?

"Why do you keep checking your watch?" Vinny shoves a shot glass my way. I don't know how many we've had. I lost count a while ago.

I reach for it and point to Diablo, then knock it back. "When you've made a bet and she is waiting for you, time becomes your new best friend."

When we first arrived, I was at the bar with the rest of the legion. Midnight was hours away and the night was young, so I enjoyed myself, making toasts and knocking back drinks. But as the hours began to tick by and the girls moved to the dance floor, Vinny and I slid into a booth to watch them, and I began counting down the minutes until the night was over.

Now that Diablo and I were together, I'd grown used to touching her whenever I wanted, and not being able to kiss or hold her for hours was torture. I'd waited for her for thousands of years, and since the night we became us, we hadn't been apart.

But if not being able to touch her for hours was hard for me, I could only imagine how difficult it must be for Diablo who had been without us for months. It told me just how important her wings were, and I wanted to do whatever I could to help them return. Even if it was adrenaline games that drove me crazy.

"So, what's the wager?" Vinny asks, pouring us another shot.

"Oh, you know," I reach for it as he hands it to me.

"Nothing but mind-numbing satisfaction."

He lets out a hearty laugh and clinks his glass against mine. "Now that is the best kind of bet."

Vinny and I liked a good game, and winning was always the best part. But I had to admit, the reason behind the one Diablo and I were playing, was just as interesting as the wager.

"Actually," I slam the glass down on the table, "we're working on her wings."

He swings his head my way, eyes wide. "No shit?"

"The adrenaline thing," I nod. "We're testing it."

"Ah," Vinny claps my shoulder. "A little prolonged, unsated desire to get the adrenaline pumping?"

"Yeah," I shake my head. "But man, tonight has really tested my resolve. I feel like I'm going to explode."

I'm willing to do anything to do anything for Diablo, but I really should have thought about the terms a bit more. I'd only been awake for less than a day and was feening for her.

"I know the feeling brother," Vinny laughs. "When that one holds out on me," he points to Lila and grins, "nothing hurts more."

"They have us by the balls," I rub my chin and check my watch. Fifteen minutes to go. "You know that don't you?"

"Yup," he nods, eyes firmly on his angel. "But there's no one's hands I'd rather they be in."

We both laugh again and take another shot. "In all seriousness though," he flicks the empty shot glass in front of him with his finger, "the way everything went down in Eden, it makes sense adrenaline could be the trigger. That shit was intense, man."

Vinny was right. What happened at Luke's was intense. I just wished I could have seen the way he ran away with his tail between his legs. The thought makes me smile with satisfaction, knowing it was my angel that sent him running. Then I'm reminded of what he wanted, and I feel a hot flash of anger.

"Man Vin," I curl my hand into a fist. "The thought of Luke living safe among the righteous, putting whatever he is planning into place, while we wait to put the pieces together," I shake my head. "Hell, no. He needs to know we're coming for him. That I'm coming for him."

"What are you thinking?" Vinny looks at me, curious.

I turn again to look at my angel. She's happy and free and it's the only existence I want for her. "Not waiting two weeks, that's for sure."

He pours a shot and studies it. "I've got an idea."

"Oh yeah?" I reply, suddenly half-listening.

Viper and Lila have sandwiched Diablo between them and are moving in rhythm to a throbbing baseline. If it were anyone else, I'd be over there in a hot second. But they're two of the few I trust most, and I'm transfixed by the way she moves to the music.

"What do you say we start a little shit?" Vinny suggests.

"Uh-huh," I lick my lips.

"Brother, are you listening?"

"Vin," I nod to the dance floor. "Are you seeing this?"

Vinny's eyes follow mine to the dance floor and when he sees Lila with Viper and Diablo, I can tell he's as turned on by his angel as I am mine.

"Well damn," he blows out a hot breath.

"Right." I hold out my hand. "Shot, please?"

He pours me a drink and I pound it, then turn to him and shake my head. "Now, what were you saying?"

"Come see me later," he says, eyes still on Lila. "I'll tell you more."

"Won't you be busy?" I raise an eyebrow. I sure as shit planned to be.

"Of course," he reaches for the bottle. "But brother, we may be able to go all night, but at some point, they need their rest. When Diablo goes to sleep, shoot me a text and we'll talk."

"Alright." He pours us two more shots and I reach for the glass and hold it up. "Here's to starting a little shit."

"To starting shit." He taps his glass to mine, and we kick them back.

"What are you two doing?" Lila bounds over as we slam the glasses down on the table, Diablo in tow.

The song they were dancing to has ended and Viper has moved on, taking up a position behind Elle, a member of the legion she's enjoyed a friends with benefits relationship with for centuries.

"Enjoying the view," Vinny reaches for Lila's hand and pulls her into his lap.

Diablo wags her finger at me in a come-hither motion and smiles slyly. "Come dance with me, lover."

"Brother," I check my watch and then push up from the booth. "That's an invitation I can't pass up."

"Tick tock," he raises two fingers in acknowledgement, as Lila wraps her arms around his neck and pulls him into a kiss.

Diablo leads me out onto the dance floor and as if on command, the music changes, and the unmistakable beat of Nine Inch Nails' Closer pounds out of the speakers.

She rests her hands on my shoulders and smiles up at me. "Foreplay's wingman."

I grin, remembering the words I said to her when I played this very song the night I claimed her, and she, me.

"Is that what I am?" I rub my hands up and down her sides. "Your lover."

She turns around and leans against my chest. "You are everything."

I moan with approval as I wrap one arm around her stomach, and move my other hand down her side, while swaying us in time to the music.

As the song builds, so does my need for her, and I slip my hand under the skirt of her dress, and between her legs–caressing the smooth lace of her G-string. She arches her back and rubs against me, and my erection gets painfully hard.

We're about two seconds away from fucking on this dance floor if I don't get us out of here. I grab her hand and yank her through the swell of dancers bumping and grinding, and down a hall that leads to the back of the club.

When we push through a steel door at the end and spill into the alley, I don't wait for it to close. I reach under her thighs, and pick her up, and crash my mouth down on hers. She wraps her legs around my waist and drapes one arm around my neck, while bracing her other hand against my chest.

"It's midnight," she hums through the kiss.

"About fucking time." Our bodies are starving for one another and feeling her tighten her legs around me, only makes me want her more.

She pulls back to look at me. "Maybe we should make up for lost time before playing games? I missed you too much to not touch you on your first day back."

"Good idea," I push her hair aside and suck on the pulse point in her neck, while taking a step towards the brick wall and leaning her back against it. "I can't stand not touching you, either."

"It didn't work anyhow." Her pulse races wildly against my tongue as her breathing picks up. "No wings."

I brush my thumb across her jaw; moonlight spilling across her face, bathing it in a halo of light. "So, we'll try something else. I know how important they are to you."

"They are," she looks at me. "To pay Luke back for what he did to you."

Her answer surprises me. "That's why you were so intent on this little game?"

"Everything I do is for you," she runs a fingernail down my cheek, drawing fire. "Even letting you have the win, when clearly it belongs to me."

"Come again?" I played by the rules no matter how hard they were because I wanted the win. Wanted to make her sexy, sassy mouth scream my name. "Pretty sure my watch, which I checked a million times tonight, knows I followed the rules to the second."

"Are you sure about that?" she asks, flashing me a wicked smile.

I replay the last few minutes in my mind. There were minutes left, and she beckoned me onto the dance floor, and when I reached for her hand, the music changed to our song. Shit...had it struck midnight yet?

"You tricked me," I shake my head, in both admiration and disbelief.

"I guess I'm bad," she shoots me a naughty smile. "Punish me?"

"Oh, I will." I tighten my grip on her ass, the idea of body being mine and only mine, to do with what I wanted, thrilled me to no end. "Just wait until we get home."

"Why wait?" she whispers.

I look up and down the alley, then back at her, knowing

well what she's saying. "Here?"

She grabs a fistful of hair in each hand and pulls my face towards her. "Yes, here. I want you. Right here, right now."

I may have won, but she wants this and she's not asking. She's demanding. Like last night when she took what she wanted and needed, it blew my mind, and she's doing it again now.

The air charges as my eyes search hers and I can't deny her. I never will. My need for her is carnal and I will do whatever she wants.

Adjusting my hold, I reach between us with one hand, and when I find her wet and ready for me, I growl with hunger. "You drive me crazy. You know that, right?"

"That's what love is," she purrs. "It's crazy and irrational and worth everything."

I can tell she is slightly buzzed, and totally aroused. It's an intoxicating combination that flames the inferno that's been building in me all night.

"Yes, it is," I agree, running my hand up and down her slick entrance as she unbuckles my belt and pulls my zipper down.

As I finally ease into her, we both moan in relief. The sensation of her tight and warm around me is a delicious payoff, and I know it feels good to her, too. I hear it in the airy puffs of approval she lets out, and the way she rocks her hips against me. Maybe we should revisit the adrenaline games, with different rules. Because this…feels amazing.

"Is this what you want?" I thrust up, filling her, while cradling her ass in my hands. "You want everyone to see me take what's mine?"

"No," she looks at me. In the light of the moon her eyes look like dragon fire. Green flames that flicker and dance, with a life of their own. "I want everyone to see me take what's mine."

Her words burn into me. The idea she too, wants me, with the same hunger, as I want her, ignites my spirit. "So possessive," I kiss her heatedly.

"Yes," she murmurs through the kiss. "Yes I am."

I slam one hand to the wall and press my forehead to hers while flicking my hips faster, and she grabs my lower back and digs her nails into my skin. The need for more, the need for us, courses through me, wild and unchecked.

I quicken the pace as I lock my eyes onto hers. "I love you angel. You are my everything."

"And you are mine," she runs her tongue along my lower lip, then pulls it into her mouth and kisses me with so much desire my nerves light up.

I wrap both arms around her again, fusing our bodies together as we fall into our own world. A world where there is no Luke, and no eternity of punishment. Just peace, and pleasure. Sweet, sweet pleasure.

12
DANTE

Once Diablo's asleep, I reach for my phone and shoot Vinny a text. When he replies and tells me to meet him in the study, I get dressed, kiss her gently on the forehead, and slip out the door.

"Well, hello," he says casually from the couch–one arm draped along the back, leg crossed over the opposite knee, and a glass in the other hand.

"Didn't drink enough earlier?" With all the shots we had, I was pretty sure my blood was more alcohol than anything at this point.

"Figured, when in Rome," he smirks.

Vinny's right. We always have bourbon when we're here late at night, just the two of us.

Not wanting to break tradition, I make my way over to the wet bar, pour myself a drink, then head back to the couch, and sit down at the opposite end.

A gentle fire crackles in the hearth, bathing the room in a warm orange glow. "So," I take a sip of my drink, savoring the slow burn as it rolls down my throat, hints of oak and caramel lingering on my tongue. "Tell me about your idea."

"First," he raises his glass. "A toast to the future. Because if tonight is any indication of what's in store, eternity is going to be fan-fucking-tastic."

"Cheers to that." I lift my drink and tap it against his. Vinny was right. Forever was going to be more than I ever imagined, and it was all, because of my angel.

Seeing her tonight free from Eden and the ties that had long imprisoned her, filled me with something I didn't think I'd ever feel-happiness. And if what happened in the alley was a sign of what's to come, something told me eternity was going to be epic.

"Tonight, was a good night," Vinny shoots me a devil may care grin.

I return his grin, with my own. "That it was brother."

Once my driver picked Diablo and I up from the alley, we were at it again in the back seat. Only, this time, I was on my knees in worship. I had her legs spread open so wide, she had to grip the end of the seat with one hand and press her other to the roof to brace herself.

"So," he takes a sip of his drink. "Now that it's just us, how are you *really*?"

I look at Vinny and know what he's asking. Today was business and tonight pleasure, but there was still a lot of shit to unpack around what happened in Eden.

I tip my head back and look up at the ceiling, blowing out a heavy breath. "I don't know, man. Obviously, I'm glad Diablo is safe, and the legion is all under one roof. But I'm angry." I pause for a moment to measure the word. "No, I'm furious. Luke took thousands of years from us, and six months from me. I know in the scheme of forever it's nothing, but for her it was."

"That's love, my friend," Vinny says simply. "What happens to us, happens to them, and we want to break something when they hurt."

"Shit, yes." I turn my attention away from the ceiling and look at him. "I will never forget the tone of her voice when she told me how long I'd been asleep. It gutted me."

He nods with understanding. "Makes you want to fight

like hell to protect her, doesn't it?"

"That's the thing…it does." I push up from the couch and Vinny watches me with careful eyes. "And it kills me when I realize the last time that I tried to protect her, it wasn't enough. Luke still ended up hurting her."

There it was. The truth I hated to think, let alone speak. I'd always prided myself on being the most powerful among the legion, but Luke challenged that when he took Diablo from me, right out from under my nose.

"I mean shit Vin, he tried to enslave the Fallen, then binds me to Diablo, knowing exactly why she fell, then keeps lying to all of us for thousands of years. And if that's not bad enough," I draw in a deep breath, the gravity of all he'd done, weighing heavily on me. "He waits for me to fall for her so he can rip her out of my bed and put her in his so she could give him an heir, then tries to kill me. Me! One who's been loyal to him since the beginning! Do you know how fucking angry that makes me?"

"I know," Vinny watches me as I pace in front of the fire. "It's fucked up. No doubt about it."

I know Vinny is angry, but he's had months to process his anger. Mine was sitting on my chest like a ticking bomb and the more I thought about it, the hotter I got.

"And yet," I close my eyes, everything I felt the morning Luke took Diablo, bubbling to the surface. "Along with this rage, I'm worried. What if he's still after her? What if he still wants her for his sick, demented idea of an heir?"

I'd never feared anything before. Not until I thought I lost her. And then that fear nearly paralyzed me. But now, the idea he may still want her burns my insides. "No fucking way!" I throw my glass into the fire. The flames twist and turn with new life, changing in color from orange to red. "He can kill me for real if he thinks that's ever going to happen!"

"Luke won't get near her again," Vinny eyes the roaring blaze. "You will make sure of it. Not to mention, the legion. And if her wings ever come back..." he shakes his head and whistles. "Luke better run again, and never stop."

"You're right," I point. "He better hope if he does try anything, the legion gets to him first because I swear, if he gets near her again, I'll chop his fucking head off. Let's see how easy that asshole heals when his body parts are in different places."

Vinny laughs and it eases the tension in my shoulders. "I'm sorry brother," he says gently. "For all of it. Maybe if we tried it your way. If I hadn't insisted—"

"No," I cut him off, knowing what he's about to say. "You're not to blame for what happened that day. You know that, right?" If anything, I'm more thankful to Vinny than ever before. He did what I asked him to. He got Diablo out of Eden.

Vinny pushes up from the couch and comes over to me. "I've replayed it in my mind a thousand times. Maybe if we'd gone in the way you wanted..."

"No," I shake my head. "You were right. There wasn't another way." I place a hand on his shoulder. "My anger is not with you. It's with Luke, and myself. I swore I would protect her. That I would never let anything hurt her. I'm the one that failed. Me. Not you."

"You didn't fail," he shakes his head. "Luke fooled us all. But I'll tell you this...he won't again. Whatever he's planning we're going to figure it out and we'll win."

He puts a hand on my shoulder, and we stand that way for a moment, watching the fire.

"When I first woke up, I was relieved," I say numbly as I stare into the flames. "Realizing we were here, and she was safe and away from Eden…it's what I always wanted. But then she told me how long it had been, and I saw the weight of those months in her eyes, and I wanted him to pay. I needed him to pay."

Vinny drops his hand from my shoulder and looks at me, contemplative. "I don't know what you went through while you were out all those months. But I do know how to give you some of that payback you crave."

"How?" I turn to him, brow raised in question.

He shoves a hand in the front pocket of his jeans and shrugs casually. "Start a little shit, while working on the bigger shit."

Stir the pot. I liked it. But there was one problem. "I promised Diablo we would do this together. She's just as angry as I am and deserves her revenge, too."

"I know she is," he crosses his arms. "And she'll have it. But you know how far Luke's network extends. We could have a little fun while working on the bigger plan that gives everyone their shot at revenge."

The part of me that craves destruction comes to life with Vinny's idea. "I do like the idea. A lot."

"Thought you might," he grins.

"When do we start?"

He pounds the rest of his drink and sets the glass down on the table. "How about now?"

My nerves come to life with fiery anticipation. "I say hell yes."

"Well then," he reaches into his front pocket and pulls out his keys. "Let's go."

***

Twenty minutes later we're in an underground club in west London. It's a stark contrast to the upscale restaurant that sits above. There is music and laughter and a vibe that's darker than the night.

"What is this place?" I look around. I'd never been here before, but the smell of corruption is strong.

"It's a place for the wealthy and wicked to explore their darkest desires and deepest cravings. Fights, sex, you name it, they make it happen."

"No shit," I shake my head with slight appreciation.

Mankind always did have a love-hate relationship with their primal instincts. But the simple fact was, at their core, they were no better than we were, and this place reflected that. The drinks were flowing, and hands and mouths were everywhere. It was a sight I hadn't seen since ancient Rome.

"How did I not know about this place?" I ask Vinny, who appears to be looking for something.

"Didn't tell you because you had your vice, and I had mine," he says simply.

"You?" I ask, not in surprise, because before Lila, Vinny was no schoolboy. But because when it came to vices, he preferred one that was different from mine.

All the Fallen carried the burn of being abandoned and had their own way of easing it. I'd once used sex. Fear-induced sex, specifically, and my appetite for it had been insatiable. Vinny however, used fighting. Only, I didn't see any fighting, just fucking.

"This isn't the only room," he leans in. "It's one of many, each with a purpose. Fighting, fetish, sex, pain...they've got a room for everything."

"Ah," I nod when I hear the room he preferred. "And why are we here?"

Vinny searches the space around us again and when he finds what he's looking for, holds up a finger. "Hold that thought. Be right back."

"Alright," I lift my chin in acknowledgement as he walks away.

A woman double-fisting drinks bumps into me and when she turns and sees me, she smiles and licks her lips. "Well damn," she looks me up and down. "Wish I bought you tonight instead of that limp dick in the corner."

Not even on my most desperate night, I think, eyes not getting farther than her smeared lipstick. "You couldn't afford me," I say flatly.

"Honey," she leans in, breath sour. "I can afford anything."

I pull my head back, amused. "Is that so?"

Her lips pull back revealing a mouth full of teeth that are as fake as her tits. "My money runs this town. If I wanted you, I could have you."

I look into her eyes, pulling her into a false sense of interest. It was a tactic that daemons had used for thousands of years to get what we wanted. I could tell her to do anything I wanted at this very moment, and she would.

I look at a man at a table next to me. He's sandwiched between two women while a third lay spread eagle on the table in front of him. "See that man over there," I point out. "He wants you to—"

"Now, now," Vinny returns, clapping my back. "Save that fun for another day. I've got something better lined up."

He grips my shoulder and steers me away, as the woman shakes her head with confusion as I leave, likely wondering what just happened.

We make our way through the room and take a narrow

hall down to a door at the end. When we open it and step inside, it's a different feeling altogether. The smell of blood and sweat clings to the smoke hanging thick in the air.

"Take your jacket off," Vinny grins. "You're up next."

I look at the ticket in his hand. "What?"

He points to a ring on the other side of the room where hundreds have gathered, shouting and whistling, as two men beat the shit out of one another.

"Hell yes," he lets out a hearty laugh. "And make me proud. I have some serious money on you."

A server walks by with a tray of shot glasses. Vinny reaches for one and hands it to me. "Here," he encourages. "Bottoms up before you go."

I've got enough alcohol in me to fuel a jet, but I take the glass and shoot it. "I thought you said we were starting a little shit."

"Have a little faith, hmm?" he smiles wryly. A bell rings and the room erupts into applause. Those who won clap, and those who lost shout profanities at the man on the mat. "Ready?"

I unzip my jacket and shrug out of it. This wasn't what I thought we'd be doing, but the idea of beating someone to a pulp sounds good right about now. "Let's go!"

"Alright," he claps, and we make our way over to the ring.

A new crowd is gathering as I hand him my jacket, then peel off my shirt, toss that to him too, and step into the ring. A shrill chorus of whistles greets me, as women stare at my inked, corded frame with fuck-me eyes, and men shoot me daggers.

I ignore both, as I move my neck from side to side, watching as my opponent steps into the ring. I look at Vinny and grin, and he salutes me as the bell rings.

I hold up my hands, palms open, and size up the way my opponent moves. He throws the first punch and the second. I block both easily and follow up with a blow to his ribs. He bellows in anger but rolls his shoulders and comes at me.

He lands a punch to my side, and I strike back with a double punch—a dance that continues for a few minutes as the shouting around us magnifies.

In no time, he begins to slow, as my punches wear down his bulky frame. But I haven't. If anything, my energy is growing.

When he throws his next sluggish punch, I grab his fist and hold it for a moment, then headbutt him with my full strength. The crowd draws in a collective gasp at the loud pop of my head hitting his. But when I kick my opponent in the sternum and he flies backwards against the ropes, pandemonium erupts.

I follow up the kick with a series of blows to his chest, ribs, and face as he stands dazed, trapped against the ropes. Blood splashes to the mat, the crowd, and on me, but I don't care. I keep pummeling, putting all my anger into the useless mound of flesh in front of me.

When he finally falls over and hits the mat, the bell rings. Vinny lifts the ropes up, and steps through, then rushes over to me and holds my arm up in victory.

"Well done, brother!" He pumps his other fist in the air and the crow goes wild as I swipe a hand across my face to clear the blood and sweat. "You just made me a mint."

"Is that what this was about?" I spit on the ground. "I need to give you a raise?"

"Right. That's what this was about." He laughs and drops my hand, pulling me closer. "That asshole you just bested is one of Luke's informants. In fact, he's the one that was watching our place the night Luke took Diablo."

Fire floods my veins as I turn my attention to the mat. "How do you know?"

"I've made it my personal mission the last few months, to find out which soulless helped Luke that morning. And he," Vinny points to the mat, "was the one who called to tell him when it was time to enter our place."

Before I know what's happening, I'm crouching down next to the soulless, my face inches from his. "That was you, you piece of shit?" I spit out. "You were the one who told Luke to come into *my* house and take *my* angel?"

He lifts his head, clearly in a daze, and it's then I see it. While he was fighting, he was hopped up, eyes lit up by whatever drug he was on. But now, it's easy to see he's soulless.

"Hey all," Vinny calls out. "Next round on me!"

The room breaks out in cheers as folks start filing out of the room and down the hall to the main bar.

"Go on," he shouts good naturedly. "Order up. I'll be there in a minute."

Once the room has emptied, Vinny comes over to me and bends down, passing me a blade. "Do what you need to do, brother."

I clench it in my hand and look at him. To anyone else he's a big guy who just came into some cash and wants to celebrate. But to me, he's being what he'd always been–my best friend. My ride or die. The one who always knew what I needed, even before I did.

He stands back up and crosses the ring, and once he's at the door, looks at me, nods, then closes it behind him.

I hold the blade to the soulless' neck, gripping the hilt tight as the memory of that morning hits me. Even now I can feel the rush of panic when I woke up and saw Diablo missing, and the burn in my lungs when I thought I'd lost her and couldn't breathe.

The piece of garbage in front of me was the one who set it all in motion. He'd been watching us, waiting for the right time, and when he saw a window, called Luke, and told him to take her.

I hold the tip of the blade to his neck and take a deep breath. Soulless may be damned, but they were not immortal. They could be killed. All you had to do was drain them of their blood. It was excruciatingly painful, but I couldn't think of anything more fitting.

I pull the blade slowly across his neck and exhale, feeling the weight on my chest lift as his skin pulls apart and blood trickles out. Sitting back on my knees I watch with satisfaction as blood pools under his head, turning the canvas mat, crimson.

Once his blood has run dry, the door opens, and I see Vinny and a man with a mop and bucket standing in the doorway. He tucks a wad of cash into the man's front pocket and pats his upper arm, then comes over to the ring and leans against the ropes.

"Ready brother? It's time for us to go."

I look up and see a folded piece of paper in his hand. "What's that?"

"Oh this?" He looks at the paper and shrugs. "Nothing much. Just your fight schedule."

I wipe the blade on my pants and stand, reaching for the list. Sure enough, it's a schedule with names. One every night for the next two weeks.

"Is that all of them?" I ask, handing the list back to Vinny.

"Sure is." He tucks it into his pocket, then hands me my shirt and jacket. "What do you say, one down, dozen to go?"

I grab both, then step out of the ring and jump down. "I say you're on, brother."

13
DIABLO

The warmth of the sun wakes me, and I reach across the bed instinctively. Feeling it empty, I open my eyes and push up, finding a note and fresh cut peony on Dante's pillow.

Morning angel,

Went on an early errand with Vin. I'll be back this afternoon.

Today, I'm training you, so try not to wear anything too distracting.

See you in the gym.

-D

PS, have I told you lately how much I love you?

I bring the flower to my nose and smile. Dante's been back for a week, and every day is better than the one before.

Since the night in the alley, we both agree, delayed gratification is an adrenaline builder, but we need to balance it alongside giving in when the need strikes. Because strike it does…daily.

We hadn't succeeded yet in getting my wings to return yet but trying never felt so good. Between our adrenaline games and making up for lost time, we're as hungry for one another as ever, hitting up whatever spot we can find when our need is too strong to ignore–the garden, the pantry, even the hidden hallway that connects the study to Dante's dark room. With its soundproof walls and easy access, it's been a great place to steal away in a pinch.

Dante and Vinny have been training hard and focused. The two are fascinating to watch as they balance Primordial with the legion and updates on the vault. They're powerful and smart and complement each other perfectly. It's no wonder they've been able to accomplish all they had the past few centuries.

I've also been working out harder, doubling my training time with Viper, and I was starting to feel it. I was more tired than normal this morning, and my muscles were screaming. Deciding to take advantage of the quiet, I get out of bed and draw a bath.

After filling the tub with lavender soaking salts, I sink into the hot water and close my eyes. It feels decadent to have this time alone, and when the water cools off and I'm ready to get out, I'm feeling revived.

After getting dressed, I make my way downstairs and head to the kitchen. When I get there, I find JJ at the counter with a cup of coffee and a croissant in hand.

"Well, hello," I smile warmly. "I feel like I haven't seen you in ages."

"That's because you haven't," he smiles back. "Dante has me working on a project, so I've been out and about."

"Oh yeah?" I pour myself a cup of coffee from the breakfast set up. No matter the time of day, there is always food and drinks at the ready. "And what project is that?"

"Did I hear someone say something about a project?" Lila breezes into the kitchen.

"Sure did," I stir in a splash of cream and sugar, then make my way over to where JJ is sitting. "Dante has JJ working on one."

"Anything fun?" she asks.

"I'm not at liberty to say," he looks at us mischievously,

then takes a sip of coffee.

"Well," I pull out a chair and sit down next to him. "Maybe he'll tell me. My powers of persuasion are hard for him to resist."

JJ takes a bite of croissant then wipes his hands. "You can try, but I think he's going to keep this one to himself for now."

I tap my fingernail against my cup and lift a curious brow. "Is that so?"

"Yup," he nods, then pushes back from the counter. "Alright, you two. I'm off. Keep my boys in line." He winks at both Lila and I, then makes his way out of the kitchen.

"It seems everyone is running an errand this morning," Lila muses as he leaves.

I look at her over my cup. "Do you know what the guys are up to this morning?"

"With those two, who knows." She takes a sip of her coffee and then looks up at the clock overhead. "Oh shoot. I've got to go. I'm meeting David like…now."

"Vault progress?"

"Not really," she sets her cup on the tray for dirty dishes. "Just a couple of ideas I wanted to run by him. See you later," she blows me a kiss, then breezes out of the kitchen, the same way she came in.

"See you," I wave back, and drink the rest of my coffee in silence.

When I'm done, I make my way to the small sitting room next to the study for my appointment with James. We've shifted from three days a week to two, now that Dante is awake, and the need for my blood has lessened.

The door is open when I get there, and when I look in the room, see James staring intently at a piece of paper.

"Diablo," he looks up when I knock on the door and sets it

aside. "Please come in."

I make my way into the room and sit down in the chair opposite the desk. "How is everything with you today?"

"Things are good." He reaches for a folder with my name on it. "Every day I learn something new. And you?"

James hasn't said much about his new existence. He's all business when here. A contrast to David, who asked questions, and was easy to talk with.

I knew how difficult it could be moving from one existence to another, and was sure James had questions, too. Perhaps he was used to knowing so much, that knowing so little about our world was hard for him to admit.

I tuck a strand of hair behind my ear, wondering what, specifically, was new for him today. "Anything I can help you with, or questions I can help answer?"

"Not right now," he shakes his head. "I'm going to focus on science. I can move on to the bigger things, like Heaven and Hell, once all this stuff with Luke passes."

Finding his word choice curious, I clear my throat and smile, but say nothing. I wouldn't call our issues with Luke 'stuff.' He'd been playing a game with the Fallen for thousands of years. A better response would be, 'once you end him.'

James pushes up from where he's sitting and comes around to the other side of the desk. "So, how is everything with you today?"

"I'm good," I say for a second time as he sets my folder down and reaches for my arm.

"And training?" he asks, placing the tip of his index and third finger on the inside of my wrist to take my pulse.

"The same." I watch as he writes down the results in my folder. "It's good, and I'm eating well, my stress is low, and

I'm feeling happy." May as well give him what he wants to know now and get the questions out of the way.

He nods, then reaches into his bag and wraps a cuff around my upper arm and starts to pump air into it to take my blood pressure. The band tightens like a snake, and just when it feels like my arm might pop, he releases the air, and the band slackens.

"How about sleep?" He removes the cuff and scribbles in my folder.

"I could probably use more of that," I admit.

"Oh?" He looks up with interest. "Are you not sleeping?"

"Not much," I grin. We look at one another for a moment and when he realizes what I'm implying, his cheeks turn pink, and he looks back down.

I can't help but let out a small laugh as he turns to the silver tray on the desk, slips on a pair of rubber gloves, and picks up a tourniquet. What comes next is my least favorite, but I take a deep breath and stick out my arm.

He ties the blue silicon band around my upper arm and taps the inside of my elbow until my veins turn blue.

"And your wings," he reaches for a syringe, and I turn my head. There's a slight prick, followed by a warm tingle.

"No luck," I take slow, measured breaths as he fills the vile with my blood, then removes the needle. "But I'm working on it."

He pulls the tourniquet free, then places a bandage where the needle punctured my skin. "How so?"

Flashes of the adrenaline games Dante and I play come to mind. "It's not very scientific. I'll keep you posted?"

"Please do," he places the vile in a plastic container, then closes my folder. "By the way, could you please tell Dante if he can't make an appointment, to let me know."

"He missed an appointment?"

"Yes," James leans against the desk. "A couple, actually."

I knew Dante wasn't completely sold on James, but he understood how important his work was, and agreed to give him a chance.

"Between the legion and Primordial, I know he's been busy, but I'll deliver the message."

James nods at me in appreciation. "Thank you."

"My pleasure," I place my hands on the arm of the chair. "Is there anything else?"

He takes a breath as if he is going to say something, then shakes his head. "Not today. Another time."

"Alright," I push up and make my way to the door. "Well then I'll leave you to your work."

"Actually," he says when I'm halfway there. "I do have a question." I stop and turn. "Sam, the one who shot Dante. I understand he has a child?"

I inhale in surprise, expecting any question but that one. "Yes," I face James, head on, and fold my arms over my chest. The child that led to Dante being shot, I want to say, but don't. "What about her?"

"Do you know much about that…situation?"

"No," I swallow to ease my throat's tightness. Sam was hard for me to talk about still. Forgiveness was in my nature, but I didn't think I'd ever be able to get the memory of him pointing his gun at Dante out of my mind. "Viper might."

James stares at me with a blank expression.

"Tall, dark hair, shaved on one side?"

"Ah," he nods. "The pretty one, with a mouth like a sailor."

"That's her." Although I'd describe her as gorgeous, fearless, and candid. "If anyone can answer your questions, she can. They were bound, and she knows Sam better than anyone."

James considers my response. "Do you know if the mother of the child is mortal?"

"Yes," I nibble on my lip. "She is or was."

He lifts a curious brow. "Was?"

"I don't know if she is still alive," I look down. "Like I said, I don't know much about the situation."

"Ah," James rubs his chin, and crosses his legs at the ankles. "And the legion? Any children?"

Members of the legion had sired children, but it seemed to be a subject no one discussed. I did know however, many had taken measures to ensure they never sired children, including Vinny and Dante.

"It's…complicated," I look up. "Why do you ask?"

"Oh," James takes a deep breath "Just, starting with the small stuff. As Dante suggested."

"Ah," I nod. "Well, if I may offer a suggestion? Don't boil the ocean just yet."

He cracks a small smile. "That complex?"

"Well," I take a deep breath. "For starters, the church has taken it upon themselves to be the authority on Heaven and the Fallen and shaped a lot of what mankind believes it knows about angels."

"And that knowledge is incorrect?"

"Yes," I say candidly. "They're not the authority on us and have gotten a lot wrong. It's no surprise though, considering who has been whispering in their ear."

Luke would do anything to paint the Fallen in a bad light, and he, a good one. The whole 'Morning Star' reference was really his own ego talking.

"What have they gotten wrong?" James asks with interest.

"Well, take the topic at hand. What they believe to be true about the children of angels, is not."

He pushes up from the desk with clear interest. "Nephilim?"

"They do not exist. Angels were not allowed to interact with mankind so they could not sire children. The Fallen however can because they are part of the mortal world."

He puts a hand on his chin, listening carefully. "And that's what makes siring children possible?"

"Yes. But not every Fallen wants to and has taken measures to ensure they do not." I hold up my hand when I see James about to ask the next logical question. "Who they are, and what they did, is their business, not mine."

"And what about female Fallen? Can they conceive with mortals, or other Fallen?"

"No," I shake my head.

"Because they can't, or because they don't."

"We can't."

"Why?"

"Not sure," I shrug. "It has been that way since the Fall."

We look at one another for a moment in silence. "Well, if there isn't anything else?" I point over my shoulder.

"Oh, no, sorry," he shakes his head. "I've kept you long enough."

"Alright," I nod. "Well, I'll deliver your message to Dante when I see him."

"Please do," he lifts a hand as I make my way out of the office. "See you in a couple of days."

"My blood will be waiting," I laugh wryly. "And answers to any more questions you might have."

"Right," he offers me a curious smile. "Look forward to it."

14
DIABLO

Later that day I'm working out with Viper and Lila in the gym and can't keep my eyes off Dante. He and Vinny are sparring on the mat, and with every twist and turn of his body, muscles ripple, sending my pulse racing.

"Earth to Diablo," Lila snaps.

I shake my head and turn to her. "What?"

She pretends to wipe my cheek. "You've got some drool right there."

"Stop," I swat her hand away and laugh.

"Oh, I'm just giving you shit. Trust me," Lila lifts her chin in Vinny's direction. "I get it. My man makes me drool, too."

I turn back to Dante and drink in the fierce determination in his jaw and the fire in his eyes. He didn't just make me drool. He made every part of me ache for his touch.

"Man, Vinny is really working him hard," Viper shakes her head. "But shit, Dante's strength is off the charts right now."

Viper is right. The force in which Dante strikes Vinny is packed with power, and yet, the speed in which Vinny moves for a guy his size, is remarkable. They're both full of energy and their sparring has captured the legion's attention.

"Maybe their errand this morning was working out," I muse, watching as the crowd gathered around the mat gets bigger. They do seem to have an inordinate amount of energy, even for them.

"Or they joined a fight club," Viper quips.

"Oh, that could be," Lila points. "Check out the bruise on Dante's ribs. That's not from sparring."

My eyes drift down Dante's torso, past the defined muscles and tattoos, and I see what Lila does. There's a shadow under the ink that flanks his ribcage. Only, it's not one bruise, but a series of them.

"Those weren't there last night?" I shake my head and turn to her. "What the hell did he and Vinny do this morning?"

"I'm telling you," Viper crosses her arms. "That's classic fight club bruising. No rules, all punches apply. How's the rest of his body?"

"It's good," I swallow past the heat creeping up my neck.

"Yeah, I bet it is," Lila nudges Viper with her shoulder and the two laugh, as heat flushes my cheeks.

"Do those places really exist?" I ask, ignoring Lila's goading.

"Well, you know what they say," Viper shoots me a wry smile. "First rule about fight club, don't talk about fight club."

I turn my attention back to the mat. "Why would either of them be doing that, when they could do what they are now, anytime?"

"Adrenaline? Boredom? Who knows," she rolls her neck from side to side. "Only one way to find out. Ask."

Viper was right. I needed to ask Dante, and the next time we were alone, I would.

"Alright," she claps her hands together. "Are we going to train or what?"

"You go on. Dante's training me today."

She arches a surprised brow. "Oh yeah? Well then, later boss," she salutes me then turns Lila around. "Let's go, red."

"Boss," I click my tongue and turn back around. It looks

like Dante and Vinny have called it quits. The crowd has dispersed, and both have grabbed a bottle of water and are standing in the center of the mat with towels around their necks.

"Who won?" I ask when he finally comes over a couple of minutes later.

He reaches out and pulls me into a kiss. "What, no good morning?"

I try not to melt at the feel of his taut arms around me and mouth on mine. "You mean good afternoon."

"Right," he hums as he nibbles on my lower lip. "Good afternoon, angel."

"Who won?" I ask again, wiping a bead of sweat from his brow.

He wipes the towel up and down his face, tousling his hair. "No one. We were just messing around."

I run my finger along his abs and his muscles constrict under my touch. "You keep warming up like that, you'll turn to stone."

"I have to find some way to channel my need for you," he winks.

"Stop," I roll my eyes. "I'm serious."

"So am I," he removes the towel from around his neck, twists it, then snaps my leg. "I told you not to distract me today, and yet, here you are, wearing that."

I look down at my workout shorts and sports bra and shake my head. "You're impossible."

I push past him and head towards the smaller room that's used for individual training.

"That's where you're wrong," he comes up behind me and wraps his arms around me as I walk. "I'm easy. But only for you."

"Well, you could have fooled me," I stop and turn around.

"What does that mean?" he laughs.

"You told me to be ready to train, but you've been…" I wave in the direction of the mat, words trailing off.

"Angel," he cocks his head and grins. "Are you jealous?"

"No," I cross my arms. "But since you're trying to get me to admit something, how about I pull a little confession out of you. Why have you missed your appointments with James?"

Dante opens his mouth to respond, but I hold up my hand to stop him. "If you're not going to make it, you really should tell him. He's only trying to help us and has a schedule to keep."

"I don't need help," he runs a hand through his hair. "I feel great. Better than great. I feel amazing."

"Oh yeah?"

"Yeah," he shoots back.

"What are we five?"

"No, five thousand," he counters. "And I've known and wanted you all that time. That's how I know," he takes a step towards me, "whatever this is right now, has nothing to do with my missed appointments, and something else."

I reach for my ponytail and twirl it around one finger. "You're wrong."

"No," he leans in. "I'm not. But you're sexy when you're angry, so I kind of want to stoke your anger and see how hot it can make me."

"If you don't like it when I don't tell you things," I toss my ponytail over my shoulder and shrug, "then maybe you shouldn't keep things from me."

"Ah ha," he smiles triumphant. "There *is* something going on."

"Sure," I nod. "With you."

"What?" he snaps his head back. "You're the one who just admitted something has you worked up, so come on...out with it."

I blow out a frustrated breath. Dante can back anyone into a corner and get them to confess anything. He'd built his corporate empire on the ability, and I'd nearly fallen prey to it countless times over the millennia.

"Fine," I lift my jaw. "Where were you this morning? And what are those bruises from?"

"What bruises?"

I point at his ribs. "Those."

He looks down, then back up and laughs. "Shit, Vinny's been rougher on me than I thought."

"Vinny?" I lift my brow.

"Yeah," Dante crosses his arms, matching my stance. "We've been training harder."

Our eyes remain locked until he rubs his chin and shakes his head. "Is this whoever breaks eye contact first, finishes last?" he grins. "Because I am more than happy to draw out pleasure for as long as—"

"I'm not playing a game with you right now, Dante."

"Fine," he holds up his hands and exhales. "You win. I left this morning because Vinny and I had something to take care of."

I raise a skeptical brow. "That's it?"

"Yes, that's it. What did you think?"

"I don't know," I shrug. "Some kind of fight club."

"Fight club?" he tosses his head back and laughs. "Where did you get that idea?"

"Well, Viper said—"

"Viper?" he shakes his head. "That's her thing, not mine."

"No?"

"No," he wraps arm around my waist and pulls me close. "You are my kind of thing. But for the record, I hated leaving you this morning and I thought about you the entire time I was out." His hand falls away and he flashes me a magnanimous smile. "Now, is there anything else?"

"Only one," I wrap my arms around his neck.

He runs his hands up and down my sides. "And that is?"

"What are we working on today? You wanted to train me, so obviously you have something on your mind."

His hands grip my sides. "Oh, I have something on my mind alright."

"Dante," I laugh.

"What," he smiles. "I was talking about defense."

"Defense?" I repeat.

"I want to teach you how to get out of compromising positions."

"Compromising positions," I shake my head. "Are you serious or is this some kind of new adrenaline game?"

"Well, as hot as compromising positions can be, I'm being serious. You need to be able to defend yourself and when I said no one touches you, I meant it. I will teach you defense. No one else."

The way he looks at me, tells me he's not kidding. "Okay," I kick my legs shoulder width apart. "I'm all yours."

"Hell, yes you are," he plants a hot kiss on my lips. "And I intend to keep it that way."

***

An hour later, Dante has taught me a handful of moves that make it possible for me to get out of any hold. He's a good teacher and I'm impressed with the focus he's maintained. Even though several of the moves have our bodies locked together, he doesn't give in to temptation. He is one hundred percent concentrated on the task at hand–my protection.

"Now remember," he instructs as he stands behind me, one arm wrapped around my torso, the other hand on my arm. "It's not about strength. It's about focus. Once you're out of the hold, then you use strength."

"Right," I nod, focusing on his words, not the feel of his touch. If he can be serious, I can, too.

"On one, ready?" he asks.

"Ready," I confirm.

Dante counts backward starting at three and when he hits one, I run through the moves he just taught me. First, I throw an elbow into his ribs, followed by a quick throw of my head back to his forehead. Once I've gotten myself out of his hold, I deliver a side kick, straight to his chest. He lets out huff and stumbles backwards.

I hate doing this to him but can't deny the way it makes me feel. All my training so far had focused on strength and offense–likely because no one wanted to touch me and suffer Dante's wrath–and it felt good to be able to defend myself.

"That was good," he takes a deep breath and straightens. "Let's do it again."

I put a hand on my hip and draw my own breath. "Can we take a break?"

"No," he shakes his head. "I want this to be ingrained so it's instinctive. No stopping until I say so."

"But I'm kicking the shit out of you. Can we do something where you're not the punching bag?"

"Angel," he grins. "You're not kicking the shit out of me. I can take a beating, trust me. But you on the other hand," he eyes me with a hint of concern. "You, okay?"

"I'm fine," I wave off his concern. "You want to go again, let's go."

"Alright angel," he waves for me to come at him. "Charge me."

We continue for a while longer, and by the time we break for the day, I have a whole new set of skills. "Thank you," I look up at him as we make our way out of the smaller room and back into the gym.

"For?" he asks, stretching one arm, and then the other, as I grab a bottle of water and towel from a table next to the door.

"Teaching me how to defend myself." I twist off the cap of my water and take a sip.

"You don't have to thank me. I want you to feel strong and confident. But if you're in the giving mood…" he gives me a wily smile.

I look at him from over the top of my bottle then lower it. "Actually, I think it's you who owes me."

He tilts his head, a smile growing. "Oh yeah, what for?"

"For leaving me this morning without—"

He reaches for my hand and cuts me off as he dips me into a sweeping kiss. It's the kind you see in movies and read about in stories–where everything goes fuzzy, and your heart skips a beat.

"There," he says when he stands me upright. "That should make up for it. But if you want to tie me up and punish me more, I'm game."

"Shhh!" I press my hand to his mouth and whip my head around, hoping no one heard him.

He licks my hand and I laugh and pull it away. "There's nothing to be embarrassed about. You as a Dom," he blows out a charged breath. "Um, yes please. Besides, liking to be in control is nothing compared to some of the stuff the others are into."

Being a leader is one thing. It's not wielding power over others. It's listening, and guiding, and seeing everyone as an important piece of the whole. But when Dante submits to me and I'm in charge of him, I can't deny the way it makes me feel.

"What the others are into is their business. What we, what I may be into, stays between us."

"It's okay, angel," his eyes flash. "Your secret's safe with me. But honestly, it's one of the reasons I wanted to work on defense with you. I've been picking up on your desire for control, and I wanted you to have it in the gym, too."

We make our way to the elevator and when the door opens, I slip inside. Dante follows, but instead of pushing the button for our floor, he hits the red emergency stop button.

"What are you—" I start to ask but he presses the hard outline of his chest against my back and grabs my hips.

"Give me an order," he says huskily.

"What?" I look up at him over my shoulder.

He turns me around and repeats what he just said, with more command. "I said, give me an order."

I look to the stop button, then back to Dante. His eyes are dark, and his heart is pounding. Right now, he wants to be at my mercy. Anything I say, he'll do.

I lick my lips, thinking of all the ways I want to own him. But there's one thing I want, and have been wanting, since I saw him sparring with Vinny earlier.

I draw in a heated breath and put my hands on his shoulders. "Get on your knees."

15
DANTE

Wills sets a black leather box down on my desk and I lift the lid and remove the items inside. "If you want to make any changes or additions, let me know and I will take care of it," he says with authority.

I shuffle through the ID, credit cards, and account ledger. Everything looks to be in order. He's an expert at this point and thinks of everything. Still, I can't help but have a question or two.

"The account has been funded with the requested amount?"

"It has," he confirms.

"And the stores we have charge accounts with?" I look up.

"She's been added to those as well."

"Excellent," I nod with approval.

I wasn't sure of Diablo's exact financial situation, but I knew she took pride in being able to care for herself. That didn't stop me, however, from wanting to give her the means to have whatever she wanted, whenever she needed.

I set the cards and ledger aside and look at the item I'm most excited about–her passport. When I took her to the opera in Italy, I'd gotten an emergency one to use on short notice. But the one in my hand is valid for the next decade, with plenty of pages to fill, and I plan to do just that.

I can't wait to show Diablo the world. All the places she's longed to go, but never could. I plan to give her an existence beyond her wildest dreams, starting with a trip to Trinity

College to see the infamous library that inspired her own.

"And her business?" I set the passport down with the other items. "How is that coming along?"

"Everything is good," Wills shakes his head. "No problems there."

When Vinny told me he and Diablo had transferred her business to Primordial after they arrived in London, I was glad to hear. I knew she hadn't touched it since leaving Eden, but she'd worked hard to build it, and I wanted it to be safe and ready for her, whenever she decided to pick it back up.

It was also a smart move on their part, to appoint Wills to look after it. He was sharp and had been working with Primordial for decades and could easily keep an eye on it. Not to mention, Diablo trusted him, and that was paramount in business. Still, I asked him to keep me informed should I need to step in and help in any way.

I set the cards, ledger, and passport aside and reach into the box for a black button and string folder. Placing it on the desk in front of me, I unwind the tie and remove the thick stack of papers inside.

Vinny had always been my beneficiary. He'd helped me build Primordial and a lot of its success was due to him. But I wanted to make sure my angel never wanted for anything, in the unlikely event of my demise.

After talking to Vinny and sharing my plans to update my trust and split Primordial between him and Diablo fifty-fifty, he agreed without hesitation and encouraged me to make the change.

I set the stack down and press my fingertips together. I can't look through the documents that would serve as the foundation for her existence without me. It's too painful to even consider a future where that happens.

"Have all the terms I requested been included?" I ask Wills.

"Yes," he confirms.

"Good." Given Diablo's generous spirit, I made provisions in the trust that would allow for her to give a percentage annually to charities of her choice, while keeping enough for her to live a safe, and easy existence.

I flip the stack upside down and set it down next to me, then grab the bottom page and flip it right side up and sign my name on the dotted line.

When done, I put the page back on the stack, flip the entire thing over, and slide it into the envelope and hand it to Wills. "Please make sure that gets processed and filed, immediately."

"I will do," he reaches for the envelope. "Will there be anything else?"

"I think we're good. You took care of everything, as always. Thank you, Wills."

"My pleasure," he bows his head. "I will send Lillian in."

Once Wills has left, Lillian enters the study. I get up to greet her and hold out my hand to the chair next to the desk. She sits down gingerly, back straight. "Is everything okay?"

"Yes." I sit back down. "Why wouldn't it be?"

When I summon her, it's usually because I need something. But I don't need anything right now. I only want to give her a long overdue thank you.

She eases slightly but keeps her steely gaze on me as I begin. "I knew when we met, you would make a perfect attendant. You had an iron fist, impeccable taste, and not about pleasantries. It was business, plain and simple, and I needed someone like that."

"No time for nonsense in Napoleon's Paris," she

remembers with a cynical smile.

"You got that right." We both smile gently as memories of the past hang in the air.

"I know the last few centuries haven't always been easy," I continue. "You have put up with a lot from me and done so without complaint. But when you cared for my heart as if she were your own and made her feel safe and protected, it confirmed what I have always believed. That I am grateful for you, more than you know."

Lillian reaches for her throat, and I can see the sentiment has caught her off guard. "It was easy to care for her, and easy to see why you do. She's made this place a home, and you, something I thought I'd never see. She's made you happy."

Lillian was right. Diablo filled both these walls and my heart with warmth. She changed my existence in every sense of the word.

"She does," I agree. "But you and I both know you more than cared for her. And we both know why."

The very reason Lillian had taken such good care of my angel was because the core of her spirit was maternal. She would always be a mother whose love had been left, with nowhere to go. It is why she chose this existence. To hold onto the love that she had for the son that she lost, not the pain.

When Lillian gave that love to my angel, I knew she hadn't done so lightly. She cared for Diablo as a mother would her child and she needed to know that I both appreciated and understood.

"So," I continue, "in expression of my literal, undying gratitude, I have made a sizable donation to the pediatric wing at Hôtel-Dieu in *your* heart's name, which will be commemorated in their new garden that you will design to ensure it honors your son's memory the way that you wish."

She looks at me, speechless, as I hand her the paperwork I'd been keeping in my desk. "I remember once, you told me a story of how your son loved to sit in the garden in the back of your boutique when he was not feeling well, and I thought it may bring you some peace to create such a place for other children to enjoy when they are not."

She reaches for the paperwork with one hand, and dabs at her eyes with the other. "I...don't know what to say."

"You do not have to say anything. Just create a space that your son would have loved. His memory deserves that, and you do, too."

She pulls the paper to her chest and closes her eyes, taking a deep breath. "Il y a de la lumière dans ton coeur."

"Light in my heart?" I shake my head. "Perhaps there is now, thanks to Diablo."

"There has always been light in you," she opens her eyes and I see they are shining with tears. "Those who know you, see it. It is why they...why *I* am loyal."

"Well," I push up from the chair. "I am glad for your loyalty because I need you. I have a special request."

"Oh?" She presses a finger to the corner of each eye and stands with me. "What do you need?"

"I need you to call Giuran and have him start working on something for me."

"The gentleman in Brussels with the diamond mine?" she asks, eyes widening.

"That's him," I confirm and reach for a folder on my desk and hand it to her. "Do *not* let Diablo see these."

"I won't," she reaches for it and smiles. "Will there be anything else?"

"No," I shake my head. "I think we're good for now."

She nods and starts to leave, then stops and turns back

around. I can see she is about to say something, but I hold up my hand and shake my head. She doesn't need to say anything. I know.

She smiles and continues to the door; Vinny walking in, as she's leaving. He reaches for her hand and twirls her under his arm, then keeps walking towards me, as she continues into the hall with a laugh and shake of her head.

After coming over to my desk and sitting down on the corner, he reaches for a pen, and clicks it a couple of times with a smug smile on his face.

"What is it?" I grab it out of his hand and set it back down.

"I just learned someone you will find of particular interest, has just arrived in London and is on the guest list for you know where tonight."

"Oh?" I perk up. The last few minutes with Wills and Lillian were kind of heavy, and I needed something to lift the weight off my chest. "And who might that be?"

Vinny reaches into his jacket pocket and when he sets a photo down on the desk in front of me, that does it. The weight lifts, and the fire that lingers in me, flares to life.

The bartender. That self-righteous prick who thought he could come between Diablo and I that first day at *Saints*.

"It would mean swapping out tonight's match with who was planned, but I thought you'd be okay with that considering who it is," he taps on the photo.

"Oh, I'm okay with that. In fact," I reach for the photo and hold it tight as my lips curve up into a wicked smile. "I'm more than okay with it."

He may not have helped Luke take Diablo that day, but I'd been wanting a piece of him from the moment he dared to look at her.

"Good," Vinny raps his knuckle on the desk. "We leave at midnight."

***

Midnight rolls around and I make my way to the garage where Vinny is waiting in his SUV. "Ready?" he asks as I slide into the passenger's seat.

"Yup," I tap the side of the door with my hand after closing it. "Let's roll."

After we've been driving in silence for a few minutes, he turns to me, brow raised. "Everything okay?"

"Does Lila know you've been leaving at night?" I look over at him.

"No," he shakes his head. "I figured if she knew, she'd tell Diablo and I didn't want to get you in trouble."

I nod and turn my attention back to the road. "I think she knows."

"Lila?"

"No, Diablo. She was all over me the other day in the gym about the idea you and I had joined a fight club."

"Well, she's not wrong."

"She's not right, either."

"True," Vinny lifts a finger from the wheel. "Fighting happens *at* the club. It is not a club *for* fighting."

"Exactly," I lean my head back against the headrest. Even Vinny gets the nuance. So, why do I feel so guilty?

"Where'd she come up with the idea?" he asks.

"Viper," I blow out, irritated. "I mean, *she* is the one who belongs to a fight club, so I get why she would mention it. But I didn't need her putting that idea in Diablo's mind."

"You know," Vinny turns the radio down. "I don't think

she would be mad if you told her what you were doing. I mean, if you said, 'babe, I needed to get rid of the assholes who helped Luke take you,' she'd probably hero fuck you."

"She already does, for less," I shoot back, and he laughs.

I look back out the window and blow out a pensive breath. "I've put her through a lot of shit over the years, man. The least I can do is honor the promises I make now."

"Here's the thing," he reasons. "We have two more on the list after tonight, and then you can go back to focusing on Luke and getting revenge, together."

I curl my hand into a fist as Vinny navigates the SUV through the empty streets. "I know, I just really hate lying to her."

"I know you do. But maybe think of it this way," he tips his head. "All that shit that was fucking with your head before–this is clearing it, right?"

"It has," I confirm. The past ten days I've felt stronger and more in control.

"Well, clearer head, means better sex."

"We don't need *any* help in that department."

"Okay," he laughs. "Then, how about a clearer head, means better focus on whatever game Luke is playing with the vault."

"Better," I turn to him and grin. "Speaking of…how's David coming along with it?" Between Primordial and some other stuff, I've been a bit busy the past few days."

"It's coming," Vinny nods deftly. "Lila's been working with him on it. She's given him a few things to think about."

"Oh yeah?" I ask, noticing the proud grin tugging at Vinny's lips.

"She's smart…and shit, she does this thing with her mouth—"

"Stop." I hold up my hand. "Keep that shit between you."

"Oh, yeah?" he laughs. "What about your 'we need no help in that department' comment? How about you keep *that* shit to yourself."

"I was going to say," he continues, "that Lila does this thing with her mouth when she's concentrating that's both adorable and sexy at the same time."

I shake my head and roll my eyes. "Sure, you were."

He smiles wider as I keep staring at him "What?" he asks.

"Nothing," I shake my head. "It's just nice to have some levity along with all the shit we've been dealing with."

"Oh, I hear you brother." He sticks out his fist and I bump mine to it. "I'm looking forward to putting Luke where he belongs and taking a long break after this."

"I know what you mean." I look out the window, thinking about the trips I'm planning for Diablo and me. "I'd love to disappear for a while, just she and I."

"You can," Vinny nods with approval. "And you should."

"I can't leave for years on end. Not with Primordial."

"Sure, you can," he tosses back. "Wills can run it in his sleep. You should think about it. At least take a break for a bit. You deserve one."

"We'll see." Truth was, I only focused on the corporation so much in the past, because it had been a distraction from what I really wanted. Now that Diablo was with me, I didn't need it as much.

Maybe I should take a break. Nothing but she and I for a couple of decades. I liked the sound of that. Just us. Just…peace.

"Well, whatever your plans, dream them tomorrow because tonight, it's on." He puts the car in park and turns off the engine. "We're here, and it's go time."

Feeling the familiar rush of adrenaline, I push open the door, hop out of the SUV, and make my way with Vinny down the dark alley.

16
DANTE

I open the door, then close it quietly, trying not to make a sound as I make my way over to the end of the bed. Diablo is sound asleep, one hand folded under her head, the other on my pillow, and my heart lurches. She is my peace, my forever, and I have to fight the urge to crawl into bed next to her, because if she woke up and saw what I looked like, I'd have some explaining to do.

I head to the bathroom and take a hot shower, giving myself time to soak in the satisfaction of tonight's fight. It's been twelve days since I began paying back those who helped Luke take Diablo from me, and just as many soulless have paid the price. It's empowering to know that I am doing *something*. Even if I am keeping it from my angel.

The club is a good cover for what we are doing, and Vinny and I have our routine down. I am the fighter, and he is the lucky patron who buys drinks for everyone after I have won. Then, once he tells me what role the soulless bastard I have beat played in Diablo's kidnapping, I end them.

I turn off the shower and reach for a towel, wrapping it around my waist, before padding over to the double sink vanity to assess tonight's damage. Staring at my reflection in the mirror, I take note of two new bruises. The only reason I have them at all is because I let the soulless get their punches in. It's part of the strategy–lure them into a false sense of confidence to boost their ego.

Some hit harder than others, hopped-up on whatever drug

they choose to fuel them with adrenaline. But in the end, their wily energy is no match for me. When they finally see what's coming for them-when their vision is no longer clouded by their high and they realize *who* I am-the recognition in their eyes is my high.

I want to tell Diablo what I'm doing. What I swore I would always do-protect her from anything that meant her harm. But I don't want to anger her for breaking my promise we would get our revenge together.

Every time she looks at me though, with those eyes that slay and steal my heart, I'm on the verge of telling her. And I nearly did a few days ago in the gym. As hard as it was *not* to- the fire and sass she gave me, stirring every damn emotion possible-I decided there was a line between the truth and a lie. If I wasn't crossing that line, I wasn't breaking my promise.

I wasn't in a fight club. I wasn't hopping into the ring for a rush. I was using fights to eliminate the pieces of shit that took her from me. It was for revenge. For her. To make up for all the pain she endured when I failed to stop Luke.

Diablo deserves peace, and once all this is over, that is exactly what I plan to give her. An existence full of it, and anything else she wants, and tonight's elimination brought me one step closer.

The bartender. The asshole who helped spy on Diablo for Luke and tried to get between she and I that first day at *Saints*, deserved to pay for what he'd done.

He was confident when he stepped into the ring. Too confident. And when I first stepped up to meet him, head down, he'd assumed I was a timid opponent. But once I lifted my head and he realized who I was, he knew his time had come.

His end brought the greatest satisfaction, and I didn't

think I could top the high I was feeling right now. Then the feel of delicate hands on my back, followed by soft lips, fill me with another rush, unlike any other.

I turn and find Diablo staring up at me, with soft, sleepy eyes. She's wearing one of my shirts and it skims the top of her thighs, and fuck, if she doesn't look adorable.

I brush my fingers against her cheek; the tattoo of her name on my hand, staring back at me. She smells like the sweetest sin and every inch of me thirsts for her. "Did I wake you?"

"No," she leans into my chest and takes a deep breath; dark hair tumbling down her back in waves. "I love your smell," she says dreamily.

"I think someone may still be asleep." I smile softly and rub my hands up and down her back. "Think we should get you back to bed, angel."

She pulls back and looks up at me, demure emerald eyes, no longer sleepy. "That's not what I need."

My lip hitches and fire stirs. There was nothing like the look in her eyes when she wanted me. Like the way she was looking at me now.

As much as I want to carry her to bed and make love to her until the sun comes up, I'm exhausted and I know she's tired, too. "You should be sleeping," I breathe her in and kiss the tip of her nose.

Diablo reaches for my hand and pulls it to her lips, kissing the ink of her name. "Do you remember what you said to me the day you got this?"

"Of course." I remember that day well. We were so full of hope. So sure, forever was right around the corner. "So, you're always with me."

"Mm-hmm," she looks up. "So, tell me…if you always

want me with you, why are you leaving our bed at night?"

The very idea I would leave her is ridiculous. I'm protecting her. There's a difference. "I'm not—"

She shoots me a look that says not to bother. She isn't buying whatever I'm about to say.

"Look," I drink in the pink of her lips and the curve of her neck. She's so beautiful that I forget what I'm about to say. "I've been…catching up on some Primordial stuff. I think better at night."

As soon as the words leave my lips, I know she won't believe me. I can run the business without thinking, and Diablo knows this.

"So, you're leaving me at night to work?" her brows pinch.

"You know it takes everything in me to crawl out of that bed when you're in it," I give her a cheeky smile. "But even I know when you need to sleep."

"Well, then," her face softens. "Come back to bed, and I'll remind you why you should never leave it."

Every muscle in me comes to life, betraying my fatigue. "You go on," I nod to the door. "I'll be there in a few."

"You know," she crosses her arms. "My Dante would never pass up that offer. He'd pick me up and—"

I close the space between us, body burning with intensity. "I am still, and always will be, yours. I will never, in a million millennia, pass up the chance to make love to you."

She arches her brow. "Are you sure about that?"

The idea I could ever deny her is ridiculous and she knows it. "How can you even ask that?"

"Well, here I am throwing myself at you and you're shutting me down. Something is up."

"Nothing is up." I curl the hand hanging at my side into a tight fist, focusing on the pressure so I don't spill my guts.

Two more fights and then I'll be done with the list, and she never has to know. "I just…need to finish here."

She looks at me skeptical, as a strange tension brews between us. "You know what," she throws her hands up and turns to leave. "If you won't answer me, maybe I'll ask one of the legion."

I grab her by the wrist and pull her to me, slamming her back against my chest. A laugh curls out of her mouth, as I lean my head into the crook of her neck. "You will go to no one for answers but me. Is that clear?"

She draws in a sharp breath, but I know it's not out of fear. She may command the legion, but I know how much she likes it when I remind her to whom she belongs.

I wrap my arm around her chest and breathe in her warmth. She can get out of this move easily. I taught her the other day. But I know she wants to be right where she is.

"You like knowing what I would do for you, don't you?" I growl.

She lets out a breathless yes, and grinds against me. "But you're forgetting something."

"Oh yeah," I kiss her neck, the sweetness of her skin, tingling my tongue. "What's that?"

She turns and draws her finger down my side and places the flat of her palm on one of the new bruises. "That you are mine and I will rip anyone to shreds that hurts you."

I swallow at the weight of her words and fire in her eyes. Fuck, I loved the way she loved me. "No one will ever hurt me, angel."

"But Dante," she places her other hand on my other side, "someone is."

"What are you—"

"These bruises," she cuts me off. "And don't tell me it's

from fighting with Vinny because I know better."

I close my eyes and weigh my options: tell her the whole truth, or a fraction of it. "We have been fighting," I exhale, then open my eyes. "You know this."

"But where?" she asks, curiosity filling her beautiful face. "And why?"

"We're building up strength...preparing for the war to come." In a way it was the truth. Getting rid of Luke's lackeys *did* help us in the long run. "It's nothing for you to worry about."

"Nothing for me to worry about?" her voice raises an octave. "Dante, I've seen you in the gym the last few days. Your strength has changed. You're stronger. And these bruises never go away. As soon as they heal, new ones crop up."

I was stronger. I felt it in my every step, every punch. Retribution had given me clarity. It reminded me of who I was and would always be–one who would strike down anyone who took from me and do anything for the angel in front of me.

"Please," she places a hand on my cheek. "Tell me what's going on."

My jaw tics and everything I feel for her, demands I tell her the truth. "I...couldn't let him get away with it," I say slowly.

She shakes her head, not following. "Couldn't let who, get away with what?"

"Luke," I exhale. "He needed to pay...for hurting you and taking you from me. So, I started a little payback. I didn't want to wait."

I brace myself, waiting for whatever she is about to say. Whatever anger she may throw at me for breaking the promise I made. To my surprise, she says nothing.

I need to fill the silence between us. Need her to know everything I did was for her. "He took you from me." I point to my chest. "*I promised to keep you safe, and he took you from me.*"

"But I'm fine," she says softly. "I'm here, and we're together."

"Yeah," I bite out. "Now. But not before you had to endure more pain."

"What do you…"

I reach for her wrist and hold it gently. "I heard your scream when he nearly snapped this bone in two and it fucking shattered me, Diablo, you have no idea." My breathing picks up. "Then he said the most disgusting, vile things to you, and I swear…. I wanted to kill him."

Memory of what Luke wanted turns my blood to lava, and I can see by the look in her eyes, it haunts her, too. "You saved me," she swallows.

"You got out," I correct. "But not before he shot me and nearly took you from me, again."

"He will pay for everything he's done," she says with fierce determination. "But we do it together. Whatever you're doing has to stop."

"No."

"Why?" she shakes her head. "Why does it matter?"

"Because he needs to know he didn't ruin us. That he didn't kill me!"

We both grow quiet, and in the silence, I hear nothing but our racing hearts.

"Don't you see…what happened in Eden may have been months ago for you, but it's only been days for me." I let go of her wrist, and place my hand softly against her cheek, stroking it gently with my thumb. "I didn't break my promise to you. When we come for Luke, we will do it together. But those who helped him take you from me, need to pay. Please don't be angry. Please, tell me you understand."

She draws in a shaky breath and puts her hand on top of mine. "I'm not angry, Dante. I'm…scared."

My angel is strong, and smart, and full of fire. But her vulnerability will always rouse my need to protect her. "You don't have to worry about me, angel. You've already worried enough for one existence."

"You think you're the only one who's angry?" she says, voice hollow. "Trust me, I feel it, with every breath I take." She places a hand on my chest and her touch lances straight through me. "He took my existence and my heart and twisted it for his gain. What you feel, I feel. My need for vengeance is so great, I burn with it. But if you do this alone and you're hurt, or he takes you from me again…"

"Angel," I lock my eyes on hers. "I am doing this, so he never, ever hurts us again."

She presses her forehead to my chest, and I lower my head to hers, breathing her in. "It kills me he took you from my bed, where you should have felt safe. Every time I think about that morning it makes me fucking crazy. But after I fought my way through his army and found him holding you, I wanted…"

She tips her face up, mouth so close to mine I feel her breath on my lips. "What did you want?"

The adrenaline that coursed through me that day sends my heart into a pounding frenzy. I love her so fucking much it hurts.

I pick her up and shove all the jars and bottles off the counter, before setting her down on the cool marble. "I wanted to kill him," I grip her thighs and push her legs apart and stand between them. "Then fuck you on top of his dead body so even in death, he knew you belonged to me. It's crazy, I know, but *that's* what I wanted."

Her mouth parts and thick lashes flutter. "Remember what I said in the alley that night? I fell for you, Dante. Abandoned the very reason for my creation because I wanted you. If you are crazy, then I am insane, because I too, would do unspeakable things for you." The energy between us charges, tingling my scalp, and pricking my skin. "There is nothing I wouldn't do for you. *Nothing.*"

Her words flood me with a combination of possession and love that's uncontrollable. My devotion to her was deep and profound and I worshipped the very air she breathed. There was nothing, no one, that could bring me to my knees. Only her.

I tear off her shirt and crash my mouth down on hers, swallowing her moan of approval. She tastes so good, like sugar and honey, and I can't get enough.

I rip off my towel, pull her to the edge of the counter and thrust into her. The feel of her tight heat feels better than Heaven and fills my head with one thought-mine.

She slaps one hand to the mirror and grips me with the other as I pound into her. "Fuck, don't stop," she pants.

With every flick of my hips, I feel her climax building, but I need more. I need to feel every inch of her.

I lift her off the counter, and she wraps her legs around my waist, showering me with kisses as I carry her to the bed. I lay her down and she rolls over and watches me with hungry eyes as I run one hand up her leg, while running my tongue up the other.

Once my body covers hers, I push her legs apart with my knees and enter her again. She grips the sheets and cries out in ecstasy as I lace my fingers through hers and move my hips in pounding, hypnotic rhythm.

I kiss the tattoo at the base of her neck; the words she had inked for us are mine, just as she is. She is my reason for everything. For fighting, for lying. But no more. From now on we will do this together.

I curl my hand gently around her throat, stroking the porcelain skin with my fingers, and when she lets go, I do too–the pleasure of release and devotion is all-consuming.

This love is crazy. Absolutely insane. And worth everything. I would walk through fire and cross time for it…for her.

"You are my beginning and end, Diablo. Those who hurt you…those who made you feel pain… we will bathe in their ashes together, I promise."

Her body is warm and beaded with sweat, and my own skin tingles with heat. But as fast as it appears, it vanishes, and in its place, a cool smoothness skims across my chest.

I pull back as Diablo looks over her shoulder, and we both see them at the same time. Her wings, they're back, and they are just as red, and strong, as she said.

We stare at them for a moment, speechless, and then her eyes find mine and I smile. "There you are my angel."

17
DIABLO

I look up at Dante and shoot him a sleepy smile. After last night, we're both exhausted and decided to take the morning off and hide from the world.

He runs a hand through the soft plume of my feathers and shakes his head in disbelief. "I still can't believe it."

"Me either," I exhale, resting my chin on his chest. "James was right. They were with me all this time."

"A Fallen angel, who still has her wings," he strokes my cheek. "There has never been another like you in existence."

An anomaly. That's what I am. And nothing ever good comes to that which should not be.

"What's wrong?" he asks when my face falls.

I should feel happy and filled with gratitude. After five thousand years of wanting and waiting, Dante and I were together, the legion was united, and I had my wings. But something dark eclipses my spirit, and I can't shake it.

I place the flat of my hand on his chest and sit up, looking over my shoulder at my wings. Every emotion from last night flows through me like a current, from wing to body.

"I don't know," I chew the inside of my cheek. "I think I'm still processing."

"It's a lot to take in," he eyes me carefully. "Are you, okay?"

"Mm-hmm," I rub my chin on my shoulder and turn back around. "It is a lot. Especially after trying so hard."

He grins and I can't help but smile, too. I hardly call our

adrenaline games trying hard. More like a not-so-guilty pleasure.

"Do you know what finally triggered them?" His eyes search mine with the question.

I pull the sheet to me and my wings fold into my back. They are part of me and under my control and command–just as they were in Heaven. "It was us," I say simply.

"What do you mean?" He sits back against the headboard.

After they appeared, neither of us could say much; both of us were too tired, too full of emotion to fully grasp what was happening. Instead, he curled up behind me, buried his head and body in the softness of my wings, and fell asleep. This was the first time we were talking about it, really.

"Last night was…intense," I say slowly; memory of the passion between us, flushing my cheeks with heat. "I've only felt such a storm of emotions like that once before. In Eden, when I thought I lost you." He reaches for my hand and laces his fingers through mine. "Both times, however, in the eye of those storms, one emotion was stronger than all of them–fear. That day in Eden, I finally knew what it felt like to give and receive love, and the idea I'd lost it, terrified me. But last night, when I thought whatever it was you were doing may get you hurt or worse, taken from me a third time, I felt that same fear."

I wait for Dante to say something, but he is listening intently, waiting for me to continue.

"I once believed Heaven took my wings away for wanting to save you." I pause to take a breath, then continue. "And in Eden, I believed they had given them back to me, so I could. But now, I don't know. It feels like my wings are connected to my heart, as they once were my spirit. Almost as if …"

My words trail off and I look down.

"Almost as if, what?" he asks gently.

"As if they have been with me the whole time," I finish the thought, quietly.

Dante reaches for my chin and tilts it up gently. "I think you're right."

"But there is *no* way that could be possible," I shake my head, rejecting the very idea I'd been unable to say aloud. "I was punished and imprisoned in this body, just as you and the rest of the Fallen."

"I know it's hard to consider," he brushes away the hair from my eyes. "But listen to me, angel. None of us have our wings. None of us have ever felt them."

"And neither have I. That day in Eden when they returned was the first time in five thousand years that I felt them. Tonight, was the second."

"Angel," he takes a deep breath and turns to me. "All the Fallen's scars are hideous because they were meant to remind us of our betrayal. But yours have never been ugly. They have always been two perfect slivers."

"But the pain," I close my eyes, trying to block the memory of bone breaking and flesh tearing. "It was excruciating. It wasn't like last night."

"I can't explain the pain you felt in Eden, and I wish I could take the memory of it away. But you have to consider the possibility that it is true."

"No," my throat burns and tears pool in my eyes. "Because if I *am* still an angel, it means Heaven has allowed Luke's torment of me to go on for thousands of years, unchecked. Why would they do that?"

"Because my love," Dante cups my face, and swipes a thumb under my eyes to stop the tears before they can fall. "Heaven made the Fallen pay because we wanted to do what made us happy. But when you chose to save me…*love me*…it was the ultimate betrayal in their eyes."

"How could love ever be an act of betrayal?"

"I don't know," he cups the back of my neck and pulls my forehead to his. "You are the very essence of what we were supposed to embody. Kind, compassionate, loyal. And your capacity to love is so beautiful, Diablo. You are every bit what an angel should be."

I push up from the bed, mind racing. If any of what Dante said was true, it meant Heaven had not forsaken me, but lied and manipulated me, and that was infinitely worse.

Dante gets up and slips on his pajama bottoms, then walks over to me and hands me the sweater I left at the end of the bed. I slip it on and sink down into the soft duvet, digging my toes into the marble floor.

He crouches in front of me and places his hands on my knees. "Talk to me, angel. What are you thinking?"

I draw in a shaky breath, trying to put words to what I'm feeling. "I've always had this bitter hatred for Luke."

"For obvious reasons," Dante says crisply.

"But if Heaven turned me mortal," I look up, "and handed me to him for his use, it means I am a pawn in a game they're *both* playing. I should be angry at Heaven, too." Dante lowers his head and falls silent. "But you already thought that haven't you?"

He sighs and rubs a hand over his face, then straightens and sits down next to me. "Let me answer your question with my own. When you fell, what *exactly* did you say?"

I shove my hands under my thighs and focus on a gray vein in the marble. "I told Heaven you didn't deserve to be punished. That it was Luke who started the War. And they said I should think whether my sacrifice was worth it because once I made the decision, I could never come back. But I didn't believe them. I didn't think…"

I stop myself from finishing the thought, but he knows what I was going to say and does for me. "You didn't think what you were doing was anywhere close to what the Fallen had done."

"I'm sorry," I shake my head. "I didn't mean—"

"We split Heaven in two," he cuts me off. "That was a crime punishable by abandonment. You were trying to save me, that was not."

"Well," I look back down, scratching the skin on the side of my thumb with my index finger. "Regardless of which was worse, they weren't lying because I never saw Heaven again."

He looks over to the desk, staring at JJ's sketchbook for a moment, then back to me. "When did Heaven take your wings? When JJ saw you shielding me, you still had them."

"Honestly," I sigh, "I don't remember. After I made the deal with Luke, I put all my energy into protecting you, and everything else just…faded away. By the time you came to in mortal form, my wings were gone, and then Luke bound us."

I can see Dante replaying my response in his head. "So, there's a possibility they didn't take them?"

"I guess," I shrug. "But why would they do that? Why would they trap an angel in the body of a mortal?"

"I don't know," he tucks my hair behind my ear. "But I think, for now, it's best if we hold on telling everyone your wings are back."

"Do you think the legion wouldn't understand?"

"Honestly," he looks down at our clasped hands. "I think it would be a distraction."

I pull one leg up on the bed and turn to face him. "Are you worried too many eyes will be on me?"

"No," he blows out a wary breath. "Well yes, maybe."

"After last night," I place my hand on his leg. "After, everything?"

"It's not that," he looks back up at me. "I know who owns your heart. I just…I know the legion. They will expect fire and fury, and—"

"You think I won't be ready," I nod with understanding. Dante's hesitation in telling them wasn't about jealousy. It was about protecting me.

"You probably need time to remember how to use them," he reasons.

I fan my wings out, then tuck them into my back. "It's like riding a bike."

"So, you don't think you will clap them out of anger and accidentally blow out the side of the building?"

I laugh gently, and when I see he's not laughing, I stop. "Wait, you're serious?"

"Yes," he levels his eyes on mine. "You said that you vaporized Luke's army in one clap."

"They deserved it," my eyes flash. "But I would never do that here. I would never use that kind of force around any of the legion."

"I know they did," he softens, "and I know you would never do anything to hurt anyone, intentionally. All I'm saying is your wings are different, Diablo. They are more powerful, and you need time getting to know what they are capable of."

Dante's right. My wings were not only different in color now, but they had a considerable amount of power.

"How about this," he suggests. "Once the vault has finished updating with all images and we have a better idea of what Luke is up to, we tell everyone. Until then, you practice."

165

I consider the suggestion and agree. "You're right."

"Yeah?" he grins. "You're not going to fight me on this?"

"No," I shake my head. "I trust you. But…" I smile softly, wanting to ease the tension of the last few minutes. "I guess this means the adrenaline games are off."

"Are you kidding?" His lips pull into a sexy smile. "We have six months and five thousand years to make up for. I plan to play every game in the book with you, angel."

He pulls me into a warm, lingering kiss, and the unease starts to fade. "I love you," I whisper.

"Angel," his lips ghost mine. "I love you so much it hurts."

I start to pull him down onto the bed when there's a knock at the door. "Hey, you two," Vinny's voice booms from the other side.

"What is it?" we call back in unison.

"David's here and has news. Get your asses dressed and get downstairs."

"Actually, smart ass," Dante looks down at his pajama bottoms. "We are dressed."

"Right," Vinny laughs. "Get dressed," he says again, then hits the door with his fist. "See you downstairs in five."

"Do you want to do this right now?" Dante sits up. "I can tell them—"

"Of course," I get up from the bed. "This changes nothing. We still have payback to plan, starting with the vault."

"Are you sure?" Dante looks at me, hesitant.

"There is nothing more important." I reach for his hand and pull him up from the bed. "Now get dressed. It's an order."

There were now two potential enemies, instead of one—Heaven, and Luke–and I was ready to take on both if needed.

18
DANTE

When we finally make our way into the study, David is sitting at my desk, staring at a tablet. He looks up when we walk in and motions for us to come over. I cross the room and stand next to Vinny, while Diablo does the same and stands next to Lila.

Before coming downstairs, Diablo and I agreed to tell Vinny and Lila about her wings. They were family and we trusted them implicitly. But we would wait until it was just the four of us. Right now, this was the focus.

"So," she taps a nail on the desk. "What's the news?"

"The vault," David looks up with a triumphant smile. "It's complete."

"Really?" I ask with surprise.

"Yes," he turns his attention back to the tablet. "Ahead of schedule, too. My contact informed me this morning. There were in fact two images with the sigil, so I went ahead and uploaded them to the album."

I press both hands on the desk and look down at the tablet. David has changed it to tile view, making it easier to see all the images. "Now that you see them all together, does it mean anything?"

"I'm familiar with each of these artifacts," he studies the screen. "But I don't see a connection."

"Other than the fact none predates the Fall," Diablo says while looking at the screen. "Maybe that Mesopotamian bowl, but the others are from the last five thousand years."

"Well, what do you know," David looks at the album with elevated curiosity. "You're right."

I wink at my angel, her brilliance never surprising me.

"Maybe they're a red herring," Vinny crosses his arms.

"Yeah," Lila smirks. "Look here, while I'm doing shit over there."

"Exactly," he smirks.

I rub a hand across my jaw and study the images. "There's a reason Luke is the one in charge of the vault and those images are marked. Why and how they're connected, isn't meant to be obvious."

"Mm-hmm," Diablo agrees. "He's literally the master of manipulation. This could be something or could be nothing."

"Another riddle on our hands, huh?" Vinny huffs. "Well, bring it on. We'll decode this, just like we did his bullshit contract."

Dante looks at Vinny and the two bump fists. Lila looks at me and rolls her eyes and I can't help but chuckle. For ancient immortals, they sure act like boys sometimes.

"Looks like we have our work cut out for us," Vinny turns back to the tablet.

"That we do," David gets up from the desk. "And five heads will be better than one. But today it will have to be the four of you. I have a prior engagement, so I'll see you—"

"Where are you going?" I ask as David gathers his things.

"I can't stay," he looks at his watch, then back at me. "I'm sorry. I just wanted to stop by on my way out of the city and share the good news."

"I don't think you understand," Vinny looks at David, eyes hard. "There is nothing more important than this. You're not leaving."

As David shifts his attention from Vinny to me, I can see

he's confused. But then the look on his face changes to something else entirely–acceptance. He didn't realize, fully, what being an attendant meant, until this very moment.

He is no longer just part of a world where he is top of the intellectual food chain. He is also part of ours. Only, he is rank and file, and not only we the leaders, but Vinny, his sire. He must follow his command. It's more natural to him now, than breathing.

"Vinny," Diablo makes her way over to David, smiling politely. "We can manage without him for one day, can't we?"

Vinny clears his throat and looks to Lila. "Give the guy a break," she says to him dryly.

Feeling the pressure from the two, he waves David off. "Oh fine, go on. But be back tomorrow."

Diablo shoots David a triumphant smile. "Tonight's the night James receives his award in research from Oxford, correct?"

"Yes," he clears his throat.

"He told me about it at our last appointment. Please tell him congratulations," she says with so much kindness it's hard to not fall under her spell. "It's a tremendous honor."

"I will. But, you're sure?" He looks to Vinny again, who waves him off a second time.

"You may report to me, but I report to her," he nods to Diablo, "and her," he nods to Lila. "They say go, then you go."

The two laugh and David eases. "Well then, we'll pick this up tomorrow." He finishes gathering up his things and shoves them into his leather briefcase, then turns to Diablo, shooting her a look of gratitude. "Thank you."

"No thanks needed," she holds a hand up. "You still have a life. Have fun and celebrate with James."

He looks at her and shoves a hand in his pocket. "I do still have a life, don't I?"

"Yup," she smiles. "And it will be a long one, and not in a good way," she adds cheekily, "if you start making your partner mad, now."

Her words send a pang of regret through me. I put her through a lot of shit over the millennia, all in the name of fealty. I really do have a lot to make up for. The accounts I set up and the project I have JJ working on will be a start. But they're only a drop in the bucket. She deserves to be spoiled for eternity and I plan to do exactly that.

"Good advice," David smiles, clearly at ease in Diablo's presence. I wonder if she can see what I do–that she's an angel on Earth. Truly, one of a kind.

"Alright, everyone," he waves as he heads for the door. "See you, tomorrow."

Once he's gone, I pull open the top drawer of my desk and remove a tablet. Diablo reaches for it and flashes me a brilliant smile. "Come on Lila, let's go figure this out."

The two make their way over to the leather couch and curl up next to one another, tablet between them. I reach into the drawer and grab a second tablet.

"Vin, I need to tell you something," I say while pulling up the album.

He's looking through it as well on his phone, flipping back and forth between the images. "Sure brother, what is it?"

"I told Diablo about the club and what we were doing."

He stops scrolling and looks up. "Oh yeah? How'd that go?"

"Actually," I think back to last night. "Better than expected."

"She wasn't mad?"

"No," I cross my arms. "But she did take it out on me." We

stare at one another for a moment and then my lips pull into a smug smile.

Vinny shakes his head and lets out a hardy laugh. "Lucky bastard."

"It wasn't too long ago I was saying those very same words to you, my friend."

I look over at Diablo. She and Lila are laying back on the couch, feet kicked up on the coffee table. I really was a lucky bastard. Probably the luckiest one in existence.

"Well," he shrugs. "It was a good run while it lasted, yeah?"

"That it was," I agree. "Thank you, brother. It really helped me."

"Don't mention it," he holds his fist out and I bump mine to it. "How about I take care of the last two? I feel the need for a little merciless payback."

"All yours," I clap his back.

***

An hour later, Wills knocks on the door with a tray of food. "Oh, great," Diablo pushes up from the couch and stretches her arms overhead. "Thank you, Wills."

"My pleasure," he nods at her. "Where would you like it?"

"Over there," she points to my desk.

"D, you're the best!" Lila jumps up. "I was getting hungry."

"Me too," Vinny rubs his stomach.

"You could have asked the kitchen to put something together," Diablo says as the three follow Wills over to my desk.

"It's better you asked. Apparently," Lila draws out

dramatically, "they're still pissed about the night I kicked them out so I could cook for you."

Wills sets the tray down and Vinny reaches for an orange. "But it was such a delicious dinner, and desert even better," he waggles his brows.

"It's better you asked anyway," Lila reaches for a bunch of grapes. "Look at this spread. They would only do this for you." She pops one in her mouth playfully and Vinny laughs as she tosses one at him and misses.

"Will there be anything else?" Wills asks Diablo.

"No," she places a hand on his arm. "Thank you."

Wills nods at her, then makes his way out of the study. As he does, I reach for an apple and take a bite. It's shiny and green and reminds me of the first day Diablo and I spent together this century. The day I inked onto my forearm so it would forever be part of my story because it was also ours.

I know she, too, is thinking about that day. I can see the glint of mischief on her face as she wraps her fingers around my wrist and pulls the apple to her mouth, sinking her teeth into its shiny green pulp.

She savors the taste for a moment, then swipes a finger across her mouth, and sucks on it. "Fuck," I say under my breath.

"You said it was worth it," she looks at me, eyes shining. They're filled with the same need for me, that I'm feeling for her. "And it is. It's worth everything."

"Tonight," I lean in and whisper low enough so only she can hear. "I'm going to fuck you first, then make love to you until the sun comes up."

"I'm going to hold you to that," she winks.

"By the way," I change the subject before I push this tray off my desk and start our night early. "I told Vinny I was done with payback."

"Ah," she lifts a brow and takes another bite of the apple. "And my wings?"

"I didn't say anything. It's your news to tell."

"What are you two whispering about over there?" Lila asks as she feeds Vinny a grape.

"My wings," Diablo says while still looking at me.

Vinny freezes as Lila pops another grape into her mouth. "What about them?" she asks while chewing.

"They came back," Diablo turns to her best friend.

Vinny's pupils widen to the point his eyes are nearly black. "Are you kidding?"

"No," she shakes her head. "I'm not. They're back and just as red as they were in Eden."

"But...how?" he looks at me. "And, when?"

"It's a bit complicated," Diablo tries to explain. "I'm not sure I understand it myself, really. But suffice it to say, they're back."

"Well, let's see them," he rubs his hands together excitedly.

"Here's the thing," she looks over at me and I nod with encouragement. "I want to work on using them. After what happened in Eden—"

"You don't want to vaporize the legion," he crosses his arms. "Yeah, probably a good idea."

"I can command them," she narrows her eyes. I know she's not mad. No one gets mad at Vinny. But the idea of hurting the legion is serious for her and she wants him to know she isn't taking it lightly. "I just want to make sure I don't hurt anyone. There are probably some differences between how they work in ethereal form, and when you're mortal."

"I'm sure," Lila laughs. "In fact, how you have them at all makes me wonder if—"

"We keep this between the four of us, okay?" I cut her off, while tucking Diablo against my side. I know what Lila was about to say and want to avoid discussion around the idea Diablo was still an angel with anyone else for now.

"Sure," Vinny looks at Diablo. "If that's what you want."

"It is," she confirms. "Nothing matters more than this. Luke aligned himself with the church and started this project for a reason. We have to figure out what it is."

Vinny nods in agreement as his phone buzzes. "Well, shit," he says after reaching into his pocket and looking at the text that's come in. "David forgot one. Says there's eleven images, not ten."

"Well, that's great," Lila rolls her eyes.

"What is it?" I ask Vinny. "Did he say?"

At this point, nothing would surprise me. The items in the album are random, to say the least. There's a spear that predates the Vikings and the Mesopotamian bowl. Even a Terracotta Warrior from the tomb of China's first emperor.

"Not sure," Vinny looks up from his phone. "He's uploading it as we speak. Said to refresh the link and it should appear once it's finished downloading."

I reach for the tablet and keep tapping refresh, and when the image finally shows up in the album, Vinny takes the words right out of my mouth. "Well, shit."

"What is it?" Diablo stares at the screen.

To anyone else it looks like an old box. Wooden, probably worthless, with etchings worn smooth over time. But for Vinny and me, it's more.

"Clearly, Luke has been working on this vault much longer than we thought," Vinny straightens.

"What makes you say that?" she asks.

"Remember back in Eden," I look at her. "When Minerva wanted to know why you fell?"

She folds her arms over her chest, clearly bothered by the memory. "Not really something I can forget."

"Well," I inhale. "The information we gave her had to do with that box. We helped get it for her...in Berlin."

Diablo arches a curious brow. "What do you mean?"

"In the late 70s West Berlin had this really gritty subculture. Music, art...all of it, was part of this chaotic underground society with no rules or moral compass, of which, an underground market that sold rare and priceless items was at the heart."

"We're talking paintings, sculptures, rare stones the size of my hand," Vinny adds. "I think there was even a Fabergé egg or two."

Lila's eyes widen and I continue. "Around 1979, Minerva reached out to us about an auction. She'd done some work for us over the years, and this was the payment she required...information on its location and the list of items planned for sale. Long story short, that box was on the list, she stole it the night before and it hasn't been seen since."

Diablo and Lila look at one another, clearly surprised by the story. "So, what information did you give her in Eden?" Diablo turns back to me. "It was obviously important enough for her to take in exchange for that which Luke wanted from me."

At the time, the information we had on Minerva was priceless. Many crime syndicates wanted the box for themselves and had been after her for decades. But information is power and knowing who wanted her head for what she pulled in Berlin, gave us leverage over her.

Whatever we needed, Minerva did, because we knew who was after her and had kept them at bay for decades. But that day in Eden, when I was desperate to break the contract so Diablo and I could be together, I realized there was nothing more important to me than her. I would trade every secret I had to keep her safe. So, I did.

"I knew there was nothing Minerva wanted more than the names of those who had been after her since Berlin, so I gave her the list and destroyed any trail that connected her to the auction."

Diablo reaches for my hand and squeezes, shooting warmth through me. There are endless words in her touch. I know because they are in mine, too.

"But why this box?" Lila looks at the image, skeptical. "It just looks old."

"It's not just old," Vinny says mysteriously. "It's believed to be made of wood from the Assyrian Tree of Life. That's why the crime syndicates wanted it back in Berlin. Dumb shits think the house that possesses it, won't have to pay for their wrongdoings."

"Really?" Lila looks back down at the image and points. "That?"

"Maybe it's not about the box," Diablo says plainly, "but what's inside."

I look at her, confused. "What do you mean?"

"It's a puzzle box," she presses one hand down on the desk, while pointing at the tablet with the other. "See, here and here," she draws circles with her finger around two dark spots on the box. "They're joints."

"Holy shit," Vinny shakes his head. "Why didn't we see that?"

I pick up the tablet and examine the markings I thought

were simply, knots in the wood. "Probably because we haven't seen it in four decades."

"Right," Lila laughs. "That's it. Or maybe, Diablo is just smarter than the three of us combined."

"That's true," Vinny laughs.

I look at my angel and there is no denying it–she is smarter, sexier, and rarer than anything in existence. "Tell me more," I encourage.

"Since the earliest civilizations, people have used them to hide their most important items. The only problem was often, they couldn't get them open again once closed."

"Couldn't they just break it?" Vinny huffs, as if the answer were obvious.

"Oh no," Diablo looks at him, eyes flashing with excitement. "Most weren't willing to try, in fear of damaging what was inside. Not to mention, with boxes that were well made, the more pressure that's applied, the stronger the wood gets, and the harder it is to open."

"So, you think there's something in that box?" I ask.

"It's possible," Diablo nods.

"How do we find out?"

"We don't," she chews her cheek. "We wait for the church to tell us."

"I'm sorry, what was that?" Lila laughs. "I could have sworn you said—"

"Think about it," she cuts Lila short. "It's a puzzle box. I don't recall seeing any other boxes on that list. There must be something inside, which means someone is working to open it. And when they do, it will likely be scanned in."

"Well, great," I step back from the desk with a new level of frustration. "More games."

"Man," Vinny shakes his head. "I'm tired of this cat and

mouse shit. The artifacts with the marking, whatever is in this box, we need to find out why they're so important."

"I agree," I look over at him. "Are you thinking what I'm thinking?"

"Probably," he nods.

Diablo looks from Vinny to me with a question in her eyes. "Angel," I smile mischievously, "looks like we're going on a mission."

19
DIABLO

When Vinny first suggested we track down each of the artifacts in the album and bring them here so we could inspect them firsthand, I thought he was kidding. But the more he and Dante talked about, the more I realized they were serious.

"Child's play," Vinny said with a laugh, when I questioned how they planned to steal eleven artifacts. Some from the world's most renowned museums and likely safeguarded by military grade security. It would not be an easy feat. Not to mention, break about a dozen international laws, maybe more.

But as he and Dante got to work, I realized they weren't kidding. They were really going to do it. By the end of the night, a plan was in place, and operations well underway, for what was sure to be the biggest global heist in history.

The next day, I'm curled up next to the fire in the study reading, while Dante and Vinny work on logistics. They'd been on calls all day and already worked through breakfast and lunch, and it looked like they would be through training, as well.

"Hey," Dante laughs, when the feel of his hand on my knee startles me. "You were so quiet over here I thought I'd check and see if you were alright."

I give him a sheepish smile and close the book lying open on my lap. "I must have dozed off."

"So, I see," he smiles softly, eyeing me with concern. "Are you okay?"

"Yeah," I yawn. "Why?"

"Your cheeks are flush." He puts a hand to my forehead. "And you feel warm."

"Well," I turn to the roaring fire next to me. "I am sitting next to the flames of Hell."

"We both know they're hotter than that," he tosses back dryly. "In all seriousness," he gets up and comes over to sit next to me. "You were warm last night, too."

"I was?" I yawn again. Why was I so tired suddenly?

"Yeah," he studies my face. "I woke up and you had all the covers pushed off you. Did you overdo it by practicing too much with your wings?"

"I don't think so," I shake my head.

Yesterday after breakfast, Dante surprised me with a space he created on the roof where I could practice using my wings. With the sky all around me and no boundaries, I could clap my wings as hard as I wanted, without someone seeing or harming anyone.

I spent half the day up there, and it was invigorating. But thinking about it now, I wondered if I had overdone it. I was more tired than normal last night and did just pass out in this very spot.

"I'm fine," I wave off his concern. "How is everything coming along with the heist?"

"Good," he smiles at the name I'd given the operation. "Our contacts are doing what they do best."

Dante's global network was impressive. I'd seen it in action when he leveraged it to find a rare book that had eluded historians for centuries, so he could give it to me, and knew he was tapping into it again now. From local government officials to museum docents, he and Vinny were doing everything they could to get into each country, swap out the real artifact with a decoy, and get out, undetected.

"And the teams?" I set my book down on the table in front of me. "How are they doing?"

Vinny and Dante had pulled together eleven teams of twenty legion members–one for each artifact–based on its location, and the skills needed to procure it. For the next forty-eight hours, they would study and review plans, over and over, to ensure each team had their moves well-coordinated, from landing to departure.

Viper was on the team headed to the Smithsonian, while Vinny and Lila were heading to China. Dante insisted he and I stay back and oversee the operation from the study, watching on a wall of monitors being set up for the legion members that would maintain communication with the teams during the operation.

At first, I figured Dante wanted me to stay behind because of his need to keep me safe. Then I realized, it was not about that. He was teaching me how to lead, which often meant being the eyes and ears, while others were the soldiers.

"Anyone having second thoughts?" I tuck my legs underneath me.

"The legion doesn't do second thoughts," he sits back and lets his knees fall to the side. "You should know that by now."

He was right. I did. The legion was more than ready for action. They'd been waiting patiently for months to make a move against Luke. While a heist wasn't their first choice, it was something to help quench their growing thirst for revenge.

"Everyone is pumped and looking good," Dante confirms. "This is going to be just another day in the park."

"Don't you mean a walk in the park?" I laugh softly.

"Day in the park, walk in the park…the point is the teams

are ready," he says with confidence.

"That's good. Oh, I talked to Hayden earlier. He's excited about overseeing the war room."

"Figured he would be," Dante runs a hand through his hair. "He's perfect for it, honestly."

Luke had remained quiet, and so far, we didn't see anything that made us believe he knew we were looking into the vault. But if he caught wind any marked artifact had been stolen, he'd know, and then we'd tip our hand and be right back where we were before Dante woke up. This meant keeping social chatter and media coverage to a zero was critical.

With a penchant and passion for all things digital, and disinterest in field work, Hayden was the ideal member to track social media and online news networks. He may be as old as the rest of us, but he seemed more innocent, and I was glad he was staying behind to manage that part of the operation.

We all believed the artifacts were critical to whatever Luke was planning and were anxious to get each back here so we could start examining them. I don't think any of us had ever wanted two days to go by faster.

"Still not planning to fill David in?" I run my hand over Dante's shoulder.

"Yes," he exhales and leans his head back and looks up at the ceiling. "You know why we can't tell him until after it's done."

As a shepherd of history and antiquities, David would never agree to what we were doing. One of the primary conditions he had in working with Dante and Vinny over the years, was that no items ever be sold illegally, and the heist broke the first part of that rule, ten times over.

Vinny insisted it would be fine however, once David heard the plan for each item's handling when they were here, as well as their safe return when done. But still, I didn't like lying to David. He'd done nothing but try to help us and hoped it didn't cause problems.

"Are you sure you're, okay?" Dante turns his head towards me.

When I find myself staring at the book on the table, I surprise myself by asking a question I didn't even know was on my mind. "Do you think my library is okay?"

"Well, I wasn't expecting that," he smiles gently and sits up. "Where did that come from?"

In remembering how Dante used his network to find the book he gifted to me–the long-believed, but never discovered, last work of William Shakespeare–it reminded me of where it was now. In a locked case, alongside my other rare editions, in the library I'd built in my house back in Eden.

"I'm sorry," I look down. I didn't care about Eden. It could burn for all I cared. But I missed the space I'd built for all the books I'd spent centuries finding and wondered if it was okay.

"Why are you apologizing?" he asks and turns towards me.

"I just hate the idea of Luke or one of his idiots getting their hands on that space I worked so hard on, or any of my books."

After the events at Luke's, Dante was my focus. I didn't think about what I was leaving behind. I just knew we needed to get out of Eden, as fast as possible. But that didn't mean I no longer cared about them or the library I'd spent decades building. I did, greatly. I just didn't have a chance to remember how much until this very moment.

Dante rubs my arm and squeezes it. "Your library and all of your books are fine," he says with confidence.

"But you don't know that." He's trying to reassure me the way he does everything, and I love him for it.

"No," he insists. "I do. Your home and everything in it, has not been touched because I have someone that I trust, keeping an eye on it."

"You, what?" I sit up.

"You didn't think I would let everything you worked hard for be lost, did you?"

"I don't know," I look at him in shock. "I mean we left so fast, and haven't been back…"

"Don't worry," he smiles. "I promise you that your home, your library, and every book in there, are safe. And when all this is over, we are going to go to Eden, and get all of it."

I throw my arms around his neck and squeeze. Dante was my knight in shining armor. The hero in my happy ever after. "Have I told you how much I love you?"

"I think so," he rubs my back. "But you can tell me again."

"I do," I pull back and drink in his magnificence. "So much."

"Ditto," he smiles warmly and steals a kiss. "Now, I need to get back to work. Can you do something for me?"

"Anything."

"Can you take the day off and get some rest? I think your wings may be taking their toll on you."

"What makes you say that?"

"You're warm, and you look tired." I start to protest but he holds up a hand and I let him finish. "I just want to make sure you're taking care of yourself."

Dante had a point. My wings could be affecting my body in a way I was not aware.

"Maybe we should tell James? It might be good to let him know now, before something shows up in my lab work. He could even run some tests to see what kind of impact they may be having."

"A few more days?" Dante reaches for my hand and brings it to his lips to kiss it. "Once the heist is over, you can tell him. For now, take today off and rest. For me?"

"Fine," I sigh and get up from the couch.

He stands up with me, but instead of letting go of my hand, he pulls me to him and looks down, staring deep into my eyes. "You are my everything, you know that, right?"

"I know," I press up on my toes and kiss him gently. "Now go lead."

He raises his brows, knowing how much I love to be in charge. "Oh yeah?"

"Mm-hmm. And when you come to bed later, I will let you lead there, too."

"Say no more." He kisses my hand again, then watches me walk out of the study.

When I crawl into bed a few minutes later, I fall right to sleep. I've never experienced such an energy crash before and can't wait for the heist to be over so we can tell James and look into the impact my wings may be having. I don't need anything slowing me down. Not now. Not when we're so close to war.

20
DIABLO

The next morning, I feel rested and ready for the day. Chalking it up to a good night's sleep, I get dressed, have breakfast, then head downstairs to meet with James for my usual vitals check and blood draw.

My adrenaline is high, and my mind is clear. Tomorrow, the biggest heist in the history of the world will begin, and when it's over, eleven artifacts will be in our possession. I'm more than ready to see what secrets they may be hiding and figure out what Luke is up to.

When I make it to the sitting room, the door is open. I peer in and find James behind the desk, staring out the window. He doesn't hear when I knock, so I clear my throat and rap my knuckle against the door a second time.

This time he hears me and whips his head up. "Hi," I smile brightly. "I'm here for my appointment."

"Diablo, right," he taps a finger on the folder lying closed on his desk. "Come in."

He appears preoccupied; whatever he was thinking about before I arrived, clearly still on his mind. "I can come back if it's a bad time," I point over my shoulder.

"No," he shakes his head. "That won't be necessary."

I make my way into the room and sit down in the chair opposite him and tuck a strand of hair behind my ear. "Are you sure?"

James is a no-nonsense guy, but even his usual limited small talk is nonexistent today. "No," he pushes up from the chair. "We should talk."

I lean back and run my hands down the arms of the chair as he walks around to the front of the desk. "How was Oxford?" I ask, hoping to break through whatever is troubling him. "I saw David before you headed out of town, and he was looking forward to the awards ceremony. He's very proud of you."

It appears to work. James smiles gently as he leans back against the desk, and the furrow in his brow eases. "It was good. He was, I mean he is, very proud."

"As he should be," I nod, pleased by the shift in his demeanor, no matter how small.

His smile remains for a moment, then fades as he looks down at the folder in his hand. Something is off. He's uneasy and it's starting to make me nervous. "James, is everything okay?"

"Yes," he nods, then corrects himself. "I mean no, I have the results of your most recent blood work."

"Oh," I straighten, wondering if the return of my wings has shown up somehow and he's upset with me for not saying anything. "Does that mean yes, it's good, or no, we need to talk?"

"It means, there's something I need to discuss with you," he says matter of fact.

I swallow over the lump forming in my throat, not liking his response. "Go on," I nod, gripping the arms of the chair.

"There was an irregularity," he says evenly. I drop my hands in my lap and look down, preparing to explain. But before I can say anything, he continues. "There's no way to say this, so I'm just going to say it. You're pregnant, Diablo."

I look up and stare at him blankly, sure I heard him wrong. "What did you say?"

"I said you're pregnant, Diablo. You're going to have a baby."

Everything around me goes quiet; nothing but the sound of my breathing, echoing in my ears. I struggle to speak. Words forming, but not leaving my lips.

Then slowly, I start to laugh–the idea is so ridiculous, he must be kidding. But when I see James isn't laughing, I stop cold. "Wait, you're serious?"

"Yes," he nods. "Very."

"I don't believe you." This is a dream. I'm upstairs, still asleep, right?

"I wasn't sure at first, so I ran your blood work a couple of times, and every test came back the same. You're pregnant."

I push up from the chair, my pounding heart, whooshing in my ears. "That's not possible."

He straightens, clearly perplexed by my response. "Didn't you tell me just the other day that the Fallen can procreate?"

"Sure," I shake my head to the point it hurts. "But not me."

He focuses on me intently, the weight of his stare making my skin itch. "Why not?"

"Dante…" I stop and take a shaky breath. "He…can't sire children."

"Is it possible he's not—"

"No," I cut him off, knowing what he's about to say. "There is no one else."

"Well then," James holds the folder out to me. "He may not have been able to sire children before, but it appears he can now. I suspected at our last appointment, but I needed to be sure."

I grasp the folder tentatively. "Is that why you asked me all those questions about the Fallen and siring children?"

"Yes," he says without apology. "I needed to know more before I could even consider this as a possibility."

"You were sitting on this information then and just *now* telling me?" I ask, my voice raising an octave.

"After we spoke, I ran a couple of tests, and the results were all the same. That's when I knew for sure. You can see for yourself," he nods to the folder. "The results are in there."

My hand starts shaking, and the folder falls to the floor. "Could it be something else? Maybe it's my wings," I search for an explanation. "Maybe their dormancy is triggering something in my blood."

"No," he bends down to pick up the folder, then stands back up and places it on the desk. "Your blood shows very high levels of hCG, which is a hormone produced only during pregnancy."

I can't believe this is happening, or what I'm about to ask next. "How…far along am I?"

"Judging by the levels of hCG detected, it would appear about eight weeks."

"Eight weeks?" I repeat. "But Dante only woke up a couple of weeks ago."

"Typically, by the time one finds out they are expecting, it is about four weeks into gestation," he folds his arms over his chest. "But I'm assuming your immortality is skewing the hCG levels higher. Given Dante's situation, you likely just conceived."

I turn back around, trying to process all of this. "I don't understand how this is possible. Dante took measures to ensure he couldn't sire children."

"Well," James considers my comment. "His blood still has traces of mortal DNA from the stardust. My guess is that's what made this possible. Or, perhaps, it has to do more with you."

I turn around slowly, his choice of words making my skin prick. "What do you mean?"

"Your wings returned before Dante was shot, right?" I nod once, not sure I like where he's going with the thought. "Couldn't that mean you're not Fallen, but an angel, making *anything* possible."

James hasn't said anything about my wings being back, yet, he suspects I'm still an angel. I didn't like that his mind went to the possibility so quickly.

My head starts to pound so I press a finger to my temple to ease the throbbing. I wasn't ready to have this conversation again. Especially not with anyone but Dante. "I gave up what I was, end of story."

"And yet, your wings returned for you to save him a second time. You can't tell me you aren't curious how that happened?"

Of course, I'm curious. But I wasn't about to tell him that. "Not really," I feign indifference, wanting to get off the subject.

"Diablo," he says with sudden excitement. "This pregnancy could change everything we know about life. An immortal, giving birth to another..." he pauses, and his eyes widen at the thought. "It could be the most important event in the history of science. You could be the most important being in existence."

Birth...creation of life. The words made my mind spin. Me, pregnant...it just wasn't possible. Angels, Fallen or not, could not conceive.

"Is there any possibility those tests were wrong?"

"No," he says with confidence. "You *are* pregnant, Diablo. There's no doubt about it."

Not only could I not process this news, but the timing couldn't be worse. The heist was going down in one day, my wings had returned, and soon, we would wage war with Luke. A baby just didn't fit in.

"Perhaps if we did an ultrasound so you could see—"

I hold out my hand. "No. No ultrasound. And we don't tell anyone. Is that clear?"

"Doctor patient confidentiality prevents me from telling anyone. But Diablo, you should tell Dante. If he is the baby's father, he deserves—"

"He is!" I clench my fists, feeling my wings threatening to appear. I take a deep breath and then another, until I feel them again, tucked safely in my back. "If I am pregnant," I say in a calmer, more even tone, "Dante is the father. But he can't know yet. No one can."

The next twenty-four hours were important. There couldn't be any distractions. Dante and the legion needed to stay focused. "I will tell him. Just, not today."

James looks at me, and seeing this is not up for further discussion, simply nods and says nothing further.

I can't breathe. Can't think. Too many thoughts rushing through my mind. "I need to get out of here."

I spin on my heel and tear out of the room and down the hall. When I pass the study and Dante calls out my name, I don't stop. Instead, I march right past the foyer, to the elevators, and press the down button repeatedly.

Come on, I tap my foot impatiently as I wait for the car to arrive. When it finally does, I bolt in and press the button for the garage.

"Where are you going?" Dante's voice echoes behind the doors as they close, and the elevator starts to go down.

When it stops at the garage I jump out, punch in the code

for the valet on the wall and grab a set of keys. Wills gave it to me months ago when riding was the only way I could clear my head on the dark days. Of course, someone in the legion tailed me on every one of those rides, but not today. Right now, I need to be alone.

Once I reach the bike that I've come to consider my own–a black and steel Ducati that was both speed and style–I grab the helmet on the seat, shove it over my head, and hop on. In minutes I'm speeding along the river, my mind racing.

I'm lost in my thoughts when a bike speeds past me, does a U-turn, then stops in the middle of the road. I apply the brakes, coming to a halt just a few feet from it, and watch as the driver jumps off and removes his helmet.

"What the hell, Diablo!" Dante storms towards me, the anger in his eyes matching that of his voice. "No leaving the penthouse alone! You know that!"

I rip my own helmet off, wind tossing my hair. My cheeks burn and tears sting my eyes. "I know."

"Then why are you leaving the penthouse!" I know he's not mad at me, rather, the idea of something happening to me.

"I needed to get away."

"Why?"

"I needed to think."

He grabs the handlebar of my bike and locks his eyes onto mine. "About?"

"I...needed to get some air."

"Okay," he looks at me carefully. "I get it. We're all a little on edge. But why the dramatics? You didn't respond when I called your name, and you know you shouldn't be out alone."

I bite my lip and look away, but he grabs my chin between his thumb and forefinger and pulls it back to him slowly.

"Angel, what's wrong?"

"What's wrong?" I laugh bitterly.

"Yeah," he drops his hand. "Is everything okay?"

"Well, that depends."

He inhales, clearly not prepared for my response. "On?"

"What you have to say when I tell you what I'm about to." He looks at me, with a mix of worry and confusion. "I just had my appointment with James."

Dante closes his eyes, as if the way I'm acting, suddenly makes sense. "Did something show up in your blood work?"

A bitter laugh crawls from my lips. "You can say that."

He opens his eyes again and levels them on me. "He knows about your wings?"

"No," I shake my head. "Not that."

"Then?" he looks at me. "Well, what is it, Diablo?" he presses when I don't say anything. "You're scaring the hell—"

"I'm pregnant."

He looks at me for a minute, expression blank. Then laughs and shakes his head. When he sees I'm not laughing he puts his hand up and steps back. "Wait…what?"

"I'm pregnant," I say again. "And before you ask, yes it's yours."

"I wasn't going to…why would you even say—"

"Because I know what you're thinking," I cut him off. "So let me stop your mind from spinning. You are the only one I've ever been with, and the only one I ever *will* be with."

"But how," he says again. "I took precautions so this would never happen. Not to mention how is it even possible you—"

"Forget it," I close my eyes. "Go home, Dante. We can talk later."

"Wait, angel," he reaches for my face and pulls it back to him a second time. "Just…give me a minute. I'm trying to process what's going on here."

"Well process faster because surprise!" I throw my hands in the air. "You're going to be a father."

He looks at me, clearly confused and surprised. "I know I'm the only one you have been with. I don't doubt that for a second. But I don't understand how this is possible. I've never…"

"Had a scare?" I quip

"Well, if I'm being honest," he shrugs. "Yeah."

"Well, you can stop yourself from worrying whether you have a litter out there or not, because apparently this just happened. Thanks to the stardust, you still have enough mortal DNA in your blood to make siring a child possible. At least, that's what James thinks. As for me, who knows how this is even possible."

Dante crosses his arms and lets out a heavy breath, then grows quiet.

"I'm sure this horrifies you," I say when his silence becomes unbearable.

"Is that what you think?" he asks softly.

"Well, yeah," I let out a shaky breath. "I can tell by the look on your face. Not to mention, I know this is the last thing you ever wanted."

"The look you see on my face is one of shock. And yes, it was the last thing I ever wanted…until you."

"What does that mean?" I ask numbly, tears filling my eyes.

He reaches out and pulls me closer, cupping my cheek with one hand. "It means, my angel, that you are the exception to everything. I never wanted anything, with anyone. But hearing you say I'm going to be a father is crazy and yet, at the same time, feels like the most natural thing in the world."

"So, you're not mad?" I ask, confused by what's happening.

"Mad?" The softness in his eyes matches that of his voice. "Is that why you ran away from me?"

"That, and I didn't want to worry you."

"Worry me?" he laughs. "You ran when you heard me call your name. That worried the hell out of me."

"Sorry," I place a hand on his chest. "But can you blame me? I mean, it's a lot to take in. Not to mention, we have a lot going on right now."

"Well," his eyes dance. "I think I get a little credit for having a damn good response, don't you think?"

He's right. His response was unexpected and caught me off guard.

"What do you want, angel?" He pulls a strand of hair from my eyes. "And don't tell me what you think I want or need to hear, but what *you* want."

I place a hand on my stomach and look down, and in that moment, my world shifts. It's as if everything I have been through, everything *we* have gone through, has led to this very moment. It shouldn't be possible, but somehow, it is, and he's right–it feels like the most natural thing in the world.

I know my answer. I want this, more than I ever would have imagined. "I want it," I look up. "I want this baby."

He places a hand on my stomach and smiles. "Me too."

"Yeah?" I smile wider.

"Yes," he kisses my forehead and wraps his arms around me, tucking my head under his chin. "More than anything."

I bury my face into the warmth of his chest and allow myself this perfect moment. A moment where it's just him, and me, and now our baby.

"I want to keep this between us for now," I say when we both grow quiet. "With everything that's about to happen, we need to stay focused. Is that okay?"

"Angel," he tightens his hold. "Whatever you want, whatever you need, your wish is my command. Now, and always. But man, when we do tell everyone about your wings and this, it will be like a bomb dropped."

"Not a bomb," I laugh awkwardly. "Just a baby."

"Our baby," he adds.

I look up and find his blue eyes shining brightly back at me. "Are we crazy?"

"Absolutely," he places his hand again on my stomach.

"You know," I put mine on top of it, "they say things happen in three. First my wings, now this. What do you think is next?"

"Forever," he says simply, then kisses me, and I can't help but think he's right. Forever is what's next. It's the third thing. I can feel it.

21
DIABLO

Dante stares at the wall of monitors in front of us, one hand splayed over his chin, the other tucked under the opposite arm. His focus is intense as he looks from one screen to the next; jaw firm, eyes set.

In front of him, legion members communicate with their teams on the ground, while Hayden and a group in the room across the hall monitor local news and communities for chatter. So far, everything is going according to plan.

With every team in different time zones, some are operating in broad daylight, while others do so under the cover of night. It doesn't faze any of them. Every team is focused and moves in perfect coordination.

"Talk to me brother," Dante says, looking at the screen monitoring Vinny and Lila's team.

While ten of the teams have one of the legion members sitting in front of us as their point, Dante and I assigned ourselves to the one with his best friend and mine.

Given their artifact's location, pulling off the heist in the evening was critical. This required them to leave before sunrise, well before the others, and arrive under the cover of night. Their boots hit the ground a couple of hours ago, and we've been waiting for them to check in from their target location.

"Six thousand," Vinny's barrel of a voice comes through the comms piece Dante, and I are both wearing in our ears. "Do any of the other teams have that many items to search through?"

Dante swings his head in my direction and grins. "Hey brother, you wanted the hardest." I can hear the relief in his response. It matches my own.

"Yeah, yeah," the earpiece crackles. "All I'm saying is don't bust my balls. We just got here."

Dante was right. Vinny did ask for the hardest artifact to extract, but he would have been assigned it anyway. Just as Dante would have assigned us to Vinny and Lila's team for comms and monitoring.

Vinny and Lila were family and we wanted to be with them every step of the way. Not to mention, Dante and Vinny had worked together for so long, they knew exactly how the other thought–an innate ability that would come in handy while operating in a country that was notoriously hard to get in and out of.

"Charming the officials here takes a special kind of skill," Vinny says with smooth confidence. "We may have been a tad late getting in, but we're on time now."

"Well, we owe someone at the airport a favor," Dante turns his attention back to the screen. "Apparently, the guy at customs took a lot of heat for waving you through."

"Yeah well, that's his problem, not mine," Vinny quips. "I have other things to worry about. Like finding a needle in a haystack."

The complex that housed the infamous Terracotta Army at the tomb of Qin Shi Huang in central China, spanned more than four acres. With three pits, larger than football fields, there were thousands of life-sized soldiers, chariots, and horses in each.

We knew the warrior we were looking for was in vault one, thanks to some information David's contact at the Vatican had found in their records. It would help narrow the search, but Vinny was right, a smaller haystack was still a haystack.

"In any case," Dante exhales. "No fucking around. In and out."

"We're fine, mom," Vinny shoots back. "Man, where's your sense of humor."

My chest twinges with the reference, and I put my hand on my stomach. As if triggered by the word as well, Dante looks over at me, with an expression on his face I can't quite make out.

For the next fifteen minutes we watch the monitors anxiously, while waiting for an update from Vinny and Lila.

"Shit, it's hot as fuck in here," he says finally.

"It's going to be hotter in about ten minutes, when those wall-mounted detectors in the pit come back online," Dante shoots back.

"Good thing we'll be out by then."

"What do you mean?"

"It means, you put my good luck charm and I on a mission together we're getting shit done," Vinny laughs. "We found it in the first five minutes."

"Why didn't you say anything?" Dante asks tersely.

"Wanted to make you sweat a bit." I can hear the smile in Vinny's response, and I can't help but crack a smile. Vinny is always the levity. Even when the shit hits the fan.

"You're an asshole," Dante barks, clearly on a short fuse.

"That I am," Vinny laughs again. "You know it, and like it."

"Yeah, yeah," Dante shakes his head. "Just wrap it up and get out of there."

"Yup, just getting warrior number three thousand and twenty-two secure in the pulley system and up he goes. There may even be time to canoodle a bit with my sweet tart and enjoy this hot, dark, sweaty spot."

"Vin," Dante warns.

"Dante," Lila cuts in. "Chill out. He's kidding. We're headed up to the roof now. We'll be back on comms when we're on our way to the airport."

"Sounds good," I reply, then tap my earpiece off.

I look at Dante who shakes his head and looks down as Hayden strides in. "Good news," he says with a cell phone in one hand, and a tablet in the other. "No chatter or media coverage of any kind."

"That is good news," I look at his cell phone. "Assume that includes local apps?"

"Come on," he grins. "Who are you talking to?"

I can't help but smile but Dante doesn't find his response funny. "Who do you think you're talking to?" He whips his head up and peers at Hayden. "She's your leader. Show some respect."

Hayden holds up the hand with his cell phone. "Hey, no offense intended."

"It's fine," I wave my hand to dismiss Dante's comment. "Keep me posted."

"Will do," Hayden nods, then turns and heads back to the war room.

Once he's gone, I turn my attention to the wall of monitors. Green lights show for half the teams, which means their artifacts are secure, every team member accounted for, and planes in the air. The others, I'm curious where things stand.

"What is the status for team one?" I ask Caro.

"They're on the tarmac," he says. "Weather in Tanzania threw them a bit of a curve ball at the last minute."

"Got it." I shift my attention to the monitor with Viper's

team. "And two?"

"They'll be at the airport in about five minutes," Azrael says. "The protest we were keeping an eye on grew and they had to reroute. Nothing to worry about, though."

I've not worked with him much but he's smart, and focused, and exactly the kind of level-head we need tonight.

"And the other two teams?" I turn to Harlan and Basel.

The two were twins and mirror images in every way, down to their tattoos. I'd learned how to tell them apart in the short time I'd known them, even though legion members that had known them since The War, could not.

They update me on their teams and when done, I take a breath. Everyone is fine. All plans are still on track.

"Have I ever told you how hot it is to see you lead?" Dante whispers in my ear without the comms piece.

"Yes," I lean back against the wall of his chest as he wraps an arm around me from behind. "In fact, I've heard you say it in the height of leading."

Knowing exactly what I mean, he growls, and leans his head into the crook of my neck, speaking lower than before. "How's the baby?"

"Everything is fine," I whisper. "But you need to relax. You nearly bit Vinny's head off."

"I know," he draws in a deep breath and kisses my shoulder.

I turn around to face him and find the same expression on his face that I saw earlier. "Hey," I search his eyes. "What's going on?"

"I just want these artifacts here already, so we can figure out what Luke is planning."

"I understand," I brush his cheek. "I'm just as anxious to figure out what Luke is up to as you are."

"I know you are," he pulls me close. "But my worry skyrocketed two days ago and now all I can think about is keeping you and the baby safe."

"Dante," I shake my head and lower my voice. "This is exactly why I didn't want to tell you until this was over. You need to focus on them right now. Not me and the baby. There will be plenty of time for that."

"Angel," he looks at me, eyes serious. "What do you think tonight has been about? I am focused on *them*, because their success and safety are how I'm going to protect the two of *you*."

"Team two is in the air," Azrael calls out.

"Great." I look at the monitors quickly in time to see the status for Viper's team turn green.

"I know whatever Luke is planning has to do with you," Dante continues when I turn back to him. "And the only way I can protect you both, is by getting those damn artifacts back here, and figuring this out so we can put an end to him once and for all."

I place my hand on Dante's cheek. I want so badly to ease his worry, but I know there is nothing I can say or do that will. I know, because for six months I worried about him, and there was nothing anyone could do to make me feel better.

I tip my head up and kiss him gently, then wrap my arms around him and hold tight. It's the best I can do right now because deep down, I'm just as worried as he is.

***

Once Vinny and Lila let us know they are on the plane and preparing for takeoff, I relieve the legion members monitoring the teams, as well as Hayden and the war room, and thank all of them for their excellent work.

After everyone is gone, I tap off my earpiece and make my way over to where Dante is sitting in the chair behind his desk.

"You did it." I run my hands down his chest and lean into his neck. "The plan worked."

"We did it," he grabs one of my hands and kisses it. "You're an amazing leader."

He tips his head up and I press my lips gently on his. It's soft and sweet at first and then grows deeper.

He turns the chair and pulls me into his lap, gripping my sides as his mouth gets hotter, then turns the chair back to face the monitors so we can keep an eye on the teams.

When our lips finally part, my lips are tingling and my body aches for his touch.

"Ever since you told me about the baby, I've been unable to think of anything but him or her," he brushes my hair back. Every muscle in his body is tight as he holds me close to his chest.

"Me too," I smile softly.

"I can't wait to see what they will look like. You, hopefully."

"No way," I shake my head. "I want to see your eyes and smile."

I finger the hair hitting his neck and place the other on his chest as our dreams for the future fill the space between us.

"You were right earlier. I was tense tonight, and not because of the heist. Something else has been on my mind." He runs his thumb along my chin as if contemplating what he's about to say.

"What is it?" I ask.

"Luke isn't the only one up to something. Heaven is, too."

I open my mouth to respond but he presses a finger to my lips and continues. "I know you're not ready to talk about this, but I have to because I can't shake this feeling...that they want you back."

"What?" I pull back, the idea is so ludicrous, I can't even believe he's said it. "They abandoned me and allowed me to be a pawn in Luke's game for thousands of years. Who cares what they want?"

"I do," he tightens his hold on me.

"Why?"

"Because what Heaven gives, it can also take away. And I swear angel if they took you or the baby—"

"The baby?" I ask icily.

"The stardust bullet may have made it possible for me to sire a child with you, but we both know only Heaven possesses the power of creation."

I'd been in control throughout the entire operation. Kept a level head and watched over the legion. But now that all but one team were in the air, I was able to let in the thoughts I'd been keeping aside all night.

The idea that both Luke and Heaven were in collusion and conspiring against me, was so unfathomable, the very idea made my blood boil. But to think they would bring our baby into it? I now understood the look in Dante's eyes earlier.

"Listen to me," I turn around and lay back against his chest so I can keep an eye on the monitors for Lila and Vinny. "They will never get their hands on me or the baby. I belong to you, and the baby belongs to us."

His body tenses as I place my hands on his thighs and scoot back, rocking my hips gently. I need to ease the burn in me. Feel something other than anger at the very thought of anyone taking from me ever again.

I take one of his hands and slide it under my leggings, moving it between my legs, while lacing my fingers through his other one.

"What are you doing?" he whispers in my ear.

I move his hand up and down, needing to feel his touch. "If they come for the legion, I will destroy them. If they come for my friends, I will crack their thrones. And if they come for you or the baby, I will reduce their kingdoms to dust."

"Fuck," he rasps, his quickly growing erection digging into my ass. "If you don't stop, I'm going to bend you over this desk."

I lick my lips and rock harder, heat building between us. "Promise?"

I press his hand down harder, brushing my clit with his finger. "Is the...door locked?" He asks, muscles in his chest constricting.

"Mm-hmm," I bite my lip.

He picks me up, kicks the chair back, and bends me over the desk, sliding one hand under my body to keep me from bearing the weight of his frame, while yanking my leggings and panties down with the other.

I kick them off my feet as the sound of his zipper makes my skin tingle, and when he nudges my entrance with the tip of his cock, my thighs burn with anticipation.

He eases into me, forehead pressed against my back, and when he is fully inside, pulls back and thrusts inside me again harder.

I dig my nails into the desk as he flicks his hips harder and harder with each thrust, hitting the spot deep inside that makes every nerve in me tingle.

"Who owns me?" I pant, wanting to hear his claim on me.

"I do," he groans while caressing my stomach with one

hand and gripping my hip with the other.

I look over my shoulder to watch him. The way he's fucking me, making me feel alive and powerful. "Say it again," I command.

"I own you," he growls, with so much heat and command, I feel the spark between my body and wings.

He crashes his mouth down on mine, and when our tongues meet, they curl and dance in a heated kiss.

"I belong to you," I bite his lip. "And our baby belongs to us. They cannot have either of us. Do you hear me?

He presses his forehead to mine as he thrusts up, over and over, our climax building. But just as we are both about to let go, static comes over the ear comms, and we both stop.

My pounding heart slams against my ribs as we remain still, both panting. "We're about to take off," Vinny says with a laugh. "So, yeah, we wanted you to know."

"Thanks man," Dante closes his eyes and swallows. "I...thought you already had."

"Not yet," he quips, way too casually for someone who just heard his friends nailing each other. I ease slightly, assuming this meant they hadn't. Then he adds, "I said takeoff. Not get off. Apparently, that was on your mind, though. PS...well done you two. That was hot."

My cheeks flush with heat and my eyes close; part of me mortified they'd heard. But the other part of me honestly, I didn't care. I'd existed for far too long with regrets. Played every day, every year, every century, cautious to a fault. Being with Dante made me feel alive in a way I never had before, and I would never feel ashamed for that. Ever.

"By the way," Vinny says good naturedly before Dante and I tap the earpieces off so we can finish what we started.

Dante presses his mouth to my shoulder, laughing softly

along with me. "Yeah," we reply in unison.

"You'll need to fill us in on when we became Uncle Vinny and Auntie Lila."

22
DANTE

When I make it downstairs the next morning, the study has been transformed. Overnight, examination tables have been set up, along with a suite of tools for safe handling of the artifacts. A few have already arrived, and more come in throughout the day, as each team lands and makes their way to the penthouse. When Vinny shows up later that afternoon, his team is the last to check-in.

"Always a bit of a mindfuck returning from Asia," he strolls into the study with a shit-eating grin on his face. "Going back in time to when you already were."

I try not to smile but it's hard given what he heard last night. I laugh and shake my head, as he makes his way over and we clasp forearms.

"Nice work yesterday, brother." I bring my shoulder to his and pat him on the back.

"Like stealing candy from a baby," he does the same. "Which, speaking of," he pulls back and looks at me, expectantly. I hold up my hand, make my way over to the door and close it, then turn back around. "Diablo is pregnant?" he asks, eyes wide.

"She is," I confirm with a smile.

"But how?" he shakes his head. "We took care of the whole siring thing a long time ago. Not to mention, how is it even possible for her to have a baby?"

"James believes the mortal DNA in my blood made it possible. As for her, I don't know man. Just like her wings, I have no clue how it's possible."

Vinny looks at me, clearly surprised. "When did you find out?"

"Right before you left. It showed up in the blood work James has been running. We didn't want to say anything and distract from the operation."

"Of course," Vinny nods with understanding. "Man," he shakes his head. "This is wild. How do you feel about it? I mean, it's huge news."

"Honestly," my smile widens. "I'm all in, brother."

"Yeah?" His smile meets my own.

"Yes," I shove a hand in my pocket. I meant what I said the day I found out. I wanted everything with her. And this baby, given the enormity of all we'd been through, felt like an incredible gift. "This happened, despite the odds. It's hard *not* to be excited."

"Man," he whistles. "This is next level mind-bending."

"Tell me about it," I agree. "Between her wings and this, I can't help but feel like something bigger is at play. What, however, I don't know, other than the obvious."

"Like the possibility she's still an angel?" he asks plainly.

The fact Vinny was thinking the same thing I had been, told me that my suspicion wasn't completely crazy.

"You know as well as I do, there is no way she could have her wings, or a baby, if something wasn't pulling the strings. And we both know what that something could be."

Vinny rubs his jaw, listening intently. "What does Diablo think?"

"She doesn't want to talk about it. The idea Heaven could be using her, is hard to process. But Vin, what if that's *exactly* what this is? What if all this is a game between Heaven and Luke, and she is at the center of it, or worse, the baby?"

"Brother," he grips my shoulder. "No one is touching her or your child. Between you, me, and the legion…they'd have to get through all of us, and that's not happening. Not to mention, I can only imagine how maternal instinct will impact the power of her wings."

Vinny had a point. Diablo's wings had reduced the soulless to ash for me. I could only imagine what they would be capable of for our child.

"Thanks man," I let out a relieved breath. I needed to hear that.

"Anytime. You know I have both of your backs, always. By the way," he looks around. "Where is the boss?"

"She wasn't feeling well this morning."

"Ah," he lifts a brow. "Morning sickness already?"

"Apparently so. I read it could start any time. Could also be her wings," I shrug. "Who knows how either will affect her."

"That's true," he agrees. "Is James keeping an eye on her?"

"He will be," I nod.

"Good. Does he know about her wings now, or no?"

"No. And do me a favor? Don't say anything about either to anyone. We want to keep this and her wings on the downlow for now. Just the four of us, except for him knowing about the baby, obviously."

"You got it." Vinny reaches for his phone, sends a text, then shoves it back in his pocket. "I just sent Lila a note, so she doesn't come waltzing in with balloons."

"Thanks," I laugh softly. It sounded like something she would do. "Where is Lila?"

"Still sleeping. My sexy kitten is exhausted this morning. She will get the text when she wakes up."

"Ah," I cross my arms. "Well, she deserves the rest. She

did well last night. You make a great team."

"We do, don't we?" he says with a cocky smile.

"Almost as good as my angel and I."

"Shit," Vinny shoves a hand in his pocket and we both laugh.

"Alright," I rub my hands together. "Where's the warrior?"

"He's in the foyer."

"Come on," I nod towards the door. "Let's get him in here."

After we've unpacked the warrior from the wooden crate and arranged him in the designated spot, Vinny and I step back, and look at each other.

"What time will David be here?" he asks.

"Any minute," I confirm.

The goal was to have everything set up and ready so David could see the efforts we took to preserve the artifacts. If there were hidden items or clues in them, we needed to know so we could start to put the pieces of this puzzle together. There just wasn't time for him to be upset over what we did. We needed to get to work.

"Well, this ought to be fun," Vinny turns back to the warrior.

"I was thinking the same thing," I smile. "In fact, I was wondering if I should wake up Diablo and have her come downstairs and tell him."

"Can't hurt," Vinny shoots back. I know he's both half joking, and half serious. David, like everyone else, melts in Diablo's presence.

When the elevator chimes, Vinny and I again look at one another. I draw in a deep breath and hold out my hand. "After you."

"Oh no man, this was your idea," he shakes his head. "After you."

"We came up with it at pretty much the same time," I laugh. "And he's your attendant. So, I repeat…after you."

Vinny rolls his eyes and goes out to greet David in the foyer. When the two walk back into the study moments later, David's eyes widen.

He looks around, speechless, and when he is finally able to say something, it's puffs of words, not complete sentences. "How did…is that…when did you…I don't believe…"

"Why don't you take a seat," I look to the couch. "We'll tell you everything."

He sits down stiffly, lips pressed together into a fine line, as Vinny and I tell him what we did, why, our plans to preserve every artifact's safety and integrity, and how we planned to return them.

David is quiet as he takes it all in, then looks from me to Vinny, speaking slowly, and deliberately. "No one touches any of the artifacts without gloves on, you will tell me as soon as every item is back where it belongs, and…" he holds up a hand, "I don't know about any of this. Is that understood?"

I must admit, I liked this side of David. He's got balls. "Understood," I nod and look at Vinny. "You?"

"Yup," he nods. "I'm good."

"Alright, well then," I get up from the couch. "Go work your magic, David."

He gets up cautiously, eyes darting from one artifact to another, then makes his way over to one of the tables at the far side of the study. Reaching for a pair of gloves, he slips them on and reaches for the artifact.

"Remarkable," he muses, while inspecting it carefully. It's

a spear and the rock of the blade is so worn down by time, it's hard to believe it once was sharp enough to cut.

He leans in to look at the hilt closely, then grabs a pair of long-handled tweezers on the table. Next thing I know, he's bringing them to a near microscopic hole, and removing what appears to be a piece of paper.

My brows shoot up as he extracts it slowly, and once it's out, see that it's a piece of parchment, about an inch long, rolled up no more than a millimeter wide.

"How did you see that?" I ask, incredulous. Vinny too, looks impressed as he comes over to us with a surprised look on his face.

"I have a finely trained eye for these matters," David says matter of fact. "Put on a pair of gloves so you can hold this."

I do as he asks and reach for the artifact as he hands it to me with one hand, while holding the tweezers in the other.

After I place it on the table, I make my way over to the examination station where David has carried the tweezers. Laying the parchment scroll down, he reaches for another pair, then very carefully uses the pincers of both, to unroll it.

"I don't believe it," he shakes his head. I look over David's shoulder and see a symbol in Enochian. "It's a letter," he looks up, answering the question he knows I'm about to ask. "An E."

"An E?" I repeat.

Vinny comes over and the two of us watch as David maneuvers the parchment between two slides, then places it under a microscope.

"Do you see anything else?" I ask.

David looks through the ocular lens and adjusts the magnification. "No," he shakes his head. "It's just a letter."

"What are you looking at?" Lila asks as she comes strolling

into the study.

"David found something," Vinny answers.

"Oh yeah?" She hurries over to where we are gathered around David and puts her hand on Vinny's back. "What did he find?"

"A letter written in Enochian," he looks up at her and winks. "An E."

"An E?" She repeats, smiling back at him.

"The parchment is old," David says while studying the slide, adjusting the magnification of the lens. "We'll have to do some tests to determine composition, which can tell us age, approximately. But I'd have to say the paper and artifact are not from the same time."

"So, someone put it there?" I ask.

"Possibly," he straightens and turns to face us.

"Well, it couldn't have been Luke because he can't write or speak Enochian," Lila counters.

"She's right," I look down at the slide for a moment, then back up. "But why a letter? And is that what we're looking for in each?"

"Well, we found something in the first one we looked at, which means there is likely something in all of them," Vinny reasons. "X, or that sigil in this case, marks the spot. Only question is, what does the buried treasure mean?"

"You're right," David takes a deep breath, "which means we need to examine all of them, but we must be very careful while doing so."

"Yeah, yeah," Vinny waves. "I got that warrior here without breaking it. Think I can handle some old ass paper."

"It's not the same," David counters. "If it's parchment, it could be older than even we know. Temperature, sunlight, any factor, really, could compromise it, or possibly, destroy it altogether. In fact, if we do find something, we extract it with great care. Is that understood?"

"We got it, Indiana Jones," Vinny laughs. "Use extreme caution."

David's lip hitches up at the corner. Vinny had called him that for years and his use of it told me the two had become more comfortable with their sire-attendant relationship.

"Hey, Dante," Lila looks at me. "Can I talk to you for a minute?"

"Sure." I motion for her to follow me over to my desk. I'm pretty sure I know what she wants to talk about. With James sworn to secrecy, David doesn't know about the baby yet, but I don't want to risk it.

"Congratulations," she whispers once we're both out of earshot, while giving me a hug. "A baby? Man, that's crazy."

"Thank you," I smile and hug her back. "But you know to keep it between the four of us for now, right?"

"Yeah," she steps back. "I saw Vin's text. Where is she?"

"Resting. She wasn't feeling good this morning."

"Ah," Lila nods knowingly. "Already?"

"Could be the baby, or could be her wings," I whisper a bit softer. "Who knows. We don't exactly have any examples to learn from if you know what I mean."

There weren't any Fallen with wings or that had conceived. Only sired. Diablo is one-of-a-kind, which makes what she's going through new for all of us.

"You're right." Lila chews on the corner of her lip. "This has to be a lot for her. How about I plan a girl's day for her and me? We can watch movies and order take out, just like we used to."

"I think she'd like that." I shoot her a grateful nod. "Thank you."

"Of course," she smiles. "Anything for our girl."

"By the way," I change the topic and with it, return my voice to a more normal timbre. "Nice work yesterday."

"Well," she beams with the compliment. "I learned from the best."

"That you did. And about the whole comms thing…"

"What whole comms thing?" she asks coyly.

I laugh and throw my arm around her shoulder, both of us knowing damn well, what she heard. "Come on," I grin. "Let's go see what Doctor Jones is up to."

***

Just before dinner David heads home for the day. I am studying the box from Berlin when Diablo comes up behind me and wraps her arms around my waist.

I set the box down and turn to find her looking up at me. Color has returned to her face, and she's practically glowing.

"Wow," I brush the back of my hand against her cheek. "You look better."

"I feel better," she leans into it, eyes shining. "Are Vinny and Lila back yet?"

"They are," I smile, glad to see she's feeling better. "In fact, they just went downstairs to pick up dinner and the kitchen is making soup for you."

"Sounds good. I'm starving."

"Yeah?" I smile.

"Mm-hmm," she nods. "Pizza sounds great."

"Really?" Given how bad she felt earlier, the turnabout's both a surprise and a relief.

"Yes," she insists, laughing slightly. "Not an ounce of nausea."

"Well, that's good." I run my hands up and down her arms. "I'll have the kitchen hold on the soup and pizza it is."

She looks around the study, taking in the artifacts. "They're all here," she says with wonder. "I can't believe it."

"They are," I take a deep breath. "We pulled it off. And guess what…you were right. David found something already in one of the artifacts."

"The box?" She looks down to the object I was just holding.

"No. The spear."

"Really?" She looks back up.

"Yup. A letter… in Enochian."

"Enochian?" she says with as much surprise as my own when I first saw it. "Well then someone had to put it there, because Luke—"

"Can't speak or write it," I nod. "That's exactly what I said."

"What does David think?" she asks and then her face falls slightly. "Oh, wait…David. How did he take all of this?"

"Surprisingly, better than I thought. Once we told him everything he got right to work."

"Yeah?" Her face brightens again. "Well, that's good. I'm glad to hear."

"He thinks it's likely there are items in all the artifacts."

"I think he's right," she nods in agreement. "And we're going to find them and beat Luke at whatever game he's playing."

"I like the way that sounds." I run my thumb along her jaw, then lower my mouth to hers.

The sound of Vinny clearing his throat cuts off the kiss. We pull back and turn to find him and Lila in the doorway, pizza boxes in hand, heads shaking with a smile.

"Do we need to lay some ground rules?" he says good naturedly, while kicking the door closed. "You know, basics like making sure the door is closed and comms are off before getting hot and heavy?"

"Probably," Diablo and I say at the same time.

He tosses his head back and laughs and we do, too.

"We have pepperoni and cheese, and Greek gourmet," Lila points to the boxes as Vinny sets them down on the table in front of the couch. "What do you want?"

Diablo tries to reach for a plate, but they both hold up their hands, refusing to let her lift a finger. "Greek for me," she looks over her shoulder. "Dante?"

"I'll get it. You go on and eat," I encourage.

Lila puts a slice onto a plate and hands it to Diablo. She reaches for it and sits down on the couch, curling her legs underneath her. "I want to hear about China."

"Nope," Lila grabs a plate, puts a slice onto it, then sits down next to her. "Baby first, trip second."

"Okay," Diablo says after taking another bite. "What do you want to know?"

Vinny and I sit down next to one another in the chairs across from the couch, slices of pizza in hand.

"Everything," Lila wraps a long string of cheese around her finger. "I want to know absolutely everything."

We fill them in on the news and when we're done, they tell us about their trip. After the pizza is polished off and we settle into our usual comfort and banter, I can't help but feel as if everything is going to be okay. With this family I've found, anything is possible.

23
DANTE

Turns out, examining every artifact was harder than we thought. Some were so old, just handling them required laborious effort not to break them. While others seemed to lack any real spot where something could be hidden.

It took nearly a week to find two items in artifacts–both also letters on parchment, written in Enochian–and another week after that, to find two more. After two weeks, we'd found five letters–an A, H, N, O, and an E–and by that point assumed the remaining artifacts had letters in them as well.

Three weeks after the artifacts arrived, I'm about to throw the box from Berlin against the wall out of frustration, when Diablo grabs it from my hand and it springs open, revealing another folded piece of parchment and letter in Enochian, which David translates as an L.

Surprisingly, the box didn't wind up being the hardest to crack. That honor went to the warrior Vinny's team hauled all the way back from China. David looked so thoroughly that at one point, he believed the team brought back the wrong one. But after painstaking effort on all our parts, the last letter was finally discovered in a hole disguised to look like a tear duct.

Each letter was written on a large wipe board David brought into the study and analyzed six ways from Sunday. But so far, we've come up with nothing. All we had was a string of letters: LEONEYUAFAH.

"Do you think we should create a word cloud?" Lila asks David one morning.

She had taken great interest in his work and rushed to the study every morning to help. To her, he was a real-life Indian Jones, and she found his work thrilling.

"Maybe seeing all the possible words that can be created, will help connect the dots," she adds as David considers the idea.

"Lila, you're good at this," he agrees and wipes the board clean. "Have you ever thought about doing it full time?"

She grins at the suggestion. "What, like being a relic hunter?"

"That," he nods. "Or a student of antiquities. I think you'd find it interesting."

"I hadn't before, but after the heist and this," she nods to the wipe board, "I just might."

I look back down at the endless stack of paperwork in front of me as Lila starts to rattle off words, and David writes them down on the board.

With Vinny spending the day preparing the legion teams for operation artifact return, I decided to catch up on work for Primordial. I'd been so frustrated at my inability to decode what the letters meant–my prowess at finding contract loopholes apparently not helpful in this situation–and decided focusing on something else for a bit would be a good idea.

"Wow," Lila clicks her tongue when I hear the squeak of the pen on the wipe board stop. "That's a lot of words."

The two roll their chairs closer to the board, as if proximity will suddenly make the answer obvious, and start to point out connections. I'm just about to finish the stack of paperwork in front of me, when Diablo strolls in.

"Morning," she comes over to the desk and stands next to my chair. I wrap my arm around the back of her thigh, and she kisses the top of my head. "Busy?"

"Business stops for no one," I look up. Her cheeks are pink, and I can feel how cold she is through her leggings. "Cold out there today?"

She's been heading up to the roof every morning to work on her wings, and from what I've seen, she's mastering their strength and power.

"Yes," she rubs her hands together. "Summer appears to skip London."

"You should go sit by the fire and warm up a bit."

"That is exactly what I'm going to do." She taps the back of my chair then walks away. Watching her, I can't help but think back to the night of the heist; the memory of her bent over my desk, shooting heat through me.

She looks at the words David and Lila have come up with, while holding her hands out in front of the roaring flames. "Smart," she nods to the wipe board.

"It was Lila's idea," David pushes his glasses up. "An excellent one at that."

Diablo shoots her friend a winning smile as she sinks down onto the couch. "You've got a knack for this."

Lila tosses her a blanket, which Diablo pulls over her lap. "Thanks D."

Both Lila and Vinny had gone into protective mode since finding out about the baby. But their attentiveness pales in comparison to Lillian's. Once she learned about the baby, I saw firsthand just how much she adored my angel.

While we hadn't planned to tell anyone aside from Vinny and Lila for a while, Lillian guessed. One night, while Diablo lay sleeping with her head in my lap as I listened to music, Lillian casually mentioned the importance of rest in the first trimester. When I looked up at her in shock, she simply smiled and said, 'women know these things, attendant or not.'

Of course, once Lillian knew, we had to tell Wills and JJ. But while we still hadn't told David, we planned to in the next few days. It was only a matter of time before one of us slipped and said something in front of him. Not to mention, Diablo was starting to show and with all of us spending so much time together, it would be hard to miss.

"Do those letters mean anything to you?" David looks over at Diablo as she studies the board.

"Yeah," she fingers the blanket. "It means Luke sent us on a wild goose chase, while he makes plans for something else. Just like Lila said."

"Don't worry angel," I push back from the desk and stand up, stretching my arms overhead. "We're going to figure this out, and when we do, he'll pay."

The reassurance is for me, as much as it is, her. I, too, am growing impatient. I want to be done with this phase and start the next one. But these letters that appear to have no meaning are making me more than a little anxious.

"Will he?" Diablo asks stonily, her voice lowering an octave. "He split Heaven in two and was he punished? No. He was cast out of Heaven and made a kingdom on Earth."

David watches Diablo with curious eyes. He's never seen her frustrated and I can tell it troubles him. But not me. We were bound for five thousand years, and I've seen every one of her emotions.

"Tomorrow," David looks from Diablo to me. "I'm going to run a query through the archives at Trinity, Bodleian, and Beinecke. Those libraries have some of the oldest books and manuscripts in the world. If there is something to be found around the Enochian symbols or this combination of letters, it's likely in one of the three."

"Sounds like a good idea," I shove a hand in my pocket.

"I'd like to try the Vatican Library," he covers his mouth with one hand, considering the idea. "My contact has been invaluable, but he does not have access and requesting permission could raise flags."

"I agree. We stay away from the Vatican." I turn to Diablo and the look of defeat in her eyes makes my chest hurt. "What do you say we take a walk, angel?" I hold out my hand. "I've been cooped up in here all morning and could use a stretch."

At Diablo's last appointment with James, we learned her hCG levels continue to chart higher than a mortal's, which can result in mood swings and energy changes. Clearly, she's experiencing the first of the two at the moment.

"Sure," she exhales and places her hand in mine, and pushes up from the couch.

"See you two later," Lila waves as we make our way out of the study and down the hall.

When we reach the garden and push through the glass doors, Diablo takes a deep breath. It is her favorite space in all the penthouse, and I know she is at ease here.

"Angel, what's wrong?" I watch as she reaches out to touch the giant leaf of a banana plant.

She turns to me, pensive. "There's something I can't stop thinking about."

"What's that?" I ask, curious what's troubling her.

"When I wanted to save you, Heaven turned me down. But, when Luke wanted his freedom, he was granted it. I was motivated by love, and he was motivated by greed, and yet, he won, and I lost."

"Well," I consider the question. "I can't believe I'm saying this, but he didn't win entirely. He did lose his wings."

"But on Earth he gained power," she counters. "You can't tell me with all he's done and allowed to do, he doesn't have more power than he had in Heaven."

She's right. Everything she said is true. Luke built a kingdom while the rest of us were punished. She, more than anyone.

I make my way over to her and rub my hands up and down her arms and kiss her forehead. "We're going to figure this out and stop him once and for all."

She chews the corner of her lip and nods, but I can see there's more on her mind.

"Hey," I tip her chin up gently. "Talk to me. What are you thinking?"

She looks up at me, eyes full of melancholy. "Why would they abandon me all this time, but leave my wings? And the baby," she puts a hand on her stomach. "What's Heaven's motivation for giving me such a gift?"

The way she's looking at me makes me want to burn both Luke's kingdom and Heaven for whatever it is they are up to. I want so much for her to be at peace. She's suffered enough. And yet, her question is the same one I, too, have been asking.

"Do you remember when you taught me how to play chess?" she asks when we've both grown quiet.

"Sure," I smile softly at the memory. "I'm surprised you do though, considering how angry you were with me in those days."

"I was never angry with you," she sighs. "I was angry at Luke, and what he'd turned you into. I didn't realize at the time, the daemon you had become, and the angel you once were, I loved, irrevocably."

It never gets old hearing her confess the truth of her heart. Especially when she was unable to do so for thousands of years.

Warmth spreads through my chest and I want to carry her

upstairs and hide for the day, doing everything and anything I can to make her smile.

"What about chess?" I smile, wanting to do or say whatever she needed me to.

"I remember you telling me that the queen was the most powerful piece. Do you remember that?"

"I do," I nod. "She is."

"Well, I'm tired of Luke winning. I don't want to be a pawn in whatever game he's playing with Heaven. I want to be the most powerful piece."

I search her eyes, wondering if I need to state the obvious. The legion, her wings, and now our baby…all were possible because that is exactly what she was. A queen.

"Angel," I cup her face in my hands, stroking her cheek gently with my thumb. "You already are."

I want her to know just how powerful she is. What the legion's loyalty truly means. But I don't know how. Yet, as I stare into her eyes and see them change from dark to light, something tells me maybe I won't have to. Somewhere, deep down, she knows.

"Tomorrow, we will tell everyone about my wings and the baby," she says decidedly. "No more secrets. The legion needs to know what we fight for, and what I am asking them to fight for, as well."

Her determination ignites a fire in me. She's right. The legion needs to know what she is capable of and the future for which we are fighting.

"And Heaven?" I ask.

"If they are watching, if what's happening to me is part of their doing, then they need to see what they've created."

"Okay," I reach for her hand and pull it to my chest. "I am behind you one hundred percent."

"No, my love," she places her hand on top of it. "You will be beside me. Next to every queen, is her king."

24
DANTE

The moment Diablo shows the legion her wings and tells them about the baby, it's so quiet you can hear a pin drop. More than two hundred Fallen angels fall silent in a way they never have before.

She looks at me and I know she's waiting for someone to say something. Then finally, one does. Viper, ever loyal, comes forward, takes a knee, then lowers her head-just like she did that day in Eden.

"I know it," she looks up at Diablo in reverence, then stands and turns, facing the legion.

Hayden is the next to take a knee, and then Caro and the twins. One by one, legion members bend their knees, until each has sworn their loyalty to our daughter.

When we break for training, the energy in the air crackles. It's as if Diablo has breathed new life into our existence by reminding the legion who they were and always would be, no matter how many millennia passed. In being led by an angel, they were no longer Fallen, but something else entirely.

Vinny and I head to the back room to do a circuit of weights, while Diablo and Viper head to the other side of the gym to train.

When I'm done with my workout, I grab a bottle of water and make my way back into the gym. My eyes find Diablo immediately, wings on display, and I'm filled with pride and possession. But then I see Viper point a gun at her, and all I'm feeling drains from my body, and I'm hit with a profound feeling of déjà vu.

Everything around me freezes, including my very heartbeat, as Viper fires a bullet, and it screams towards Diablo. Just before it reaches her, she dips a shoulder and it hits her wings, and falls to the floor.

Air rushes into my lungs and everything around me starts moving again, as Diablo looks at Viper with a triumphant smile on her face.

"What the fuck, Viper!" I yell, fists clenched at my sides.

She whips her head in my direction and lowers the gun. "Did you see that?" she points excitedly. "Her wings are like steel. Nothing penetrates."

"Yes, I saw, which is why I am going to say it again. What, the fuck! You shot her."

"I shoot everyone," Viper puts a hand on her hip. "I am the Master of Arms. It's my job in case you forgot."

"Dante, it's fine," Diablo crosses the mat, wings tucked behind her. "We've been testing it, and—

"You what?" I seethe. If this is how they tested her wings when I wasn't around for a few minutes, I could only imagine what they would do if I were gone for longer.

"First, it was a blank," Viper shakes her head. "I would never, in a million millennia, shoot her with a live bullet."

"Now wait," Diablo looks at Viper. "I don't want you to change how you're training me. Real rounds are important, to assess their speed and strength."

"Diablo," Viper shakes her head. "No. He'd have my head."

I listen to the two go back and forth as they debate the benefits of live rounds versus fake. Just when I'm about to lose my shit, I shout at everyone to get out. "Training's over!"

Diablo looks at the clock overhead. "We've still got a

couple of hours."

"I said, everyone out, now!" I yell again.

Viper looks from me to Diablo, then sets the gun down on the table of weapons next to her and whistles and claps her hands. "Yo, everyone, time to go."

The legion stops everything they're doing and one by one, makes their way to the door. Most of them look in Diablo's direction and wave, or nod, or place their hand over their heart and lower their head. She acknowledges each, even Vinny and Lila who salute her on the way out, until there is no one left but the three of us.

"Dante," Viper puts her hand on my shoulder. "I would never do anything to hurt her. None of us would. The sooner you realize this, the sooner we can teach her what she needs to know."

Viper nods at Diablo, who watches her leave, and once she's gone, turns to me, hands on her hips. "Before you say anything—"

"Stop." I hold up my hand, cutting her off.

"In case you didn't notice," she fans out her wings, "they're like steel. Perhaps even stronger."

"Please," I look at her, trying to make sense of what I'm feeling. It's intense but it's not anger. It's something different, and more powerful. "Just...stop."

"Dante," she takes a step towards me, and folds her wings into her back. "I have to train. I was the only one who could stop Luke in Eden and may be the only one who can again."

"No," I shake my head. "Not this time."

She crosses her arms and meets my eyes head on. "What do you mean?"

"You're done training."

"I'm what?" she asks, eyes flashing.

"This isn't up for discussion, Diablo." I hear the words and I hate that I've said them. My angel can't be tamed, and it's one of the things I love about her. But this is for her own good. For our baby's own good.

"In case you forgot," she says with a venom in her voice that I've never heard before, "you don't make the rules."

"You're right. I don't. But I do love you, and our child, and that should trump everything."

She inhales sharply and the fury in her eyes gives way to love. "It does," her voice softens immediately. "Of course, it does. But you can't ask me not to fight. Not now."

If anyone deserves their vengeance, it's Diablo. And I did promise her we'd do this together. But that was before the baby. Before I learned just how deeply I could love.

"We need to end him," she reaches for my hand. "Don't you see, as long as he exists, he will be a threat to us. To...her."

"I know, but—" I stop, realizing what she just said. "Wait, what did you just say?"

"I found out at my appointment this morning," her mouth pulls into a luminous smile. "James had a new test he wanted to run for chromosomal conditions, and he let the gender slip. I hope you're not—"

I pull her into my arms and cut her off, kissing her gently, yet fully. Before today, it was a baby. But now, it's a girl. And for the first time, I see the future clear as day–Diablo, me, and our daughter. My family.

"We're going to have a girl?" I ask when we pull apart.

I think of that tiny heart, growing next to the one I already love more than anything, and a part of me cracks. That feeling earlier was dread, and the threat Luke poses to the two I love most, fills me with a kind of fear I've never felt before.

She places my hand on her stomach and puts her other one over it, eyes searching mine. "I hope you're not mad I didn't say something earlier. I wanted to surprise you after training when it was just the two of us."

"No, I'm not mad," I shake my head. "How can I be mad? I'm going to have a daughter."

She looks down at our stacked hands and then back up; her smile filling the space between us with warmth and light.

"I never expected this. Not in all this existence. But as crazy as it sounds, I feel like my wings came back so I can protect her."

I look at Diablo and see my world. But now that world includes another. "I already worry about you, and you can take care of yourself. I can't even imagine what that worry will feel like when this baby is here, and she can't."

"You trust me to take care of myself?" Diablo's eyes flicker.

"Of course. Just because I want to, doesn't mean I don't think you can."

"That's one of the sexiest things you've ever said to me." She throws her arms around my neck and pulls me into another kiss.

I rub my hands up and down her back and laugh gently. "That turns you on, huh?"

She rubs her nose against mine. "Add it to the list."

She pulls back and cups my face in her hands, eyes searching mine. "This baby is going to have not only a mother who will fight for her, but a father, and a legion. Not to mention, an aunt and an uncle, and Wills and Lila and JJ. She is going to have so many that will support and protect her."

"And love." The confession is so heavy it presses down on my chest. "Because I do, angel. It's why I panicked when I saw

Viper pointing that gun at you. I didn't think it would be possible to feel more love than you make me feel, but I do. I love this child already, so much."

"I feel the same," she takes a deep breath. "Which is why I know you understand the lengths I will go to protect her. I will do everything in my power to make sure she doesn't have an existence where she is always looking over her shoulder. If I can make that happen, if *we* can, we must."

I know what Diablo is saying is true. But I can't tell it to my heart. Can't convince it that either of them will be okay.

"You have always been part of me, Dante. But now I feel your strength in her, too," she locks her eyes onto mine. "You, us, our love…it makes me stronger. I can do this," she insists. "I would never do anything that would put us or her at risk. That's why I know this is right. I can fight Luke and beat him."

"But I've seen what Luke is like when he is after something he wants," my throat constricts. Just the idea of Luke touching either Diablo or our child fills me with anger and fear. "I can't even think about what I'd do if he took either of you away from me."

"I know what desperation feels like," she says, looking at me with so much love and tenderness, it makes my chest ache. "I've felt it, twice. Both times I lost you was a pain unlike any other. So, trust me when I say I will do anything I can to protect this life that our love created and make sure we never feel that pain again."

I think about everything she's said, and Diablo is right. Our love made all this possible. Us. Our tenacity and strength and desire to be together. We were unstoppable. And the angel in my arms, stronger than even she knew.

"I have to tell you something," I reach for her hand. It was time she knew in her lie a power that could help keep her and our daughter safe. "Remember when David asked what happened to Hell since the legion swore their loyalty to you?"

"Yes," she nods slowly.

"Well...you do."

She looks at me confused, clearly not understanding what I'm saying. "What do you mean?"

"When we broke the contract and the legion swore its loyalty to you, their power deferred to you." I tighten my hold on her hand and continue. "Hell was created by a powerful energy–the light of all the Fallen–and that light now belongs to you."

"What?" she swallows and shakes her head. "What are you saying?"

"I'm saying you command the power of Hell, Diablo, and I think you should claim it to protect our daughter. Between it and your wings, there is nothing that could harm either of you."

"Dante," she closes her eyes and shakes her head furiously. "I can't be a queen of Hell. Not when I was, or maybe even still am, an angel."

It's the first time she's admitted what I'd long suspected, which tells me she suspects it, too.

"Hell doesn't have to be what it is," I brush her hair aside. "It's only ever been dark and desperate because that is what Luke wanted. But you can make it what *you* want it to be."

She looks at me, shock and disbelief clouding her beautiful face. "Why didn't you tell me this sooner?"

"I wasn't sure how. But now that you're determined to fight, I want you to have all the protection you can have."

"The souls he's taken...the blood he shed..." she says shakily. "Can I correct the darkness and suffering caused by his hand?"

"You cannot change what was," I lock my eyes on hers. "Only what will be."

She grows quiet while considering my answer. "Okay," she says finally. "If I can use that power to protect her, I will. How do I claim it?"

I hold her hand tight. "I'll help you."

I knew the lengths Diablo would go for me. It was the same as that which I would go for her. But for our daughter, I would help my angel harness the fires of Hell.

But before we claim an ancient power, we need answers. We need to know more about the letters from the artifacts in the vault, and what Luke wants with them.

25
DIABLO

The following day, Dante and I are about to head upstairs to change for the gym when David comes running through the elevator.

"Oh good! I'm glad you're here." He's out of breath and his eyes are wild with excitement. "I have something to show you."

"What is it?" I ask, curious why he's so worked up.

"Come," he waves while hurrying down the hall. "I found something."

Dante and I look at one another then follow him quickly to the study. When we enter, legion members are packing up the artifacts and double checking the connections to the monitors. Tomorrow, each of the teams will swap the real artifacts with the decoys. Dante and I will monitor from here like before and Hayden the war room, and when the sun comes up the next day, it will be like they were never gone.

"Could you excuse us for a minute?" Dante asks the members.

They stop what they're doing and make their way out of the study, smiling at me as they close the door behind them.

Once they're gone, David drops his leather briefcase on Dante's desk and removes a tablet. "I ran a query through the archives at The Royal College of Physicians. They have the largest collections of John Dee's work in the world. I figured if we're looking for Enochian, we should search the archives of the one who brought the language to the world."

According to Dee's accounts, many secrets had been dictated to him by the angels. While some considered his revelations to be the ravings of an eccentric scholar, there was no disputing he'd been in touch with our kind. Enochian *was* the language of the angels.

"I'm glad I did," David continues, while entering his password and tapping on the screen. "Because the query found this."

He hands me the tablet and I reach for it, looking down at the image he pulled up. It's a page written completely in Enochian, and scrawled across the top, symbols that look like those on the wipe board.

"What is it?" I look up.

"Before I reveal that, I have a confession." He looks from me to Dante. "I...made an error."

Dante looks at David as if he's never heard the word before. "A what?"

"I had a few of the letters wrong." David removes a folded-up piece of paper from his briefcase and hands it to Dante. "It's not LEONEYUAFAH," he points to a second row of letters. "It's LEONEWVAFAH."

"Okay," Dante studies the two rows of letters. "And?"

"In the Enochian alphabet, Y and W can be represented by the same symbol, and U and V the same. When I ran the queries with our original string of letters, it returned nothing. But then I remembered, two of the symbols could mean one of two possible letters. When I ran a new query with a different variation of those letters—one swapped out, then the other, then both—it returned that," he nods to the tablet.

"Hey brainiacs," Vinny strides in. "Someone called a Mensa meeting and leave me off the invite list?"

Vinny laughs at his own joke and Dante motions for him

to come over. "David found something."

"Oh yeah," Lila follows Vinny. "What did you find, Indy?"

"He's about to tell us." I look up.

She comes over and rests her chin on my shoulder, looking down at the tablet. "Hey, a few of the letters are different?" she points to the letters at the top of the page.

David explains to Lila what he just did to Dante and me, and when he's done, she reaches for the paper in Dante's hand with the two strings of letters and shakes her head.

"I knew something was off. No offense, Doctor Jones," she looks up and smiles. "But the other day, I kept thinking what a shame it was that two of the letters weren't different because if they were, you could create all kinds of words, especially one very important one." We all look at her and she shakes her head as if the answer is obvious. "Heaven, duh. See."

"Well shit," Vinny smiles and shakes his head. "Baby, you should do this for a living."

"She should," David agrees.

Preening with the compliment, Lila beams as I hand David back the tablet. "So, tell us, what does this say?"

David taps on the home icon, then pulls up a different app. When he finds what he's looking for, he hands the tablet back to me. "Here's what I have been able to translate so far."

There are a few words scrawled across the top of the page, while the rest is filled with lines and phrases. At a first glance, it appears to be nothing more than incoherent sentences.

"Why are these words circled?" Dante asks, pointing at the screen.

"Well," David looks from him to me. "The text is written in boustrophedon."

"Come again?" Vinny asks.

"A style of writing where alternate lines are reversed or written in mirror-style. It was used in many ancient civilizations and has also been used for secret communication throughout time. I think, that is what Dee was trying to do, because the circled words are those that are most like words we use today, but the rest of the text is puzzling."

"And the rest of the text?" I look up.

"It will take some time to figure out. The diction is unlike any I've seen before. I will need to consult a few languages to find commonalities and establish a nomenclature."

"What are the words?" Vinny asks the question I was about to ask.

"Kingdom and inherit," David stops and clears his throat. "And…Earth, and Hell, as well as Heaven in the title, which Lila pointed out."

I look up at Dante and his eyes widen. "What do you think it means?" he turns to David.

He looks at the four of us, and then rests his eyes on mine. "I think it is some kind of decree or law…from Heaven."

I swallow to ease the tightness in my throat. "Why do you think that?"

David crosses his arms and rubs his chin. "In all the text, those words are the only ones that are clear. They're sign posts. Words that are meant to guide and give meaning to the document."

"And you think it's some kind of law?" Vinny scoffs.

"Yes," David says deadpan. "I do. With the words Dee uses as signposts, it's hard not to."

"It would make sense," I second the idea. "If it is something Heaven communicated or wanted mankind to know, Luke would want it. The question now is, how does he know about it? And how does he know the artifacts would point to this text?"

"Well," David reaches into his briefcase again and pulls out what looks to be a pamphlet and hands it to us. "Funny you should say that."

Dante blows out a frustrated breath, grabs the trifold, and opens it. It is an invitation, with glossy images of the artifacts that fill this very room.

"In three weeks, The Vatican will hold the gala where they will feature artifacts from their prize project, the digital vault. I don't believe they were for show. They were bringing them to the Vatican to search for what we already found."

"Well, well, well," Vinny snickers. "Look who's behind the eight ball. I say we stuff them full of our own little messages and send *him* on a little goose chase."

I can't help but agree with Vinny. For the first time in what feels like a long time, we are finally one step ahead of Luke.

"So, what's next?" I ask, eager to get to the bottom of whatever Luke is up to.

David turns off his tablet and stuffs it back into his briefcase. "I am going to run my translation of that text through the archives and see if any of the lines resonate with other collections and get to work trying to make sense of the text. In the meantime, the artifacts go back as planned."

"And if Luke needs them for something else?" Dante asks.

Fear of losing our upper hand tells me to keep them. But the promise we made to David says they should be returned.

"We promised David they would go back, and they should. But we don't want to tip our hand. He doesn't know we have them. Let it stay that way."

"She's right," Dante places his hands on my shoulders. "As much as I'd like to leave that asshole a note to find, he can't know we've had them."

"Alright," Vinny claps his hands and turns to Lila. "Babe, get ready for terracotta tryst number two."

***

When we go to bed that night, I can't sleep. I keep tossing and turning, my mind racing a million miles a minute. As soon as I try to focus on one thought, another one comes to mind. When I've had enough of my sleeplessness, I get out of bed, wrap my robe around me and slide into my slippers, then head downstairs.

When I reach the foyer it's quiet. Not a security guard or legion member in sight. Even the delicate clap of Lillian's ballet flats on the marble is absent in the night.

After making myself a cup of tea and drinking it in the silence of the kitchen, I make my way back down the hall and continue to the garden. When I push through the glass doors, I'm greeted by the gentle trickle of water and immediately feel at ease. Dante created this space for me, and every time I'm here, I'm reminded of the lengths he would go for my happiness.

A cobblestone path wove through lush foliage and beautiful flower beds, and a small stream ran over shiny river rocks, meeting at a waterfall in the center that served as a life source for the space. It was my very own paradise, and I couldn't wait to share it with our daughter.

I make my way along the path, running my hands over the thick leaves, and come to a stop at the door on the far side of the garden that leads to my practice space on the roof. I open it and climb the stairs, and when I reach another door at the top, push through.

The area is massive, with a training pad on one side, and

an outdoor sitting section, with a firepit and topiary trees with lights wrapped around them, on the other.

When I began practicing, the space was empty. But as I gained control and didn't worry about damaging anything, I created a sitting area. I loved the garden, and it was my favorite space in the penthouse. But up here, I felt weightless, and one with the sky.

Closing the door gently behind me I make my way over to the loveseat and sit down, turning my face up to the night sky. It's cool, but not as cold as it has been, and a small crescent moon hangs against a blanket of stars that look close enough to touch.

I put a hand on my stomach and drink in the night, moved by its beauty. "One day sweet girl, I hope you find your moon. And when you do, if you have to fight for it, you fight with everything you've got. Don't ever back down, no matter what because that love will be worth everything."

I smile and look down at my stomach, thinking of the little girl whose heart is beating next to mine. I already love her so much, and to know Luke threatens the world I want for her, fills me with a protective fury.

"I believe someone asked me not long ago, why I was leaving our bed at night." I look over and see Dante in the doorway, smiling at me. "Is this your very own fight club, or a group for star gazers?"

The sight of him in loose fitting pajama bottoms and tight T-shirt, sends butterflies fluttering in my stomach. "How long have you been standing there?"

He comes over to where I'm sitting and sits down next to me, putting a hand on my thigh. "Not long."

I lace my hand through his and turn my attention back up to the sky. "I don't think I've ever been this close to the stars before."

"Now angel," he smirks, "we both know that's not true."

I smile, remembering the way they appeared as we looked down on them from Heaven. "I meant here, from Earth."

"Ah," he grins. "Right."

I lean my head on his shoulder and draw in a gentle breath. "What do you think about what David found today?"

"Honestly," he sighs. "I'm relieved everything with the artifacts wasn't a goose chase. But I'm anxious to know what it means."

"Me too," I admit, and lift my head. "Do you think it's possible all of this has nothing to do with us?"

"No," he shakes his head gently as his eyes search mine. "Luke thinks I took you from him and you took his legion and with it his power. He wants payback. But how that payback relates to what David found, I have no idea."

"Well, like I said before," I drop his hand and slide onto his lap. "You did not take what you already owned. And the legion is better off without him."

His eyes flash as I reach for the sash of my robe and untie it. "What are you doing angel?"

I let it fall from my shoulders and he runs a hand up my chest and wraps it around my neck. "Just, taking advantage of the quiet, and privacy."

"Well, you keep that up," he groans when I lean in and kiss his neck, "and we're going to give the stars a show."

"Then let's give them a show," I whisper dreamily.

He moves his other hand between my legs, while gripping the back of my neck tighter. "Like this?"

"Mm-hmm," I suck on his lower lip as he strokes the inside of my thigh, then dips a finger inside me.

"You really should put on pajamas when you walk around

the house late at night," he moans while thrumming me.

"What's the point?" My breath hitches and hips buck with his touch. "You're just going to take them off, anyways."

"True." He lowers his mouth to my breast as I rock against his hand.

"Shit." I hiss, as he grazes his teeth against the pebbled skin.

He looks up in surprise, mouth full of my breast. "Did that hurt?"

"My body is sensitive everywhere right now."

"Oh yeah," he shifts me from his lap and lays me down gently on the loveseat. "Then I guess we'll have to be careful."

"Not too careful," I grin as he lowers his body between my legs and kisses me softly.

I ran my hands through his hair and down his back, relishing his warmth. The sun will rise in the morning, bringing with it the light and what lies ahead. But right now, it's just him and me and the night sky above, and in this moment, it's all I need.

26
DANTE

It's been a couple of days since David found Dee's text and we're all on edge. The optimism we felt originally has been replaced by anxious anticipation as we wait for Luke to make a move.

Thanks to David's contact, we know the real artifacts were sent to the Vatican the day *after* Vinny and the legion teams returned them. It was close timing, but we still have the element of surprise on our side. To our knowledge, Luke never knew we had them. However, we didn't know if his examination of the artifacts had begun.

To stay focused, Diablo trains with the legion and practices using her wings, while Vinny and I come up with plans, scrap them, then make new ones. But none of it seems good enough. We need to do more. *I* need to do more.

I never wanted to care about anything other than destruction and desire, but Diablo changed me in ways I never would have imagined. This family we're creating means everything to me, and I'll do whatever it takes to protect it.

It was time to play the card I'd been holding onto for a rainy day. Only, this wasn't just a rainy day. It was a mother fucking monsoon.

While Diablo is in the gym with the others, I slip out and head down to the garage. When I get there, a dozen legion members are waiting. They are dressed like me in head to toe black and stand next to a motorcycle identical to mine.

I stride over to my bike and reach for my helmet, ready to

get this show on the road. "Everyone clear on the plan?"

"Clear," they answer in unison. If we were being watched by any of Luke's army, I didn't want to make it easy for them.

"If you think you're being tailed, do whatever you can to lose it. Is that understood?" All twelve heads nod, while holding their helmets tight. "Alright, let's go!"

I slide my helmet on and swing a leg over my bike, revving the engine a couple of times before speeding down the circular ramp. Once we hit the ground level, we spill onto the city streets, breaking off into different directions.

As I race to my destination, I think about everything Diablo and I have been through since Eden. It feels like a lifetime, not months, and given our relationship these past five millennia, that's saying a lot.

I heard what she said the other night on the roof, and I know how much she wants this baby. I do too and would make a deal with the devil himself to keep them safe. Only problem was he's currently preoccupied with being a duplicitous piece of shit, so that meant I'd have to make one with the next best thing–his wife.

When I first considered talking with Lilith, I thought I'd lost my mind. I never really understood her motives for befriending Diablo in Eden, and she'd proven countless times over the millennia that her loyalty was to herself. But the more I thought about it, the more I began to see it was our only option. No one knew Luke better than Lilith, and if there was anything that could help us, she'd be the one to know.

Only, she wouldn't offer up information freely. I'd have to bring something to the table.

After shooting a text to Minerva and letting her know I needed to talk to her mother, I received one back from an unknown number. It was Lilith, and after offering her a deal I knew she would not refuse, agreed to meet.

After navigating my way through the East End, I come to a stop outside a murky hole in the wall pub. I knew the place. It was a favorite of the nefarious and wasn't surprised Lilith chose it, or that she was in London for that matter. She had a habit of lurking around where she wasn't wanted or needed.

After removing my helmet, I tuck it under my arm and head inside. She is already here and hard to miss. Black fur, long red hair pulled into a bun, and perfume so strong, I could smell it from the door.

I cross the bar and make my way to the booth in the back and slide into the bench seat across from her.

"Well, hello," she smiles coolly, as I set my helmet down and unzip my jacket.

"Lilith," I nod. "It's been a while."

"Indeed," she taps a long red nail on the tabletop, while raking her eyes over me. "This century certainly suits you."

She slips out of her fur, revealing a red silk halter top, which dips low in the center, and a black pendant. Lilith's got the goods if you're into the type. But I wasn't, and never had been. She was more trouble than she was worth.

"You're looking well," I offer, knowing the nicety will get me one step closer to what I came here for.

"Well thank you, lover," she purrs.

I bristle at the name the legion had given me one particularly indulgent century. It had stuck for a thousand years, and I did not want it to come back. "Don't call me that."

"Oh, come now," she leans against the table, peering at me with infernal eyes. They were sky blue, with pupils black as night, and a red flicker in the center. "Chaste does not suit you, Dante. Your appetite has always been one of your more appealing qualities."

I sit back confidently, remembering why I'm here. "That's not who I am anymore."

"But who we were, is always a part of who we are," she tilts her head. "Is it not?"

I hated to admit it, but she was partially correct. I was insatiable, and still am. Only, my hunger is now, and forevermore, for Diablo.

"Well," I shrug. "You've got a point. Once you find the one that wants you for who you are, those old habits don't die hard, but instead, find their way home."

"Well, well, well," her eyes flash. "I didn't think it would be possible, but then again, love can tame even the greatest of beasts."

I stare at her and say nothing; the comment is exactly why I'm keeping my guard up. Lilith loved Luke. Between them existed an unbreakable, albeit fucked up connection. I'm still not sure this conversation is a good idea, but I'm already here, and at this point, willing to do anything.

"I can't say I'm surprised," she continues. "There is something about your angel that is hard not to like. Perhaps it's her innocence. Tell me..." she lowers her voice, and a wicked smile tugs at her lips. "Is she as sweet as she looks?"

I thrum my fingers against the table, answering her question with my own. "Are you ready to talk business?"

She tosses her head back and lets out a throaty laugh. "I always liked you," she points a long nail at me. "That is why I agreed to this meeting. You remind me of my beloved. So serious, and yet, sexy."

The hair on the back of my neck stands up. I am nothing like Luke. But getting into a battle of who I was and who I am now, is not why we're here.

"Now Lilith," I lean in. "We both know you're here

because I have something you want. So," I reach behind my back and remove the folder I'd tucked into my jeans and set it on the table in front of me. "Shall we?"

"As you wish," she sits back and watches me open it.

I remove a piece of paper and push it towards her. On it is the sigil from the images of the artifacts that led us to the letters. "What do you know about this?"

Right now, we were one step ahead of Luke and I wanted to keep it that way. If Lilith were working with him, or if he were somehow watching, I didn't want to ask about the letters we'd found. He could easily find someone that could read and speak Enochian, and then we'd be right back where we started.

The sigil, however, had been used to mark those images for a reason, and while it hadn't come up in any of David's searches, I had a feeling it meant something to Luke.

When she reaches for the paper and her eyes flicker in recognition, I know I'm correct. "You've seen it before," I say matter of fact.

She draws in a breath and sets the paper down. "It has been the bane of my existence for centuries. Not to mention, my beloved's obsession with it, is why every crime syndicate in the world is after our daughter."

Lilith had gone to great lengths to keep Minerva's parentage a secret, which told me she would do anything to keep her daughter safe.

The ace up my sleeve. The card I saved for a rainy day.... Just as Minerva wasn't honest about why she wanted the box all those decades earlier, I wasn't in Eden when I said we'd given her all the information we had.

In exchange for a meeting, I promised Lilith the address of every crime syndicate looking for Minerva. With it, she could eliminate her daughter's enemies for good. But I wouldn't give it to her yet. I needed to know more.

I tap on the paper, wanting to keep her focused. "Explain. How has been the bane of your existence?"

"My beloved believes that symbol is his destiny," she answers without reservation, which tells me Luke is neither listening, nor watching. "It's why he has done all that he has-the war, bedding me, even betrayal of his own daughter. It is also why the relationship between us is what it is, currently."

"What do you mean?" I shake my head. "Luke divided Heaven over free will."

"The war was a red herring," she laughs haughtily. "My beloved questioned Heaven's authority, long before the Fall, and believes that symbol is the key to the power he needs to challenge it."

It's clear Lilith is meeting with me because she has an ax to grind. Deciding to use it to my advantage, I press my finger down on the paper and continue. "You said it was his motivation for everything. How so?"

"My beloved believes there is an authority greater than that of Heaven, and when combined, creates a source of energy that rivals all others in the universe."

"What kind of energy?"

"The blood of man, spirit of Heaven, and fires of Hell," she says drolly. "That is why he wanted your angel. And, why I helped you in Eden."

"Helped me?" I reply tersely, her comment loaded with two statements, of which one, makes me angry to even think about. "How exactly did you help me?"

"I made sure the two of you were nudged in the right direction, so to speak."

"*That's* why you were spying on her?" I sit back,

incredulous.

"I wasn't *spying*," she emphasizes. "Only a fool could not see that you are destined for one another. I merely helped things along."

Lilith's eyes flash and I realize then, that the bartender may have bugged Diablo's place, but she was the one watching us that day in the library.

I move my head from side to side, trying to lessen the burn of that realization. "What exactly did you do, Lilith?"

"When Minerva told me Diablo had contacted her to find the contract that bound the Fallen, I asked her to hold off. I knew where my beloved kept it hidden, but had gotten to know your angel, and could see she had feelings for you that ran deeper than she would admit. I wondered if perhaps, this was the century you two finally found your way to one another. And if so, would it put a stop to his fascination with her."

I sit back and cross my arms, irritated by how well-informed Lilith had been of my relationship with Diablo. And, of her true intent in befriending my angel.

"When the bartender at *Saints* told me about your first meeting," she continues, "I knew I was right. And just in time, too," she waves a hand, dramatically. "My beloved had played his game well, but I was determined to beat him. So...I told Minerva to give Diablo the contract because I knew you wanted to break it to be together, not apart, and voilà. You're welcome, by the way."

I couldn't believe it. Without Lilith's interference, we might not have found the contract so quickly and Diablo would still be in Eden, under Luke's thumb, or worse, in his bed. She really did nudge us in the right direction.

"Why would you do that?" I ask, curious what would

make her betray the one she'd been loyal to for thousands of years. There had to be a bigger motive other than beating him at his own game.

"Minerva is my child," she says solemnly. "I would do anything for her. And when her father rejected her for not possessing the power he craved, he needed to know what that felt like-the burn of disappointment."

Her confession stuns me because even though its Lilith and lies are her forte, I know it's the truth. The very reason she is here is what drives me now. For the love of her daughter. My child is not even born yet, and I would do anything for her.

"I did my part," she continues. "I was mortal. But somehow, it was *my* fault he did not possess the spirit of Heaven. Perhaps my beloved should have checked the fine print when he started the war and lost his wings."

"That's why he sired Minerva? He thought she would possess the power that could challenge Heaven?"

Lilith doesn't respond. She simply looks at me, stoic-as if she has both said too much, and not enough-and that's when it hits me. Luke sired Minerva because he believed between him and Lilith, their child would have the power needed to challenge Heaven. But when she did not have it, he turned his attention to Diablo. *That's* why he wanted her.

"I don't know why he thought siring a child with Diablo would be successful. She fell, just like the rest of us, and neither of them are mortal. His need for her was pointless."

"No," Lilith says crisply. "But for a spell he can be, as you very well know. As for her wings, I think you and I both know they did not simply return. What Heaven takes away...it does not give back."

It takes a moment for her words to register, but once it

does, the pieces I'd been struggling to put together, slide eerily into place.

Diablo's wings…they are the spirit of Heaven. Which means if Luke wanted her to sire his child before they returned in Eden, she'd had them all this time, and he knew. And how I'd been able to sire a child with Diablo…it's how he planned to.

"Now," Lilith straightens when she sees I've finally realized what she could not say outright. "I gave you what you came here for, it's my turn."

There is so much more I need to know, but Lilith has said all she plans to. There is a fine line between love and hate, and no matter what Luke had done to her, she loved him, and would not cross a line from which she could not come back from.

I take a moment to clear my head, then fold up the paper, stuff it into my pocket, and hand her the folder. A deal is a deal. I need to honor it and then get back to the penthouse, quickly.

She reaches for it and pulls it to her, opening it slowly. "That list has the address of every crime syndicate looking for Minerva. She has the names, now you have the locations. Remove the locations, you wipe out the names."

Lilith stares at it for a moment, and the relief in her eyes is obvious as they light up in a way I've never seen before. "The moment I saw her, I loved her," she says softly. "And her father, too. She could do no wrong in his eyes, and her smile lit up the room."

Her words strike a chord, and a familiar twinge, tugs at my chest. It is that of adoration for my own child, whom I had not yet met, but already loved. Her smile would no doubt light up a room. She will be her mother's daughter. How could it not?

"But I cannot let her incessant need to please him be her undoing." Lilith's eyes again turn dark and her voice, cold. "I have to protect her, even if he will not."

I did not want to give Lilith any indication that I understood. She should remove the threat to her daughter. Even if that daughter was Minerva. "Then you should do what you need to do."

"Mmm," she nods, studying me for a moment. "Tell me Dante, what will you do?"

I zip up my jacket and reach for my helmet, preparing to leave. "About?"

"Knowing your child is in danger," she says pointedly. "What lengths will you go to protect your daughter?"

Her lips pull into a knowing smile and a chill shoots through me. There is no use in feigning ignorance. Her comment was clear.

"Just as my beloved has people on the inside of your community," she continues, "so too, do I in his. What he knows, I do."

The revelation stuns me. Luke knows Diablo is pregnant. Someone has been feeding him information. "Who?" I reply tersely. Whoever it was, I would rip their head from their shoulders.

"Oh Dante," she tsks. "You know I cannot tell you. There are things I will do, and then there are things I will not, for obvious reasons. But make no mistake," she says grimly. "He will do whatever it takes to achieve what he believes is his destiny. Even if it means destroying what you love most."

Son of a bitch! Luke didn't just want her back in Eden. He was still after her. And not to get back at me, but because he believes she is the key to his destiny.

I knew Luke would stop at nothing to get what he wanted. The fact he was willing to hurt his own child, meant he wouldn't hesitate to destroy mine if she's in his way. And if he wants Diablo to sire a child that he believes will give him the power to overthrow Heaven, our daughter was directly in his path.

The realization sends my heart slamming against my ribs and fills me with raw fury. "The fuck he will."

I don't wait for Lilith to respond. I push up from the booth and storm out of the bar. This changes everything.

27
DIABLO

I take a deep breath, filling my lungs with the lush smell of flora and soil, and fade into the garden's richness. When I'm here I lose track of time.

I don't know how long I've been here. Afternoon has given way to twilight, bathing the sky in magnificent shades of pink and orange, dusting the garden in a warm, soft glow. But when strong arms wrap around my waist, I'm pulled back to the present and I realize it's been hours.

"There you are," I lean back and close my eyes; the familiar scent of orange and spice surrounding me. "I was wondering when you'd be back. Did you take care of what you needed to?"

"I did," he says with tired breath, pulling me closer.

Detecting the fatigue in his response, I turn around and see the weight in his voice, matches that in his eyes. "What's wrong?"

"We need to talk."

"Is everything okay?"

"No," he shakes his head. "Not even close."

I cup his face in my hands and he closes his eyes and presses his forehead to mine. "What is it?" I ask, growing more concerned.

He hesitates for a moment, then takes a deep breath before answering. "I met with Lilith."

"You what?" I drop my hands and step back as his eyes fly open and find mine.

Lilith…Luke's duplicitous paramour. She'd played her own game with me in Eden, which even now, I didn't know its purpose, and because of this, her very name drew ire.

"Why would you go see her?" I cross my arms angrily.

"No one knows Luke better than she does," Dante explains. "And I had to know if she knew anything about the vault or Dee's text."

"And did she?" I ask, eyes narrowing.

"Yes," he nods sharply. "More than I thought she would."

"Well, what did she say?"

"She'd seen the sigil before."

"And Dee's text?"

"I didn't show her or reveal anything about the artifacts. I didn't want to tip our hand should she be working with Luke."

"Smart," I bite out.

"I've known her for a long time, angel. I know the games she can play. I wasn't going to give her anything that may somehow make its way to him and give him an advantage. I would never do that."

"I know," I soften slightly and draw in a pensive breath. "I just…don't trust her."

"I don't either. But she had something I needed, and I had something she needed."

I lift a brow, not liking anyone needing anything from Dante. "And that was?"

"I gave her a list of the crime syndicates after Minerva. And it worked," he adds when I open my mouth to interject. "She sang like a canary. Or a crow," his lip hitches up slightly.

"Well, out with it," I wave for him to continue, ignoring the joke. "What did she know?"

He hesitates for a moment, as his eyes search mine. "Do

you want the bad news, or the bad news first?"

"No good news?"

"No angel," his smile fades. "It's Luke. It's always bad."

"Well then, bad news."

He closes the space between us and puts a hand on my stomach. "She knows about the baby, and Luke does, too."

I clutch his hand and a shiver runs down my spine. "How?" I ask, voice faltering.

He looks at me, eyes cold. "Someone told him."

"What do you mean, someone told him? Are they working together?"

"They're not working together," Dante answers crisply. "Someone has been feeding him information. And Lilith has a spy on his team, who in turn tells her everything."

"What?" I seethe, my wings shooting straight up. "Who would do that? Who would tell him about the baby?"

"I don't know. I've been wracking my brain, trying to figure it out."

Heat shoots from my back to my wings, radiating through every plume. Someone I know and trust had betrayed not only us, but our daughter.

"She's innocent," I grip his arm. "This isn't her war."

"Angel," he takes a deep breath. "This may not be her war, but she is very much involved."

My nails dig into his skin as my body shakes with rage. "No!" I clap my wings once in anger and the leaves in the garden twist and bend with the force. It's a tenth of what they're capable of, yet powerful enough to bend the trees to the point their trunks creak under the strain. "Whoever betrayed us and put her in harm's way will pay."

"Trust me," he puts his hands on my shoulders. "I feel the same way."

I clench my fists, feeling a fierce kind of fury emanating through me. "I didn't think I would have to go to war like this, but Shield-maidens fought while they were pregnant, right?"

"What?" Dante shakes his head, and his hands fall away. "You're not getting anywhere near Luke or his army now."

"What?" I straighten. "But you agreed."

"Things are different, Diablo."

"How?"

"Because!" he shouts. "Luke still wants you. Only now he sees our child as being in his way!"

"She told you that?"

"Yes."

"And you believe her?"

"After what Lilith told me about the way he used and discarded Minerva," he looks at me, face serious. "Yes. I do. He thinks you're the key to his destiny."

"It doesn't matter what he thinks," I straighten my wings for emphasis, with a pop. "There's nothing he can do—"

"I said no!"

I snap my head back, staring at him in both anger and disbelief. "Did you just yell at me?"

"No," he holds up his hands. "I'm not yelling at you. I'm just…fuck!" He runs a hand through his hair and blows out a heated breath.

I reach for his hand and hold it tight. "First, if you ever raise your voice at me again, I will kick your ass." His eyes flash and lip twitches. "And second, I would never do anything that would put our daughter at risk. You know that, right?"

"Of course," he sighs. "But Diablo, Lilith was clear. Luke discarded his own daughter when she didn't live up to his expectations, and he won't hesitate to harm ours if she's in his way."

"Why would she be in the way?" I shake my head, not understanding. The way he's looking at me, I know whatever Lilith told him, has him angry and ready to go to war.

"Luke has been obsessed with Heaven's authority since before The Fall. He believes a power that combines the spirit of Heaven, fires of Hell, and blood of man will challenge it. He believes he could sire a child with that power, but when Minerva did not have it, he set his sights elsewhere."

"But the spirit of Heaven was in our wings. His were stripped when—" The thought stops abruptly as my mind races ahead. "My wings," I cover my mouth.

"And your claim on Hell," Dante holds up a second finger. "And when I was shot with stardust and it gave me mortal DNA," he holds up a third.

"No," I close my eyes, dread filling my veins.

"And now he knows you're pregnant, which means he knows that siring a child with that combination is possible and he wants his own."

"But he's not mortal," I protest, angry tears filling my eyes.

"That's why he was testing the stardust on himself, and why he shot me."

"But why would that kind of power even exist? If Heaven is the universal authority, why would they allow a power that could challenge it?"

"I don't know," he admits. "But those very words were used in Dee's text, and I believe that's why Luke was looking for the artifacts. Somehow, he knew those specific items would lead him to it, so whatever is in that text, must be significant."

Everything Dante is saying makes sense. I chew on my nail nervously.

"We can't risk it, Diablo," he watches me with careful eyes. "I won't put you or our daughter's life at risk. We have to come up with a plan, and fast."

The tears I'd been holding back spill free. "He wants to take her from us. He wants to end her life before she even has a chance to live it."

"No," Dante pulls me to his chest and wraps his arms around me. "That's not going to happen. He's not getting his hands on either of you."

"How are we going to stop him?" I clutch his shirt, wanting to keep our daughter where she is right now. Safe between us.

"We beat him at his game before he even has a chance to play it."

"Then we need to tell Vinny and Lila," I look up. "They can help us figure out what to do."

"Agree," he swipes a thumb under one of my eyes and then the other.

Before we make our way to the door, he holds my chin with his thumb and forefinger. "You are my light angel. No matter the darkness. I won't let anything hurt my girls. Do you hear me?"

I nod and grab the back of his neck and pull him into a quick kiss, then we hurry out of the garden to find Vinny and Lila.

When we find them in the game room, they're laughing, shooting a round of pool. But when we come in, and they see the look on our faces, they stop and their smiles fade.

"Well," Vinny sets his pool stick down on the table. "That conversation went as well as expected."

"What conversation?" Lila asks.

"I went to see Lilith," Dante responds.

"You what?" Her eyes narrow.

"It's a good thing I did," he shoots back, "because she knew more than I anticipated."

"Oh yeah?" Vinny straightens. "What did she know?"

Dante grabs my hand and holds it tight. "Luke knows about the baby."

"He what?" He crosses his arms and flexes his biceps.

"Wait, there's more."

Dante fills Vinny in on all he learned from Lilith, and it takes a moment for him to process everything. But once he does, he picks up one of the balls on the table and hurls it at the couch.

"A spy!" he says angrily. "We have a fucking spy?"

"I know," Dante nods. "Can't believe it myself."

"But you've seen the way the legion is with Diablo and now, the baby," he shakes his head. "That loyalty can't be faked."

"I know," Dante exhales. "But it has to be true. There is no other way he could know."

"I know," he rubs his chin. "You're right. And an heir," he looks up at me. "One that can unseat Heaven's power?"

"Wild, right?" Dante lets go of my hand and makes his way to the wet bar in the corner. After pouring a drink he knocks it back and then pours another and a glass of water for me.

"You know everything Lilith told you she wanted you to know, right?" Vinny watches as Dante makes his way back over and hands me the glass. I wrap my hands around it, glad to have something to hold onto.

"I know," he nods and takes a sip of his drink. "But she told me all she did because she's pissed. Luke discarded their daughter like she was nothing. I may not have understood that once upon a time, but I sure as shit do now."

"How about what she didn't say?" Vinny asks while Dante stares into his drink.

"She didn't say anything about where Luke was, or if he knew we found the letters and translated them."

"Did she say how Luke knew Minerva wasn't the child he thought she would be?"

"She didn't harness the wind, throw thunderbolts, rain fire…I have no fucking idea." Dante lifts his drink and takes a sip. "But she did make one thing perfectly clear," he says after swallowing. "He wants to sire a child with Diablo, and he won't hesitate to remove any obstacle that is in his way."

Lila puts her hands on her hips. "Well, that's not going to happen. No one is touching a hair on my niece's head."

"He tossed his own child out on her ass," Dante says flippantly. "He would like nothing more than to take from me, the way I took from him."

"Only, you didn't take from him," I correct. "I was *never* his."

Dante looks over at me, the confirmation in his eyes, matching that of my declaration.

"Okay," Vinny reaches for one of the balls on the table. "I need a minute to think."

As he tosses it back and forth between his hands, Dante comes over to me, kisses my forehead, and squeezes my hand, reassuringly.

"So," Vinny says after a couple of minutes. "First problem, we have a mole, and we need to figure out who."

"Agree," Dante finishes his drink and sets the glass down on a side table.

"And second, he's coming for Diablo. We don't know when, or how, but he is."

Dante clenches his jaw so tight, his teeth gnash. "Yup," he bites out.

"I've got an idea," Vinny looks to Dante and then me. "To find the rat we have to set a trap, right?"

"Go on," Dante waves for him to continue.

"You're not going to like it," he sets the ball down and presses both hands onto the pool table.

Dante looks at me and I nod, then he turns back to Vinny. "Try us."

28
DIABLO

I look out the window at the blinking lights of the runway as Dante reaches for my hand and squeezes it. "This was the only way," he says with reassurance.

I turn to him and sigh, knowing he's right. But that didn't mean I liked it. "Any word? The meeting should be over by now."

"Vinny just sent me a text," he confirms.

"And?" I chew my cheek nervously. "How did it go?"

Dante rests his head against the back of the seat and takes a deep breath. "They took the news hard."

I couldn't imagine the weight in the room when Vinny told the legion we'd lost the baby. The idea hurt to even think about but to hear the words would've been unbearable.

"It feels wrong," I shake my head sadly.

"When we beat Luke and they see our child alive and well, they will understand. Trust me," he says with authority. "It was the only way."

I hated to admit it, but Dante and Vinny were right. The only way to keep our daughter safe was to root out the spy by telling a lie.

I close my eyes and rub my stomach. "I can't wait for the day when all this is behind us."

Dante puts a reassuring hand on top of mine and warmth passes between the two. "You and me both. Hopefully, we will know who the rat is soon."

"Dante's right," Viper flops down in the seat across from

him. "It's better this way. Now we can narrow down the list of suspects."

"Speaking of, I haven't ruled you out yet," he shoots her a smirk.

"Yes, you have," she kicks him with the toe of her boot. "Diablo trusts me. It's why she asked me to come with you, and not bestie number one."

"Number one?" he arches a brow. "Am I to assume you are number two?"

"That's right," she reaches for a travel size bottle of vodka in the basket on the table next to us, and twists off the cap, downing it. "Where can I get another?" She looks up and down the Dante's private jet. "No hot number in high heels and a short skirt, passing out peanuts and whatever else I need?"

"You get it yourself," Dante reaches for his cell phone. "Low on radar means only necessary staff on the plane."

"Fine," she pushes up from her seat. "I'm going to go look in the back and see if I can find another bottle or two before takeoff. I'll be back."

"Can't wait," he grumbles as I smile softly and watch Viper make her way to the rear of the plane. "I can't believe you find her amusing."

"Are you kidding? She's the best." The past twenty-four hours had been intense. Between plotting and packing there hadn't been much to smile about and it felt good to at least do that.

"I don't know if she's the best," he pulls my hand to his lips and kisses it. "But she makes you smile and that's all I care about at the moment."

I reach up and put my hand on his cheek, then exhale and turn to the window. We haven't moved an inch. "We're in the same spot we were ten minutes ago."

Dante leans over and looks out. "Don't worry, angel. Paradise will be there waiting for us, whenever we get there."

When Vinny first suggested we go to Dante's place in Bali to lay low until the spy was identified, I groaned. I'd been on an island this entire existence and wasn't exactly thrilled with being sequestered to another one so soon. But as we packed our bags and prepared to leave, I started to warm to the idea.

Our history may have been long and complicated, but as a couple there were a lot of firsts Dante and I had yet to discover. There was a part of me that looked forward to it being just he and I for a bit, despite the danger that loomed.

From what he'd told me, the house was amazing. A beachfront villa with unobstructed views of the South Pacific, sounded like something right out of *Architectural Digest*. Come to find out, it had been.

He saw it a few years back and bought sight unseen. It had five bedrooms, a gourmet kitchen, decks, and covered terraces on every level, as well as a spa, plunge pool, and tropical gardens. Plus, no one knew about it but Vinny, which meant we'd be safe.

I turn back to him and try to think of this as nothing more than a vacation, rather than running and hiding. "Having you to myself for a bit sounds like paradise enough."

"Now that sounds like music to my ears. Just us," Dante's eyes smolder, "and you in a bikini every day. What's not to love?"

My cheeks warm at the thought of spending all day in bed and late-night swims in the ocean. "Won't you have to be on your best behavior since Viper will be with us?"

"She'll have plenty to keep her busy." He leans over the arm of the seat and kisses me; lips lingering on mine. "We won't even know she's there."

When it was decided only Vinny and Lila should know where Dante and I were headed, I pushed for Viper to be included. Surprisingly, Vinny and Dante agreed with little argument. With Vinny and Lila needed in London, we needed someone with us should anything come up and Viper was my first, and only choice. Dante may have been giving her a bad time earlier, but he trusted her. If he didn't, she wouldn't be here.

"Well, get an eyeful while you can," I laugh, "because soon, a bikini is the last thing you will want to see me in."

"Oh, come on Viper," returns with a handful of bottles and sits back down, this time in the seat across from me. "It's only a couple of months."

"Nine months is hardly a couple," I shake my head. "And have you seen how the human body changes during that time? Say what you want about mankind, but anyone that goes through pregnancy and childbirth is a hero, as far as I'm concerned."

"What are you talking about?" She twists off the cap to a miniature bottle of gin and takes a sip. "You have what, three months left? You'll be back in shape in no time."

"Three months?" Dante looks at Viper, confused.

"Sure," she nods, holding the bottle loosely in her hand. "Sam's baby mamma went from peeing on a stick to having a baby in like, four and a half months."

"What?" I straighten.

"That's how it is for all children of the Fallen," she nods.

"How do you know that?" Dante sits up straighter.

"How do you not?" she counters.

"Well," he considers the question, looking from me to Viper. "Once siring was off the table for me, I didn't pay attention to any of that."

"Okay," Viper slumps back in the seat and lets her knees fall to the side. "Well, I did, and the others tell me things because I'm the cool one."

He shoots her a dirty look. "Are you insinuating I'm not cool?"

"No," she shakes her head. "I'm saying it."

Dante's eyes narrow and she laughs. "Oh, come on...you've always been the serious one. I mean, you're the most successful of all the Fallen for a reason. The brooding daemon thing has worked for you. But I'm the fun one. Everyone knows this, which is why they tell me everything."

Dante rolls his eyes. He may be annoyed by the comment, but she hit the nail on the head. He had been brooding for thousands of years.

Viper on the other hand, was strong and confident and fun. Combined with striking good looks, mortals and Fallen alike, were drawn to her.

"Well, one thing you said is right," he grins begrudgingly. "I am the most successful."

"We know, we know," she groans.

"So, wait, V," I clear my throat, trying to steer the conversation back to the bomb she just dropped. "You're saying children of the Fallen are born in fewer months than mortals?"

"Yep," she nods.

"How many?" Dante presses.

"It's about half the time," she says simply.

"Well, shit," he sits back and looks at me.

I look at him, too stunned to speak. But the more I think about it, the more it makes sense. That's why my bloodwork showed me as farther along when James first told me the news, and how he was able to determine the baby's gender so early. It's also why my morning sickness started as soon as it did, and why my body seemed to be changing every day. I was around nine weeks now, so I was actually... eighteen months?

"So, our daughter could be here in only a few months?" I ask, voice lifting an octave. "And when she's six we'll have a pre-teen on our hands?"

"No," Viper sets the empty bottle in her hand down and reaches for another. "Once they're born, they age as if mortal, but their body stops aging physically at eighteen."

I grip the arms of the seat and stop breathing for a second but when Dante puts his hand on mine, the air rushes back into my lungs. "Hey, you, okay?"

I nod but have trouble finding my words. All this was a bit much to process.

"We have to tell Vinny before we take off," Dante reaches for his cell phone. "This changes a few things."

"And James," I swallow to ease the tightness in my throat. "He also needs to know. Maybe even Wills and Lillian, so they babyproof the penthouse while we're away instead of months from now."

"We can't," Dante shakes his head while sending a text to Vinny. "We agreed, only the five of us, and James, can know about the plan."

I close my eyes and look down as guilt slams into me. Of all those we were keeping in the dark, it was Lillian I hated lying to the most.

He reaches for my chin and tips my head up slowly. "I hate not telling them, too, but you know why we can't. They would never forgive themselves if something happened to you or the baby because of information they had."

Dante, Vinny, Viper…they'd been at this game a long time and knew how duplicity worked. But Wills and Lillian, while smart, and tough as nails, weren't as experienced in matters of treachery like the Fallen. They could so or do something to tip off the spy and then Luke would know what was going on.

"It's because I trust them with the most precious thing in the world to me, that I don't want them to know," Dante said when he first suggested who should and should not know where we were going. "Luke would only use their loyalty against them, and they wouldn't know, until it was too late."

Once Dante explained this to me, I understood. Still, like the lie, I didn't like it.

"He's right," Viper unscrews the cap on a new bottle in her hand. "You can't be too careful. Only James should know besides the five of us. But I'm sure he already suspects."

I look down at my stomach and Viper is right. My body was changing every day and James probably did suspect and was trying to figure out how to tell me.

"Now that we know the baby will be here earlier than expected, it speeds up the plan," Dante says while typing on his phone. "The sooner we know who's betraying us, the sooner we can finish Luke once and for all. I don't know about you, but I'd like to welcome our daughter into a world where he's not in it."

I liked the sound of that. An existence without Luke and his lies was the only outcome I would accept. There was no place for him in our forever.

The captain comes over the intercom and tells us we're the next in line to take off. Dante checks my seatbelt to make sure it's fastened before doing the same with his.

"Viper, could you make a list of all the children of the Fallen, and when they were born? I want to know who they are, and their ages."

"Sure," she leans her head back. "But if you want to know about Sam's daughter, you could just talk to him."

She watches me carefully as I wait for Dante to answer. "Maybe," he responds without looking up.

"Viper's right," I encourage. "You should talk to him."

Dante looks at me. "He took me away from you, in case you haven't forgotten."

"I haven't," I put my hand on his arm. "Bur forgiving and forgetting are two different things. And the legion is stronger when together, not apart."

The legion was a family. Sam may have not been part of it for long, but he was in the beginning, and that warranted at least a meeting to hear his side.

Dante looks at me, considering my comment. "I'll talk to him when this is over," he leans back. "Okay?"

"Good," Viper smiles. "And I'll work on that list when I wake up. We've got what, a seventeen-hour flight ahead of us? I've got time. Until then," she closes her eyes and flashes us a peace sign.

I'm quiet as the plane taxis to its spot at the end of the runaway. "What's wrong?" Dante asks noticing my silence.

A strange mix of excitement and nervous anticipation hits me. "You do realize, we're going to be parents much sooner than we expected, right?"

"I know," he smiles.

"Are you ready for that?"

"Ready to be a father?" he laughs. "No. Not in a million millennia. But what I'm ready for, and what I want, are two different things."

"What if it's too much for her?" I think about our existence and all we'd had to endure. "What if this world, our world, is too much?"

"It won't be," he says with certainty. "She will have us, and Vinny and Lila, and a whole extended family behind her. The legion will protect her, just as they do her mom."

I've never considered the strength of the community our child would be born into. And knowing there were other children out there, I wonder if perhaps they could be part of it, too? Perhaps she will be the beginning of something new.

"Trust me." He wraps his hand around mine and pulls it to his lips. "We got this."

I knew Dante wanted this. From the moment I told him about the baby he was all in. But I hadn't realized until this very moment, that he is already everything a father should be–strong, confident, and protective–and my love for him feels infinite.

"Oh!" I jump as a tiny flutter, moves my stomach.

"What?" He looks down, alarmed. "Everything okay?"

I place his hand on my stomach and hold it there for a moment until it happens again. "Is that…" he looks up.

"Yep," I laugh. "She must know we're talking about her."

"Wow, we can feel her already?" He looks up at me in wonder. "She's strong, like her mother."

"Don't forget her father," I add.

"If she takes after me in any way, the world is in trouble."

We both laugh as it happens again and when we look up and our eyes meet it hits me. Dante and my daughter are everything, and what we're doing is right. Her safety is worth every lie we must tell.

Before I know it, we're racing down the runway and climbing into the skies. It doesn't matter the game Luke is playing. Knowing who we were now playing for, there was no way in Hell that we would let him win.

29
DANTE

Diablo walks out of the bathroom and my jaw hits the floor. She's always been beautiful but seeing her pregnant with our child fills me with a consuming combination of possession and love. She's never looked more radiant and takes my breath away.

I rub my jaw as she crosses the room, sun-kissed skin, glowing. "If you only knew what I was thinking."

She closes the space between us and presses both hands to my chest and tips her head up, long hair spilling down her back. "Oh, I know, because I'm thinking it, too."

We've been here three weeks already, and in that time, her body has changed nearly every day. Thankfully, we learned what we did about the baby's gestation, or it would've been alarming to see her pregnancy advance so quickly in such a short amount of time.

I run my finger under her chin then lower my mouth to hers. Her kiss is sweet and warm, and I can't stop myself from sweeping her off her feet.

"What are you doing?" she laughs as I carry her to the bed.

"Shouldn't you be off your feet?" I nibble on her neck.

"Please," she laughs softly as I lay her down. "You know I feel stronger than ever."

She's right. I do know she doesn't need to rest. She's now twelve weeks along, which is twenty-four weeks for the baby, and what ailed her weeks ago, no longer does. Her nausea and fatigue have passed, and her energy is high.

Picking her up and laying her down so I can admire her was all me. While I never could keep my hands off her before, now, her body makes my mouth water. She looks particularly ravishing today in her white bikini and its barely there top with two white triangles stretched across fuller breasts, and floss-like bottoms, which sit low on rounder hips.

I lay my head on her thigh and she runs a hand through my hair, as an island breeze stirs the large banyan tree out back and fan whirls slowly overhead.

Another reason for her radiancy is Bali. She loves it here. It's different from Eden in every way and it only took her a few hours of being here, to see why it was the perfect escape.

The ocean stretches out endlessly, everywhere you look, and the smell of plumeria and spice clings to the air, and a smile as warm as the sunset lights up her face, all day, every day.

Despite whatever Luke is up to looming over us, this time together has been exactly what Diablo and I needed. We're more in sync than ever. Sleeping in, walks on the beach, dinner under the stars… I'd never known such peace. I could stay here like this forever and it would be more than enough.

"Can I tell you something?" she asks when we both grow quiet.

I look up and find my angel's questioning eyes on mine. "You can tell me anything,"

"I'm…worried."

"About?"

"Messing this up."

I smile and dismiss the idea. She is perfection and meant for greatness. "You could never mess this up. You are a queen."

She reaches out and runs a finger down my cheek. "I am

what I am because of you."

"Your destiny was written in the stars," I smile warmly. "I am just here for the ride."

"And what a ride it is," she smiles wickedly.

I don't have to think too hard to know what she means. I know exactly by the heat of her words and the look in her eyes.

"What's on your mind, angel?" I ask coyly, heat stirring in me.

"I want you," she purrs.

"You always want me," I laugh softly, and it's not a lie. While the human body experienced hormonal changes over the course of nine months during pregnancy, Diablo was experiencing them at double the rate and in half the time, and her sex drive was through the roof.

I'm not complaining. I'll make love to her every day, all day, for as long as she wants. And right now, there is no end in sight to her insatiability. It's the best side effect of pregnancy.

She bites her lip and looks at me, knowing well how the seemingly innocuous act stirs my need for her. "I can't help it if I know a good thing."

I press my lips to the soft skin of her hip and run my hand up the inside of her thigh. She lays her head back on the pillow and sighs melting under my touch. She was perfect before, but now…the things I want to do have no limits. I could devour her from head to toe for hours and still not get enough.

Pulling the ties on her bikini bottoms free, I peel the scant fabric away, then toss them over my shoulder and push up on the bed and do the same with the top. Her ample breasts spill free, and I bend down and pull one into my mouth and then the other, sucking each of her no-longer sensitive nipples for a moment, before trailing my lips down her body.

When I reach her stomach, I stop and hold her growing bump with both hands, kiss it gently, then continue making my way down between her legs, and push them open. She's already wet and wanting and when I run my tongue up the length of her warm entrance, the taste of her tickles my tongue. She's sweeter now, and gets aroused faster, and it's not long before she is moaning in pleasure as I flick my tongue against her clit.

We've had sex all different ways, in all kinds of positions–even tried some new ones on account of her growing stomach–but seeing her like this, spread out before me full of desire and trust, is one of my favorites. It makes me want to get up on my knees, throw her legs over my shoulder and bury my cock inside her. But instead, I give her what she wants.

Pushing up, I lay down on my back next to her, and when I reach out, she's already climbing onto my lap to take control. As she sinks down on me, my abs constrict with the sensation of her tight and wet around me, but once she adjusts herself so that she's fully seated, she starts to rock her hips back and forth and my body settles into its pleasure.

I know it's the most comfortable position for her right now, and a preference to be in control. But fuck, if I don't enjoy it, too–both the view and feeling her press her hands onto my chest so she can take me deeper and own me.

It isn't long before her breath starts to come out in short, quick puffs, and when I press my thumb to her clit, she detonates, letting out a cry of pleasure as she tips her head back and digs her nails into my skin. Feeling her clench and pulse around me, nearly makes me come, but I wait until she is fully sated, before getting my own release.

When both of our breathing has slowed back down and we're lying side by side, I can't help but shoot her a dazed grin. "How long will this side effect last you think?"

"Who knows," she says mischievously. "Maybe I'll hold onto it."

"Fuck," I blow out a charged breath and grab her chin with my thumb and forefinger and kiss her.

She laughs softly and curls her hand around the back of my neck and squeezes, as our skin connects, sending off a charge.

I stroke her cheek with my thumb as the kiss lingers, and then she grabs my hand and pulls it over her as she flips onto her side. Tucking one hand under her head, she sighs as I press my chest against her back. "Do you think Viper is okay?" she asks dreamily.

"I'm not really thinking of her at the moment," I smile. "But yes, she's fine."

Viper had made herself scarce since we stepped off the plane, but I knew she was keeping watch. Her devotion to Diablo was total, and because of this, so was my trust in her.

She checked in daily and was laying low, while managing to have a bit of a good time herself and was planning to stop by later to say hi in person.

"And back home?" Diablo takes a deep breath. "Is everything okay?"

"Everything's fine," I whisper.

Just as it was quiet here, so too, was it at home. Luke hadn't made a move, which meant one of two things: the spy wasn't on the legion, or the spy knew we were on to them. Either way, quiet wasn't good, but I was trying hard not to think about that.

"How about dinner on the deck tonight?" I suggest. "We should probably take in as many romantic dinners as we can now because when the baby comes, we'll be at her beck and call."

Diablo turns her head up and looks at me. "Lillia's assured me once the baby is here, she gets to watch her at least four nights a week. I'm sure we could get her to five."

"Really?" my brows shoot up. "Man, she really must adore you."

"She must," Diablo winks.

"Speaking of adoration," I remember the gift I was planning to surprise her with before she walked out of the bathroom in that bikini and made me lose all track of what I was doing. "Stay here. I'll be right back."

"Um," she looks down at her languid, naked body. "I don't think I'm going anywhere."

I hurry to the closet, rifle around in the closet for the package Lillian sent yesterday, and remove the black velvet box inside, and make my way back to the bedroom.

Diablo sits up as I reach for her robe at the end of the bed and hand it to her, while keeping my other hand behind my back.

She looks at me curiously, while sliding one arm into the sleeve of her robe, and then the other. "What are you doing?"

"I have something for you," I grin.

She returns my grin with her own. "You just gave me something."

"It's bigger than that."

She arches her brow. "Bigger?"

"Not that." I sit down on the edge of the bed and shake my head, laughing a bit, while pulling my hand out from behind my back.

She looks down at the black velvet box lying in the palm of my hand. "What's that?"

"I don't know," I shrug. "Guess you'll have to open it and see."

She looks up at me and I encourage her to take the box. When she reaches for it hesitantly, I nod for her to open it. She lifts the lid slowly, and when she sees the ring staring back at her, her eyes widen.

She's quiet as I take it out of the box, reach for her hand and slip it on her finger. It's a perfect fit and looks stunning. Giuran outdid himself.

Her hand starts to shake a bit and I hold it steady as her luminous eyes look up and find mine. "I could have bought you anything in the world, but I wanted something special. Something that fits who you were, and who we are. So," I draw in a breath, "I designed this. It was once a whole diamond, which was then hollowed out and made into a band. There is no beginning or end, just flawless and continuous, like us."

She looks up at me, eyes brimming with tears. "It's...too much."

"Too much?" I wipe at one that breaks free. "Angel, it's not enough for all you have given me. And it's just the beginning of all I plan to give you."

"Are you proposing?" she asks nervously.

"Proposals are for mortals," I smile. "And we are no mortals, Diablo. We are forever. Our connection, our bond, our promise...it's stronger than any marriage ever will be. This ring reflects how much I love you, and how much I will always love you. Speaking of," I get up and make my way over to the nightstand on my side of the bed and pull out the paperwork I had Wills draw up. "I had a trust created for you and the baby, to ensure you want for nothing should anything ever happen to me."

She shakes her head and looks at the black envelope in my hand as I sit back down next to her. "What?" she asks, slightly confused.

"If something were to ever happen to me, I wanted to make sure you and our daughter never wanted for anything. As owner of fifty percent of Primordial, the two of you will be set for eternity."

"But Vinny…" she shakes her head. "He's been with you since the beginning. He helped you build Primordial."

"As owner of the other fifty percent, he and Lila will want for nothing," I tuck a strand of hair behind her ear. It is just like Diablo to think of others. "He already knows and agrees with my decision."

She places a hand on the folder and closes her eyes. "I don't know what to say. Wait, no," she looks up and her eyes find mine. "I do. We will not need the trust. You are not ever leaving us."

"Angel, I don't ever plan to leave you," I place the flat of my hand against the side of her head. "But after what happened in Eden, I need to know both of my girls are protected." She places her hand over mine and my heart lurches. "This is part of my promise to love and spoil you, now, and until the end of time."

"You don't have to spoil me," her lip starts to quiver. "I only need this. You, me, and our daughter. That is all I need."

I put my other hand on her stomach and feel the same way. If everything were gone tomorrow–all the money, and luxuries, and power–it wouldn't matter. I'd still be the richest asshole on the planet because I would have her and our daughter.

As if hearing my very thoughts, the baby kicks and I look down and laugh. "Man," I shake my head. "She's full of fire today."

"Yup," Diablo laughs. "She is her father's daughter."

"And her mother's." I think about the little girl who will soon be the center of our universe. "Man, the world doesn't stand a chance."

"We don't stand a chance," Diablo puts a hand on top of mine. "She's already got us wrapped around her finger."

"Now that is just like her mom." I pull her to me and hold her close; the promise of forever wrapping around us.

As I look out the folding glass doors, drinking in the ocean and dreaming about the future, the horizon appears endless. Not a cloud in sight. But in the back of my mind, I can't help but think this is the calm before the storm.

30
DIABLO

When I wake the sky is a beautiful shade of pink and orange. It's not been long, a couple of hours maybe, but it feels like in the time I was asleep, the baby has grown again.

Her movements have gotten more pronounced-the flutters I began feeling weeks ago, turning into tiny kicks-and we are on opposite schedules. When I sleep, she is awake, and when I am awake, she is asleep. A tiny kick to my ribs is what woke me, but now she seems blissfully asleep.

A part of me wonders if it is a sign of things to come, her tiny kicks, a part of my daughter's tenacious and willful spirit. Without having to think hard, I smile and think yes, of course it is. She's our child, and Dante and I are anything but passive.

I smile and rub my stomach, anxious to meet this little girl that has stolen both of our hearts. "No matter what you throw at us little one, we're ready."

The ring Dante slipped on my finger earlier shines back at me and I move my hand so the facets of the diamond catch in the muted light. Even in the warm glow of twilight, it shines bright, and I know that's why Dante designed it as he did. He calls me his light, but he too, is mine. This ring is us, through and through.

I didn't need jewelry or expensive gifts to know Dante loved me. But something about the way it sits prominently on my finger, makes his promise of forever feel unbreakable. As if this ring can shatter anything that threatens our happy ending. If only I could use it to eliminate Luke from existence. Then forever wouldn't seem so far away. But until he is gone, it is a little further out of reach than I would like, and I have to remember to not let the daze of his incredible place, or these amazing weeks, let my resolve slip. We must be ready for anything.

After pulling the sash on my robe tight, I make my way out to the deck. Dante is sitting in one of the lounge chairs, a gentle twilight breeze rustling his hair. Even from behind his presence stirs longing in me and I fight the urge to crawl into his lap and have my way with him.

I'm sure he feels like a stud horse at this point, and the thought makes me laugh because well, it's Dante, and I know how much he loves sex. But a part of me enjoys my need for him. By wanting him morning, noon, and night, I'm satisfying a need I'd kept hidden for so long. Not to mention, erasing every sexual experience he had over the past five millennia, and filling it only with us.

I come up behind him and run both of my hands down his chest. "Hey beautiful," he tips his head up and smiles.

While here, Dante has opted for loose-fitting shirts, or no shirt at all. The thin linen button-up he has on today, makes it easy to feel every ridge of his chiseled chest.

I bury my head in his neck and draw in a deep breath, filling my lungs with him. "Hi."

He reaches up and places the palm of his hand on the back of my head and pulls me in closer. "Have a good nap?"

"Mm-hmm," I sigh. "Did you rest at all?"

"I just woke up a few minutes ago."

I kiss him softly and then straighten, coming around the side of his chair to ease down into the one next to him. "I would have slept a bit longer, had your daughter not woken me."

"Oh yeah?" He flashes me a smile. "Giving us hell, already?"

"Like you wouldn't believe," I rub my stomach. As I do, the last light of the sun catches my ring and casts prisms across his face.

He holds his hand up to block the refraction from hitting his eyes. "Maybe I should have thought twice about a diamond," he smiles. "Maybe have something else made that isn't so bright?"

"Don't you dare," I pull my hand to my chest. "I love it."

"Do you really?" he asks with more seriousness.

"Yes," I look down at it. "It's a little bigger than necessary, but it's perfect. I love it."

"Well, you do like big things," he wags his brows.

"Stop," I groan and lay back in the lounge and stretch my legs out.

"You weren't asking me to stop earlier. In fact, I do believe–"

I reach over and clap my hand over his mouth. He laughs and pulls my hand away and I can't help but laugh, too.

The gentle lull of the waves and light breeze come together to create a symphony that calms my spirit, and I find myself wondering for probably the dozenth time if staying here forever would be possible. London is home, but this island has stolen my heart; the time we've spent here together, unforgettable. Maybe we could spend half the year here, and half there.

"Can I get you anything?" Dante turns to me.

"No." I wiggle my toes and stretch. "This is perfect. What are you working on?" I nod at the notepad on his lap.

"Nothing," he pulls it closer. "Just something I'm working

on with JJ."

"Oh yeah?" I sit up slightly, curious if it's the project JJ mentioned in the kitchen that day. "Can I see?"

"Um, no, miss nosey."

"Come on," I laugh, sitting up a bit more to reach for it. When he pulls it away, I fall onto his lap.

"If you're going to stay there, I have something else you can do that's a hell of a lot more exciting than what's on this notebook," his voice smolders.

"If you're good," I reach for the notepad, "I'll spend as much time in your lap as you want."

"Promise?" he swallows.

I reach for the notepad and set it aside, then reach for the waistband of his shorts. Just as I am about to pull them down, Viper strolls up the backstairs.

"Oh, hey," she covers her eyes. "Catch you two at a bad time?"

"Yes," Dante and I say in unison.

"I can come back," she points over her shoulder.

"No," I sit up and flash her a smile. "We're kidding. It's good to see you."

I let go of his shorts and Dante adjusts the way he's sitting. "Speak for yourself."

I swat Dante's arm and get up from the lounge, giving Viper a hug. "It's been a few days."

"It has," she nods and tosses a package down on the side table.

"What's that?" Dante asks.

"Not sure," she shrugs. "It was waiting outside the front gate."

"Probably something from Lila," I reach for it and shake my head. Ever since she found out we were having a girl she'd been seeing pink. Between her and Lillian, our daughter was going to have more clothes in her closet than me by the time she was born.

"How is the little one?" Viper looks at my stomach. "Growing like a weed, I, see?"

"By the hour," I add. "If you hadn't told us about the rate in which Fallen children grow, I'd be seriously freaked out right now."

Viper's eyes drink in my robe covered stomach and widen. "No disputing it now. You're well and good, pregnant."

"She's never looked more beautiful," Dante winks.

"You're glowing," Viper agrees. "I'll give you that. Then again, angels always do."

Dante has always called me angel. I'd always secretly loved his term of endearment, but now, it held even greater meaning.

I still wasn't sure what to think of the idea I was still an angel but even I knew now it was hard to ignore. There was no way I could be pregnant with our daughter or have my wings, had Heaven not deigned it.

Still, I hadn't *really* thought about what it meant, or why. It was still too hard to wrap my head around. To know Heaven had not abandoned me, all this time, left me conflicted to say the least.

"I'm glad you're here," Dante says to Viper and reaches for the notepad.

"Oh yeah?" she grins. "Miss me already, big guy?"

"No," he shoots back without missing a beat, then gets up from where he's sitting. "I need a favor."

"I need you to take care of this." Dante rips off the top sheet of the notepad and hands it to Viper as I turn the package over in my hand. It's white, with the address label computer-printed and a red air mail sticker slapped on both sides.

"You got it," she reaches for it, and tucks it into the pack pocket of her shorts. "What else?"

"That's it for that specific...request," he says slyly. "Anything going on at home I should know about?"

"No," she shakes her head. "The legion is still sad, and Luke is still a dick," she smirks. Dante laughs once and she continues. "In all seriousness, it's super quiet. To be honest, I'm having a hard time seeing any of the legion as a spy. They are all still really bummed about the baby."

Dante draws in a deep breath and rubs his chin. "What about David? How is his work on Dee's text coming along?"

She leans back against the deck railing and rests both elbows on the handrail. "When I talked to him yesterday, he said it's like reading hieroglyphics written in sand, which were blown away by a storm."

"I take it that means it's difficult," Dante asks.

"Beyond," she confirms. "He's never seen anything like it before."

Dante leans against the railing next to Viper, staring in the opposite direction, across the water. "What about the artifacts?" he says after a moment. "Has his contact at the Vatican heard anything about whether Luke has looked into them?"

"Not a word," she crosses her arms.

Dante looks at me and I know what he's thinking. The longer it takes to find the spy, the closer we get to my due date.

Deciding to focus on something other than what's happening back home, I open the package and reach inside. There's a box, the color of a robin's egg, with a white satin ribbon tied around it, and a card attached.

I open the envelope and remove the card, knowing whatever my best friend has written will make me both laugh and cry. But the moment I see the words staring back at me, I drop the box.

When it hits the deck, Dante whips around and looks at me, confused at first, and then alarmed when he sees I'm frozen.

He rushes over, fast as lightning; brows pinched together in concern. "Diablo, what is it?"

I try to speak but my heart is pounding too hard to get the words out. Instead, I hold the card out to him.

He reaches for it and as he reads what it says, his eyes turn murderous. "Son of a bitch!"

Viper comes over and grabs the card, reading the message we both just read, aloud as Dante picks up the box and hurls it into the ocean.

```
I hear congratulations are still in order.
What a relief. I am glad to hear no harm
befell her.
Tell my daughter, daddy will see her soon.
```

The ground feels like it's liquefying under my feet as his words fill my veins with fire and ice.

"We're leaving," Dante reaches into his pocket and removes his cell phone.

"And go where, back to London?"

"Yes!" he shouts. "He knows the baby is fine, and that we're here. What's the point of staying?"

"But the spy. We need to know who it is?"

"Maybe this is a good thing. By returning home, I can root out the rat bastard myself."

"Dante," she holds up a hand. "You can't go accusing all the legion. That scar will last longer than you think."

"Well, do you have another way that doesn't involve being sitting ducks for Luke? We have seventeen-hours. Between us, I'm sure we will figure something out."

She looks at me and I start to shake. Luke has finally revealed his hand. He doesn't want me, or our daughter gone. He wants *her*. And the thought fills me first with dread, and then anger.

My wings shoot out from my back and before I know what is happening, I've clapped them once and then again, cracking the large banyan in half. It topples into the ocean and sends the waves pounding against the beach.

"Angel," Dante sticks his hand out. "Calm down."

"No!" I scream, hands clenched at my sides. "He wants our daughter! *My* daughter!"

Dante and Viper hold onto the handrail, as my wings flap again. They're not out of control, or even unbridled. I am controlling the strength of every clap and they're more powerful than ever before."

"Diablo," Viper looks up at me, eyes pleading. "He won't touch her. I promise you. None of us will let him near her. But you must calm down or you are going to create a tidal wave."

I look to the ocean and see the height of the waves picking up with each clap of my wings. She's right. If I clap with enough force, the waves will recede at such a velocity that when they return to land, it will be ten-fold.

I close my eyes and take a steadying breath, and when the howl around me dies down, my wings straighten.

Dante takes a deep breath and closes the space between us, clearly concerned. "Diablo, you need to breathe."

I nod and when I feel the baby kick, I close my eyes and put a hand to my stomach, folding my wings into my back.

One tear, followed by another, rolls down my cheek.

"He…can't …have her," I stammer, as heavy sobs bubble up in my chest and shake my shoulders.

"Angel," he cups my face in his hands. "He will not touch her. I promise you."

"If he takes her or hurts her in any way…"

Dante pulls me to his chest and tucks my head under his chin. "Could you call the pilot and tell him we'll be leaving tonight."

"Sure," she reaches for her phone and comes over to put a hand on my back.

Between her touch and Dante's, my breathing steadies, but the fear and anger are just as strong.

"He just started a fucking war," Dante says angrily, tightening his hold on me.

"Fuck yeah he did," Viper rubs my back.

Luke just made his biggest mistake. Last time when I came for him, he ran. This time, he would be wise to run again, because he threatened my daughter, and I wouldn't just send him running. I would hunt him down with the power of Heaven and Hell and reduce him *and* his kingdom to ash.

31
DANTE

We're on the plane waiting for takeoff and I'm ready to come out of my skin. If I knew where Luke was right now, I'd kill him with my bare hands. My daughter…he wants my daughter? Hell. Fucking. No.

"She's resting finally," Viper says as she sits down across from me.

"Good," I exhale and look over at Diablo. She's lying quietly on a divan-one hand cupping the bottom of her stomach, the other resting gently on top of it. Her wings are wrapped around her like a shield, and she looks serene.

It's the first time she's been quiet since Luke sent his sick little package. I don't think I'd ever seen her so angry before; her wings possessing the most incredible display of power I'd witnessed in them yet. I was blown away, nearly, and had Viper not been there to help calm her down, I think she would have gone after Luke herself, right then and there.

"How do you think he found out where you were?" Viper sits back in the seat and rests an ankle on the opposite knee.

"I don't know," I rub my jaw, trying to figure out the answer to that very question for the past couple of hours.

My first thought was Minerva. Perhaps she was trying to get back into her fathers' good graces and hacked our system. But I knew that couldn't be it. When Vinny said the new security was impenetrable, he meant it. He'd tested it against some of the world's best hackers-equal to or better than Minerva-and they'd all failed, deeming it frustratingly foolproof.

My next thought was perhaps, whomever it was, saw Vinny or Lila's phones and was able to figure out where we were from photos either Diablo or I sent. We'd been keeping them apprised of how things were going, Lila particularly anxious to see her best friend's growing stomach. It was a long shot, but I suppose it was possible.

"Well," Viper reaches for her phone. "I was careful. And we know I'm not the rat."

"I know," I exhale. Viper's loyalty went into overdrive the moment she saw how upset Diablo was, only now leaving her side because she was resting.

"But man, Dante," she leans in, "those wings are unbelievable. Did you see how big they appeared?"

Viper was right. When Diablo's wings stretched out, I'd never seen anything like it. Not when practicing. Not even in Heaven, when wings were a kind of bragging point, and angels did whatever they could to make them appear larger. It's like Diablo's wingspan grew when under threat to a width I didn't know was possible.

The pilot comes over the intercom and tells us we are ready for takeoff. Viper and I both fall silent as the jet fires up the engines, and then speed down the runway. Once we have climbed high into the sky and at our cruising altitude, Viper starts talking again.

"Maybe it's David, or James?" she suggests.

Admittedly, the thought had crossed my mind for a moment but where David was concerned, I quickly dismissed it. He'd been a good contact over the years and was now part of our community. He'd been working hard to figure out the mystery around Dee's text and had proven his loyalty, even when we went behind his back with the heist and did something we said we never would.

James on the other hand, was a wildcard. I didn't know him that well. Just because he was David's partner, didn't necessarily make him trustworthy. But just because he was serious, didn't make him not, either. He did have access to Diablo's health records, which meant he could have told anyone about the baby. But James being the spy seemed too obvious.

Shit! I wanted to figure this out before we landed so I knew what we were walking into. Maybe even divert our flight to the furthest place on the planet so Diablo and the baby were safe while I ended both the rat *and* Luke.

I still couldn't believe we had a spy. This was worse than being shot by Sam. At least then, he pointed the gun at my chest. But this was someone pointing it not only at my back, but my angel, and my daughter, and that was infinitely worse.

I look over at Diablo again and when I see her sleeping peacefully, draw in a deep breath and ease some of the tension in my shoulders. "I swear, Viper. I'm going to kill him. No more of this wait around bullshit."

"You know you can't do that," she shakes her head.

"I can do whatever I want. He made it clear he wants my daughter!" I shout-whisper. "That's a clear declaration of war."

"I know!" She shoots back. "But we have to be smart. This could be exactly what he wants. Draw you and the legion out, so she is vulnerable."

Damn it, I close my eyes. She's right. "When we get back, we need to stop messing around and get a plan together. No more waiting."

"Okay," she looks at Diablo. "But she won't be happy if you do something without her. You know that right?"

"I know," run a hand through my hair and blow out a frustrated breath. "But she will understand. She knows how important it is to protect the baby, at all costs. She can be mad at me for as long as she wants, as long as both she and our daughter are safe."

"At the same time," Viper smiles wickedly. "She could end him in seconds."

"Don't you think I know that?" I say matter of fact. "But it doesn't matter if her very breath set him on fire. There is no way in hell she's getting anywhere near Luke. None."

"I don't like it either," Viper agrees. "But she seems to be the only one that is capable of stopping him."

I knew this and part of me wondered if that was Heaven's plan all along. Use her as their weapon, not their pawn. But again, it brought me back to the same question—why. What was Heaven and Luke at war over, other than the Fall? I couldn't even think about that whole situation right now.

"Even the strongest armor has an Achilles heel, Viper. You know this better than anyone. And I'm not willing to find out what that is."

"You're right," she is the one to agree with me now. "Just, keep a cool head. Once we get back, we will figure this out."

I clench my fist and look out the window. Fuck a cool head. I wanted to explode. I'd never felt so helpless. No one knew what this felt like. Except…. Sam.

I pinch the skin at the bridge of my nose, trying to push away the thought, but it was no use. It was front and center; an immovable boulder that begged to be addressed.

Only Sam knew what it was like to have Luke after your child. Only he knew the lengths you would go as a parent, to get your child out of his clutches.

When Sam accepted Luke's gun, he was trying to protect

her by doing whatever was necessary to get her back. I'd have done the same. For my daughter and her mother, I'd do the unthinkable, just as he did.

"Viper," I swallow, the anger I'd held onto for so long starting to fade. "Call Sam. Tell him we'll do whatever it takes to find his daughter but that it's time for him to come back where he belongs. Tell him we need him. That *I* need him."

Viper doesn't say anything. She simply looks at me with confirmation. But when she kicks the toe of my shoe, I know she heard me-really heard me-and I don't have to say anything more. My anger isn't with Sam. It is with the one who was after both of our children. And I will do whatever it takes to make sure Luke doesn't get Sam's. Just as I hope he will do whatever it takes to protect mine.

***

When we finally arrive back at the penthouse nearly a day later, the three of us are exhausted. It's hard not to be, between anger, worry, and the long flight.

It's early morning when we walk through the door and the legion is waiting. Vinny has told them everything and there is no anger on their faces. Only relief. They all watch Diablo with reverence as she climbs the stairs to our room, and I know each of them would give their life for her. Not one of them is a spy. I feel that truth in my bones. Luke's contact is someone else.

Diablo and I fall tired into bed, while Viper takes one of the guest rooms in the other wing. She needs her rest, too, and I insist it's under our protection. With all she has done to protect Diablo, she is family now, and under my watch.

Two dozen legion members stand guard on each floor of

the penthouse as we sleep, while teams of two stand guard at every entry point in the building, and dozens scour the London streets, keeping an eye open for Luke and the soulless. Vinny also lowers the titanium security doors for added protection, with he and Wills keeping watch of every team member that comes and goes.

That night, after sleeping through the afternoon and well into the early evening, I'm rocked awake by a nightmare. In it, Luke has my daughter and he's holding her over the fire pit in his throne room. She's crying so hard, her little voice has grown hoarse, and Diablo lays lifeless at his feet. He's snuffed out her light and taken my daughter's as he strokes her cheek with his long bony fingers.

I feel broken, lost, and hollow. Luke has taken everything that matters from me, and there isn't anything I can do but stand there and watch. It's a feeling I haven't felt since the Fall–when the world was dark and my existence, bleak. Only, this time, Diablo isn't there to save me. I try to call out to her, but she won't respond.

When I shoot up in bed, I'm covered in sweat and my hands are curled into angry fists. After checking on Diablo to make sure she's okay, I shove the covers off me and reach for a pair of sweats at the end of the bed and put them on, then slip downstairs.

When I reach the foyer, I'm surprised to find the light in the study on and voices inside.

"Vin," I push open the door, finding he, Lila, Wills and Lillian in a heated conversation in front of the fire.

Vinny turns, clearly surprised to see me. "Hey brother. You, okay?"

"What's going on?" I look at the four of them, answering his question with my own. "I don't like the look on their faces or the tension in their shoulders."

"There's something we need to tell you. Why don't you come on over–"

"I'm fine here," I cup him off and cross my arms. "What is it?"

"Dante," Lila says gently, then stops. For the first time I can see she is at a loss for words.

"Oh, come on," I look at each of them. "Is it the spy, do we know who it is?"

"Well, yes," Vinny says matter of fact.

"Well then spit it out," I motion impatiently for him to continue. "What the fuck are you waiting for?"

"It's...not that easy," he says stoically.

"Look," I blow out a tense breath and point at the door. "My very reason for existing is upstairs right now, likely dreaming about losing our child to the monster who punished her for five thousand years. And I know that's what she's probably dreaming about, because it's the same nightmare I just had!"

"Dante," Vinny takes a step towards me, and I hold up my hand to stop him. "Not one of you knows what it feels like to have a lunatic after your fucking daughter!" My words are charged and my muscles tight. I'm breathing so hard my lungs struggle to keep up. "So, I'll ask one more time, if you know who the spy is, if you know who put my heart, and my child in danger, I suggest you tell me right…fucking…now!"

The four looks at one another, and when all eyes settle on Vinny, he takes a deep breath and turns to me. "JJ," he says sadly. "It was JJ."

My ears ring and the room starts to move around me as my heart stops beating for a moment, then thumps deep once in my chest. It's followed by another thump, and another, until it's pounding.

JJ…the one who saved us, has betrayed us? It can't be possible. "This has to be some kind of a mistake," I shake my head. He adores Diablo. Her very presence changed his existence. He would never hurt her, or me, or our daughter.

"No," Vinny looks at me, face more serious than I've ever seen. "It was JJ."

"It can't be. He would never…could never…."

"Even though we broke the contract," he cuts off my denial, "JJ was soulless. He was bound by his contract to Luke first." I step back, rocked by the words coming out of Vinny's mouth. "I thought when he became an attendant," he continues, "that his connection to Luke would be broken. And we all assumed when he was able to leave Eden and his health approved, that had happened. But apparently not. JJ is still connected to Luke, and like any soulless, what he sees, Luke does."

A surveillance system. That's what Diablo said Luke called the soulless. His eyes and ears are everywhere. And he has had eyes on us the entire time and we didn't even know.

I think about everything I've said to JJ over the past month…my excitement at becoming a father and my plans to make Diablo a partner at Primordial. I've shared with him so much and to think Luke has heard every word, infuriates me.

"Her house," I shake my head.

"What about it?" Vinny looks from me to Lila, confused.

"He's been working with me to pack up her house and bring it here. So that I can rebuild it for her. All her books, that library she is so proud of, everything, down to the floorboards."

"You what?" Lila looks at me with so much sympathy in her eyes, it makes my chest constrict.

"I didn't want everything she worked for to be lost, and he's the only one who knows how to get in and out of Eden without being seen. He's been helping me."

"And you've been in touch with him the whole time you were away?" Vinny asks carefully.

I sink down in a chair next to me, lowering my head, and gripping the sides of it. I did this. Me. I brought the devil to our door. To my girls.

I want to explode. I want to tear into something and make it bleed.

I shoot up from the couch and storm over to the wall system on the far side of the room–the one with the collection of music I've amassed over centuries–and start pulling albums off the shelf. One after the other, like they're nothing, until finally, I find what I'm looking for.

Berlioz's Symphonie fantastique, fourth movement. A haunting score I've seen performed many times, yet each time I listen, new layers unfold. It's dark and raucous, yet tender and light. A brilliant, nuanced piece that carries from ecstasy and despair, to obsession, and murder.

I put it on the turntable and close my eyes, putting my hand on the shelf, feeling the vibration of the music. Slowly, my maniacal thoughts begin to fade, and an airy calm settles over me.

When the piece ends, I turn and find four sets of eyes trained on me. Vinny, Wills and Lillian have seen me at my worst, but Lila has not, and the expression on her face is one of not fear but worry.

"Brother," Vinny approaches, sticking one hand on my shoulder and the other on my chest when he finally reaches me. "We will do whatever it takes to make this right. We will not let anything touch either of them."

"I know," I nod soberly. "But you know what," I look up at him. "Maybe this is a good thing. Now he knows the lengths I will go to protect what's mine. No," I correct. "To protect my family."

"Now you're talking," Vinny's eyes flash as he grips my shoulder. "So, what are we going to do about it?"

I look Vinny in the eye. "We talk to JJ and let Luke know we're coming. He wanted a war, he fucking got one."

32
DANTE

I storm down the hall and when I reach JJ's room, the door is open. He's sitting at the edge of the bed, head down, and his hands on his knees. But when he hears me, he stands up quickly.

I hold up my hand to stop him from speaking so I can ask the one and only question I have. "Did you know?"

"No," he closes the space between us. "I swear to you, Dante, I didn't know. She has always been your angel, but in a different way, Diablo has been mine, too. I would never hurt her. I would never hurt either of you or that child. I think of her as my own granddaughter already."

I study him with my arms crossed, and don't have to look hard to know the truth. I can see it written all over his face.

I exhale and I look down, nodding with relief that JJ was still who I'd always known him to be.

"I would never have agreed to become an attendant if I knew it came at a cost to her, or any of you," he puts a hand on his chest. "But now that it does, I need to leave. I can't stay here. I can't risk knowing or seeing anything that would put any of you in harm's way."

"It's a little late for that." The comment isn't meant to be fatalistic. It's the truth. "Whether it was you, or someone else, Luke would have found out. It was only a matter of time."

Vinny echoes my sentiment. "It would have been nice to not have the fucker breathing down our neck so soon, but you're off the hook, old man."

JJ places both hands over his ears. "I don't want to do any more damage. I'll pack—"

I reach for JJ's hands and pull them down slowly. "Open your eyes, old friend."

A smile pulls at my lips for the first time since Luke sent his little gift, as his eyes open carefully, and I lock mine on his and speak deliberately. "I know he can see and hear everything. I want him to. I want him to know his time is coming to an end. If he thinks for one minute, he is ever getting his hands on my daughter or Diablo, he has another thing coming. They're mine," I point at my chest. "Mine! So, you better get ready because I'm coming for you. And when I'm done, there will be nothing!"!"

I can see JJ is worried, but he doesn't need to be. Luke is the one who should be. He doesn't know what's about to hit him.

"Stay here," I put my hand on his shoulder. "You are not a prisoner, but I am asking you…please, do not leave this room. Is that understood?"

He nods plainly and looks at Vinny. "I'm…sorry."

Vinny holds his hands up. "It's not your fault."

"I just—"

"No more," I hold up my hand, then turn and walk out of the room.

Vinny follows on my heels. Once we are out of earshot, he turns to me and stops walking. "What are you going to do?"

"Are you in? No matter what?"

"Of course," he crosses his arms. "You know that."

"Call Draven."

Vinny's brows shoot up with the command. "You sure about that, brother?"

To draw out the devil, you needed to bargain with a beast,

and that is exactly what I was going to do. "I'm sure. Call him."

***

I meet Vinny in the foyer at sunrise and after briefing everyone on security while we're gone, including Viper who is under strict orders not to leave Diablo's side, we head out.

Two hours later, my black Aston Martin navigates the sweeping drive of a baroque estate in the English countryside. I've been here before, but to collect. This is the first time I've requested an audience.

When we finally come to a stop in front of a row of tall hedges that flank the mansion's entrance, two men in black suits walk up to the car and open both the driver and passenger side doors. Vinny and I place confident feet onto the stone driveway, and get out of the car in unison, adjusting the ends of our jacket sleeves once standing.

Vinny and I are dressed for the occasion. We're both wearing black tailored suits, cut to perfection, and dress shoes that reflect the early morning light. I'm wearing a green silk tie and the emerald cufflinks I wore the night I took Diablo to the opera. It reminds me who I am doing this for, just as Vinny's blush colored tie and matching cufflinks, remind him who he is. Until Luke is eliminated, none of us will be safe, and that includes his heart, too.

We make our way up the estate's massive steps, passing a row of guards on either side, each with a military grade gun in their hands, and comms in their ears. They stare straight ahead as we pass, neither interested nor curious why we are here-their focus instead, on protecting the man with whom we've come to see.

I keep my jaw tight and shoulders back as we reach the top and come to a stop in front of a set of wrought iron doors. A large dial in the center of one turns and a bar that runs across both pulls back, and then it swings open.

An oppressively tall man steps through, wearing a midnight blue suit and tie. His dark red hair is slicked down and gray eyes at ease, and he clearly commands the attention of every guard lining the stairs. They pull their feet together and grip their weapons tighter in unison; a coordinated effort that makes the man smile.

"Dante," he sticks out a hand as he makes his way over.

"Draven," I reach for it and shake it firmly. "It's good to see you."

If it were anyone else, I'd assume control of this greeting. But this was no one else. The man before me was an invaluable part of my network, with one of his own, and perhaps the only mortal I regarded with more than a modicum of respect.

Throughout history there were many men whose machinations matched those of Luke's. Ideologues and sycophants obsessed by money and power. But men like Draven played the game differently. He was a ghost in the shadows. Shadows that reached around the world.

While I considered him a part of my network, the way he worked was a favor for a price-and that price was usually paid for in blood. Normally, I'd laugh at any service that came with that kind of demand, but Draven was not just any man. He could make even the devil's life miserable because the simple truth was, he did not fear him. When you did not fear the devil, you were your own infernal beast.

"Tell me…" he claps me on the back. "How is business?"

"It's good," I say simply. "And you?"

"It is good," his lips pull into a thin smile.

Draven had made a comment or two in the past that suggested he suspected what Vinny, and I truly were. He was a man whose ancestry believed in daemons, but Draven had never pressed the matter.

"Vincenzo," he sticks a hand towards Vinny. "Good to see you."

Draven knows how much Vinny hates the name, but he's not afraid to use it–and Vinny always lets it slide because well, he knows how to play the game.

"Draven," he takes the man's hand and gives it a shake.

"Come," Draven turns. "Let's talk."

We make our way through the massive doors, and I look up at the fresco on the domed ceiling of the foyer. A remnant of the home's former owners, it has been restored and shines down from above, a focal point of the estate's opulence and grandeur.

As we make our way into his office, a little boy with dark hair and eyes identical to Draven's, runs into the room.

"Pappa!" he throws tiny arms around Draven's legs.

Draven bends down and speaks to the boy at eye level. "Declan," he smiles, the only sign of softness I've ever seen the man display. "Where is your mother?"

"She's still sleeping," the boy smiles and turns to me and Vinny.

"And Yaya?" Draven asks.

"Making breakfast," the little boy says while focusing his attention on me. He tilts his head and smiles, and my lip can't help but hitch up in response. "She wanted to know if you had eaten yet," he says after turning back to his father.

"Tell Yaya I am fine, but you should eat my boy."

The little boy cups a hand to his father's ear and whispers into it. "Is that right?" Draven pulls back and looks at me for a moment. "Well, I'll have to remember that. Now run along," he pats the boy on the cheek and stands.

The little boy runs off and Draven watches him. "Men like us, we are built of the same mold. We seek power, and control. But when it comes to the ones we love, we will do whatever is necessary to protect them."

I adjust my jacket and watch as he makes his way over to a large marble desk and sits down behind it.

We have seen his son and he has offered us a truth. I need to do the same. I unbutton my suit jacket and straighten my shoulders.

"I need your help protecting someone who means the world to me." Draven presses his fingertips together and looks at me with great interest as he leans back and waits for me to continue. "I am about to be a father. Only, someone wants to take her from me."

"A daughter?" Draven arches a brow.

"Yes," I nod. "She and her mother are my world, and I will do anything to keep them safe."

Draven looks to the door again and then smiles. It's the same as his son's but older, and wiser.

"What do you need?" he says as he turns back to me.

I reach into my suit jacket and pull out a photo and set it down on his desk. "I need him, neutralized."

Draven reaches for the photo and looks up. "A cardinal?"

"Cardinal Lucius Raphael Giancarlo," I nod with confirmation.

Draven taps a finger on the desk while rubbing his chin. "You do know that will be an act of war?"

"I do," I say crisply. "And it's one I'm willing to both start and finish."

Draven considers my answer then turns to Vinny. "And you, Vincenzo? What do you think of this?"

"His enemy is my enemy," he says simply.

"So, the wolves have come out to play, hmm?" Draven sits back and smiles, then spins his chair around and looks out a window, which overlooks the back of his property. "That is what they call you…wolves. But they are mistaken," he turns back around after a long pause. "You are not predators that hunt in the shadows. You are the shadows."

I hold Draven's stare, neither yielding nor confirming, and it's a move that commands admiration. "I will help you," he says finally, rapping a knuckle on his desk.

"And your price?" I ask.

"Nothing for now. Only, a favor in the future."

"A favor," I repeat.

Draven clasps his hands together, holding them tight. "My son likes you, and that is worth more than all the money in the world. When you become a parent, you will see that currency is more priceless than any." He pushes up from the desk and sticks out his hand. "Do we have a deal?"

Vinny and I stand up at the same time, and I take Draven's hand firmly in mine. "We have a deal."

"Call this number," he hands me a card. "Leave a message with whatever it is you need done and it will be done."

I don't have to look at the card. I know what's on it. A number. Nothing more, nothing less. It's the same card he's used for years.

"Gentlemen," he adjusts his tie and makes his way to the door. "A pleasure, as always."

Vinny and I exchange a glance and then watch as Draven walks to the door and disappears around the corner. Seconds later, a guard enters the room. Unlike the men outside who hold their weapons proudly, his gun is concealed in a holster at his side.

"This way," he sticks one hand out.

The guard escorts us out of the house and once Vinny and I are back in my car with the doors closed, he turns to me. "Are you prepared to owe him a favor?"

I reach for the seat belt and pull it across my chest. I know why Vinny is asking. A favor could hang over your head like the blade of a guillotine, coming down when you least expected it.

"I am," I start the car and the engine hums.

"What if when the time comes, it is something you are not willing to do?"

I put the car into drive and navigate away from the estate and back down the sweeping drive. "That's why I have you."

We both laugh and when his smile fades, he looks out the window and asks the question again. "I'm serious, man. What if it is something you are unwilling to do?"

"It won't be," I take a deep breath.

"How do you know that?"

"We understand each other."

"Oh yeah?" He turns to me as the trees lining the drive start whizzing by. "And what, pray tell, do you understand about Draven?"

I remember something I told Diablo back in Eden when we were trying to break the contract. "Word choice is important, and he was clear–it was a favor, not a price. And something tells me the favor will not be about something, but *someone*."

Vinny looks at me and it takes him a moment but then it dawns on him. "His son," he nods.

"If or when the time comes for him to ask me for that

favor, it will be because he has no other choice. And I will honor it because I know what it is like to be in that position. Besides, he's a cute kid. How big could a favor involving his son be?"

"Big bad wolf turning soft now?" Vinny laughs.

"Not soft." I shoot him a wry smile. "A father."

Vinny smiles at me and turns his attention forward. "Wolf," he laughs.

"I have to admit," I laugh. "It has a better ring to it than daemon, don't you think?"

"Hell yeah," Vinny sticks his fist out and I bump it.

As we make our way back to London, Vinny leaves a message at the number on the card with our orders. Tonight, the sun will set on Luke's kingdom for the last time. And when it rises, his reckoning will have begun.

33
DIABLO

Lila and I are coming down the stairs when Dante and Vinny exit the elevator. The minute I see them, I know something's changed. Their body language has shifted from tense, to confident, and the worry that's haunted Dante's eyes since we left Bali is gone. They both possess an authoritative countenance, and a powerful charge is in the air.

The moment Dante's eyes find mine, my stomach flips. We may be facing the biggest challenge of our existence, but he will always be my first and only love. His very presence, stirring warmth and butterflies.

"Where have you been?" I ask as he crosses the foyer, body moving with intent towards me.

"Putting an end to this shit once and for all." He reaches for my hand and pulls me into his arms. "How are you feeling?"

"Tired," I admit, breathing him in.

"Baby?" he asks, chest rumbling with the question.

"No," I look up. She's been quiet this morning. "I think we're both a bit jet lagged."

He kisses me softly and squeezes a bit tighter. "I can still smell the plumeria in your hair."

"As soon as she's born, I want to take her there." I close my eyes, channeling the sounds of Bali in my mind. The melody of birds outside our bedroom window in the morning, and the gentle island breeze stirring the leaves in the trees at night. "Fill her first days with its peace and beauty."

"We will," he kisses the top of my head. "We will give her the world and then some."

The dream of our future comforts my restless spirit. "Where did you two go this morning?" I ask for a second time.

He starts to answer but as if remembering something, he pulls back. "Where's Viper?" Dante asks, brows furrowed as he turns his head to look down the hall one way, and then the other.

"Cool your jets man," she says while coming down the hall, coffee in hand. "Just fueling up."

"Good," he lets out a relieved breath. "I need you in peak form from here on out. We're talking, Fall-level strength."

She looks from Dante to Vinny. "Seriously?"

"Very." Vinny confirms, while canoodling with Lila.

"Alright,' she takes a sip of coffee. "I'm going to need you two to fill me in on what's about to go down."

"We will," Dante turns his attention back to me. "We will fill everyone in shortly. But first, I need to talk to Diablo, alone."

"That's our cue to leave," Vinny hoists Lila over his shoulder. "How about we go and grab a bite to eat, sweetness? I didn't have breakfast before we left."

"Vin," she taps his shoulder as he reaches for the handrail on the stairs. "The kitchen is that way."

"I'm not talking about food." He grabs a handful of her butt cheek, and she yelps, then laughs.

Despite the heaviness of what looms over us, I can't help but smile as he hurries up the stairs, taking two at a time.

Vinny and Lila had their own kind of love that was full of fun and magic. I could not wait for our daughter to meet them, because I know she'll adore them as I do.

"Walk with me," Dante says once they've disappeared, sliding his hand in mine.

"Alright," I look up, drinking in his calm strength as warmth surges between our palms. "Where to?"

"How about the garden?" he suggests, as I wrap my free hand around his upper arm.

"Sounds perfect."

"We'll be back," he says over his shoulder to Viper as we make our way down the hall. "Can you tell everyone to meet in the gym in an hour?"

"Will do," she holds up her coffee in acknowledgement, then makes her way to the elevator.

Dante and I head to the garden and when we push through the doors, I look up and drink in the afternoon sky through the glass ceiling high above. It was good to be back in this space. I missed the simple beauty and stillness of Bali, but this space was special beyond words and always filled me with hope.

"Did you manage to get any sleep last night?" He reaches out and tucks a strand of hair behind my ear."

"Mm-hmm," I look down from the ceiling and turn my attention to him. The way the light falls across his skin warms his face, and he looks like a god. "But I had some unsettling dreams."

"Me too," he admits. "How's the baby?"

I grab his hand and put it on my stomach. "Better now that you're back. But it was a good thing you sent Lillian in with tea this morning to deliver the news you'd left, or she and I would have been kicking up a storm."

"I'm sorry I didn't wake you," he strokes my cheek lightly with his finger. "But time was of the essence. That's why I sent my secret weapon to deliver the message. I knew you could never be mad at her."

"Clever," I narrow my eyes. "So, did you get done what you needed to?"

"I did," he looks at our stacked hands resting on my stomach.

I watch him carefully, and it looks as if he is trying to memorize every second of this moment.

"It's time, isn't it?" I ask. The question is simple, but heavy.

"I promised you that our daughter would be born into a world where Luke does not exist," he looks up. "And I intend to keep that promise. When Luke sent that gift, he signed his death wish. Today, I summoned the executioner."

I knew this day would come, and now that it has, I'm feeling a rush of emotions. My heart starts to hammer hard against my ribs. "What do I need to do?"

"Nothing," he says simply and looks up at me.

"What?" I shake my head, not understanding.

"Diablo...if you love me, if you love our daughter, you will do as I ask and do nothing. You stay here where I and the legion can keep you safe."

I dismiss the idea of doing nothing. "But we talked about this. I might be the only one who can stop him. You can't expect me to stand by and watch. Especially since we know Luke is after our daughter."

"I do," he replies crisply.

"Dante–"

"Angel, listen to me. I think that's why he showed his hand now. He knows you will do whatever it takes to protect our daughter, and he will use it to his advantage. You're an easy target."

"You saw my wings in Bali." I protest. "I am *not* an easy

target. I can defend both myself *and* the legion."

"Diablo, I am begging you," he presses hand down on top of our daughter. "Sit this one out."

His eyes search mine. "That's why you made the trust, isn't it?" I ask angrily. "It was always going to be this way."

"No," he presses his forehead to mine. "I began putting the trust together the day I woke up and saw what my being gone had done to you. But when Luke found us in Bali, it was clear he would do anything to get his hands on our daughter. Even if that means taking you. So please," Dante's words cut off, catching in his throat.

It's the first time in five thousand years he has shown any sign of weakness and it guts me. "Okay," I concede, and lean into his chest.

He exhales heavily and presses his lips to my head and pulls his hand from my stomach and wraps them both around me. "Hopefully, this will be over before it even begins. But if not, I need you to listen to me. If something happens, and I say leave, you leave. Do you understand? Do not ask questions, and do not fight me." I nod and he continues. "I mean it," he pulls back. "Angel, promise me."

"Okay," I swallow, the seriousness in his eyes alarming me. "I promise."

"You will be safe," he swipes a thumb along my cheek. "You have the legion, a family who loves you, and me, who loves you so fucking much, I will smite an entire army to protect you and our daughter."

"Why are you telling me this now?" I look up.

"Because we are going to brief the legion shortly and you are its leader. I want you to be informed. It is also why I want you to know everything."

"Okay," I nod. "What else is there?"

"There…was no spy."

"What? But how–" I start to ask, and he cuts me off.

"It was JJ."

"What?" I step back. It wasn't possible. JJ had watched over us for thousands of years. He would never betray us. Not in a million millennia.

"Luke saw everything through his eyes. JJ is an attendant, but he is also soulless, so his connection to Luke remains. Luke has seen and heard everything JJ has.

I close my eyes, guilt flooding me. "I did this." I was the one who insisted we make JJ an attendant. I brought the devil to our door. My daughter is in danger because of me.

"No," Dante rubs his hands up and down my arms. "If anything, it's because of me. I have been in touch with him since we left." My head spins as the realization Luke used JJ starts to sink in. "The project I had JJ working on…it was packing up your place in Eden. It's how Luke found out where we were. I'd been in touch with JJ when we were in Bali. *That's* what was on the notepad. Some items I wanted to make sure he didn't forget."

"I can't believe you did that," I shake my head in disbelief.

"That morning after I woke up when I asked if you had been back to Eden and you said no, it angered me to think you left everything behind. That all you worked for was just lost, because of Luke. He'd already taken enough from you. I didn't want him to take your home, too. So, we got it all. Everything is packed up, from the books in the library down to the fireplace you love so much. Apparently, that was a real bitch, but we got it, every damn rock."

I stare at him in disbelief, nor knowing whether to laugh or cry. How much time and money had Dante spent trying to pack up my home?

"I'd assumed Luke had made Eden impenetrable after all that happened. How did he get in and out without being seen?"

"JJ knows Eden better than anyone. He is the only one who could get in and out without being seen. Only, now we know Luke did see what JJ was doing. He just didn't care because his eyes have always been on another prize."

"Our daughter," I say numbly.

"Yes. But he won't get his hands on her," Dante insists. "And when this is over, everything in your house, down to the studs, will be unpacked from the ship it is on at Vinny's dock down in Tilbury, and rebuilt anywhere you'd like, exactly as it was. I just need to know what to do with the house."

"The house?" I repeat.

"Tonight, every one of Luke's strongholds will burn to the ground. Even Eden. And I need to know what you want me to do with the studs for your house, and the property."

His words from our first night together echo in my mind. *I would burn the world for you, you know this, don't you?*

Now I know why he thinks Luke will strike back tonight. Eden was his glory. His crown jewel on Earth. And when it burns, he will retaliate. "You're drawing him out."

"Yes," Dante confirms. "No more hiding. This ends tonight. And when he comes, we will be ready. I just need to know what you want us to do with your property. Do you want us to put a firebreak around it?"

I stare back at him, my heart full of too many emotions to process–anger, pain, hope, sadness. But the one I feel most, is love.

I'd always loved my home in Eden. But thinking about it now, I realize it was not a home. This was–the penthouse and all the people I cared about, who also considered it a home. It was where we would raise our daughter, surrounded by everyone who I would always fight for, and in turn, would always fight for us.

Eden was a place where I had been imprisoned for five thousand years, and I loved my home because my love had nowhere else to go. But now I had so much love, it flowed through every inch of me. For Dante, and our daughter, and our family, the legion...everything I had now was real. Whereas that structure of wood and stone was nothing more than a skeleton of a place that never really existed. A sadness, and desolation, which was my torment.

"Burn it," I say simply.

"Are you sure?"

"Yes," I insist. "My home is here."

He trails a finger along my jaw and grips my chin with his thumb and forefinger. "Your wish is my command."

He presses his lips to mine and kisses me. It's fueled by the fire of what's to come, and my need for him flares.

"We have some time before we meet with everyone," I whisper through the kiss.

"Oh yeah?" he grins. "And what do you propose we do with that time?"

I lace my fingers through his and lead him to the door that connects to the roof. When we reach it, his mouth is already on my neck as I punch in the code into the digital lock.

We never make it to the roof. By the time we're mid-way up, he's got me pinned against the wall, cradling me safe in his arms as he fucks me against the wall. It's carnal, and full of heat and exactly what we both need. It eases the anxiety of what lies ahead, and the need we both have to be as close to the other as possible.

Dante promised to burn the world for me and tonight he is making good on that promise. But if anything happens to him by striking the match, I will light up the universe with an inferno, to the likes it has never seen.

34
DANTE

I sit at the end of the bed in a chair facing the door, gun in one hand, cell phone in the other. The gun is loaded with rounds filled with every element known to do us harm, including our own version of a synthetic stardust James has been working on, while my phone has a live stream pulled up.

Draven's network has not disappointed. Once the sun set, Luke's fortresses around the world began to fall. One minute they are standing, and the next, engulfed in flames; the crackling fires and imploding structures, filling me with a wicked sense of satisfaction as the feed shows each of his domains falling one by one.

Regardless of how much it pleases me to watch Luke's empire burn to the ground, I tighten the hold on the gun in my hand, remembering to be ready. He could retaliate at any minute, and I don't want the element of surprise to be what puts Diablo or our daughter in harm's way.

The legion is ready. They've been training for this since they learned Luke lied and made a mockery of their loyalty and Viper has made sure I and every other member are weaponed up. I've got two semi-automatics in a back holster, two more in holsters on each thigh, and daggers in both boots. There were also weapons stashed all around the penthouse if needed at a moment's notice, and every legion member was wearing a comms piece in their ear.

Still, you can never be too careful where the master of deception is concerned, and I've added my personal security team to the arsenal of legion members stationed at every point of entry in the building. As former special ops they're more than used to thwarting militant warlords and itching to put their skills to the test on what I said was the worst one they'd ever face.

I look over my shoulder and check on Diablo for the dozenth time. She's resting peacefully, with hand cradling her stomach, and her wings wrapped protectively around her like a shield. After watching Eden burn, she passed out from exhaustion and there was no reason for her to be up. I had her back.

To be honest, I wanted her to be as far away from here as possible but sending her away came with risk. Luke could divert his energies to wherever she was, and we needed him to come here. That was the plan. But if it comes down to it, I have a helicopter waiting on the roof's helipad, ready to whisk her away to a secure location that only Vinny, myself, and the pilot know the coordinates for.

The very idea of sending her away makes me tense and I hope it won't come to that. I hope all our training and preparation can put an end to Luke swiftly. Still, it was best not to underestimate Luke. Losing every stronghold he'd amassed over the millennia, would incense his ego. But losing Eden would provoke his rage. Especially since JJ-taken there while blindfolded-would be the one holding the match and giving Luke a front row seat to seeing his beloved island go up in flames.

Fire and ash. That's what I said I'd do to the world if anyone ever hurt Diablo. And in one night, I was honoring that promise by doing it to Luke's. Eden was his pride and joy. A place he created for to torture my angel and claim souls. It was his world and burning it to the ground would be a start to giving her spirit the absolution it deserves.

He'd been hiding way too long, and I was sure tonight would draw him out. But when sunrise hits and he still hasn't shown his face, a strange prickling sensation crawls up my back and settles in my neck.

What are you up to? I wonder. The question plaguing me all day, and into the next, when he still hasn't made a move.

One week passes. And then another. Two weeks since we set fire to his empire, and Luke still hasn't made a move. David's contact at the Vatican hasn't seen nor heard from him, and the artifacts that were on display in its haughty, gilded halls after the gala, have all been sent back to where they belong.

Some members of the legion think he may have been caught inside one of the fortresses, while others think because he came up empty-handed with the artifacts, he'd scrapped his plans and was busy pulling together a new one. David thinks the answer is in Dee's text, which he continues to study, trying to figure out its unique linguistics.

I, however, know Luke's silence does not denote his complacency or elimination. He's biding his time and there's a reason. I wrack my brain daily, trying to figure out his angle. And before I know it another week has passed, and it's been a month since we burned his empire to the ground.

Then one night in the middle of Diablo's sixteenth week of pregnancy–thirty-two weeks for the baby–the reason becomes painfully clear.

"How are you feeling?" I ask as she crawls into bed. She's still radiant, but her movements have slowed, and her energy noticeably, waning.

"Your daughter is rolling up a storm tonight," she says as I plump up a pillow behind her, then motion for her to lean back.

I place my hand on her stomach and sure enough, the baby does what feels like a barrel roll. I can't help but smile. In all that looms over us, she's the promise of the future for which we are fighting.

"Are you taking it easy?" I watch her cautiously as she closes her eyes and takes a deep breath, rubbing her side gently.

"I am," she turns to me and smiles gently. "You don't have to worry."

"I will always worry about you," I brush my finger against her cheek.

"Oomph," she winces and grabs her side.

"You, okay?" I sit up, alarmed.

"I thought our daughter listened to you. She just kicked the hell out of me."

"Hey princess," I place both hands on either side of Diablo's pregnant stomach and press my lips to it, softly. "Give your mom a break, for me?"

"Wow," Diablo looks down and breathes a sigh of relief. "You have the touch."

I look up and wink. "We already knew that."

I settle back against the headboard, and she rests her head on my shoulder. "I wish I knew what he was planning."

"Me too," I blow out a frustrated breath.

"She'll be here in just a few weeks, and for all we know, he's planning to show up in the delivery room as one of the doctors."

My stomach plummets at the very idea. "First," I shake my head. "That's not happening. And second, oh yeah, not happening."

"When you say it, I believe it," she tips her head up.

"Because you know I will do anything to keep you safe." I lean in and kiss her, and she places a hand on my cheek. "You know what I want?" I say after pulling back.

"I think I have a pretty good idea," she grins.

"Well, yes," I flash her my own wicked smile. "That. Always. But also, I want to take you on a trip. See all the places you've always wanted to go to."

"The pyramids?" she asks with a flash in her eyes.

"And the Northern Lights," I nod.

"The Library at Trinity?" she adds with more excitement.

"Angel," I smile. "It's first on the list."

"I assume you're talking about after she arrives," Diablo looks down at her growing bump.

"For sure," I smile. "Strap her into one of those carrier things and we'll take her everywhere."

"Really?" She laughs at the idea. "You're going to be that dad?"

"I will be anything you want me to be."

"Just you," she kisses me again. "But there's one small problem with your plan."

"Oh yeah?" I look at her, brow raised. "And that would be?"

"Well," she claps her hands and rests them on her belly. "I don't have a passport. In fact, I've always wondered how you managed to pull off our trip to Italy that night."

"Ah, well," I reach over to the top drawer of my nightstand and pull out the items I planned to give her in Bali: the passport, bank ledger, and credit cards. "Funny you should mention it."

I close the drawer and turn back to her, holding my hand out. "For Italy, Wills pulled a few strings and was able to get you a temporary passport. But this one is real and ready to go."

She looks down at my hand, a look of surprise filling her face. "What's that?"

"I was planning to give them to you in Bali, but well…" My voice trails off and I know I don't have to say anything more. The shit hit the proverbial fan and the focus has been on the war he started, ever since.

"Anyway," I clear my throat and continue, "I want you to have everything you need for when all this is over, and you are free to exist. You have a whole department to play with at Primordial, and now you have the resources to get whatever you need, whenever. Use the account and cards, or don't. It's up to you. But the passport we will be using, as much as possible once the baby is born."

The moment I say it, the answer to the question I'd been asking finally hits me. He's waiting for the baby to be born so he can take her. It would be the ultimate retaliation to let me hold and love my daughter, and then take her away.

The prickling sensation that's lingered in my neck for weeks grabs hold and squeezes, as if confirming I'm right. Pulling Diablo closer, I kiss the top of her head, filled with new purpose.

Tomorrow, I put a new plan into place. I'm not sitting around and waiting any longer. Vinny and the legion can take care of Luke. But Diablo and I need to disappear.

***

The next night we're rocked awake by an explosion. Jumping out of bed, I hurry to Diablo's side and help her get dressed, then yank my own clothes on, grab my guns and gear from the chair next to the bed, and reach for my phone. There are three missed calls from David, with a voicemail marked urgent.

Shoving it into my pocket, I grab her hand and race out of the suite; keeping her close to me as we hurry down the hall and head towards the stairwell at the end of the wing on the other side of this floor.

When we get there, Vinny and Lila are waiting by the door as planned. Yesterday I'd filled both in my suspicions for Luke's silence, and they agreed–leaving was the only thing that made sense for Diablo and the baby's safety.

It wasn't like me to run from a fight, but Vinny had my back, always. And it "wasn't running," he said once we were all in agreement on the new plan. "It's saving your family. Let us handle Luke. You keep your angel and my niece safe."

"What happened?" I ask, pulling open the door. He appears as surprised as I am.

"Missile launcher at ground level. Hit the 30th floor. Elevator banks down and the titanium doors for the stairwells were activated."

"Shit!" I blow out a tense breath. That meant we were down half the legion, and nearly every one of the special ops team.

The sound of glass shattering and explosions below us, sends Diablo's brows, shooting up to her hairline. "Ok angel, up you go," I point at the stairs.

"No," she says adamantly. She won't let go of my hand and her grip is like ice. She knew this moment was coming and now that it has, she doesn't want to part with me, just as it is killing me to part with her.

"Please," I beg. "We talked about this. I'll be right behind you."

"Dante, we can't leave them," she insists. "They need me."

"The legion will be fine," I say urgently. "They divided Heaven, remember. This is just another day in the park." I offer a small smile, hoping the play on words from that day in the study before the heist will ease her resistance to leaving.

"No," she shakes her head, tears welling in her eyes. "I can't abandon them. Not when I have the power to end this."

"Listen to me," I cup her face in my hands and press my forehead to hers. "I love you, angel. Both of you, more than anything. But we have to leave now before it's too late."

Viper swings open the door at the top of the stairs leading to the roof and charges down, reaching for Diablo's hand. "D, come on. He'll be right behind us."

She'd followed the plan to the letter, as I knew she would. First sign of chaos, get to the roof. And she did.

"Diablo," Lila encourages. "Dante is right. You need to get out of here."

Her wings jut out, strong and red as she looks from Lila to me. "Why do I have these wings if I can't use them when I need them most?"

"I don't know," Lila shakes her head, steadfast. "But you need to get out of here. So up you go," she nods to the stairs.

"You heard Viper," I nod with confirmation. "I'm right behind you."

I look at Viper and nod as she reaches for one of Diablo's hands, and the other one slips from mine. As they climb the stairs, another explosion rocks the building. This time, the ceiling of the stairwell collapses behind them as they reach the door at the top, and the impact throws Vinny, Lila, and I into the wall of the hallway.

"Nooooo!" I shout as I scramble back up and pound on the now closed door.

Rubble and dust fill the hall and Lila waves her hands

around to clear the air. "Dante, it's no use," Vinny grabs my shoulder. "Come on. We'll go through the garden and use the stairs to Diablo's practice space to get to the helipad."

"Angel!" I shout. "If you can hear me, I'll be right there."

There is no sound on the other side of the wall and my heart starts to hammer in my chest as I reach behind my back and grab both guns out of the holster and start to run down the main stairs.

Vinny and Lila follow close behind, each with a gun in both hands, and when we reach the foyer, it looks like we're in a war zone. The glass of the floor to ceiling windows behind the stairs is gone and a wicked breeze rips through the space.

"Alright," I bang the ends of my guns together, preparing them to shoot. "I need to get to Diablo. We head to the garden as planned and you take that son of a bitch down while I head to the roof. Okay?"

Those who can, raise their fists in acknowledgement, and follow up down the hall as we check, then clear each room along the way.

The garden had been ground zero for the first plan, and it would now, as well. We would use the glass to our advantage–the reflection showing a thousand legion members, while a handful would be making their way through the garden and come up behind Luke and inject a lethal amount of stardust into his veins and turn his blood mostly mortal, so we could then execute him.

Vinny and I push through the glass doors of the garden, followed by dozens of legion members. "I'm here you son of a bitch!" I shout out as the legion files in behind me. "Come and get me!"

I stand at the ready, guns in both hands, and when the leaves part towards the back side of the garden, my head swings around and there he is standing in front of the door I need to get to.

"Dante," he smiles as if we're old friends, seeing each other for the first time in years. "How is my daughter doing? I do hope tonight's events didn't cause any duress."

I move my neck from side to side as Vinny tightens the hold he has of both guns in his hands. "Get out of here man," he says through clenched teeth. "I got this."

I know he does. Vinny can handle anything. But something about wanting to end the bastard that had hurt my angel endlessly, picks at the need in me for revenge. Not to mention, he's blocking the door I need to get to, and I don't want to tip him off that it's exactly where I am trying to get to.

"You know," he taps his cane. "I was impressed with that little switch you pulled with the artifacts. It's made things more complicated, that's for sure. But impressive, nonetheless. Especially since you weren't so quick to understand my connection to your oldest friend. Then again, when all you're focused on is fucking, you tend to miss the obvious."

"Shut your mouth." I tighten my hold on each gun and keep my focus.

"I don't blame you," he smiles wickedly. "I got a taste of her skin in Eden, and it was delectable. I can only imagine what she tastes like everywhere. Perhaps I will find out for myself once my daughter is born."

"You will not touch Diablo or *my* daughter, do you understand me? Your existence ends tonight."

"Now see, that's where you're wrong," he sneers. "She will be my child and I will take your angel to my bed. The heir and my whore. A broodmare, for my dynasty, which will reign over all eternity."

My blood is boiling. I want to kill him. I want him gone and buried. "You will do nothing but die. Your time here is over. Over!"

"No," he reaches into his pocket. "Your time is over. All of you."

He starts firing bullets and the legion does in response. For every bullet that strikes him, he hits a legion member with his own. Our bullets push him back, but his bullets...they destroy.

As they hit the legion, they scream and then in seconds, right before our eyes, they turn into ash.

Vinny dodges a bullet, watching in horror as Hayden is struck in the shoulder with one. Hayden sticks his hand out and I reach for it, only to have the ash of what were once his fingers, slip through mine.

"No!" I look in horror at the pile of ash where his wily self once stood.

I look at Luke, shocked by what I've just seen. "Your angel left something behind when she eviscerated my army in Eden," Luke says gleefully. "Who would've thought angel wings could be turned into bullets? Then again, who would have thought an angel could have a baby. I guess when you're Heaven's pawn, anything is possible."

Her wings? Luke made bullets out of her wings. And now he was using them on the very legion she swore to protect with them.

I start shooting again and when my guns run out of bullets, I shove them into the back holster and reach for the ones attached to my thighs.

Luke is too busy shooting his guns like a deranged cowboy, giving me a slight opening to jump to the left where the glass creates a reflection of me all around the garden.

Hundreds of me. Luke's worst nightmare.

Vinny shoots and navigates the crossfire and I know he'll be all right. But the others...losing them will not only hurt but anger me beyond reason. They didn't live through the Fall to have their existence snuffed out by Luke. This needed to end, now!

Making my way around the perimeter, I come up next to Luke and slide the guns in my thigh holsters quietly, then lunge at him, grabbing his neck with both hands.

When he feels my hands on his throat, he swings his eyes in my direction and laughs. "You think you can kill me with your bare hands?"

"No." I press my fingers into his jugular, pushing so hard it draws blood. "But it feels really fucking good to make you bleed."

"I'm not one of your soulless opponents," he sneers. "You cannot fight me to the death or slit my throat when I'm down, like a coward."

"Coward," I clench tighter, and a trickle of blood seeps out from under my thumb. "The only coward I see is you. Hiding and waiting for the moment to pounce. That's a bitch move if you ask me."

"Only you Dante, would have the audacity to challenge me, the prince of Hell." He grips at my forearms, trying to pull them off. But I'm stronger than ever before and fueled by an adrenaline which has one life source-my family.

This time it's me who laughs. "Diablo is the queen now, or did you forget? All you have left is that ridiculous, which I'm going to enjoy shoving up your ass."

"You really should have paid more attention," Luke slowly pries my fingers away from his neck. "She does not have the power source...yet."

I look at him, confused, while at the same time, applying new strength to my hold. Of course, she did. She had the legion's loyalty. Binding her spirit to the light merely gave her control over Hell. It did not matter we hadn't done that, yet.

"Do you know how to do anything but lie?" I spit out. "You're really–"

I don't get a chance to finish the thought. Something crashes through the glass roof and when it lands between Luke and me, I see it's not something, but someone.

Diablo. My angel…literally. Her wingspan extends from one end of the garden to the other, red like fire, and she's more breathtaking, more badass, than ever before.

But then I look to Luke and seeing the way he is looking at her, my heart stops and I go numb. She's put herself between he and I, and I've never felt more helpless in all my existence.

35
DIABLO

"Enough!" I clap my wings and send the plants and trees of the garden bending with the force.

"Do not tell *me* enough!" Luke shouts back. "I have spent an entire existence waiting for this moment, and you will not ruin it for me!"

"You don't have a choice." I clap my wings again, and the glass behind him shatters and his feet slide backwards.

He slams the tip of his cane down and it breaks through the stone, rooting him in place. "I learned from your parlor tricks last time. "You will not run me off again."

Dante reaches for the guns on his thigh holsters and trains the barrel of each on Luke's chest. "You may want to rethink that decision."

"She cannot hurt me. Just as you cannot. Your reckless behavior is about to end."

"Reckless?" I pull my wings back, preparing to deliver another powerful clap. "That's rich, coming from the most impetuous being that ever existed."

"That tongue of yours is so cunning, Diablo. Tell me," he licks his lips. "Did you know I, too, am a cunning linguist?"

Dante clenches his jaw and cocks both guns. "Shut…your…fucking…mouth."

"You know," Luke trains his eyes on Dante. "This may be my least favorite side of you, Dante. You used to be fun. A real fucking good time, if you know what I mean," Luke wags his brows with the implication. "But you have become predictable, and predictable is nauseating."

"When someone is trying to steal your child, it tends to take the fun out of things," Dante barks back.

"Oh, now see," Luke's eyes flash. "That's where you're mistaken. I am not *trying* to take her. I will. She will be mine."

"Over my dead body," Dante closes the space between him and Luke.

"Don't tempt me," Luke's face lights up in wicked satisfaction.

I pull my wings back and prepare to strike again but Luke holds the gun in his hand up and wags it back and forth. "I would not do that if I were you. One more clap, and I fire off a round. You saw what these bullets are capable of. Who could it be next? Your eternal beloved, or your best friend?"

I look from Dante to Lila, who is being shielded by Vinny, and he is watching Luke with eagle eyes. Luke will not shoot her or Dante. He knows if he does, I'll unleash the full wrath of my wings, and something tells me he fears the power. But the thing was.... I too, knew their power now, and he should be scared.

He may have harnessed a plume for his bullets, but I'd been harnessing all of them for weeks–practicing day after day, while we waited for him to make a move. I knew well what they were capable of and was about to show him.

I turn my wings down towards the floor and bend my knees, then push off the ground, and fly up through the broken glass of the garden's roof and into the sky. Feeling the clouds among my fingertips, I soar weightless, and roll, gathering them around me.

When I'm done, I shoot back down towards the garden and just when I breach the roof, I pull my wings back and send the clouds hurtling towards Luke. They wrap around him like a net, pulling tight as a snake would its prey. His gun falls to the floor, but he grips his cane with ferocity.

Dante watches me, speechless, and totally in awe. "You think you can chain me up and take my daughter?" I shout. "Kill my friends and take Dante from me a second time? You will never touch anyone I love ever again! No way in Heaven. No way on Earth. No way in Hell!"

With each declaration, I clap my wings harder, and the clouds tighten their hold. Luke struggles for a moment and then stops, a small laugh curling from his lips.

"What's so funny?" Dante sneers. "She's kicking your ass."

"I'm wondering how you will feel when you know the truth," Luke continues to laugh. "When you learn every century, every second of your miserable existence on Earth, has led to this very moment."

The look in his eyes, and hint in his question, makes my skin prick. "What are you talking about?"

As if channeling all his strength, Luke pushes his arms outward and breaks from the restraint of the clouds, then yanks up his shirt sleeve and reveals a tattoo of the sigil.

"I know all about your obsession," Dante stares at it angrily.

"It is not my obsession," Luke says with defiance. "It is us."

Dante steps in front of me protectively. "What is us?"

"To answer that, you must go back to the beginning."

"To the Fall?" I pull my wings back, preparing to strike his lies from his tongue.

"No," Luke's lips pull into a menacing smile. "Before even that."

"What are you talking about!" I demand

"Here," Luke taps the tip of his cane on the ground twice. "Let me show you."

***

It is cold, and dark. The beginning of time. I remember because it is lonely, and my existence without light. Then the sun appeared, followed by the moon, and I was alone no more.

Before man. Before the time of angels, it was us: the stars, the sun, and the moon. We were its first children. Not man. And Heaven cherished us. But then the stars fell in love with the moon, and along came jealousy, and with it, Heaven's scorn.

I look at Dante and the depth of my love for him, radiates from my heart out to the tip of every plume. There is a reason my spirit was drawn to his in Heaven. A reason he has always felt like my other half. Because he was. A part that had been cleaved, long, long ago, in the beginning, when our story began.

He reaches out to touch my wing, gun still in hand, and when he does, light shoots through me. It is the light of creation and in it, the memory of him and I.

Confusion haunts his face, and pain clouds his eyes, and I know he is seeing what I am–memories of an existence taken away and a story erased. A story that began, well before everything.

The pull we have on one another, the pull we will always have, is beyond cellular, beyond spiritual, beyond even time.

Dante's inherent anger with mankind now made sense. For him, his reason for rebelling against Heaven was not about free will. It was a deeper knowledge in his very core, that he was meant for something more. *For me.*

When Heaven pulled us apart to watch over man, they stole from us one another, and that need for me festered in his spirit, just as my need for him had festered in mine. He longed for me, just as I had, for him.

"How could we forget?" he asks, shaking his head in disbelief. "All that time."

I draw in a shaky breath, the weight of countless forgotten millennia, pressing down on me. "In Heaven, my job was clear. Watch over mankind, nothing else. But then, one day, there you were, and in an instant, everything shifted. It was as if my spirit knew my reason for existence had been missing. That you had been missing."

"Because it had." Dante removes his hand from my wing and locks his eyes on mine. "Watching them wasn't your reason for existing. We were."

The moment I saw Dante in Heaven, his light consumed me. My spirit felt for him, more than it ever felt for man. Just like in this existence, when I tried to stay away each time he was in Eden, something always pulled me back to him.

I choke back angry tears; forgetting a previous existence was hard to swallow, but remembering it all at once, including who helped make it happen, was devastating.

"You?" I curl my hands into fists and turn to Luke. "You did this. How could you be so cruel? You betrayed us."

"Me," he says incredulously. "*You* did this. You betrayed us! When it was the three of us it was fine. No power greater. Just equal. Then you fell for his light, and it changed everything."

It was true. I did fall for Dante's light, because the stars were always destined for the moon. But the heat of Luke's domain now, was what it had been in the beginning. The sun, so hot and blinding. Its power grew more oppressive by the millennia as his jealousy grew.

"The sun, the moon, and stars," Luke says angrily. "We were Heaven's first children and they treasured us. But then you fell for him, and that harmony was at risk and Heaven could not allow us to be out of balance. The moon and stars could not be together–it would have destroyed the universe."

"That's why you tormented me for thousands of years, because you were jealous of what I had done in an existence I could not remember?"

"Yes!" he shouts. "You didn't just lose your existence when you chose him. I did, too. In your incessant need to love him, I lost me the greatest power in all of existence. We each paid for your crime."

"That's what Lilith meant by the war being older than the Fall," Dante turns to Luke. "You have been angry with Heaven since the beginning of time."

"But how…" my mind races. "How do you remember, and we didn't?"

"Because I did not betray Heaven. I only suffered the consequence of your choice. My punishment was to remember all I had been."

"Is that how you became The Morning Star?" Dante's eyes narrow.

"Heaven believed that by giving me a fraction of the light I once possessed, I would lead and watch over their second children, the angels. With their benevolence and purity, they believed the problem of selfishness displayed by their first children had been fixed. Yet, in that existence, you fell for him, again," he looks at me with hatred. "Despite your place in the angel hierarchy. And I could not allow you to bring us down a second time."

"The Fall," I say numbly. "Was it because of us?"

"I knew Heaven would not tolerate a second act of defiance from its first children. That it would be an act that got us banished forever. But also knew the power of the angels and the freedom being cast out of Heaven would grant me. With the light of the Fallen, I planned to build the kingdom for which I was destined on Earth. But then you fell for him a second time and nearly foiled my plans. So, I created a way that ensured you could not."

"The contract," Dante says angrily. "You bound us to a contract bound by lies."

"Mmm," Luke nods in confirmation. "And it would have helped me achieve my plans, had my wretched daughter and her mother not helped you find and translate it."

My mind is racing, trying to keep up. The Fall had been devised to keep Dante and I apart? The contract, one part of a larger plan for power?

"But how did you write the contract in Enochian? None of us can read or speak it."

"An angel's light does not diminish within moments. It takes time for both what we knew, and our light to fade. I wrote it when we had just fallen, and I could remember our language–"

"And when we still had light to steal," Dante says through gritted teeth.

"That's when Heaven would have taken my wings," I look at Dante, answering the question he asked the night after my wings reappeared.

Luke's eyes flash with recognition and he can see we are putting everything together. "But they didn't," I look back at him. "Heaven only made me believe they had done so, and you knew. All this time, you knew."

"Angels were not allowed to walk on Earth. You were an abomination," he spits out, and the word makes me cringe. "That's how I knew they were up to something."

"She is not an abomination!" Dante seethes. "She is the most incredible being to ever exist. You are jealous she chose me. That in every existence she chose me, and that I too, have always chosen her."

"Jealousy can be an ugly beast," Luke muses. "It is true. But it can be an incredible source of power. When wielded alongside deceit and greed it can raise armies and build empires, which is exactly what I did. When Earth and Heaven are mine, Hell will rule, and my soulless will feast on both."

Dante and I stare at one another. Luke's anger and plans ran deeper than either of us imagined.

"I assume, you're wondering how your child plays into this?" Luke asks when neither of us says anything.

Not wanting to give Luke the satisfaction of knowing he is right, I say nothing, and neither does Dante.

"It seems, the very thing they broke us apart for in the beginning, was how they planned to put a stop to me and my empire. Inspired by your sacrifice, Heaven devised a plan. They shared our language with one of their choosing and told him their greatest secret–the key to their power."

"Dee," Dante whispers.

"Many believed he was crazy. His claims of speaking with angels, nothing more than the machinations of an eccentric mind. But see," Luke holds up a finger. "Heaven knew this. They did not want their secret to get out. They wanted it hidden away, and that is exactly what Dee did. He wrote the secret down and created a key that was the only way to decode it."

"How did you find out?" I ask, neither confirming we

knew about Dee's text or the letters, which I assumed were the key.

"Dee was at one time a favorite in Queen Elizabeth I's court and traveled all over Europe in service to the crown. In every city he visited, he talked, and when you are me and have eyes and ears all over the world, I heard every one of his stories."

"That's how you created the list for the vault," Dante blows out a frustrated breath.

"Turns out, Dee didn't hide pieces of the key to his text in places, but items. Items he would have access to as one of the crown's most trusted confidantes. It took centuries to compile this list, and by the time I finished, many of the items had changed hands as regions and territories did. That is when I decided to work with the one group with the reach and power to help me procure them."

"The church," I shake my head. "You claimed to hate them all these centuries but were in bed with them the whole time."

"As they say, the enemy of my enemy is my friend," he smiles. "And they were all too happy to embrace my idea of a vault that would serve as a backup for mankind's official story, should the originals ever become destroyed. The church had been foretelling doomsday since its creation. It was the perfect hook to reel them in."

Dante tightens his hold on the guns in his hands. "All this time. All these years. You have schemed and plotted and worked with the church, all to find this secret you believe will give you Heaven's power? How do you know it is not just a lie?"

"Because.." he looks from me to Diablo. "The power the secret hinted at, the elements needed to achieve it, make sense. Heaven's kingdoms have always been Heaven and Earth, but my power was Hell. It is exactly something they would do–enable the creation of one with their powers and mine, to take away all I have built and irrevocably bind it to another. It would be the ultimate retaliation for your betrayal!"

"My betrayal?" I pull my wings back. "You are the one who created Hell! You are the one who has played with mankind and built an army and empire! If Heaven communicated the secret to their power with mankind that is on *you*, not *me*."

"No!" He grips his cane angrily. "The whole reason I fell was to keep you two apart!"

"The reason you fell was for power!" Dante shouts back. "And the reason you were mad in the beginning was because you lost your power. Both existences, your anger was driven by jealousy and power. Don't put your bullshit failures on us or our daughter. That is all you!"

The anger coming off Luke and Dante is palpable. I need to do something before it is too late.

"You have always been in the way," Luke stares at Dante. "Had the moon not come along, the sun would have reigned. Had she not seen you in Heaven, I would have remained the brightest star in the sky. Had you and the Fallen not stolen the artifacts that Dee stashed the key to his text in, I would have claimed your daughter for myself by now."

Dante smirks. "Payback's a bitch, isn't it?"

"It is," Luke bites. "That is why I am here. I need her ready for when I find the key and secret hidden by Dee. So, Diablo, come with me willingly, and I will make the next few weeks tolerable. I may even allow a doctor to assist you when it is time for you to give birth. But if you refuse, when I capture you, I will pull that child out of your womb myself, ready or not."

I look at Luke in horror as Dante takes a step towards him. "Say one more word and this bullet goes in your head. Understand?"

Luke grips the top of his cane, and the entire thing lights up red, glowing as if it were on fire. I look from the gun in his hand to the cane and back again. Luke has not fired even when he could, despite his anger, despite the words he and Dante have exchanged, he hasn't fired because the bullets aren't his true source of power. The cane is. I may have the legion's loyalty, but the power of Hell is in the cane. Whatever Dante thought I needed to do to claim it wasn't it at all. I just needed the cane.

I know now what I must do. I have always known it would be me that has to end Luke. I am the only one that can absorb the power in that cane.

My spine tingles and my wings fan out. I know they will protect me, and I know my daughter will be okay. She is strong and has her father's blood and spirit in her. But Dante needs to let me do this. He must get out of the way so I can end this–for him, for me, and for our daughter.

I push past Dante and before he can stop me, I reach for the cane. When I wrap my hand around it, malevolent energy surges through me like an electrical current, passing through every cell, out to my wings.

"Nooooo!" Dante screams as hurricane force winds shatter the glass walls of the garden, sucking what is left of the foliage into the night sky.

Luke looks at me in shock, then disbelief, and then finally fear, as fire passes from his cane to me, ripping through my body, igniting every plume on fire. As my wings go up in flames, his eyes narrow and he shouts out a dozen words, none of which I can make out.

Then right before my eyes, as his own glow an infernal red, he starts to disintegrate. First his hair, then his clothes, then his shoes, until nothing remains but dust.

I look down at his cane in my hand and then out to my wings, as one by one, each plume burns down to the stem and crackles, then rains down ash on my face and arms. My desperate heart beats fast in my chest, watching as my wings disappear, and when the last plume turns to ash and rains down, I fall to the ground.

The cane rolls from my hands and light returns to the garden, as the legion looks around, as if they are not sure what is going on. But as I look up through the hole in the roof and see the moon and stars shining down, I know this is right. I know this was meant to be.

36
DANTE

I look at Diablo lying motionless on the ground and rush over to her and kneel, holding her head gently in my hands. "Angel, can you hear me?"

When she doesn't respond, I pull her into my arms carefully, then push up from the ground, and hurry out of the garden–racing past the legion members who look at me in a daze, wondering what just happened.

"Dante," Vinny calls from behind me as I race down the hall, with Diablo tucked against my chest.

I look from room to room quickly, stepping over plaster and glass, trying to find one not devastated. But they too, like the garden, are destroyed. Painting hangs from the walls; the furniture ripped open and overturned.

Seeing the sitting room next to the study is the least damaged, I race in and lay her down gently on the sofa, then grab a throw from the arm of a side chair and toss it over her.

I rub her arms and legs to stimulate warmth, and notice my own arms covered in blood. I pat myself down, confused where it is coming from, then realize it's not mine, it's Diablo's.

I reach for her shoulder and sit her up carefully to look at her back and she lets out a small whimper. It's a good sign she's conscious, just barely, but her back is in bad shape. Her shirt is burned, and her skin, charred, and the slits along her shoulder blades where her wings once jutted out are open, the flaps of skin on each side pulled apart, revealing bone.

My head spins and hands shake as I ease her back down gently to check on the baby. When I place both hands on her stomach and feel the baby moving, I blow out a relieved breath.

"Our girl is fine," I say to Diablo, hoping she can hear me. Normally, she smiles when the baby moves but her response is a faint murmur, which worries me.

"How is she?" Vinny races up behind me with Lila next to him.

I can't put together two words, let alone a sentence. "She's…um…blood…and burned…"

Lillian rushes in and puts a hand on my arm. It's a relief to see her okay, both because she is safe, and because she is the one that tended to Diablo's back after Eden and the only one who can help her right now.

She sits down gingerly on the sofa next to Diablo and places a hand on her cheek. "Oh, mon cher," she soothes.

"How is she?" I ask shakily as Lillian looks at what she can see of Diablo's back.

"We need to clean her back and stop the bleeding and she needs water," she says matter of fact. "Go to the kitchen and bring as many bottles of water as you can find. Vinny," she turns a serious eye to him, "in my bathroom, there is a medicine cabinet. Bring everything inside. Bandages, scissors, sewing kit…all of it."

Vinny nods and grips my shoulder. "Come on."

"No," I shake my head. "I'm not leaving her."

"Dante," Lillian looks up. "She needs hydration. Go, now."

Vinny grips my other shoulder. "Come on brother. We'll come right back."

Somehow, he manages to pull me out of the room, and we

race down the hall. When he reaches Lillian's room he hurries inside, and I continue to the kitchen.

When I get there, the sound of someone moaning catches my attention. When I look down and see Wills on the floor next to the stove, I rush over and kneel next to him.

"Wills, are you okay?" He's got a cut in his head and a nasty gash on his arm, and he looks confused.

Wills reaches up to touch his head and then holds his hand out to look at it. When he sees blood, he blinks once, then again. "Yes," he says with as much authority as he can muster given his state. "I...think so."

I grab his uninjured arm and pull it over my shoulder, then place a hand on his back and help him to his feet.

Once he's standing, I put one hand on his chest. "You, okay?"

"Yes," he replies, more alert. "Is everyone okay?"

"No," I shake my head. "Diablo is hurt. She needs water. Everyone needs it, actually."

"Pantry," he points with a shaky hand.

I race over to the end of the kitchen and yank the pantry door open. Wills comes in behind me and does what he does best–takes charge. He pulls a handful of bags from one of the shelves and starts filling them with bottles of water, and when done, starts filling more with anything else he can get his hands on: fruit, nuts, protein bars, chips.

Once we have more than a dozen bags full, I grab a bunch in each hand and sling them over both shoulders. "I've got these," I nod. "Go."

We head back down the hall and when we get back to the sitting room, Vinny is standing next to Lillian, with her actual medicine cabinet in his hands. "You said bring as much as I could, and well," he offers a half-hearted grin. "I did."

Lillian shakes her head as he sets it down next to the sofa and she opens it, pulling out bandages, wound cleaner, a sewing kit, ointment, and scissors.

"Dante," Lillian looks at me as Wills gets to work passing out food and water to the legion members lining the halls. "I need you to keep her upright while I clean her back and stitch up the wounds."

I drop the bags on the floor and help Diablo into an upright position, as Lillian cuts what's left of her shirt and peels it off. I pull the blanket up to cover her as Lillian starts to clean the wounds.

"Vinny," I look up. "Can you get her robe from our room? It's at the end of the bed."

"You got it." He races out of the room and pats a couple of legion members on the shoulder as he passes.

"Lila, can you get her some water while I keep her still for Lillian?"

"Of course." She reaches into one of the bags on the floor and screws off the cap, hand shaking visibly as she looks at her friend.

"Angel, you need to drink something," I instruct. Her eyes flutter in response, but her breathing is still shallow and she's pale.

Lila holds the bottle to Diablo's lips and tips it. A bit spills down the side of her mouth, but feeling the cool water, Diablo licks at her lips slowly.

"That's good," I encourage. "More," I nod at Lila, and she tips the bottle again.

Diablo licks her lips again, and this time, swallows a bit. When the water hits her throat, her eyes start to open, and when they find mine, a rush of relief washes over me.

A tear leaks from her eye and rolls slowly down her cheek.

"Shhh," I pull one of my hands from propping her up to wipe it away. "Don't cry, angel."

She licks her lips again and I nod to Lila, and she brings the bottle back to Diablo's mouth so she can take another sip.

"Are you in pain?" I ask gently and she nods as another tear breaks free.

"Okay," Lillian says, tossing down a handful of dirty gauze. "Wound is clean. I need you now to hold her very still. This is going to sting."

Lillian threads a needle and places one hand on Diablo's shoulder and begins to sew up the first wound. Diablo yelps when the needle pierces her skin and every muscle in my body tightens, wanting to stop the pain.

"It hurts," she whimpers, and closes her eyes, as another tear breaks free and rolls down her cheek, carving a path in her soot-covered skin.

"I know, angel, I know." It guts me that I can't help her. That I can't make it better. "You're doing so good. Just a little bit longer."

It seems like forever, but finally, Lila's done sewing up the open wounds, and gets to work applying the ointment and bandages. When she's done, we ease Diablo down gently onto the sofa, as Vinny races back into the room with her robe.

"What took so long?" I ask while stroking her forehead.

"The place is a wreck, man." He holds the robe out and I grab it. "It took a while to get upstairs."

I look at him and I can tell from the expression on his face that he's sugar-coating it. I'm sure it's destroyed, but right now, the damage to the penthouse is the least of my concerns.

"Thanks," I reach for the robe and shoot him a look of apology.

"How is she?" he asks.

"Lillian stopped the bleeding, but she's in a lot of pain."

"Can she take anything for it?"

"Nothing we have here," Lillian looks up. "Not with the baby."

I rub a hand over my face and wish we could do something.

"Diablo, do you want us to help you with your robe?" Lillian asks.

She nods but doesn't say anything. Deciding to let her rest, Lillian pulls the blanket back and starts to cut off Diablo's pants. Vinny and Lila turn their backs while we peel them from her legs and then ease her into the robe and pull the blanket back up.

She's resting peacefully for a while when out of nowhere she sits upright and grabs her stomach and howls out in pain. "What is it?" I look at Lillian in alarm.

Diablo reaches for my hand and squeezes. "The baby..." she pants through what appears intense pain.

"She's probably moving around," I say, trying to ease her fear. "Kicking up a storm after the night she's had. You know how much she likes to–"

"No," shakes her head, eyes wide. "My water...it just broke."

This can't be happening, I think, looking up at Lillian. This is the last place and the worst condition she could be in, to give birth to our daughter. Diablo should be in a soft, warm bed and free from pain. Not in the middle of a war zone, with her body damaged.

Lillian smiles and places a hand on Diablo's cheek. "Are you sure?"

Diablo nods and a fresh tear rolls down her cheek. "It's too soon."

She's alert now, rocked by fear, and I can't believe I'm saying this, but a part of me wishes she were still out so she didn't have to feel any of this.

"Babies are born early all the time," Lillian says with encouragement.

Diablo appears to ease with the reassurance. "Really?"

She was a mother and knows how to calm a child when they are scared and in pain. And that is how Lillian thinks of Diablo. As her daughter. And she's trying to keep her calm.

I look up at Vinny and Lila and shake my head; my nerves pulled so tight they may snap at any moment. "I can't believe this."

"Ready dad?" Vinny grins slightly.

Before I can respond, Diablo places both hands on her stomach again and howls. She's having contractions. Shit, the baby really *is* coming.

Once the contraction passes, Vinny's phone rings and he pulls it out of his pocket and looks at the screen. "It's David."

He answers the call and walks over to the corner for a moment, then returns and shoves his phone into his pocket. "David and James were hit, too. Before us, apparently."

"I saw a few missed calls on my phone right after we were rocked awake by the explosion."

Vinny nods. "He said they tried to warn us, but no one answered. Also said he has news, I think. Couldn't hear him well. They'll be here shortly, although they'll have to take the stairs when they get here, so it may take a while. Lights are on thanks to the backup generator, but the elevators are down."

"Doesn't matter as long as he gets here."

Despite everything, it's a bit of good news. James can give Diablo something to ease the pain and help deliver the baby. From what Vinny just said, we weren't getting out of here anytime soon and it looked like the baby was coming, whether we liked it or not.

"Well," Lillian unscrews the top off a bottle of water and douses her hands. "He better get here soon because her contractions are getting closer."

She rubs her hands together, then reaches into the medicine cabinet, pulls out a bottle of alcohol, and does the same.

"Have you done this before?" I ask, something telling me this isn't the first time. "I mean…delivered a baby?"

"Yes," she says, frankly. "My own."

Another contraction hits and when it passes, Diablo turns her head to me. "I'm sorry," she says slightly out of breath.

"For?" I reach into the bag next to the sofa for a fresh bottle of water. I hold it out to her, and she shakes her head no, so I twist off the cap and down the entire thing.

"I said we'd do it together, but when I realized his power was in the cane, I knew what I had to do."

As much as I hated to admit it, she was right. Her wings were the only thing that could absorb his power, and therefore, end him.

"How did you know the cane was his power source?" I'd always assumed we would transfer his power the way we did with attendants–through an incantation.

"I don't know," she shakes her head. "He was always holding onto it like a life source. But Dante," she whispers, "I felt the fires of Hell pass through me. And I can't explain it, but I feel it in me now, and in her."

Another contraction hits Diablo and when it passes, she closes her eyes. "Could you tell our daughter to ease up a bit?" she asks through ragged breath. "She listens to you."

I stroke her forehead and press my lips to it gently, then

move down on the sofa and place both hands on her stomach and lean in. "Hey princess, it's your dad."

I've said her name in my mind dozens of times, because that is what she is–a princess. The daughter of a queen. But it's the first time I've said the word dad, and it makes me falter a bit.

"I know it's been one hell of a night," I continue, "and we want to meet you more than anything. But you need to let your mom build up her strength a bit. Do you think you can do that for me?"

Another contraction hits Diablo, but this one doesn't appear to be as intense. When it passes and Diablo's sighs with relief, she looks at me. "See, I told you she listens to you."

I hold Diablo's hand tight as the next few contractions come and go. "Has anyone seen Viper?" she asks tiredly.

Hearing her name, Viper pushes through the crowd of legion members gathered in front of the door. "I'm here!"

She rushes in and hugs Lila and Vinny, then comes over to us. She grabs my shoulder first, then stands next to the sofa and looks down at Diablo. "Hey warrior," she smiles proudly. "You kicked some ass tonight."

"I don't know about that," she draws in a shallow breath. "My back is charred like barbequed meat."

"So, you can get a killer back tattoo to cover it up like Dante," she winks. "Only, your wings really will have been flames. Or wait," she laughs. "I know…something that says, 'I vanquished the devil.' That would be awesome."

Another contraction hits and Viper looks at me. "Baby's coming," I say wryly. "Can you believe it?"

"Well," Viper shakes her head. "I guess that's the cherry on top of the fucking sundae."

I can't help but laugh at her choice of words because she's right, and as she always manages to do, she makes Diablo laugh as well, and its music to my ears.

Diablo holds her other hand out and Viper grabs it. "I'm glad you're okay, V."

"Me too," she squeezes her hand back.

We're gathered around Diablo talking, helping her with humor as the contractions come and go, when James and David finally arrive. The collective relief is evident as we all jump up and welcome them.

"Could you maybe think about moving to a place with one level?" David puts a hand to his chest while trying to catch his breath and patting me on the back with the other. He's wheezing and sweat rings his collar.

I look around and considering the state of the penthouse, think about buying an estate in the country while we rebuild. Somewhere my daughter can run free and feel the grass on her feet.

Lila hands David a bottle of water as James comes over to the sofa, sets a bag down, and gets to work checking Diablo's vitals. He appears unaffected by the climb up the stairs, and I'm impressed.

"How far apart are her contractions?" He asks while checking her pulse.

"About three minutes," Lillian says.

James sets Diablo's arm down and leans over to inspect her back. "Who did these sutures?"

"I did," Lillian says proudly.

"Excellent work," he nods with approval. "Were you a nurse?"

"No," she laughs gently. "Just, experience helping the wounded in Napoleon's Paris."

James arches a brow, clearly curious by the reference. "We will have to talk when this is over."

"I would be delighted," she nods.

"Her contractions were painful at first but seemed to have calmed down a bit," I say as James digs around in the bag at his feet.

"That's good," he removes a bottle and a syringe. "But they can change with intensity the closer to labor she gets. I can give her something to ease the pain of both the contractions and her back if you would like?"

He looks at Diablo, then me. The day we met, I yelled at him for touching her. Now here he was, about to deliver my daughter. I considered him and David now, like everyone else in this room–part of my family.

He may not be a baby doctor, but James had been steadfast in his care of Diablo from the moment we found out she was pregnant. I could say now, without reservation, that I trusted him.

"Give her whatever she wants," I nod.

"Please, yes," she exhales with gratitude. "My back hurts more than the contractions."

James gives Diablo a dose of Demerol and within seconds, her face softens. "Oh, that's nice," she lays her head back as if resting it on a cloud.

"Alright," he places the syringe back into his bag and pulls on a pair of gloves. "Let's see how much she's dilated."

James instructs Diablo to pull her legs up and Lillian tents a blanket over, as Vinny, Lila and I turn our backs to give them privacy.

"Well," James removes his gloves once he's done. "Eight centimeters. She's in active labor."

"How much longer?" I ask.

"Two more centimeters to go and then she starts pushing. Could be minutes, could be hours?"

My eyes widen at the idea of minutes. "So soon?"

"Soon," Vinny shakes his head. "She's been having contractions for hours."

"Really?" The world felt like it stopped after the battle with Luke in the garden. I must have lost track of time.

James and Lillian talk at the foot of the sofa as I sit next to Diablo, holding her hand. More contractions come and go. Then one hits that despite the pain killer, sends Diablo shooting straight up.

"Well," James pulls on a fresh set of gloves after it passes, and Diablo's breathing picks up. "Looks like it might be show time."

I hold her hand tight as James again, checks to see how far she is dilated. "Alright," he looks up. "Ten centimeters. Time to push, Diablo."

Lillian stands up next to James, with a blanket in hand and looks at Diablo and nods with encouragement. When the next contraction hits seconds later, she bears down and I can tell the strain hurts her back, but like a warrior, she digs her nails into my hand and pushes through the pain.

For half an hour she pushes with each contraction, her cheeks growing flushed and face sweaty, but just when I'm about to lose my shit from seeing her in pain for so long, Diablo pushes and lets out a cry that's louder than any of the others. It's followed by an eerie stillness and then a small cry, breaks the silence.

The sound pierces my chest and grabs hold of my heart, and for a moment everything stops. Then James sits up with our daughter in his hands and places the tiny infant in the blanket in Lillian's outstretched arms.

They wipe her off and suction her nose and mouth, and when they're done, she's screaming her little lungs off. Lillian brings her over to Diablo and places the baby in her arms, and the moment she feels her mother, she grows silent.

James asks me if I want to cut the umbilical cord and I swallow and shake my head no, my eyes on the beautiful miracle in my angel's arms.

"She's here," Diablo looks up at me and smiles, tears pooling in her beautiful green eyes. "And she's perfect."

The feeling that hits me when I see the two of them is so powerful, it nearly knocks me over.

"Would you like to hold your daughter?" she asks.

I nod unable to speak. But when she places her in my arms and I stick my finger out and the baby's tiny finger wraps around it, I laugh. Diablo's right, she's perfect. For the first time in all this existence, I feel as I did in the beginning. Before the fall, when I was the moon, and Diablo the stars. I feel full of hope, and love, and as if we have been waiting for this moment since the beginning of time.

"The world is in trouble," Vinny pulls Lila to him, and I couldn't have said it any better myself. My little girl was meant to be. Her destiny, written among the moon and stars.

Lila kisses her friend on the head, then me and whispers in my ear. "We bet on our girl that day in Eden and she won."

I look up at her, then Vinny, and the others...Lillian, James, Viper, David. Even JJ who I see in the hall for the first time, head down, still scared he will reveal more secrets to Luke, unaware their connection has been broken. "No," I shake my head and look back down at my daughter. "We won."

Who we were before Heaven will stay between Diablo and me; a story we tell our daughter at bedtime. But she and I...we will remember it every day of our eternal existence, so that we never forget it again.

37
DIABLO

We're gathered in the sitting room, legion members milling around eating and drinking a mix of food and I can't keep my eyes off our daughter.

"She's beautiful," David smiles, coming over to sit at the end of the sofa. "Just as Heaven predicted."

Dante and I look up at the same time, a curious expression on both of our faces.

"Dee's text," he clarifies. "That's what I was calling to tell you before everything happened. I deciphered the language finally. The Law of Nevaeh, as Dee called it...it's about her."

"How to get her power?" I ask.

"No," David shakes his head. "She is the power."

"What?" Dante shakes his head.

"Here," David reaches into his pocket and pulls out a piece of paper and unfolds it. "It says, 'A child born with the blood of man, fires of Hell, and spirit of Heaven, will end the war still to come. With hair like the night, and eyes the color of the darkest sky, she will bridge the kingdoms and bring about peace.' There's more, but basically, the secret was never a way to harness the power of Heaven, but the foretelling of her arrival. Either Dee shared what he believed it meant," he holds the paper out to Dante, who reaches for it, "or falsely communicated it as a power, to throw whoever may one day look for it, off its trail. Who knows...maybe Heaven told him what to say."

I look down at the miracle in my arms and feel an

overwhelming sense of affirmation. "They did all of this," I smile and brush my finger against her tiny cheek. "My wings, the letters in the artifacts, Dee's text, your mortal DNA..." I pause and look back up at Dante. "They gave us what we needed to end Luke because we represented the best of Heaven. It's why they asked me if I was sure the day I fell and why you lived when Luke shot you. They wanted to make sure we were worthy, and we were. We were never the problem. Our love was the solution that created her."

"Then that should be her name," Dante places a gentle hand on our daughter's head. "Nevaeh."

"Nevaeh Lillian," I look up at the woman who helped bring my daughter into the world and smile. "I love it."

Lillian reaches for her throat and swallows, looking from me to Dante.

"You have not only shown me every kindness possible, but loved me like a daughter," I hold out my hand. "You are the closest thing to a mother I will ever have. Let us honor you this way, please?"

Lillian's eyes fill with tears as she reaches for it. "It would be my greatest honor."

"Well then sweet Nev," I kiss my daughter and inhale her sweetness. "Welcome to the world, precious girl."

She appears to purse her tiny lips, which to me, looks a lot like a smile. "I think she likes it," Dante leans down, and kisses the top of my head.

Despite the broken space all around us, and the members that we lost, I know everything is going to be okay. The little girl in our arms was given to us for a reason. She is our peace and the promise of a new beginning.

Dante and I are lost in the little girl that we've been waiting for, that only when Vinny comes over, do we look up.

"You won't believe it," he says with a hint of wonder.

"What is it?" Dante asks.

Viper makes her way to the door and steps into the debris covered foyer, where she is embraced by Sam. They pat each other on the back and when they pull apart, Viper kneels, and a little girl comes up and hugs her.

"Is that his daughter?" I ask.

"Must be," I look at the exchange and smile.

As Viper hugs the little girl, a group of children surrounds her and Sam. "Who are all those kids?" I ask. There must be more than three dozen, and they range in age, from toddler to eighteen, maybe older.

"They're the children of the Fallen," Dante says, as one by one, they're greeted by the legion member I can only assume is their father.

"You did this, didn't you?" I whisper.

Dante looks at me and then our daughter. "Since that day on the plane when I asked Viper to make a list, we've been working to unite the Fallen with the children they sired. I did it for them but also for her. I wanted her to have a community. Friends who would support her, as ours do, us."

I shake my head, heart swelling with love at the father he already is. "You know, they're not only that." He looks up at me in question. "They are her legion. The legion of a queen."

Our daughter is destined to one day inherit a power greater than any in existence. One that gives her the ability to walk between Heaven, Earth, and Hell. She will be a queen, and the legion that awaits her, an army.

But if anyone tries to hurt her, or them, her father and I, along with her family and our legion, will have their backs. Because she is our daughter, and they are our family. And no one fucks with family.

Epilogue
DANTE

Three years later...

"Make a wish, princess," I look up from where I'm kneeling and encourage Nev to blow out the candles on her cake.

"Go on, sweet girl," Diablo smiles at our daughter. "You can do it."

Nev looks from her mom to me, then sticks a finger into the gold icing and laughs. I can't help but laugh back.

"Don't encourage her," Diablo sticks a hand on her hip and shakes her head. But I can see she is amused, too. Our daughter is only three and she's already cheeky.

I still can't believe it's been three years. Where did the time go? One minute I was fighting for both of their lives, and the next, here we are–surrounded by friends and family, and so much pink and gold, our family room looks unrecognizable.

It's hard to believe at one time, a century seemed to drag on endlessly; the time between the days when I could see Diablo again, painfully slow. Yet, three years had passed in the blink of an eye, and sometimes I had to stop and just be in the moment so I could remember it before it passed.

Each day has been full of more love and happiness than I ever thought I needed or deserved, and it's because of the little miracle that was part me, and part Diablo. I'm so in love with my girls and thank Heaven for them both every day.

They broke the mold when they made our daughter. She is as beautiful as she is mischievous, and has everyone wrapped around her finger, including her Uncle Vinny.

I look at my best friend and shake my head in disbelief. His brawn is a stark contrast to the glittery cone-shaped birthday hat on his head and yet, he's never looked happier. Between him and Lila, they take their role as aunt and uncle seriously, and Nev lights up whenever either of them walk in the room.

Lillian brings a stack of plates over to the table and rubs her nose against Nev's before cutting the cake. She's smitten by the girl she helped deliver, and Diablo was right–Lillian is always up to watch our daughter, so we take her up on the offer when we need some alone time. And we still do. We're still as hungry for one another, as ever.

"I want an end piece," Vinny rubs his hands together. "Give me that frosting."

"Yes," Lillian rolls her eyes and plops down a big piece of cake onto a plate and hands it to him. "I know."

Diablo wipe's Nev's hands and then pretends to pinch her nose. She laughs and the sound reaches into my chest and squeezes.

I love that little girl so much; she has no idea the lengths her mother and I went to protect her. Someday she'll know the power she possesses, but until then, we relish these moments. These simple, sweet, perfect moments I never knew could be more priceless than anything.

Diablo runs a hand down my arm and squeezes, and I know she's thinking the same thing. "We did good."

"You did good." She rests her head on my shoulder and I stroke her cheek with my finger.

Diablo is still my stars, and I her moon, just as we were to one another in the beginning. And our story is one we tell our daughter at bedtime.

"I can't get over how much she looks like you," Diablo smiles.

"Me?" I turn to my beautiful angel. "That face is all you."

Nev has her mother's hair and my eyes. But her mouth is a perfect pink bow, just like Diablo. She's a gift from Heaven, there is no doubt about it.

"Hey," Luca points at Kai as he sticks a finger in the side of the cake. "You can't do that. It's Nev's birthday, not yours."

"Boys," Diablo makes her way over to the table. "It's fine."

I laugh as the two boys shoot each other dirty looks, then smile up at Diablo. She may have lost her wings, but she still has the angel effect on everyone.

"Is Luca being a pain?" Caro comes over, shoving a spoonful of cake into his mouth.

"No," I pat his back. "He's fighting for the honor of my daughter's cake. That's a good boy right there."

Nev didn't just create our family when she was born but changed the way the Fallen embraced their own offspring. When the legion saw the lengths Diablo and I were willing to go for our daughter, they too, started fighting for their kids.

Luca is Caro's son, who was born only a few years before Nev, and Kai, surprisingly, is Sam's second child with his daughter's mother. It's a long story he said one night after too many drinks at *Riders* and so, I don't ask about it. I just embrace him as I do all the kids.

My daughter has what Diablo predicted–her own legion that she belongs to–and one day she will inherit them as her own army. They will have her back if her power were ever to be challenged. But for now, they're all children of the Fallen, and they're a beautiful, mischievous, curious group.

"Sir," Wills comes over. "There is someone here to see you."

"Who is it?" I ask, annoyed that anyone would dare interrupt this special day.

"It's Mr. Draven," he clears his throat.

"Who?" Diablo asks, coming back over while wiping frosting off her hands with a napkin.

I never told her who made the night we burned Luke's kingdom to the ground, possible. In the precarious month that followed, the details fell away. But she knew we had help. Just not what it cost.

"I'll take care of it," I say to Wills. "Show him into my study and I'll be right there."

"Is it Primordial?" Diablo looks at me.

"No," I say simply and something about the look in her eyes tells me she will table it for now, but later, she will want to know everything. "I'll be right back," I kiss her softly. "Save me a piece of cake."

"Okay," she watches me leave as I make my way out of the study.

Nev cries out when she sees me walk out the door, and my chest tightens. I hate it when she cries, but I can't be angry. I knew the terms of the favor I owed Draven, and that it could come at any moment. And it looked like that moment was here.

"Draven," I make my way into the sitting room, hand outstretched. "It's good to see you."

"Wolf," he nods with a smile as he takes my hand in his and gives it a firm shake. "You have a beautiful home."

I smile at his name for me and shove a hand in my pocket. "Thank you. That's very kind of you."

The penthouse has been totally remodeled since our war with Luke. It took a crew of hundreds more than a year to repair everything, down to the marble floors. This sitting room and the study have been restored to what they were, but there had been changes.

A family room was added next to the study and the kitchen was blown out to make way for an eat-in dining area. We'd also remodeled the second floor, which was now Nev's bedroom, mine and Diablo's suite, and the space of the suite I had built for her, turned into a recreation of her library in Eden, down to the leather tufted sofas in the center and shiny wood floors.

The garden had also changed and took a lot of effort to get back into its former glory. But with patience and a huge budget for the gardener, it too, was again thriving and beautiful.

"Can I offer you some cake?" I ask, curious why he's here. "It's my daughter's birthday and we're having a party."

"No on the cake. Thank you," he holds a hand up. "But wonderful on the news of your daughter. I am glad to hear our work was successful."

"It was," I say with appreciation.

"Now that she is here, I gather you understand the need to sacrifice for her happiness and safety, no matter the cost."

"I do," I nod. It is one of the few truths I do know.

"Then you will understand what I have come here to ask you."

"The favor," I say simply.

Laughter wafts down the hall from the family room, and I make my way over to the doors and close them. It's then as I turn, I see a young boy on the chair in the corner. He's taller than I remember and hair darker, but it's him all right. It's Draven's son.

"Declan," I smile, remembering how gentle the boy had seemed when we first met, three years earlier.

The boy casts his eyes down and swings his legs back and forth on the chair as Draven speaks. "I once said to you that our children's trust was a currency more priceless than any in the world. That currency is why I'm here. I must leave, Wolf, and you are the only one I trust to watch my son while I am away."

I look at Declan and he looks down at the words his father has just said. What is he now, six, seven years old?

"Where are you going?" I ask, not knowing what else to say.

"Away," Draven says simply. "But I will be back."

I cross my arms, knowing the only answer I can give him is yes. "Okay."

"He's bright and won't be any trouble to you. And he has his mother's heart."

Draven looks down and it hits me as I look at Declan...he's sullen because he lost his mother, and his father is about to leave him, too.

"I have to ask," I turn back to Draven. "Your reason for leaving...will it become a problem?"

"You're worried about your daughter," he says with understanding.

"Yes," I reply with complete candor. "I am."

"Do not worry. This problem is at my door, and there it will stay. But it is that very reason, why I must leave, and you are the only one I trust to keep my son safe. Something tells me you have been doing it longer than any of us even realize."

I look up and meet his eyes and I have a strange feeling he knows what I am. Or what I was. And yet, he's put his son, the one he loves most in this world, in my care.

"It will be my honor to welcome Declan into my home. He can join the other kids at the party and Lillian can help him get settled later. He can even have his pick of any of the guest rooms."

"That is too kind," Draven lets out an audible sigh of relief.

"It is the least I can do, given all you did for me. Come back safely," I stick out my hand.

Draven shakes my hand, turns to speak to Declan, and then just as fast as he arrived, he's gone.

The room is quiet, nothing but the sound of my breathing and Declan's filling the space. Then the sound of steps coming from down the hall get louder and in walks Diablo.

"Dante," she comes in. "Is everything okay?"

"How do you feel about having a little company for a while?" I ask.

"More than what we already have?" she laughs.

Diablo's right. There is always someone here, between the legion and its kids, and Vinny, Lila, Wills, Lillian, and JJ, who has his own place and shop in the city, but stops by so often, he may as well still live here.

"What do you mean?" she asks, clearly confused by the question.

I nod to the chair in the corner and her eyes widen when they see Declan. "Oh," she smiles. "Hello there."

He looks up at the sound of her voice and a small smile pulls at his lips. This time it's not the angel-effect. It's the mom one.

She turns to me, questions in her eyes, and then back to Declan. "How long will you be with us son?"

He shrugs.

"Well," she makes her way over to him and bends down in front of the chair. "We're having a party in the other room. Would you like some cake and play with some kids your age?"

He nods and reaches for her hand, and she stands up and leads him out of the study. "Be right back," she winks.

When they're gone, I blow out a heavy breath. Draven left his son in our care. A boy who was only a few more years older than my daughter. What could make him do such a thing?

"He's playing with Kai and Lucas," Diablo says as she walks back into the study and shuts the door.

"Good," I say absently, racking my brain, trying to figure out what trouble Draven was in. Given the company he kept, it could be anything.

"So," Diablo comes up to me, and places a hand on my chest. "Do you want to fill me in now, or later?"

I look into her beautiful green eyes, knowing I need more than a few minutes to explain, and not wanting to miss Nev's party. "Later?"

"Okay," she reaches for my hand and laces her fingers through mine.

"Are you okay with him being here?" This was her home, too, and she had a right to tell me if she wasn't comfortable with assuming the care of another child.

"Of course," she smiles. "We have the space, and there are lots of kids here these days. We'll figure it out."

"You're amazing?" I cup her cheek. "You know that?"

"I do," she smiles wider. "Now, can I tell you what I came in here for?"

"What's that?" I grin.

She grabs my hand, and heat passes between our palms as she leads me to the door in the wall to the hidden hallway.

We tumble inside and once it closes, she pulls my mouth down on hers and draws me into a searing kiss. This love was worth everything and together we were crazy, insane-and exactly what I wanted for my daughter one day.

COMING SOON...BOOK 3!

Thank you for reading Legion of the Queen! If you enjoyed it, please leave a review on your favorite retailer or book community, blog, or website. Your support means the world to me!

I look forward to sharing more of Dante and Diablo's world with you. Keep a look out for the next book in the After the Fall series, an exciting three book why choose romance, with characters introduced in this book.

ACKNOWLEDGEMENTS

Thank you to my readers for embracing Dante and Diablo and their story. I am forever grateful and humbled for your support of this world I've created and enthusiasm for my writing. You are why I write!

I also want to thank my PA Christina Santos. You came into my world, and forever changed it, and I am so grateful we met, clicked, and all you have done for me!

Also, thank you to my Street Team, Danielle's Darlings, without your encouragement and excitement, the last few months would have been rough. I look forward to more adventures together.

I also want to thank Rebecca at RFK Designs for another beautiful cover. Your vision for this series is breathtaking and I am so lucky to have you in my corner.

To my family and friends, thank you for your support, encouragement, and patience. It means the world.

xo,
DM

ABOUT THE AUTHOR

D.M. Simmons is an international award-winning author of adult, new adult, and young adult fiction. She creates lush, atmospheric worlds, which tell captivating stories filled with complicated but swoon-worthy relationships, characters to fall in love with, and heroes to champion. Fascinated by the indelible power of love, romance is usually at the heart of her stories and the narrator's journey. She believes in love of all kinds: new, old, young, lost, unrequited, irrevocable, forbidden, enemies to lovers, friends to lovers, star-crossed, soulmates, and everything in between. You can expect a HEA, but she makes her characters work for it. When she isn't writing, she can be found reading, binge-watching TV shows, listening to music, running her kids around, creating aesthetics, and wondering where the time goes.

ALSO BY D.M. SIMMONS

After the Fall Universe
Book One: Fealty of the Fallen
Book Two: Legion of the Queen

The Lake Haven Series
Book One: Evoke
Book Two: Ravel
Book Three: Coming soon!

Printed in Great Britain
by Amazon